P... ...RASHA

More vivid tha... ...Skousen's attention to deep detail in describing not only events but Rasha's times makes The Search for Rasha a compelling recommendation that's hard to put down.

—D. Donovan, Senior Reviewer, *Midwest Book Review*

Paul B. Skousen tells the story of The Search for Rasha *with a polished economy of writing rarely seen today, and certainly with a poetic beauty and sense of presence mastered only by experience. It may seem hyperbolic praise to add: This book reeks of intelligence and knowledge. Academic authenticity saturates this high-paced thriller with immediacy and belief.*

—Joel R. Dennstedt for *Readers' Favorite*, Five Star Review

Books in the *Bassam Saga*

Bassam and the Seven Secret Scrolls
Zafir and the Seventh Scroll
The Search for Rasha

The
SEARCH
for
RASHA

The SEARCH *for* RASHA

THE BASSAM SAGA, BOOK THREE

PAUL B. SKOUSEN

IZZARD INK
— PUBLISHING —

Other books by Paul B. Skousen
How to Read the Constitution and the Declaration of Independence
The Naked Socialist
Comrade Paul's Socialist Bathroom Reader
Treasures from the Journal of Discourses

Contact Paul B. Skousen at info@paulskousen.com.

Published by:
Izzard Ink
PO BOX 522251
Salt Lake City, UT 84152
www.izzardink.com
info@izzardink.com

LIBRARY OF CONGRESS CONTROL NUMBER: 2018936326
Designed by Alissa Rose Theodor
Cover Design by Andrea Ho
Illustrations by Shreya Gupta
Cover Images: Indian Collections/Shutterstock.com MarcelClemens/Shutterstock.com
R-O-M-A/Shutterstock.com Yevtushenko Serhii/Shutterstock.com

First Edition: October 30, 2018

eBook ISBN: 978-1-64228-008-1
Paperback ISBN: 978-1-64228-009-8
Hardback ISBN: 978-1-64228-010-4

"Bassam" is pronounced "Bah-SAWM"

To My Rasha and My Bakra

Mäp Of Ammär

HENRI

If someone had ventured into the museum that night they would have stumbled upon a curiously contradictory sight.

There sat Henri cross-legged on the cold cement floor, his head invisible underneath a 2,000-year-old sarcophagus, and a tangle of cords, tubes, and a laptop computer in a jumble at his feet.

The old caretaker was stuck. His fumbling and fussing with one technology wasn't helping him unravel the other. And at 77 years, his brand of technology was caught in between.

"It's like rocket surgery," he mumbled, peering into the dark access hole under the clay casket. "Or is that brain science, or . . ."

There was a problem with the endoscope and turning the little camera. He pushed it deeper into the casket's gloomy cavity. "No, it's a labor of love—patient, painful, excruciating love—I think."

Lying next to him was a laptop he borrowed from Dr. Lincoln. He touched the mouse pad. "Wake up, wake up, are you broken too?"

The screen flickered.

"About time. So . . . what do we have here?"

The image was mostly black with sweeping blue streaks and darting images.

"The camera should be right there, in the cache vault, is that it . . .?"

Henri let the camera focus then tried to make sense of the abstract angles and shapes playing across the screen.

"Endoscope," he muttered. "I know what you are." He pushed the insertion tube another inch, finding a corner but pressed up against an obstruction. "I know exactly what they do with you, why are you making this so difficult?"

He backed off a fraction then turned it for a slow look around. The colors and corners of the interior were smooth and finished. "That's a strange attention to detail for something meant to stay closed for eternity," he mumbled.

Henri twisted the tube, directing the camera toward the lower portion of the sarcophagus, the part he couldn't reach before.

"En-do-scope," he said. "Why does the good doc need this in a museum? Yes, yes, the very thing I'm doing here—looking, probing—to find . . . to find things meant to stay hidden until . . ."

Just then the little lamp cast a sharp cone of light on what appeared to be the curled corner of something like dark brown leather.

"Ah ha!" Henri said, reaching with his foot to turn the laptop for a better view.

"I knew it, I knew it! I'll just bet they wanted me to find this the last, if it is the last—"

The scroll was nestled deep in a corner as if wedged there after some violent movement. It was wrapped in the same fashion as the other two, but maybe fatter.

"More story?" he wondered. "It better be . . ."

He reached for his penlight and put a beam on the scope's handle controls.

"Okay, okay, what now?" he mumbled. "Here's the what? Suction valve? No, no, what else—angulation—angulation control," he said, and twisted it a fraction. "Angulating—angulating closer, almost there."

He guided the tube forward and the camera obediently turned downward. "Not bad," he said. "Just a little to the right . . . down . . . a little more . . ."

The tools at the end of the scope were agile, but were they strong? Henry put his thumb on a slider switch and watched three tiny prongs extend like grasshopper legs into view, beautifully illuminated so he could guide them exactly where he wanted. He pulled the slide back, closing the prongs on one of the leather ties. With a slight tug, the scroll moved.

"I should have been a doctor," he mumbled, working the scroll to the opening. "If this was a real colonoscopy, I would have just scored my first polyp . . . and it's huge."

He pulled gently. "Just like catching fish . . . Here's the good doctor's $48,000 hook, and I'm the net."

Carefully dragging the scroll toward the small opening, he reached in and manipulated it this way, then that, and finally the right combination to free his prize. He carefully drew it out and cradled it a moment to examine.

"Ah! Heavier than the others," he noted, and glanced at his watch. "There's still time," and stood to pop his spine back into place and rub life back into his sore muscles. Finding his balance, he shuffled his way to the reading room.

"Here we go again," and slumped into his favorite leather chair. The lamp clicked on, casting a warm glow.

"Identical wrapping, the same leather ties," he said, turning the bundle under the light. "And me, the first human eyes to see this in what, 2,000 years? No, 2,200 years, an odd time in history, a glorious time."

The scroll was packed as the others with the same attention to neatness. "Certainly part of the collection—three scrolls, three stories? I hope so."

He produced his little dental tool and began picking at the knots.

With the last tie released he laid back the leather, then quite by surprise, two small objects rolled out, landing right in his lap.

"What is this?" He picked them up to examine. "Fruit pits? Ha!" He held one to the light. "Somebody's lunch ... quite curious, though—white as snow, I've never seen pits like these. I'll have to look more closely..." and tucked them into his apron.

Bringing the papyrus into full view, he saw the parchment was aged with spots and wear, but still, beautifully preserved. Henri felt for the leading edge and gently slid his fingers beneath.

"Well, well, my friends," he breathed, "What have you to tell me tonight?"

STEALTH

"My dearest Bassam, come for me, I am taken away to a dark place. It is the end of my life. I have nothing but this script to console—and my thoughts of you. If these words find you when it is too late, let them comfort you for your life without me at your side.—Forever yours, Rasha"

I am Rasha.

It was a year and 259 days after my father's great trek to the east with my beloved Bassam when the bandits came to our Rekeem.

Our watch was only two that night but two others slept. Our men gave no thought to that quiet train of camels and their riders who poured from the Siq. Their lighted torches spoke peace in their casual, friendly waves as they filed quietly into the confines of our sleeping village. It was a large train, lightly fitted out, but at such a late hour, no alarm was assumed.

The strangers smiled with glistening teeth behind shiny black beards, and nodded as they passed. The watch held their torches, noting them strangers who seemed on a familiar errand, and let them pass.

The few who saw their arrival thought them just another trading caravan seeking hospitality. Had the watch considered their lack of baggage and trade goods, that the camels carried only men with swords, my story might be different.

By the end of second watch, more than 200 riders had funneled into our canyon city. None were challenged or checked. Slipping by a multitude of dark dwellings with slumbering residents, the sojourners continued by torch to the far side of Rekeem.

Along the way, others joined—men who were waiting, who emerged from shadows to guide the train into darkened pathways toward the dwellings far beyond the market square. They divided into groups and slipped quietly into blind alleyways and streets, finding in silence their places of rendezvous.

None were awakened by these activities, for such is common in our little canyon home. Night traffic comes frequently enough that no one gave this group any unusual consideration.

I was awake when the train came, seated at a table with a small lamp, writing dreams in my journal—dreams for when my Bassam would return to me.

It was then I heard the rustle of movement and the snorting of camels.

"That's strange," I thought, and extinguished my lamp to watch through parted fabrics.

I could see shrouded men atop camels, waving arms and pointing in muffled discussion under the light of torches. Six of the camels knelt for their riders to slip off. The men turned toward our door, motioning the others to spread out. I could think of no reason for strangers at this late hour except—Did they bring news of Bassam? Or Father?

But to my horror they drew swords and started up our steps. I hurried to awaken Bassam's parents.

"Kateb! Dalal! Get up! Strangers!"

The two had barely risen when the men stepped through the doorway with torches ablaze. Long darting shadows danced everywhere.

Kateb motioned Dalal and me to stay behind, then parted the curtain to confront the men in the main room. He held out his hands in peace, squinting into the light.

"Who are you?" Kateb asked. "What do you want?"

A large man draped in black stepped forward. "Are you Kateb?" he growled. The grizzled leader had a scar parting the black whiskers on his left cheek.

"I am," he said. "What do you want?"

"We are looking for the daughter of Zafir. Where is she?" he demanded.

Hearing the words, I drew a panicked breath.

"With her mother," Kateb said, "South to Saba', tending to her mother's illness. Three weeks. We expect her back any day."

Dalal and I could hear awful noise of distant fighting in the dark—shouting, screaming, hooves hurrying toward us, awful sounds of an attack.

"What could be happening?" I whispered to Dalal. "Is it an army? Bandits?"

Dalal shushed me and froze to listen.

My mind raced with a thousand questions. First came father's warnings about danger—a network of men who served the Abdali-ud-din in the caravan season. If an emergency comes, he had said, I should flee to his steward, or to his cousin's home, or escape through the Siq. If that failed, notify Al Kalimat.

I hurried for my journal and tore a corner to scribble a message.

"Dalal," I whispered, "Al Kalimat?"

She understood immediately and pulled a leather pouch from a small table. I shoved the note inside and inked the secret emblem of Al Kalimat on its outside—a weighted cross with two dots on the right. I hurried it to the door, and laid it face down partly covered by my shawl.

"If you must get a message to me and can't deliver it safely," my father said, "don't hide it. Evil men will look for things hidden. Leave it in plain sight and mark it with this emblem," and he drew it for me. "If you cannot get to safety, leave what you can and my men will find it."

Just then a torch flooded the hallway and our curtain was ripped aside.

"Come!" a voice ordered. More men squeezed into the narrow corridor.

We obeyed and joined Kateb in front. The many torches made it smoky and my eyes stung.

"You!" the man in black said pointing.

I stayed in the shadow behind Dalal.

The man motioned to another to bring forward a torch.

"Step aside, woman," he ordered.

Dalal shifted, exposing me to their full gaze.

"And who is this?" he asked, pointing at me.

Kateb waved his explanation rapidly. "As I have explained, she's our daughter," he said. "You must travel to Saba' for the daughter of Zafir. Her mother took ill, and . . ."

"Shut up old man," he shouted, and shoved Kateb to the wall.

He gestured and one of his own came forward. He was a shorter, younger man who pushed his way from the back. A shawl hooded his head, burying his face in shadow. The grizzled man held the torch near me. I felt the heat of the flame and raised my hand in protest, then noticed the big man had a finger missing, cut off at the middle joint.

"Well?" he ordered.

The shorter one looked at me and then stepped back into the shadow.

"It is she," he said.

Two of the men pushed Dalal aside and grabbed me by the arms and pulled me to the door. I gasped and screamed. Others pushed back at Kateb who stood to resist, shouting protest. I began kicking and fighting and they wrestled me to the entrance.

"No!" I screamed. "No! NO! Help me, Help!"

Behind me I heard a great ruckus erupt in the shadows.

"Hold him!"

"Where are you taking her?"

"Shut up old man."

"No—don't!"

"Oh be quiet woman or I'll kill you."

"Rasha! Rasha!"

I struggled as they dragged me out the door and into the cool of the night. I fought all the way down the steps, screaming to awaken neighbors, the watch, anyone. Then one man threw a hand on my mouth to muffle me. I bit down hard and he snapped it away shouting a cursing oath. He wrapped his arms around me tightly and threw me to the ground, his heavy body landing on top, crushing my breath away. A meaty hand pressed my head against the sandy gravel and a voice shouted, "The rope and rags, quick! "

"This will shut her up," another panted, producing a gag.

I fought against their strength, groaning more against the sorrow of betrayal than my suffocating fight for freedom. That voice, that shadow, that figure in the shroud, how could he do this to us? Why? Why would he come to us hidden with treachery and number himself among such men? And we had trusted him. Was everything a complex lie? Bassam would be so ashamed of you. How could you be the traitor of friend and family and do this to us, *Faris*?

THE NOTE

Al Kalimat verified — +:
Wadi-Anen to Zafir

Acommunique to Zafir, to the event of his kidnapped daughter. By my seal, affixed.

Zafir,
We do not rest in the search for your daughter.

The expected notes of ransom were received in 'Adan by courier, and the original is held for your inspection in Rekeem. It is dated the 14th day of Odar, and the text follows:

> *To the tyrants of Abdali-ud-din, death to you all.*
> *We possess treasure for sale. You may purchase her for 10,000 talents of Egyptian gold in three payments. We will tell you when and where to deliver your pieces of treasure, or we will deliver our treasure to you in pieces.*
> *I am Sutekh*

The second note was received in 'Adan by courier, and the original is held for your inspection in Rekeem. It is dated the 1st day of Nison.

To the Tyrants of Abdali-ud-din, death to you all.

You will give to Masaharta and his men a tribute of 1,000 talents of Egyptian gold in leather pouches at a place in Avalites that we will tell you.

If you do not deliver your pieces of treasure we will deliver our treasure to you in pieces.

I am Sutekh

We concur with Al Murrah on the following points:

It is the work of the Tauri of the Pontusl.

There is no reason to doubt their claims of possessing your daughter.

The name Sutekh is Egyptian, an evil god who creates chaos.

They demand the gold in portions, probably to fund a delay tactic, and to guarantee some payments.

Their mention of Avalites leads us to believe she is held in Nub'ah, a tactic to dilute a possible rescue.

They did not send additional communication.

I am your trusted friend and servant at this urgent time,

—Wadi-Anen

THE LONG WAY

Shamar shifted in the saddle, making his camel snort in complaint. The shabby beast turned her head with the irritated sneer she'd exhibited these past three weeks. Shamar gave her a firm swat with his riding stick.

"Keep your pace, old girl," he warned, "there's a storm coming, and no room for you in my tent. I might have to eat you, so step lively."

A gust caught Shamar's beard and he tucked it back. It was always windy and cold along the shores of the Egyptian Sea during this season—storms could blow to a frenzy in just moments, turning calm to torrential rains. The coastal paths were pockmarked with standing water, and the camels growled their objection. They opposed the long days of sloshing through the icy puddles. Sensing his camel's hesitancy, Shamar whacked her a good one and she leapt at the sting.

"Forward!" he ordered, and her pace quickened.

Despite his seeming gruffness with the camels, Shamar was perhaps the kindest man who led the caravans. He carried a soft spot in his heart for the beasts that knew no better than the sharpness of his whipping stick.

Shamar couldn't hide his love of the scenery at this part of the trek. The images of distant peaks, mirrored waters, and painted skies along the shoreline were unmatched in the world, yet ever changing. Each day was a new painting of natural beauty.

Shamar filled his lungs with the crisp, salty air. Ahead he saw the next marker, those same old ruins that seemed unchanged over the decades, emerging from the melting fog on the distant shore. The ancient pier guarded an abandoned harbor, once the busiest port on the coast. Was that a thousand years ago, or was it two? Change comes so slowly in these parts, he thought.

The fresh-water wadis were all behind them now, and coastal desert lay north for another week. The Yan'bah trade had long ago moved from this place for a better crossroads to the spice and incense.

"I don't blame them one whit," Shamar mumbled. "Whatever beauty once lured their need for a settlement in these desolate parts is long gone."

As the train plodded through the historic ruins, Shamar imagined the abandoned villages, the thousands of homes that had served so many industries over the centuries that now lay crumbled and broken. "So much life and so much death all in this same place," he sighed.

The ruins marked the halfway point in his journey to the Nilus and the great city of Noph. Eight weeks at least, maybe seven if the weather was fair. Shamar was anxious to be done with this strangely brooding group and their secretive ways. They had been a difficult bunch since departure and kept themselves distant from his friendly banter.

"They're hiding something criminal," he whispered to his camel. "I've seen this kind before."

He set eyes on the band's leader, a grizzled black-bearded man they called Rakbah. Shamar wondered if his clients could see in these passing scenes the same lessons of history—the remains of human futility against the wind-blown climes of nature's worst. The broken rock walls and foundations and stoops and roadworks standing as a metaphor for truths eternal. No hand raised against the laws of nature can long survive, and here lay the proof. Or were such historical philosophies too hard for men of such suspicious calculations? Were their cares too deeply bound up in whatever vice drove them to hire his little transportation business?

The signs of ulterior intent were all there—a payment in gold, a suspicious off-road path that involved the risky trek across Sinai's Mountains of Moses—making theirs a needlessly long and arduous trip to Egypt.

Shamar tried discouraging the men by increasing his fee, but they insisted. "A more direct route is the way of honest trade," he thought. "They must be running from something."

Shamar had a keen eye for human nature. "Noph is a direct trip, a short trip, an easy trip—especially when in company with safer men. Not so for this group . . ." His camel ignored the lecture and flicked her ears.

For his safety Shamar kept a pleasant countenance for the duration, but in his heart he didn't trust a single one of them. He slept with his knife unsheathed.

The day was cold and damp, and the sun never showed his face. This was not unusual for the season. All manner of weather was to be expected along this stretch, from storm to shine to fog to a terrific wind that sinks the fishing boats—in just one day. He had seen it all. Today the air was heavy with dampness. Its chill clawed through robes and coats down to the skin. Churning clouds warned a storm was coming, but the gray shroud hung just high enough to keep its tricks well hidden.

The little train crested a slight rise about midday and began the long descent to the broad coastal plain that stretched off for 100 stadia. Shamar nodded his silent goodbye to the familiar harbor stonework and looked for the next collection of ruins that would soon appear.

Such cities in this place, he thought, such industry and trade. Where have the people gone? What becomes of the works of such men?

He steered the group through an ancient common grounds of jutting foundations and toppled columns. The abandoned streets of the old city were sparsely covered with thin sheets of wind-blown sand. The camels' footfalls changed to hollow clopping across the rutted pavers.

"The sand is slow. It works to bury their glory," he told his camel "—the dunes hide the walls that I saw standing just five years ago. It's a sure sign the desert continues her slow crawl northward, ever laboring to bury the trespass of men. Do you see it, beast?"

What vibrancy this city must have generated—noisy, crowded market squares, untold thousands of sojourners working these streets by foot or donkey.

"My sirs," Shamar called back. "Do you see these old stone pillars? This was the old fortress of Al Nakhij, many centuries ago. An important place."

The men looked up, annoyed at the interruption. Rakbah's face was travel-weary and annoyance burned in his eyes. His disdain was palpable though no words were spoken. Shamar shook his head. They are not circumspect, he said to his bakra. They have no respect, they have no honor.

Shamar had been counting. Eight more weeks and I'll leave them to the graces of the Nub'an rock and royal granite. And then? And then I will be rid of them for whatever evil they plan, and be more discerning when selecting my next client.

Shamar's train was seven men plus a younger woman and her older escort. The two women rode separate camels and were pulled at the back of the caravan. He was never allowed to talk with them, but gave them names just the same—Suwr ("zoo-r") for the older woman. It meant strange woman for strange she was—too free with her mean and spitting words. The younger one who was treated with so much rudeness, he named Cala ("Kay-lah"), meaning castle of protection. A fitting name not just because she was there against her will, but she had an inner strength and resolve they couldn't defeat. She stood like a castle, protecting her dignity and virtue, a bulwark against injustices. He could see it in her countenance and the way she took the taunts and abuse from her captors. She was youthful, solitary, obedient, and plainly dressed. Her features were covered in the traditional fashion, and her head covered with a shawl. It was her hands that betrayed her age—young, unfettered, and unaccustomed to the saddle she rode.

Is she a wife? A sister? A slave? Or was she being led to a prince who has bought her for his harem?

Only eight weeks more and that answer would reveal itself.

Until then, his bakra would have to bear the telling of his history lessons because the long hours on the trail could fashion intense boredom into such exaggerated specters that even the rocks themselves would cry out for some diversion.

"These broken columns," he mumbled aloud, "the stela and stone-wall etchings, and countless thousands of cast-away tablets and markers, they are the reminders. Do you see it?" he whispered to his bakra, tapping her lightly on her neck. "All of this wreckage, they are memorials—no, they are more than that. They are monuments to the haughty emancipators of the civilization that dwelt here, a ruling power who thought itself invincible, as if they were wiser than God. And their remains, like so much graffiti, teach the lessons of lost humility that we, the witnesses to their demise, should see and learn from and never forget nor repeat."

He smiled at the brilliant poetry of an old man riding an old camel along an old trail in an old time.

"Bakra? If I had some ink," he mumbled, "I should write these prosaic words for the future. I would sign it 'Shamar the philosopher and historian, driver of caravans for rent.'"

A STORM OF SECRETS

Nothing stops a line of camels and their determined masters unless they will it so, for such is the mettle of the desert nomad. However, as all wise travelers know, when the torrent and wind are so heavy as to drive the camels to refusal, then an exception to free will must be made. And for the sudden downpour and raging wind that finally broke loose, Shamar made one of those rare exceptions. He hurried the company to a nearby sagging shelter of ancient stone. The cold gales made the dismount difficult, but the camels were pleased to drop their loads and huddle behind a wall to snort their discontent.

Rakbah barked his orders and the men hurried to raise their tents in the drenching downpour.

In this muddy confusion Shamar witnessed Suwr exhausting a storm of her own, thundering her stern words with one of the men, then confronting Cala with the same. The girl bowed her head and took it. With Suwr's vitriol finally vented, the two women entered their tent and sealed out the torrent.

Shamar was soaked and left alone to erect his tent. He managed it quickly enough, and placed it so the women's tent stood between his and the men's. He quickly changed to dry clothing then rummaged about for some fruit and cheese—comforts he hoped to share with Cala if her escort would allow it. A bribe, perhaps, to learn why there was secrecy and abuse. He looked to the portions, estimating enough fruit for both women, and set it aside.

The pounding rain did not abate, and the darkening dusk made it clear that sleep would be the only activity for that evening—no fires or tea or travel until the storm had passed.

Shamar sat cross legged on his rug wondering about this band of strangers. He lit the brass lamp and strung a rope to hang the wet clothing.

"They make no secret of their treachery," he said aloud. "Will Cala need help from me, or is such help to be found in Noph?" He looked at the chunk of cheese and the fruit. Perhaps, he thought, this will buy an answer.

The storm pelted and pushed against his tent, making the center post creak. With each gust, a light mist blew through the fabric. For another long hour, Shamar kept vigil, hoping that with darkness he could venture a trip to the women's tent with his offering.

The timing had to be just right. Could he manage some contact without the men seeing him?

He was content to wait longer, an art of patience long standing among the desert caravans.

The steady drumbeat on the canvas continued, prompting Shamar to unlace the door, then he paused. "Anyone watching? I'd better make one last check," he whispered.

At the wall nearest the women's tent he placed his sleeping mat and lay flat, pressing his face to the ground. With his riding stick he carefully lifted the fabric and peered outside. In the momentary flashes of lightning he could see that the two large tents drooped heavy in wetness.

No man or movement stirred the shadowy gray. Icy water cascaded down the fabrics, a thousand splashing sparkles that ignited with each silent flash. Little rivulets racing in courses misted his face with cold spray. He wiped the droplets and squinted into the wet. It was quiet enough, but suddenly . . . slight movement at the women's tent. The wall nearest him sagged. Was it the wind?

Shamar lowered the fabric to a mere slit and watched. Just then, another flash and he could see slender fingers reaching beneath the edge of the wall, lifting it upward, hesitatingly, just a palm-width. A shadow filled the opening, and for a moment in the flashing strobe of lightning appeared a young face, Cala masked in a tangle of long black hair. Her eyes were bright, blinking away the splashing droplets. Shamar raised the opening of his tent a fraction more to be seen, and gestured. Her eyes grew wide and her tense lips moved, mouthing three words in desperate silence, "Help me—please."

"She spoke!" Shamar whispered, dropping the fabric and drawing back into the dark of his excitement. For him the night suddenly became alive with wonder and fitful agony.

"Help me please," Shamar whispered. "Help me from what?" He squeezed his hands in frustration and paced around the center pole. "She's caught, she must be. How do I free her? Was she seen just now? What if they take her in the night and I'm unable to follow?" He played out a hundred ideas. None of them promising.

When he finally closed his eyes, he was already forming a means to protect the circumstances of that night and to expose no suspicion that he had become aware of a kidnapping underway. Patient he could be.

They awoke to a cold and thick overcast. A misty morning fog clung to the camp.

The group was relieved to find the rain had stopped and glad the thirsty ground had swallowed it dry. A morning fire was arranged and a generous tea was served among the men. The camels found shrubs to munch, and the wet goods from the night before were hung at the fire to dry.

Shamar resumed his routine chores, and retreated a distance to allow the women a chance alone at the fire. He feigned disinterest as Rakbah and one of the men scolded Cala and shook her by the arm. The others were hunched about the orange flames, sipping their teas and watching impassively at the verbal assault until Suwr interrupted. She made some demand, but did nothing to stop the abuse. Moments later, Cala was seated near the fire and given tea and food.

Shamar stood afar, plotting their trek forward. He made another quick calculation and grew concerned. If her plea for help was to be answered, then eight weeks to Noph might be too long to wait. Somehow, he needed to talk to Cala. He needed to talk to her now.

Day 641
My Dearest Rasha,

I am coming for you. Do not despair. Zafir is guiding us across the seas. We have not seen land since learning of your danger, and follow the stars directly west. Our boat is sleek, two masts and worthy of the great ocean. It's fast, my Rasha! We cover many hundreds of stadia in the day, and many more at night. It's our best speed so long as the wind blows at our backs.

Your father is sick with worry and talks of you often. I fear it is bringing his grey hairs down to the grave. We speak of happy times and we laugh and remember. I put that scorpion down your dress. Do you remember it? I thought it a great prank for my friends, but you were so angry with me. I could not tell you today how sorry I am that I tormented you so. I didn't know how much I loved you then as I do today.

I'm writing you somewhere west of the Indus waters. The winds have been favorable and help us in our haste to reach you. We reckon by the stars, and right ourselves by the setting sun. We're alone here and stay far from the Roman shipping lanes so we may continue uncontested.

Ammar's southpointer is a gift from God. He is our captain and keeps our course. He orders us into precision, and we're fast to obey. He is a good friend, but a funny old man. Every moment he is not pushing us about, he is sketching places on the parchment, looking to build another set of maps for this part of the world. He makes a good record of our journey.

There's fish near to shore but few will find us this far from it. Fawzi has crafted several ropes and manages to pull up ugly *creatures from far below. It's our only food so we prepare it as best we can. We dry it in the sun or eat it raw. But our desperation for food and water has not exceeded our anxiety to reach you as quickly as we can.*

Your father has consented to our marriage, did you know that? So many secrets. I was shocked. I'm still shocked. But I'm overjoyed. He told me this just a few months ago. I wear his ring and will bear his name for the family we will raise together.

I'm afraid for you, my dearest Rasha. Have they harmed you? If you are hurt, you will heal and be happy. Have they forced you? If you are, you will find comfort and joy in my arms, a future in a home that is yours, and together we will put all that is dark and ugly behind us. The scrolls point the way for us, my Rasha. There's hope and healing from all things.

I will find you and I will preserve you. I'm coming as fast as this sleek boat and the winds that push her will take us. Do not fear. Have peace, have courage, and know that I am coming.—Bassam"

NOTES IN THE NIGHT

Two days more and Shamar's caravan had reached the broad coastal plains leading to Abu Zenime'. This lone post was one of several shipping-off points, a coastal village right on the seashore where traders loaded barges with their wares—ores, metal goods, spices, and incense for Egypt. It was a two-day trip west to cross the sea.

Abu Zenime' had grown into a busy place since Shamar first visited. So busy, in fact, his routine encampment area was now filled with stone huts and a boulevard. The crowding pushed his little caravan to new camping grounds well beyond the village outskirts.

Abu Zenime' was an ideal crossing place, one from which he had sailed many times before. Calm seas, stiff wind, and good harbors both here and at Al-Jarf.

But this wasn't the place where the men wished to cross, and Rakbah made that clear. Shammar tried to convince them. Those shipping for Noph always crossed here. It was the shortest and safest route. Rakbah wanted to go farther north for reasons he wouldn't share, to a lesser-known harbor village. It was a four-day trek that would bring them through another dozen villages, but Rakbah seemed determined. Shamar graciously assured him a safe trek would be theirs, but they must first restock their supplies and rest a night here at Abu Zenime'.

With tents erected and dusk descending, Shamar prepared for sleep. He leafed through his maps one last time.

"Not many more days," he said, tracing a dotted line leading to Egypt's coast and the port of Al-Jarf. "Two days across the sea, then westward through the broad valley, around the mountains, then into the Eastern Desert—that trip down the Nilus, the winds have to be right." He tapped the map nervously with his stylus, wondering what additional detours Rakbah might suddenly command. "That's a week on the river to Noph, even if I have to row it myself—and then? And then I'll be free to go home . . . but what about Cala?"

As the shadows grew long across camp, the din from the village with its nighttime revelry faded to quiet and darkness fell. Torches dimmed and the road traffic melted away to just an occasional walker. The snorting of nearby animals mixed with the calming sigh of the night breeze, thus inducing sleeping time upon everyone.

Feeling the fatigue conquer his resolve at last, Shamar decided to bed down and reached for his lamp to set it away. Just then his tent wall rippled ever so discreetly. He looked over and saw a narrow opening appear at the bottom. A small feminine hand reached inside and placed a folded parchment, then quickly withdrew. Shamar blew his lamp to darkness and froze.

"Cala!" he whispered.

Nothing—no sound, no footsteps.

A few heartbeats later he retrieved the note then peered under the fabric. The adjacent tents were black cutouts against the shimmering night. The stars glistened like crystals, but shed no light or shadow.

"This can't wait." He felt about for his sandals. "The torch by the road, I'll read it there."

The light made the ideal guide, helping Shamar step through the maze of slumbering travelers. A few camels took notice, but kept their cuds in silent disinterest.

Alone beneath the yellow flame, he glanced about for followers. Finding none, he unfolded the parchment. The message was scrawled in charcoal.

"I am taken for ransom. My father will pay you. Help free me. Tonight—Al Kalimat."

Shamar's eyes stopped on the last words.

Al Kalimat? Al Kalimat! He took a breath. His heart pounded. "Al Kalimat," he whispered. "How does Cala know of Al Kalimat? Only a select few of the Abdali-ud-din know of Al Kalimat. Why would she think that I could possibly know about that?"

His mind went racing through a thousand possibilities. This new information changed everything. She was no ordinary peasant girl. She was not just a young prize to be traded away at the slave markets to the highest bidder. Her captors, these men, they know exactly what treasure this is. If she's Abdali-ud-din, she could be a treasure worth a kingdom. This is more than a kidnapping. This is a king's ransom. Abdali-ud-din won't rest until she is found. There might be an entire army chasing after these men right now. I must get this girl some help.

Shamar stepped back to the shadows and folded the paper into his robe. He looked across the black field that bristled with the peaks of so many tents, stoically holding vigil over the safety of hundreds now slumbering through the night. "Tonight," she wrote. "Free me tonight."

How? He walked in a slow circle.

"Wait. Yes, that's it. She will find me. Certainly she will. She will do something to make her way from the tent, and I must be ready. She won't be alone. That woman, Suwr, will have to accompany her, and I must be ready for that, too."

Shamar hurried back to his tent and made just enough gentle rustling to transmit a soft signal to the women's tent.

He felt about for the most necessary supplies—his coins, some morsels of food, both his knives, two of his blankets rolled under his arm, and his satchel of maps and lamp. Bundling them together as best he could, he strapped them over a shoulder and stepped into the dark. Shuffling his sandals just loud enough, he tried to draw a sound picture away from the tents, away from the light and toward the toilet area beyond the nearby rise. He coughed and kicked some rocks and made as straight a path as he could. Some 200 paces away he found a suitable hiding place on the shadowed side with a good view of the camp. "This will do, this will do just fine—if she can find me."

He spread out a blanket to spy. The distant torch made silhouettes of the camping grounds and a good view of anyone's approach. He sat down to wait.

The minutes grew to an hour. It was second watch and the tents remained still. The yonder torch was burning low, and no one came to attend it. Shamar supposed it was there for security, for campers returning late from town, but it was otherwise neglected.

"I'll need that light," he mumbled. "Who keeps the light? Will a man come replenish it? If not, my coins for this camp are in vain. I will have to complain," he said. "A poorly run camp, they should be ashamed, I'll tell others to avoid it."

More than two hours dragged on, maybe three.

Fearing he might fall asleep, he started pacing in the shadows, keeping just enough view with a sharp eye—but doubt and fatigue took over. There had been some activity, singular figures walking toward the toilet and back again. But for the past hour, nothing moved from the direction of Cala's tent.

Daylight was still three hours away, and sunrise probably an hour after that. It meant there was still time to wait. Should Cala's rendezvous discover a sleeping sentinel, that would not bode well for either of them. An awake sentinel he must be. For an old man feeling the many years on the trail, losing a night's rest was always a costly risk, but a familiar one.

Did she even hear him as he noised his way to the place of the rise?

A man did finally come to change out the torch, and the weakening shadows suddenly took life again.

"It's about time," Shamar grumbled. "If this was my camp, I would tend to my customers with kinder dispatch so they'd come again. It's only fair. . ."

He began to worry that Cala's plan had somehow been foiled. Perhaps it would have to be tried again on another night, somewhere up the road a distance?

Should he abandon the plan and return to his tent for some sleep, or stay longer? Suddenly—was that movement? From the direction of his tent?

He ducked low out of the light and held still. There were dark shapes against dark tents. He could make out a singular figure, slender, silhouetted against the distant torch. That must be Cala. And then came a second—round, about as wide as she was tall. That would have to be Suwr.

Shamar watched them negotiate the long walk toward his hiding place. It appeared that Cala had listened well to his footsteps because her path was pointed directly to him. He reached for his other blanket and clutched its corners, preparing to spring.

As the two women neared, Shamar could hear angry whispers as Suwr spat her sleepy complaints and insults at the girl, telling her she would be left for the wild dogs if she didn't start cooperating. Both women had shawls over their heads. Suwr complained about the long walk and Cala mumbled something in return. In the dim of dark Shamar could see the girl's eyes darting left and right, hunting for a sign, some signal he was there.

With Suwr's face turned down, Shamar quickly raised a hand into the light and waved. Cala saw it. She betrayed no reaction, but carefully drifted to her left to draw Suwr within reach. The angry woman followed unaware.

CAPTIVE

Just as the pair crested the rise Shamar leapt from the shadow and threw the blanket over Suwr's head and tackled her to the ground. He tightened his grip around her head so forcefully that the woman didn't even have breath to scream. She kicked and struggled, but he held her tight, muffled, and trapped.

"Shush old woman," Shamar growled in her ear. "I have a knife and I'll slice your throat if you make a single word."

He loosened his hold and the woman finally stopped her fighting and lay gasping for breath, panting with fear.

"Cala!" he ordered. "The rope, the rags, bring them—there, see, in a pile? Bring them."

"Cala?" she asked, delivering the implements to his outstretched hand. "That's not my name, I'm not Cala. . ."

"You are to me, and it's just that, well, never mind!" He leaned in to Suwr again.

"Now, listen to me carefully old woman," he said. "You're outside of earshot if you try to scream. And if you try, I'll slice your throat so fast the rats will slide down for dinner, lap up your blood, and build a nest in your stomach. Do you understand me?"

The woman grew still and nodded.

"I'm going to remove this blanket. The cold pain you feel on your throat is the blade of my knife just waiting to slice through your flesh—and I will, you're an easy kill. My blade makes you gurgle while you die. Blood is salty. Did you know that? If you lie still, I'll put this rag around your mouth so you can't scream. You let me do that, and I'll put my knife away. Otherwise, I spill your blood right here right now, and the land crabs that come out just before sunup will find your body and pick it raw to the bones. Even the vultures will feel robbed. Do you understand me?"

She nodded again and whimpered.

Shamar gagged the woman and tied her hands behind her back.

"What will we do now?" Cala asked.

"That's what I've been working on," Shamar said. "First, we take this old woman with us."

"What? Why would we do that?"

"She might serve our purposes," Shamar said. "We can always cut her throat later if she tries to flee. I'm fast with my blade," he whispered.

The terrified look on Suwr's face was enough to scare a scorpion back to its nest.

"You'll follow me and not make a sound," Shamar ordered.

He lifted the woman to her feet and replaced her shawl and veil in a manner that masked the gag on her mouth, and draped the blanket to hide her tied hands.

"We must reach the loading docks before daylight," Shamar said. He pulled the woman along, away from the sleepy camp. "I estimate it's half an hour's walk. We shouldn't dally."

He turned again to Suwr and breathed into her ear, "I have my long knife here in case you can't keep up old woman. We could go much faster without you."

Suwr nodded and hurried her step.

Shamar kept within the shadow of the hill until they reached the main road and then walked directly toward town and the docks that lay some distance farther.

"Cala," Shamar said, "if we should be asked about this woman, she's our slave. We have traveled from the Sinai, and you are my oldest daughter. If anyone asks, her name is Suwr. We caught her stealing so we are taking her to the marketplace at Noph and will dump her to the highest bidder. Do you understand?"

Cala nodded and took Suwr firmly by the other arm, leading her through the dark toward the shore of the sea beyond.

MORNING BARGES

The dock was already busy in the pre-dawn dark, and Shamar found several crews loading by torchlight for an early departure. Among their numbers he luckily fell upon an old friend who occasioned the wharf as captain of his own barge. Sadad was a good man, a fine acquaintance from several years back.

"So, my long-lost Shamar, are you running this time or are you chasing?" he asked with a slap on the shoulder.

"We're running, my old friend," Shamar said. "It turns out I was guide for an ill-gotten cause, and we just made our escape. When they awake, I'll need to be far away."

Sadad's friendly smile dissolved. "Then safe on my barge I will make you." He looked at the two women. "I gather the portly one was the escort?"

Shamar nodded. "She can't be seen, either."

"A hostage perhaps? I see her hands were getting in your way. I know what to do with her."

Shamar looked about nervously. "Yes, and we should get out of sight soon lest others tell of three together seen at your ship."

Sadad agreed and with a strained groan he helped lift Suwr over the rails and onto the deck. "We have small guest quarters, but you'll have to stay together in a single room," he said.

"I'm most grateful," Shamar said. "Let me get her secured to a post. Then I'll put Cala on guard, and fetch some fruit for the trip."

"Ah, good—the captive becomes the captor. I love it when that happens," he said. "Fetch your food from that third booth down. That's my cousin. He should be there already. Tell him Sadad sent you and to give you the family price."

"And for that, you'll please take this," Shamar said, pushing a small leather pouch into Sadad's hand.

"Oh no, not when you're my guest."

"I promise to be your guest next time, but for now, let me save my honor and bring this young lady to safety under my own labors. It would mean much to me."

"Very well, then." Sadad smiled wide. "For you, my old friend, I'll help you just this once and keep your silvers. The next time you'll bring your wife and it is my treat including a dinner in Al-Jarf."

Shamar took the two women into the guest quarters where he tied Suwr securely, gave Cala his knife, and left for food.

"Cut her throat if she tries to bribe you," Shamar said.

"No problem," Cala replied. "I've wanted to do that for two months."

Shamar stopped. "Two months?" he asked.

She nodded.

"We need to talk. I'll be back."

The sky was light when the barge pushed from the dock. Large sails billowed up the masts and a dozen men hurried about the decks tightening the lines and ropes, turning the sheets to catch the slightest breeze. The heavy-laden craft pulled slowly from the pier and soon caught the stronger winds farther from shore.

The trio was well engaged in breakfast—a large melon divided among them, a small bunch of grapes, khitana-fruit, a clutch of figs and dates, dried fish, bread.

"So, old man," Sadad smiled at the door, "Don't tell me you're hungry?" Shamar offered a melon slice, but Sadad declined. "Tell me about this secret mission of yours. What ill-gotten goods do you trade this time?"

"This is my daughter, Cala," Shamar said.

Cala wiped her mouth and smiled a sweet hello.

"A daughter? Why I thought . . . Oh, I see." Sadad looked at her a moment, then at Shamar, and gave a slight nod. "This is getting more interesting all the time . . . and the old woman?"

"A slave," Shamar said. "I might have to slice her up for your fishermen. Do you need bait?"

"Slaves make good bait," Sadad said. "If she gives you any trouble, send her body to my men. They know what to do. Eat well, old woman. The fish are big and they are hungry."

"Tell me," Shamar asked, "how long do your trips take you now?"

"This is a good place to cross the sea. It narrows for a fast journey. Last you saw me I was farther south, but the trade moves here, and so I ship here. There's a good connection to the caravans. It's a better place to cross. We'll tie off before tomorrow sundown. We have a good wind," he said. "The trip west is fast. It's coming back the other way that takes all the trouble. The winds don't work with me."

"Then we'll leave you to your return trip and find you again some day soon," Shamar said.

"And you, my friend, bring me up to date. It has been too long— what, maybe three years? Four?"

"Six," Shamar said. "I've been taking my clients north. I don't have much call for a trip across the Sinai—too hot, too long."

"Not for Moses and his children of Israel," the captain smiled.

"No, not for them. Perhaps I'm just getting too old."

"Old? And Moses was 80? No, you're not too old. Maybe fat, but not too old."

The men laughed while Cala remained poised. Her food held neatly in her lap.

"Here, here," Sadad said finally, waving them back to eating, "you finish your breakfast and I'll come visit again," and disappeared from the doorway.

GENEALOGY

It was midday when Cala came on deck to find Shamar. She was greeted by the barge's great sails bulging overhead like massive white clouds, popping and sighing in their strain at the masts. The wind churned the choppy sea with small whitecaps that bubbled to life then dissolved to lacy threads of foam.

Shamar was at the front leaning against the rail, basking in the fresh sea breeze, a fruit basket at his feet. The morning sun's sparkle was a rolling carpet of twinkling emeralds cast upon the deep in lazy blue hues and patterns.

"Shamar," Cala said approaching him.

"Good morning, Cala," he said standing straight. "Did you sleep well?"

"Yes, the best in a long time," she said, and took a deep breath, savoring the fresh air of freedom. She instinctively looked west, scanning the horizon.

"No one is following," Shamar said. "Let your heart rest a moment—have this," offering her figs and a sliced bakul. "How is our prisoner?"

"She snores."

"So I noticed," he said. "In fact, she does so with great vigor."

Cala smiled. "It's been that way for a long time. I'd know that snore from anywhere," she said.

Shamar picked another small melon and tested it for ripeness before cutting. He handed a slice to Cala. "When she awakens, we'd better feed her."

"In a while," Cala sighed. "I just want to … it's been so long," and glanced west again. "If we're safe, that's all."

Shamar nodded. "None of these barges are fast, I can promise you that!" he smiled. "My friend Sadad has men with swords. He is faithful, and watching. You can trust him."

"We must hurry," she said. "I want to find land, and hide."

"And that's exactly what I wanted to talk to you about," Shamar said. "This great mystery, this trip to Noph. I have questions, you've caught me in quite the trap."

"They will kill you," she said.

"Ah, only if they catch us, and I have more friends here than do they. We'll be safe enough."

She accepted another slice and found a place to seat herself. "I wondered if you knew of the Al Kalimat," she said, testing a fig.

"You're a puzzle," Shamar said. "Al Kalimat is a secret to most people, not well known. How is it you came to know of it? And why did you think to ask me? Now, no fibs or those fish will have a fresh breakfast, too."

She smiled. "I can tell you anything you wish to know," she said. "And yes, I am Abdali-ud-din."

Shamar picked through a juicy ruman, peeling back the red seeds from the white pulp. He eyed her with some degree of suspicion. "I am long on the road in these parts, Cala," he said. "I recognize your accent. It's from a place I know, and that's another puzzle. Tell me more. Where is your home, where do you come from? Perhaps I will know of it."

"And I need to be able to trust you, Shamar," she countered. "How do I know you're not part of the scheme I've been trapped by for these months on the trail?"

Shamar smiled through his grey beard. "All right, fair enough," he said. "I'm connected to Abdali-ud-din in several ways, so I should know anyone of significance whom you might mention. Try me."

Cala took another fig and chewed it, working a puzzle in her head. Then she looked into Shamar's eyes for signs of trust. The old man's gray eyes were kind and alive with honesty, fairness, and mercy. They were comfortable, and she began to think she might be able to tell him.

"I know of a man," she said. "His name is Suoud. Do you know him?"

Shamar nodded. "I do know of a Suoud. He performed great feats of bravery, even while still a young man. He carried the sword at an early age, a great honor. Many know of him, his fame is well known far and wide. So the story of Suoud is not enough. You could have heard of him in many places. You must do better than that."

Cala pursed her lips and looked out to sea. "All right, another," she said. "How about a man whose name is Humam."

"Ah, Humam! I know him well," Shamar said. "He is an infrequent visitor to our parts, a healing man of the medical arts."

Cala's eyes brightened. "Yes," she said, "That's Humam. He knows everything!"

"Well, I'd say he knows enough to amaze all the medicine men I've ever met," he said. "Yes, we've crossed paths several times. I haven't seen him for some time." Shamar picked at a bleak cluster of small yellow grapes, fingering for the ripe ones. "Okay, Humam, I know him. Now, who else?"

"I am from Rekeem," she finally said.

"Rekeem? Oh my! Why yes, I know Rekeem, I have kin there. I have been there a few times," and breathed a whistle. "You, Cala, you're a long way from your home and your people," he said chewing at the rind of another ruman.

Cala nodded and looked down. "It's my home and I need to return." She went quiet for a moment, then looked up. "Have you ever heard of the man Zafir?"

Shamar stopped chewing and looked at her with a red-stained smile. "Why, yes! Yes, I know of Zafir. He is also a great man. However, you could have heard of him anywhere as well, I must quiz you about Zafir. And you can't trick me there. He is a cousin of mine."

Cala gasped and froze, her eyes unblinking. "Your cousin? How?"

"Well, not a close cousin. His mother who is dead was a niece of my father, and it brought us close enough over the years—Rekeem, Saba', Leuke Kome. We met on his travels or mine. I've been to his home once. He would know me were we to. . ."

Cala sprang to her feet, scattering her morsels to the deck and threw her arms around Shamar, almost knocking him over. "Shamar! Shamar!" she cried with joy.

"Here, here!" he said, reaching haplessly at her arms. "It's okay! You'll break the neck of an old man if you squeeze any harder!"

"Shamar! You know Zafir. You know him. You're his cousin?"

"Well, um, yes, I said so," he stammered, pulling her off and holding her in front of him. "Certainly, he is well known. He is Abdali-ud-din. I've known him all my life. You know of him?"

Cala clutched at Shamar's sleeves, tears rolling down her cheeks, hope shining in her young blue eyes. "Zafir! Zafir, yes! Oh, Shamar, Zafir is my father!"

STRATEGY

The words tumbled from Cala almost faster than she could speak, and Shamar sat on the rail transfixed as her tale unleashed frustrations trapped much too long for a young spirit so filled with life and hope. He pondered what forces of fate and chance had brought him to this redeeming time, an unexpected chance to help the daughter of his cousin.

"Rasheeda is my mother," Cala said. "I was named after her. Rasha is my name. Everyone knows me by Rasha."

"Rasha is a lovely name," Shamar said. "I can see it was well chosen for you, a beautiful name. May I suggest some caution? We must be careful about listening ears and watching eyes." He thought a moment, looking around. "We're not out of danger, and won't be for a while. For your continued safety, I think we should call you Cala lest those who know of you hear your real name and discover you again."

Rasha nodded and doubt began clouding her face.

"Now, now! Be of good cheer," Shamar said. "We'll get you home, Cala. You must have hope." He took her hand in a firm hold. "We're a full day ahead," he said. "The next barges didn't leave until this morning. We'll be on shore a full day ahead of them. Have faith, Cala. A day on water is two days for us on land. We'll lose them, we will."

She forced a smile.

"So, you should know," Shamar said, changing the subject, "you should know that I met your mother Rasheeda many years ago, when she was Zafir's young bride. And much later, I remember hearing about you," Shamar said. "Zafir was hoping for a son and brought into his fold some additional wives, three or four?"

"Just two," Cala said. "But they gave him more daughters."

"Yes, yes, your other sisters, and that was the problem. He wanted a son for the scrolls."

Cala was surprised. "You know about the scrolls?" she whispered.

"I only know of them, perhaps more than I should," Shamar said. "Our bloodline crosses through the scrolls, but it didn't mingle. We had other things to do."

"How can that be?" she asked. "Are you not Abdali-ud-din?"

"Not precisely," he said. "We claim it, indeed. We're a branch of it, and that reputation carries a great deal of honor where the name is well known. We've joined forces many times over the years, but most of my family runs these sorts of service treks—camel caravans, boats, foot traffic. There's plenty of wealth in the business, and we help Abdali-ud-din all the time, but we ourselves don't move commodity like your father. And he didn't share the scrolls with me, nor did he offer—and I never asked."

"But you know of Al Kalimat and the secret ways?"

"Oh yes, that's all part of the family. No one else knows, and we don't betray those things that slip or are shared otherwise," he said. "That's why I was shocked that you knew of it and dared risk it on a total stranger. I thought there must be a connection somewhere."

"I felt inside that you were a kindred," she said, "and it was my last chance. I had to try."

They fell silent, watching the ship gently rise and fall as an errant wave moved across the sparkling waters. A trio of lazy gulls passed overhead squawking for a handout.

"Cala," Shamar finally said, "We can't do this alone."

"Why do you say that? Can't you just take me home?"

"That's what I want to do, but we've got some problems," he said.

"What problems?"

"I am me, just me, all alone," Shamar said. "Your father never travels unless he carries with him hundreds of extra swords, and that to protect his gold and incense. All I have is my knife."

"Does it matter?"

"Yes, it matters a great deal. You are his greatest treasure, and I have nothing but my wits to protect you, at least until I can find one of Zafir's stewards, someone who can hide you while I build a guard to escort you home."

"Where are my father's stewards? Are there any along these coasts?"

Shamar walked to the railing, reached for a taut line, and gazed out over the edge. "I'm not sure," he said. "I think I know how to locate his steward in Noph, but there are others, Al-Jarf, maybe Waset, Luxor, Thebai, up the Nilus, down the coast. I know there are many more, but that's all I know."

"You're worried about Rakbah, aren't you?"

"He knows your value, Cala. And not just your value to your father, and that's priceless, but also to any conspirator who wants a part of it. You're the prize. They won't stop at anything to find you and get you back."

"Then how can I get home?"

Shamar looked at the girl with a distant stare, his mind working a strategy that could be calculated for only so many days out.

"I believe Rakbah is on the sea right now, wondering the same thing," he said. "I'm sure he's plotting which way to dispatch his men."

Cala scanned the horizon, fear turning her pink cheeks to ashen gray.

"Here, here," Shamar said, putting a hand gently on her shoulder. "I won't have you buying trouble before its time, right?" He bent down to catch her eye and smiled. Cala's gaze broke and she looked at him, worry pulling at her hope.

"We'll make it just fine," Shamar said, "but we'll have to do it carefully. First, as we discussed, you must be anonymous. You must answer to Cala and nothing else."

"Yes, I can do that," she said.

"Second, we must have everyone think that you're my daughter, and we'll have to dispose of Suwr as soon as we land."

"Kill her?" Cala asked.

Shamar smiled and shook his head. "I've never killed a thing in my life," he said. "Okay, maybe some insects or a scorpion or two, but never a man."

"Or a woman?"

He shook his head and grinned behind his great whiskers. "That talk of mine was all just a lot of blow and bluster to keep her scared," he said. "It's easier to keep them under control when they fear you. My goodness, I could never do that. I wouldn't even know where to begin to dispose of a woman like that. Would you?"

Cala scowled. "Not me. I just wish she would go away. I never want to see her again."

"Very well, then," Shamar said. "That's exactly what we'll do at the first opportunity. Now, I need you to tell me about these kidnappers. Would any of them know about your family back home, any other information that could help them set a trap, or find us on the way?"

"Yes," Cala said sourly. "Faris. He was a childhood friend and betrayed me into the hands of Rakbah and his men."

"I think I remember him," Shamar said. "Wasn't he the scrubby youth who labored so hard to grow a beard?"

Cala nodded. "Yes, that was him."

"I noticed him. He rode apart, didn't talk much. He seemed too young to be party to those bandits—out of his normal element."

"Yes. He knows about my mother's family in Saba', and my father's business and his great trek to C'ina. He knows that father carries the scrolls. He knows enough to betray me and my family, and he knows where I would hide from him. And . . ." The words caught in her throat.

"And what?" Shamar asked.

"And he knows about my Bassam," she said.

"Bassam?"

"Yes."

"And who is this?" Shamar asked. "Someone close to you?"

"If he knew what Faris has done to me, he would kill him."

"Where is this Bassam?"

"With my father, far away, learning the scrolls. I sent a message."

"Al Talimat?"

She nodded.

"Oh, the scrolls. Then this young Bassam stands in the place of a son, and you and he are . . ."

She nodded again.

Shamar scratched his beard and gave these new developments a patient review. The many names and facts and disjointed pieces were coming together, and that brought concern about what else might be afoot—things unfolding beyond the communication channels of coastal Egypt and the regions of the great sea.

"Then this young betrayer, this Faris, and the rubbish with whom he has thrown his lot, they won't be successful," Shamar said. "For what this boy knows, and for what you know too, we might be able to use that knowledge against him. He becomes the leader to guide them until they have no further use of him, then will they destroy him. Until that time we can anticipate their moves . . ."

Cala went quiet and turned her face to the breeze and closed her eyes.

"Do not worry my daughter," Shamar said, taking her hand gently in his and giving it a confident squeeze. "We will return you to your Bassam, I swear it."

It was dusk when Sadad's men rolled sail and rowed the last short distance to the dock. They bumped along the pier and found places to rope off. Torches lit the wharf while stiff-legged passengers helped each other onto a steadier platform. The coastal outskirts of Al-Jarf glowed with activity. Distant windows and doorways shined like an array of tiny yellow stars scattered across the hillsides, outlining the boulevards of the busy trading places and quiet destinations.

With Sadad's crew busy dispensing their bundles for trade, Shamar arranged to hide his departure. The goal was to remove their "slave" into the dark and disappear without notice. Sadad directed them with God-speed to a discreet boarding house beyond the coastal traffic and beyond any spying eyes.

SLIGHT OF HAND

Their boarding house was especially Spartan, offering little more than old stained pillows and cheap stick furniture. It was Sadad's idea, not so much for lack of better accommodations as it was for the inn's distance from the center of the village—and its lack of frequent visitors. Privacy in these coastal villages, Sadad said, was as good as secrecy, and a good night's rest would pay them well. The weariness of the two-day sail had taken enough toll that despite it all, the three travelers slept deeply.

At daybreak Shamar was already away, and Cala was left in charge of Suwr. The old woman awoke to discover she was not yet dead. Suspecting her captors had no intention of doing her serious harm, she regained some of her old bluster.

"Let me go and I'll see that Rakbah goes easy on you," Suwr said. "You know he's coming, you have my word on it."

Cala was busy poring over Shamar's maps.

"I can arrange it," Suwr persisted. "Rakbah is a rough man, but I know him from a long time back. He will listen to me, but only if you let me go now."

Cala turned her back.

"Are you listening Rasha?" she scolded. "I said I can do you this one favor."

"It's Cala," the girl said without turning.

"Rasha, Cala, I don't care, and neither will Rakbah when he finds us. You know he has his spies everywhere," she said. "They probably heard your every word to that man on deck."

Cala examined the faint lines running across the map of Egypt, tracing with her finger the several indistinct routes connecting the regular trek from shore to the Nilus. She estimated 6-7 days down river to Noph.

"Ever been to Noph?" Cala asked without looking up. Suwr pleaded more forcefully.

"Untie me and I can help you escape," she said.

"But Noph," Cala insisted. "Have you ever been there?"

"No," the old woman said. "But I have relatives there who can help, they can help us get back to your Rekeem. And Rakbah won't be the wiser for it if we leave now, before he finds us."

"Sorry," Cala said, turning. "We'll keep you as our slave if we need to, and when we arrive in Noph no one will know you until we have made our escape. And should any misfortune befall us, we'll have you to get us out of it."

"And what awaits you beyond Noph?" Suwr asked. "The sea? What will you do then? You can't go back home. You can't return to Noph. You can't challenge the Romans. Those are their waters. Or the Greeks, those are their coasts. If you're captured, they'll use someone like you in ways you only hear about in whispers and shame, young Rasha. You must let me guide you to friends who will protect you, who will set you free, and save yourself."

"No, I don't think so," Cala said as she measured distances on the maps. "No, I think Noph is best. It's large, a place to get lost in for a while. That's where we must go."

Suwr sat back in a huff. Her hands remained tied behind her back, and she slouched to relieve the discomfort.

A short time later, Shamar breezed through the door. "All is set," he said. "Let's get going."

"You found passage?" Cala asked.

"Yes, at mid-day, the earliest, and we'll soon be rid of this baggage," he said, looking over at Suwr. She frowned.

"We've got an eight-day's hard ride ahead of us," Shamar said. "A caravan west will take us to the Nilus, and there we will find regular dhows for hire to Noph. A week or so on the water is all," he said.

"What about her?" Cala asked. "What about her screaming and complaining?"

"I've taken care of it," Shamar said. "If she starts up again, we'll bind her mouth for the camel trek. No one will care. We'll tell them she's a slave. Once we're on the dhow, she can scream all the oaths she pleases. We'll stow her in an animal room behind a locked door. Passengers are accustomed to such yelling and false promises."

"Then I'll gather our things," Cala said.

Crossing through the eastern desert was tedious. Vast plains of briny flatlands thinned out in all directions. Ancient wadis carved across the plains made great basins of stony ground. Perhaps this had been a vast stretch of swamplands in eons past, but stony passages for now—hardly a growing thing could be seen anywhere. The heat was humid with sea smells perfuming the arid expanse for that entire first day.

Only the shallow rises over small hills or the unending plains of dormant sands gave occasional respite from the colorless terrain. Cala was impatient for what awaited them at its end.

"Shamar, what is this place? Does the man know where he's going? Does he lead us into some trap?"

Shamar awoke from a concentration of sorts, and tried to share in her despair and boredom.

"I've taken this way once before. It does not get better until we reach the valley of Nilus," he said. "Fields of basalt outcropping, etched hillsides, stony paths, it's a way I would not take were it not in our best interests right now. We're in good hands. Only a few days more, then our work begins."

"And this detour south, it makes our trek much farther . . ."

"Bandits," Shamar said. "They've controlled the great Kush deserts for as long as I've traveled through here. We'll be safe enough in the river villages, but it costs us a detour south."

The low sun shone directly into Cala's face and she drew her covering. In her hands she held some colorful silken threads. It was a long braid, woven as a memorial to the long, forced trek that carried her west and farther from home.

"The desert hides the horizon, have you noticed?" Shamar asked. "See the haze, swallowing the sun? That's a part of this wonderful land, a thick horizon that hides the rising in the morning and the setting at night, just as pharaoh would have it."

They were interrupted with a happy hubbub from the front of the train. The troupe had come upon an oasis that had suddenly materialized out of nowhere.

"How does our captain magically find such places?" she asked.

"They've crossed these lands for thousands of years," Shamar said. "There are many secrets here, and we must find at least one of them."

She smiled at the audible groans as her fellows stepped from their kneeling camels. It had been a long, hard day on the road.

They pastured their camels and set camp. Suwr was led away to toilet and returned for some food. Small dung fires brought life to the gathering and a simple evening meal was prepared, each company supplying food to their own.

There were exchanges with others, some with accents from lands too distant for the map. Their host brought a biting green tea that was shared among all, a calming finish to the day's difficult work. Friendly banter carried into the dark as the sky grew black and its jewels appeared above. The early sleepers were soon quiet as the fires blinked out.

With Suwr's complaints finally silenced, Cala and Shamar sat at their fire. The yellow flame of an oil lamp danced shadows across an old map.

"Here we board the dhows," Shamar said, pointing with a small stick to a well-marked place on the map. Then, gesturing toward Suwr, he traced a line northward toward Noph. "About six days' travel on the river," he said quietly. Tracing a line in the opposite direction, he whispered, "And we'll find help here," and stopped his pointer at Cyene.

Zafir had rehearsed many tales about the river city Cyene. Cala had longed to visit it, and here she was approaching the place from a most unusual circumstance, the last she might have imagined. The city was a place for taxing the traders leaving Upper Egypt and headed north.

"It's an ancient treasure place," Zafir had told her. "Valued for its quarries of red granite. From these were the Egyptian gods given birth, first as large stone blocks, then barged down the Nilus to temples and shrines where the royal stoneworkers placed their images, then set them as sentinels to keep order and obedience."

Cala had never dreamed to visit such a place. It made her smile to remember her father's tales.

"Do you see how we'll travel?" Shamar asked, pointing far south, keeping their true destination unspoken lest Suwr be awake and listening.

"I see it well," Cala said. "Noph must be a short stop."

AKHETATEN

The eight-day trip ended abruptly with the appearance of the great desert river—distant, broad, gray and still. The mighty Nilus.

As they neared, Cala closed her eyes and smiled at the sounds and smells of the lush river, its crowded banks, the growth of blossoms, green, wet, rot.

"Shamar!" Cala said. "Look at that! A wonderful city over there!" she said pointing across the river. "Do we travel there?"

"Not if we can avoid it," he smiled. "That's where they bury the dead."

"The dead? In that great place?"

"It's their religion," Shamar said. "The temples are on the east bank, and their tombs on the west. That's no city for the living!"

"The River of Death I hear about?"

"That's it," he said. "They follow the sun, rising at birth, setting at death."

"That seems backwards," she said.

"Perhaps. The king's spirit follows the sun, stopping at the river to pay the trespass, then finds rest in his tomb at sunset to renew himself," he said.

"Some rest is what I want right now," Cala said, "even in a tomb, if it will get me out of this heat."

"Yes, tombs are good for that," Shamar smiled.

The two went quiet as the descending sun slowly dissolved into the layers of desert haze, changing its disguise from white to yellow to orange. Its muted reflection shimmered widely in the river, a thousand distortions softly disappearing.

It was first watch when they pulled into Akhetaten. Torch bearers stood ready. Suwr was awake on her camel and looked about to beg an escape. A sandal-footed man pulled the reins of the lead camel, taking them to a camping spot not far from the river's edge. It was a lush meadow surrounded by palms.

"Be good, old woman," Shamar said. "I'll let you loose soon enough, but not here, not until we get you inside a cage bound for Noph. If you give me trouble, I'll give you to the deb and his mates. They don't trust intruders on their hunting grounds. But you? He might think you're one of his herd."

Cala shot a look at Shamar. "You're getting mean with your teasing, Shamar."

"Who says I'm teasing? There's a whole herd of river horses wading out there, just waiting to come feed. Do you see them?"

Cala scanned the mirrored surface of the still water. Its color was quickly changing toward gray, matching the sky above. In the distant reflection, she could see tiny bumps bobbing in the water, the heads of some 20 debs settled low, just enough for their snouts and eyes to keep watch.

"They'll forage tonight on land," Shamar said. "It's unusual for them to be this far north—normally there's not enough green, too much desert." He counted their number. "Twenty-four."

Just then an old bull sprayed a great mist over his companions and rose to expose his great fat head.

Shamar turned to Suwr. "When he comes to graze, old woman, I should put you out for his meal."

Cala shook her head and looked away. "Now you're acting like Bassam," she said, glancing ahead for their camping place. The group hurried through stands of ancient stones and columns. Mounds of drifted sand piled around the base stones like old cobwebs, the rest of the works were swallowed up in the dark.

"It's like burial grounds of ancient skeletons," she whispered.

Shamar nodded. "It's a poor harbor that greets you, Cala—a few diners, a few inns, but in its day? Glorious! Magnificent!"

Small bats circled above in great wild swoops, snatching insects lost for a hiding place. At the river's edge, a pair of boats made shore by torchlight.

"The river and her gifts," Cala spoke softly. "It's a secure life with days and nights to eat and sleep—a rhythm that needn't be bothered by the cares of the world. I can almost feel that harmony—ancient peace, distilled quiet, ingrained beauty—and freedom." She sighed and smiled. "The Nilus and her home in Egypt. This must be a part of heaven."

TO THE RIVER

Dawn over the Nilus was breathtaking—the desert haze mixed with the river mist slowly emerged as an orange-tinged curtain that spread across the eastern horizon.

Cala breathed the cool humid perfumes, resting her gaze on the glassy river. A hesitant breeze teased gently at a few errant strands of her hair, and for a moment she closed her eyes to the sounds of the awakening waters—the darting tweet of a small black-winged bird

swooping in great circles to complete her work of the night before—
the distant hollow clunking of men loading a boat—a frustrated camel
somewhere by the shore chewing her cud with a grunt. And then the
great snorgling trumpet of Suwr's snore heralding the moment that
she was waking up just as Shamar came walking briskly from the
shoreline.

"It's an old Roman barge," he said breathless, pointing down the coast
a few hundred paces. "Right there, can you see it?" he asked smiling.
"It's no trireme, but it will get us to where we're headed."

Cala picked out the large mast rising above the rest.

"A crew of 20 or so," he said. "Mostly oarsmen. It's the fastest they've
got. We'd best be getting on our way."

He pushed a sack of fruit and cheese into her hands. "Enjoy!"
he said. Then turned to Suwr. "Roll those old fat bones into action,
woman! Get up and get out or I'll leave you for the pirates." Shamar
turned and winked at Cala. She grinned back, shaking her head in
modest rebuke

The sun was glaring on the boat's decking when Cala stepped on board.
She quickly worked her way to the bow for the large awning. Several
passengers seated themselves in similar fashion among the deck cargo,
finding enough comfort to doze until departure. There was a long bench
by the railing where Cala spread out her things. Her blanket made a
nice cushion, and she settled in.

Shamar had the captain trapped in conversation, gesturing and
working some plan of his. She smiled at the captain's impatience. He
nodded, stepped back, smiled, waved, stepped back again, then cut it
off with an abrupt nod and turned to the business of launching his craft.

Before Shamar could even reach the bow, the routine shove-off
finally engaged and the large craft moved from the dock. Long oars
beneath the main deck lowered into action.

It took just a few minutes for the oarsmen to pull the boat into mid-
river where a slight breeze finally caught and the boat leapt forward. At
last, we're on our way, Cala thought. The knot in her stomach relaxed.

Cala watched the shore drift away, shrinking from a crowded metropolis of rugged activity to become just an ant colony of men and their boats blurring into the thin line of the receding shore.

"Did you do it?" she asked as Shamar sat down next to her.

"Yes, all taken care of," he said.

"Does she suspect anything?"

"I doubt it," he said, leaning to his left to peer beyond the mast and superstructure. "That's her boat there, just pulling out, the one with a single sail . . . do you see it? The blue streamer at the top?"

Cala watched the distant shape turn down-river.

"So, she heads to Noph, but she'll tell Rakbah of our ruse, won't she?"

"She'll have it figured out by tonight's first stop," Shamar said. "I paid the captain copper drachmas to continue the secret. I've seen him a few times before. He knows me. I think I can trust him."

"You know that my father will pay you back," Cala said.

"Oh, it's not the money I'm worried about," he said. They watched the foaming caps of river water break against the hull and melt into the next wave. "I'm not convinced Rakbah will fall for it. Too many eyes and ears around here. When they tie in at Noph the captain will evict the old woman, and tell the authorities she was a stowaway or an escaped slave woman. They'll take her away. Even if Rakbah follows her unknowingly, it's a large river, hundreds of stops. Finding her—let alone hearing of her—would be a miracle by itself."

"We could use a miracle," Cala said.

"And we're making one," he said. "We'll hurry south, anxious, as if he might be closer than we want, but glad that we have put this much distance between us. No more ships are headed south today. They departed this morning, we're alone."

"And how far?"

"At least 12 days."

Cala draped her arms over the railing resting her chin, and invited the cold misty spray from the slapping waves to touch her face and cool her skin. The oarsmen would continue for a while longer until the winds blew and the sail could do the work.

When Cala awoke it was midday and the sun was straight overhead burning her face dry. She opened an eye to see that Shamar and the captain stood by, yet again engaged in something of mild concern.

"You're awake!" Shamar smiled. "Captain, my daughter Cala." "Is there a problem?" she asked, working her tongue against a sticky dry mouth.

"Here," Shamar said, handing over a clay mug of river-water tea. She let the swampy taste cool the parch in her throat, her first drink from the Nilus itself.

"I've been telling your father about this old barge," the captain said smiling. "We've had this craft in dry dock before. It might be time again."

"Why?" she asked.

"These old barges the Romans liked to call river-worthy boats don't keep out the water like we're accustomed. Here, let me show you," and he knelt down by the bench to remove a board along the railing. Behind it Cala could see the inside of the planking that skinned the outer hull. Blackened fibers of old rope were woven in and out of grooves in the planking, and pulled tight with knots.

"See this rotting stuff?" The captain asked. "This is papyrus rope. It's an old design, but they use it to hold the planks. It works well, actually. The planks fit together nicely, a mortise and tenon joint all along here," he said, tracing a joint with his finger. "Keeps them in place—strong, but see? This rope here . . ." and he bent down to look more closely. "See how it frays?"

Cala could see fibers cut and splitting away.

"It's a tight hold and an old science," the captain said. "But for this old barge some new ropes are much preferred to old science."

"A lot of rotting," Shamar said. "Do you take on water?"

"I like to say we don't," the captain answered, standing up to replace the plank. "So we keep watch on it—we have been for the last month. For a day at a time we are sea worthy. We had them caulk it last time at dry dock. The problem is these old planks move and bend with the weight. That puts a lot of strain, the joints need that lashing to hold."

"Is it something new you just found?" Cala asked.

"No, but it's getting worse," the captain explained. "Water accumulates faster than we can bail it. We've got each night to work it along the way, my crew will see to that, but we'd hoped one last trip to Cyene and we'd dry-dock for a complete going over—or set it all ablaze for a month-long fire to cook our meals, I'm not sure."

Shamar smiled.

"We'll be fine, Cala," he said. "I'm sure the captain will take things carefully for the next 12 days. It's not a long time for an old boat."

"I'll deliver you as promised," the captain said. "Tonight, then, dinner when we dock, with me and my officer?"

"I'll look forward to it," Shamar said, and the captain left.

Cala looked at Shamar with concern. "Are we going to sink?"

"With all this wood?" Shamar laughed. "Not possible! What you should worry about are the krokodilos if this old boat does come apart. In these waters, they'll grow as long as the boat," he said, measuring with outstretched arms. "They've been known to swoop out of the water and snatch people right off the deck. Swallow them whole. Without chewing. Honest."

"So that's how this is going to go," she said, adjusting herself away from the railing.

'ADAN

"Wake up donkey butt," Fawzi said, kicking my foot. "We're here, get up."

I had been dreaming a long and detailed adventure with color and talking and movement, a sure sign of badly needed rest.

"Bassam! Did you hear me?"

I rolled over to my knees and stretched. The sun had baked me dry. My tongue was stuck to the roof of my mouth. A nearby goatskin quenched my desperate thirst, but it's foul-tasting stuff when it gets warm, and I spat some on the deck.

I blinked my eyes and saw for the first time the magnificent sea-mountain wall surrounding ancient 'Adan.

I was told about this famous seaport, a city built inside the blackened cavity of an ancient volcano. I let my eye trace the towering peaks that leered down at us from high above the ocean—sheer cliffs streaked with the black striations that made the setting so famous. It was mysterious, almost mystical. The valley below was busily engaged in the noisy life of exchange, even at this late hour.

I held to a mast line as the boat bumped against the pier. A great sense of relief spilled over me at the same time. At last, I breathed, 'Adan! Without mishap—we made it. I could feel the desert heat not far from this little metropolis. It felt so close to home.

The captain snapped some orders and his crew leapt to action. The passengers crowded to the railing.

The air was pungent with the quaint smells of the fishing village—a wafting reminder of where fish-eaters dwell, with a mix of salty brisk air—so unique to a seaport. Zafir held to Ammar's arm for steadiness. "We have urgent business with my steward. Follow me," he said and stepped off the boat.

Fawzi picked up Zafir's bundle and threw it into my arms. "Avenger of Suoud, be a cousin to your donkey family and carry this, would you?" This time I didn't object. All of us were anxious and weary. That last stretch took us three straight weeks at sea and we badly needed a break.

The city of 'Adan was well patrolled by the port authorities. They stood in twos or threes, eyeing us with stern suspicion as we made our way to the receiving agent. For the many merchants who came, it was clear that the city did not allow the squabbling of disorderly patrons to export their rudeness to the business sectors of 'Adan.

I followed the others, leaving for good that creaky, smelly boat that had tested our endurance these many months. Were it not for Ammar's south pointer and Zafir's experience, we would have been constrained to follow the shorelines in the traditional fashion, tripling our travel time. Timely bribes encouraged the captain to let us navigate, hastening our arrival.

'Adan's wide streets were crowded with men and women in clusters of commerce. These masses were intermingling, going, coming, buying, selling, laughing, arguing. Such a pleasant annoyance compared to the tomb-like silence of our desert caravans. I smiled as we followed Zafir toward the market. I loved to be around people, a great engine of prosperity and survival, all of them inspiring in their multitude of ways.

"What are you grinning at, yak dung?" Fawzi asked.

"It's nice to be home," is all I said.

"We're not home, fish phlegm," he answered. "We've got another three weeks on the water, maybe four, unless you can fly."

Four weeks. Maybe three if the winds blow north this time of year, maybe then we could travel faster . . .

Zafir was anxious. He passed by all the diners and inns, even the street carts that could give us a meal. He headed straight to the northern section. It was markedly quieter here. A stone-paved boulevard with many open-air stone buildings led to an average-sized structure plastered in a light blue daub. Zafir left us standing on the pavers beneath some palms while he went to the door. There was a nice calm in this place—peaceful, breezy, quiet.

"He knows all these stewards?" I asked.

"Not all, not personally," Ammar said. "Wadi is a good friend from years back. He's the one who watches over Zafir's family when he sends them for the season."

Moments later an older woman appeared, greeting him with a surprised smile. They exchanged words for a few moments. Zafir explained our purpose. She smiled and waved us in.

"This is Nida," Zafir said, "my dear friend, and the widow of my dear friend Wadi, who I just learned has died just last month."

"I can't tell you how much this sorrows me, my dear friend," he said, taking Nida's hand and holding it affectionately. "You and Wadi have been guarding this post as your home for what? Forty years?"

Her eyes grew red, but she smiled. "No, I think it's only 39," she said, and we laughed politely.

"I am just now informed of this," Zafir said. "It breaks my heart. I had so wanted to greet him again with fond memories of our many shared adventures."

"You are all most welcome here," Nida' said. "Wadi would have liked to have seen you, too. We miss his great warmth and industry."

We nodded at her loss. She led us into the great room to some wooden chairs. Zafir was given the cushioned lounge.

"Tea for anyone? You must be tired from your long journey."

Zafir told her not to bother, but that he would return to take her and her daughter to a dinner later on.

"We're anxious for any word," he smiled weakly.

"I expected it so," Nida' said, and crossed the room to a squat cupboard in the corner. "We were shocked and horrified at the news at Rekeem. We've been in frequent contact with them," and pulled out a leather pouch, wiping the dust with a small towel. "Everything we know is here, as of a few weeks ago," she said, handing it to Zafir. I noticed it was identical to the pouch Arja gave us in Tamralipta. It carried the same mark.

Zafir drew out a thick packet of reports and began reading. We watched his face for clues. Several minutes passed and he furrowed his brow as if working through some difficult problem. Setting the documents on the table, he sat back hardly breathing a word. We all looked in anticipation.

Finally, after a long silence, he announced, "My friends, our plans must change."

"We're not heading to Rekeem?" I asked.

"Not directly," Zafir said. "No, not yet."

PARTING WAYS

"A man and a girl have been spotted in the past weeks traveling south on the Nilus," he began.

In Egypt? My heart sank.

"They were first seen at Al-Jarf and later, the first cataract. That much is good news," he said. "It seems this could be our Rasha, and she could be in the company of my cousin. More important to me," he said, pulling one of the messages, "are the ransom notes," and handed them off to Ammar. "These are dated before the sighting on the Nilus."

Ammar took the notes and read Wadi's letter, now a month old. "Then their threats were not . . ."

"That's right," Zafir said. "She has escaped, for this we can be grateful, for this we must think that she still lives, and . . ."

He paused, tripping over his thoughts and emotions, searching for the right way to present his concerns.

"What is unknown has complicated things—" and he looked directly at me. "This man and girl were pursued by the Tauri, certainly by the same men who took her from Rekeem. Their leader is well known. He was seen by several and goes by the name Rakbah. A description is provided here," and he hefted the leather pouch as if to weigh the value of the news.

"My advisors believe the ransom scheme was to deflect our attentions to Avalites, when in fact, they took her north into Egypt, therefore . . ." He paused.

A tired strain shadowed his face. He put his fist to lips a moment to re-compose, and cleared his throat. "They wanted a ransom. Therefore, they would not harm Rasha. That's good. They were observed making their way toward Noph. And then, somewhere along the way, she escaped. The man seen with her afterwards is described as one known by my stewards. His name is Shamar, my relative."

"I know Shamar," Ammar said, looking at Zafir then me. "A good man, Bassam. A good husband and a good father."

"His family hires out their caravans, guiding travelers east and west," Zafir said. "What we don't know is what became of him and Rasha, and here is the trouble."

Zafir said the reports told of several sightings of a fair-skinned man and girl who were seen on the Nilus traveling south. "Those messengers knew of the attack on Rekeem, but not of Rasha's kidnapping. They assumed him to be from our region. He was noticed only because of his unusual hurry, but there was no reason to suspect his involvement in any crime, only that he was in the company of a girl and both were in a rush. They were traveling alone—not on a supply barge, and that seemed unusual."

Zafir paused. He looked as if he was drawing a map in his head, illustrating where events took place and where the two might have journeyed by now.

"My steward at Gebtu became suspicious because strangers came asking at the river villages about a fair-skinned slave-girl escaping upriver, and asked if she had been seen. My steward reported this activity, and that brings us up to date according to this report."

Why didn't they just rescue her right then and there?

Fawzi saw my concern. "Bassam, if they had known who she was or what she looked like, they would have taken action. There are many people traveling the Nilus at any given time, fair-skinned and not. These things happen so quickly."

He was right. I was frustrated and angry.

Zafir rehearsed the dangers of the Nilus, the difficulties of passage, the crossings, and the pirates. He said a flight south on the river does not lead to the Egyptian Sea. There are no escapes to the open sea in that direction. It leads only to the jungles.

"They would have to cross the Punt by caravan," Ammar said. "That's ten days, two weeks, depends from where they embark."

Zafir furrowed his brow. "I wouldn't know if Shamar is aware of this problem; though, he would ask, I'm sure he would. He might also choose to hide in a village. If the Nub'ah are kind, perhaps they would protect them, or show them the way home."

Zafir reached for the lounge to sit. His face was ashen, and his eyes looked tired and grey. We waited quietly. "Al Talimat reports no other sightings for three weeks. No one knows what has become of Rasha and Shamar. I'll send a better description of Rasha, that will help."

I felt sick and didn't know whether to be angry or fearful or regretful or . . .

Zafir straightened up and squared his shoulders, making a fist with his right hand as resolution returned to his countenance. "Here, then, is my decision. I need your help, my dear friends," and he looked each of us in the eye.

We began unfolding a plan in simple words, direct tasks, and he made it clear—the odds were seemingly impossibly against us having success.

I discreetly reached for Suoud's sword that hung at my side, and wrapped my fingers around its hilt. Would it see yet one more day of duty in the service of this great and kind soul?

"However, I can't go with you," he said.

The three of us gulped.

"I must admit this," Zafir continued. "My leg, my age, I am good on the desert leading men at a camel's pace, but I would not be good in the land of the Nub'ah. That place is for men still in the strength of their youth. It is a curse upon the elderly that when they become old they are still young! And you Ammar, I'm not sure if you're up to this. You're no spring lamb yourself, but I need you, my old friend. I need you to guide this journey. They will benefit from your knowledge. Will you do it?"

Ammar nodded. "With all my heart, you can count on me. I've wanted to see those jungles since I was a boy."

"Then it's settled," Zafir said. "My wives are in Saba'. I will start for there tomorrow, and gather up my family. We'll return to Rekeem, reclaim our lands and possessions, and bring order to our city."

He stood and pointed west. "And you, tomorrow, you'll take the next boat to Punt. They have a busy port at Avalites with much trade.

Ammar, will you get your map? Let me show you the shortest way to the Nilus from there."

Day 712

Dear Rasha,

We returned to our part of the world yesterday. Your father is sick with worry. So am I. He will return to your mother and take the family to Rekeem. Ammar and Fawzi and I begin our search for you at the southern part of the Nilus. I refuse to believe you have been taken from me. I will not rest until I have found you. Do not despair.

—Bassam

PATIENCE

None of us slept that night. The urgency of the trip kept us staring into the dark or pacing around the oil lamp. I was stewing in my fear that Rasha was in danger. Ammar was preparing for the new lands and the maps he would draw, and Fawzi was out late bribing our way to an early start. He left twice to wander the docks for any captain willing to leave before sun up. All of them refused.

"They must be accustomed to men like us," Fawzi said upon his return. "Men in a hurry become easy spenders, and I couldn't pay enough for early passage." He replaced the coins to their hiding places.

Ammar looked up from his map. "That sounds right," he said. "It's quite the place—treasures from the whole land converge through here. Lacking gold is probably not much of a problem here as it is for others."

"How do you convince the man who has everything?" Fawzi said with frustration.

"I'm told it's been this way for centuries," Ammar said. "Vast loads of gold, skins, incense, spice, animals, slaves—dispatched to ports around the world. Such wealth must leave behind plenty of crumbs. I'm guessing for these captains of the boats a full night's rest means more than a bribe in gold."

He told us nub is the Egyptian word for gold. Thus, Nub'ah means a whole land named after gold. "Maybe we've got things in Rekeem they don't see here," I suggested, "and that will make for a good bribe some day."

Fawzi scowled and threw his hands up like I was a complete fool. "Oh Bassam, you smelly heap of freshly piled bat dung. Bribe them with what?! A few empty caves? A bushel of sand? A look at the scrolls? Sometimes, I really wonder about you."

That made me smile. Despite my fears, I fell asleep knowing I had two friends who would make this a memorable journey no matter the challenge.

That next morning Zafir gave us some last instructions.

"My stewards in Egypt are few," he said. "Atbara, Cyene, Noph, these will help you along the way. They won't be hard to locate. You must be cautious to ask carefully. Rasha and Shamar won't know you're coming and will be hiding from strangers, staying in shadows. You must ask in confidence lest you alert her captors or their spies to your intentions."

We reviewed the maps once more, and changed out some of our supplies.

"You better leave your journal with me," Zafir said. "This is not a time for much writing. I will keep them safe."

I agreed and rummaged through my things for the bundle. "I still want to take notes, a journal of our travels. I'll leave this with you, but keep a few sheets. It won't slow me, I promise. If that's okay."

Zafir took my bundle. "Then you must use this," he said, handing me a large empty water skin. "Dry it for your writings. We don't want another mishap in the water," he said waving his arm toward C'ina. "Tie it up tight. You'll be safe on the Nilus." At that, Ammar lifted his map pouch and pointed. "Yes," Zafir said, "like Ammar's maps, it works well."

I took the skin and began experimenting to see if the supplies would fit. "I'll make it work."

"This too," Zafir said, handing over a brass Egyptian lamp and some wicks. "Bassam, you'll take your fire drill and preparations. This won't be a time for luxuries or carelessness. Travel light. Travel swift. Keep these protected and they will serve you on the water and across the deserts. You might cross Punt or Kush or Egypt, wherever this journey takes you. You have learned much since we left home. Do not let these lessons become lost on another river."

Zafir took a smaller skin of lamp oil, checked its seal, and pushed it to Ammar. "Don't forget this," he said. Then turned to me. "Bassam, you must leave with them, my son. I know this is a difficult errand and you might suffer for your sacrifices. Know this, no matter the ending place of your journey, I love my Rasha so much, and if . . . and if . . ." Zafir's voice broke. He put a clenched fist to his lips and cleared his throat. "And if she has found her place with God and you must discover that, I pray your safety to return quickly to your home. And if by God's will she be found safe and you return her to me, how blessed and how benevolent is the goodness of him in our lives. No matter his will in this labor, the ring on your finger must stay. You are my heir, my son, and you're under covenant to return to me alive, to fulfill your promises. Fawzi, Ammar, do not let this boy test your patience with undo risk. Do you understand me? If he should, I give you permission to teach him a lesson with the broad side of the Sword of Bassam."

"Happy to help, any time. In fact, we can start right now," Fawzi said and reached for my sword.

"Broadsides fit better the baggy flat side of old men," I said, stepping back. "Let's try that on you."

"That's the spirit," Zafir said, then straightened back his shoulders in renewed determination to push us on our way.

"Then you're prepared, my friends," he said. "Be safe and well. Peace, joy, courage."

I embraced Zafir, vowing to fulfill his every expectation. He held me a moment and then pushed me to my duty.

A pair of men waited to escort Zafir to his family.

"Farewell," I said, and Zafir turned with a smile. I saw restored hope shining in his eyes.

CYENE

Shamar estimated by the sun it was just past midday when the boat maneuvered to a wide pier. The dock was built on dozens of large stone pylons jutting from the water that supported a heavy deck of thick planking. It was one of several such piers, stretching out into the Nilus for several hundred cubits. A passenger said that in ancient times it was the busiest port of the whole eastern shore.

Cala and Shamar were already on their feet when the boat bumped into place. The leaking hull had turned the 12-day trip into 18, and that constant worry of swamping had created impatience.

"I don't see any of those dangerous cataracts everybody talked about," Cala said as the crew slung ropes and barked instructions.

"Oh, they're here, most certainly," Shamar said, "but not anything that you're thinking of."

"Let's not take the time to find out," she sighed.

The captain instructed the passengers to remove their belongings for the portage around the cataract. By morning, he assured them, his men would have the boat ready for departure, first light.

"I just want to put more distance between us and..." Cala said, scanning the blackness eastward. "I can't eat or sleep any more . . ."

"Remember, my daughter," Shamar said, "they can't move any faster than us. We're safe. It's time to rest from your worry."

With the boat cinched to its moorings, Shamar stepped out and offered Cala a hand. It was good to stand on something solid again.

"Shall we?" he smiled, and led the way.

As they neared the market the crowding grew thick with passengers coming and going, handcarts of goods, cattle, load-bearers slowing the way. Cala glanced about for anyone dangerously familiar. "How do we know it's safe?"

"It's safe enough," he said. "See the rod-bearers?" and pointed to two large men with spears standing post. "This busy place isn't about to tolerate the mayhem of men like Rakbah. Let's search out a spot to set our things for the night, find some food, and then look for help."

"Help?" Cala asked. "Do you know anyone here?"

"Yes and no—I know Abdali-ud-din employs several stewards along the Nilus. But here in Cyene? I just don't know. We'll be discreet and ask around—someone will know."

There was a small inn beyond the noise of the market square where an opening toward the back let Shamar keep an eye out for shadowy people. They found a round table under an awning. It was good to sit at last. They ordered a meal and took time to breath in the new smells and noises and traffic of Egypt's famous Nilus Valley. Bread was brought with a fruit jam while they waited for their fish.

"They don't eat a lot of fish," Shamar said.

"What? On the river? Why not?"

"It's just not part of their regular diet—we're the unusual ones, stopping for a well-prepared fish almost every night."

"And what about these ram heads I see everywhere. They're on everything," Cala said. "Do they eat them or . . .?"

"You, young lady, are looking upon Khnum. He is the reason we're all here, according to the Egyptians."

"So, he's some kind of god?"

"Yes, a ram's head on a man's body. Power. Deity! And not only that, did you know he made everything on a potter's wheel? Oh, that it was that simple . . ."

"But the ram . . ."

"For virility and power! But Khnum wasn't alone, mind you. He had help."

Cala chewed the bread thoughtfully. It was a new taste, a new mix of grains.

"Satis? Anukis?" Shamar asked. "You've never heard of these gods? They made the world, you know, and all that's in it."

"No," she said with disinterest. She drank from the barley mix, and it made her face sour. "There's one God," she coughed, "and I ask him to watch out for my Bassam, and now to watch out for . . . what *is* this horrible drink?"

"Better make that last a while," Shamar said. "It's their special recipe and I never trust special recipes . . ."

Their meals were presented—a boiled fish covered with sauce, coriander, and dill, boiled cabbage with green peas and lotus, sliced apple and some grapes. More bread and a dipping oil with crushed sesame.

"You would never eat so well in the desert," Shamar said. "Everything is for the gods in this place—the green leaves are the gift of Khnum. They call him Min for short—and the onions? Yes, those will keep away the demons of disease. So, eat well and live."

Cala tried to smile. "Too many gods, a god for just about everything." She suddenly stopped chewing. A rotund man with a white head wrapping was paying her too much attention. He had been leaning in their direction ever since they sat down. Cala mentioned it quietly and Shamar turned to observe. When the man saw he had their attention he smiled, pushed back his chair, and stood to approach.

"Uh-oh," Cala mumbled under her breath. Shamar reached beneath the table for the bag that held his knife.

"Please, do forgive this intrusion," the man said, speaking in the perfect diction of Rekeem. "But I could not help but notice from your language that you come from the east. You're not Egyptian. Are you beyond the Sinai?"

"You're correct my good man, the high deserts," Shamar said warmly. "And your language, I think you're from there as well?"

"Indeed!" he said. "It's good to hear someone familiar. It's a delight to the ears, a joy to the soul of a wayward traveler!"

Shamar smiled. "This is my daughter," he said. "We're returning to our home in Saba."

"Ah!" the man smiled, pointing east. "I know Saba, a nice village now grown into a large city, is it not? I'm there once in a year, or twice, to trade." He offered his hand, "I am Narmer, not the great king who united this hot, scorpion-infested land, but I do unite with new friends from afar. If you will excuse my intrusion, it's nice to speak with people in my own tongue."

"Not at all, Narmer," Shamar said. "This is Cala. I am Shamar. We, too, are happy to speak with someone from our side of the sea. Won't you sit?"

"Indeed!" he said, pulling a chair from another table. "I would be pleased to enjoy your company for a few moments this afternoon."

Cala looked alarmed, but Shamar welcomed the congeniality from someone closer to home.

"I was just telling Cala about the quarries," Shamar said.

"Ah! The quarries," Narmer said. "I should take you there. It's the most amazing of places." And turning to Cala, "All of the royal stone the pharaohs ordered for their carvings, all of it left from right here, this place—red stone for the gods, their images, their temples, by riverboat. Can you imagine it? Pylons the weight of a mountain, moved down river on boats of cedar and papyrus? It amazes me what men have done here."

Cala glanced at Shamar.

"Perhaps we should see those some time," he said.

"I'll take you!" Narmer said.

Cala's eyes went big. Shamar smiled. "Take us?" he asked. "You must be a guide."

"No, no guide," Narmer said, "I live here with my family, but I know my way around this city. There's much to see. Your travels should wait a day. You might not get back here again." He took a drink and smiled at Cala. "The Egyptian gods left a mighty obelisk in the quarry, made to their honor—more than 100 cubits long. You must see it! The largest in the whole world! They say it boasted too much in its pride and it made the shrine to Khnum look small and weak. So the gods decreed it could not be moved, and shook the earth until great cracks appeared, and it lies there still, locked to the earth."

"Fascinating," Shamar said. Even Cala was carried away.

"You'll like Cyene," Narmer said. "You should stay and see it, and there's more. Have you been to Khere-Ohe?"

"Where?" Cala asked, suspiciously.

"Ah, that's its ancient name. You may know it by the Hebrew's name of Noph."

"No," Cala said.

"Yes," Shamar laughed. "But not together. It's a long trip from here."

"Longer than 4,500 stadia," Narmer said. "Three weeks if the wind doesn't fight you. The pyramids, the sphinx! A wonderful place!"

"That's a trip for a future time," Shamar said. "We're on our way home and must go the other direction, upriver. We need an outlet to the sea."

"You cannot reach the sea from here," Narmer said.

"That's what people are telling us. They say there's an outlet farther south."

"Too far south, you would be on the other side of the world," Narmer said. "You should take the caravan from 'Gena to Leucus Limen, the white port. It's the coast, a busy place, many boats there. You may take your choice."

"We're actually pressed for time, and looking to stay on the river. Is there such a way?" Shamar asked.

"There are no direct rivers from the Nilus to the Egyptian Sea. Much difficulty with the cataracts—farther south is the same," he said. "You must cross Kush Desert by caravan. It can be done, safe, easy, seven days. I've traveled it many times."

Shamar fell quiet. He did not want to risk an overland route, not now in these foreign regions.

"Then my good man," Shamar said, risking some private information, "do you see any of the Abdali-ud-din pass through these parts?"

This time Narmer went quiet. The two men studied each other a long while. Cala watched them eye one another quietly. She grew nervous. *What are they doing just looking at each other?*

Just as the silence became awkward, Narmer quietly asked, "Are you a man of a particular worship?"

Without reacting, Shamar nodded his head.

"Then I should like to ask you," Narmer said. "Is your praise of God in the seventh?"

Cala looked at Shamar for translation. "By my oath, it is in the seventh." Then he bowed his head. The stranger looked upon Shamar and nodded. Shamar lifted his head and repeated the same question. "Is your praise of God in the seventh?"

Narmer answered the same, "By my oath, it is in the seventh," and bowed his head toward Shamar.

The mysterious ritual left Cala feeling frustrated, in the dark. "What are you doing?" she whispered to Shamar, poking him in the leg.

Shamar smiled. "My daughter, if I'm not mistaken, I do believe we have come across the official steward of the Abdali-ud-din for these headwaters at Cyene."

Narmer and Shamar extended hands and shook. Cala saw their cautions melt away and a countenance of a different sort come across both of their faces.

"Indeed, the steward!" Narmer smiled with a new softness in his voice. "And welcome to you, my friends. Now I extend to you a new greeting and a new welcome!"

MAKING A PLAN

By nightfall, Cala arrived at the door of a modest mud-brick home, welcomed by a woman her mother's age. Standing to her side was a girl, probably 13 or 14.

"May I introduce you to my family," Narmer said. "My wife, Kiya, and our daughter Ana."

The woman smiled. Ana seemed glad to have a guest close to her age, but Cala could feel the girl's anxiety at the presence of strangers.

"Please, seat yourselves," Narmer said, gesturing to large cushions on modest chairs.

"It's not as hot in here," Cala said, surprised that the stifling heat had so quickly abated inside the spacious stone dwelling.

"Thank you, young lady," Narmer said smiling. "It can be most hot this time of year, but we invite the breeze whenever she will visit us!"

Large windows on either side let the southern breeze pass through unobstructed.

"You are our guests. We'll enjoy our evening meal, and you'll tell us about the east," Narmer said. "Perhaps it's time we thought of returning there ourselves, to follow you. A few months more, after the caravan season," he said, smiling to his wife.

Kiya's face was worn down with the labor of being away from home, assigned to a land not of her ancestors. Even so, she had a warm smile for her guests.

Cala waited in a chair, her hands folded neatly with pretended interest as the men's conversation changed from a retelling of personal histories to an in-depth comparison of genealogies.

An hour later they were seated for dinner. Hot barley bread and a dipping oil with ground sesame and spices, slender strips of roasted chicken on rice, roasted papyrus tubers, with melons and dates to round out the modest feast. The smell was delicious.

"So, tell us Cala," Narmer said, "tell us about your family and why bandits would want to take you to Noph."

"It wasn't me," she said, "but the ransom they hoped to win from my, um, uncle," and looked over at Shamar who nodded.

"Do I know of him?" Narmer asked.

"His name is Zafir, a chief among the Abdali-ud-din," Cala said.

Narmer thought a moment and reached for another bread. "Yes, I might have heard of him, but not directly. Perhaps I'll meet him one day."

"He travels to the east most of the time," Cala said.

"Ah, that explains it," Narmer said, chewing. "And I'm a steward here in the west."

As the sky darkened, lamps were lit, and the two men engaged in a strategy session. Narmer's maps showed the long winding Nilus, the obstacles created by the half-dozen cataracts, and dangerous places where bandits preyed on travelers. There were vast tracts where no city or wadi was marked—great stretches devoid of life and water.

"The more I listen to you, the more I'm sure of this, that we'll accompany you south," Narmer volunteered.

"Oh, no, too much danger," Shamar said. "We are well on our way. We'll be well enough."

"I don't think so," Narmer said. "Abdali-ud-din has another steward living about four weeks upriver. I'll travel with you that far. It will bring us to The Belly of Stones, a long stretch most dangerous this time of year, a place to leave your boat behind. There you'll join a caravan to the sea, and there we'll bid you goodbye."

"That's eight weeks before you return here," Shamar said. "That's a long time from home."

"I'll be glad to be rid of him," Kiya said, and everyone laughed. "It's not that unusual for my husband to be gone," she said. "It's part of his duties."

Kiya took the plates and brought an evening tea.

"These are bad days for this land," Narmer said. "A wicked king rules, a boy king—ruthless, bullied by his regents and a terror to all."

"It seems peaceful enough," Shamar said.

"We're too far away," Narmer said. "He attacks the lands in the sea north and there's fighting among his generals. A year ago, he bribed the allegiance of his temple priests so they would intercede between him and heaven. He put his decree into a black stone in the center market for all to see."

"A tablet?"

"A hard-stone stela, you can't miss it—the dead writings of the figure language of the Temple priests, the same message in their own language, and a third version for the Greeks. I have no question the king wishes all to know of his power over mercy and justice. Nevertheless, a bad man. Ridding the land of him and his strongmen is good for all," Narmer said.

"Then we're glad to leave while the fighting stays north," Shamar said. "Perhaps this is a good time, then, for you to return to your homeland?"

"Not yet, but soon," Narmer said. "The fighting has gone on a few years. The garrison here is lazy—they'll tax you for your travel south. I'll help you pay it, but I must station here until the caravan season has ended, and then I'm released from my oath. We'll return to our homes, but not yet. That's for you to do. Tomorrow!"

"That soon is good," Shamar said. "I'm still not convinced we haven't been followed, and all I have is my little knife. The sooner we're back on the water, the better for us all."

"Then we'll take you south to El-khartoum. It's a wonderful city, the place of the two rivers. Abdali-ud-din has a steward there.

"Will it connect us to the coast?" Shamar asked.

"Yes," Narmer said, circling with his finger a group of dots on his map. "There are others but this is the most traveled. You would have done better to stop at Gebtu, the Wadi Hammamat leads directly to Al-Qusayr, a great trading port, popular for shipping. Would you consider it?"

"Not anymore," Shamar said. "We're still not far enough from our enemies to risk going back, if you can steer us south, that's our desire."

"All right," Narmer said, pointing a stylus in the general direction of Atbara. "We'll take you here, or just here, you decide when we near it, and I'll bring Ana, she's been anxious for another trip."

Narmer retrieved an exquisitely detailed white carving from a table by the wall. Shamar had noticed it upon first entering. "Farther downriver you'll find much of this," he said, handing it off carefully.

Shamar took it with both hands and hefted the cylindrical sculpture. It was heavy like stone, hard like pottery, but was the purest white he had ever seen. A rotund lahpaš was portrayed rearing up on its hind legs, its great khartoum raised in revenge, with small images of men with spears as if hunting it. The grasses and trees were perfect—elegant, fragile, exquisite, carved into the strange white material—too light to be stone, too strong to be wood.

"It's an emblem of their island city," Narmer said.

"Beautiful . . ." Shamar replied without looking up.

"Other garrisons manage the trade," Narmer said. "They let pass only those things that do well for the king. Animal pelts, incense, resins, even feathers from a large exotic bird that lives in the jungles—all these may pass. You should look for them."

"Amazing work. I can see why the trade is watched," Shamar said.

"And slaves, there are many to buy, for your journey east, many people do," Narmer said.

"No slaves. We've had our fill of captivity," Shamar said, looking at Cala. She wasn't listening. Her thoughts were far away.

Cala felt the length of the journey catching her, and let her gaze wander. Her attention was caught by a stone bowl made of beautiful polished marble. It held several dozen tiny balls of glass, marble, clay, granite, and onyx. She stood to examine it closer, fascinated by the colors and shapes. She picked up a few and let them roll about in her hand. Narmer watched and smiled.

"Ah, so you found our nuts," he said.

"Nuts?"

"Oh yes," Narmer said, joining her at the table. "Not to eat but that's what we call them," and reached for one. "They're for games or for the soothsayers telling their tales. Do you see? Made of many things, but in the beginning, they were just that—nuts."

"Real nuts, that grow?" she asked.

"This one is old. It's a real hazel," he said, choosing another. "Plucked from the tree—beautifully round and if you're good at it, you can flick it across the ground—games, sport, fun. And, look close here, you can see where they polished them, smoothed off the ridge, the imperfections. It's perfect for a perfect little ball. Then they started manufacturing them from stone or clay, and you know what? They kept the same name—nuts."

Cala reached into the bowl and gently stirred them around, letting them clink their different little notes and sounds.

"Most of these are gifts from traders, visitors to our little community from all over the world, like yourselves."

Narmer saw the fascination grow in Cala's eyes, and grinned. "Tell you what," he said, "you may choose one as a parting gift, a token of our new friendship."

"Oh, I couldn't."

"No, I insist. And I'm sure that it will bring you good luck," he said. "Choose one and I'll tell you its story. Each has her own tale—choose and I will tell."

Cala peered into the shimmering collection and spotted one that stood out from all the others—larger, as clear as pure glass, but in its center was a strange blue glow.

"What is this light? Do you see it?" She held it for Narmer to see.

He smiled. "Ah! Yes! You have chosen the Lordstone, a good choice my young Cala. She has a curious story."

THE LORDSTONE

Narmer invited Cala close.

"You have heard of the great prophet Nu'h," he began, "and the boat he was commanded by God to build?"

"To save the animals?"

"Yes, and all his family, from the flood."

"I've heard of it," Cala said.

"There's a part of that story that's seldom told. You won't find it in the ancient writings—the Hebrews, the Greeks, none of them. Yet, it is in our traditions that Nu'h and his wife Nu't were commanded to build such a boat before the rains came to drown away all living things except the eight souls who were spared."

"Yes, and the animals," Cala said.

"And the animals. A big job, no?"

Narmer reached into the bowl and plucked a round ball and held it in front of Cala, delicately balancing it between finger and thumb.

"This is why we call them 'nuts', to honor his wife, Nu't. Our legend says these little orbs are her children because of the light." He dropped the marble back in the bowl with a clink.

Cala rolled the small blue ball in her palm and held it to the oil lamps to test its translucency. Its soft blue glow seemed to grow stronger.

"Imagine your place in the world at such a time," Narmer said. "Imagine that you are commanded by God to build such a great boat, to survive a great flood that's coming. And you have been given a plan for its size, its length, its breadth, its height, its chambers, its floors, its windows, its decking, its roofing, its keel, every cubit of its construction. The feed, the fodder, the straw, the victuals, the forks to muck out the stalls, the means for tender care of new-born life that may appear along the way, the preparations, things consumed, all things for a journey of how many days it does not say, but of enough, a long time. All of this so they could live through the greatest torrent to visit the earth since its creation. A torrent to wash away the filth and corruption of every living thing except what lived upon the great boat."

Narmer paused. He took Cala's hand with the glass ball and held it in his.

"Tell me, young daughter," he said. "After all of this, all of these many preparations, what thing is lacking?"

Cala pondered a moment.

"I can't think of it," she finally said. "Was there something missing?"

Narmer opened Cala's hand and took the round sphere and cupped it in his, letting it roll in the creases of his palm.

"When Mother Nu't gave consideration to the long journey ahead and all the difficult needs of tending to her loved ones and the animals and worried about the promised rain that was to come for days and days, her first concern was light."

"Light?" Cala repeated.

"Yes. Light for when the windows were shut for they had no glass in those ancient times. Light for when the sun was set at night, light for when the storm billowed with such power they dare not open a window. Remember that it says the rains fell and the storms blew for many days on end? Think of it. Many days and nights without light."

"Light in the darkness—yes, certainly!" Cala said. "It would be a terrible time without light inside a large boat. I supposed there were torches or candles, but fire inside would . . ."

"Exactly!" Narmer said. "Animals bedded down with straw, all the pens and floors and ceilings and walls, all of it wood, seasoned wood—dry dust in the air, easy to catch a wayward spark—it was a box of kindling just waiting to catch."

"I wouldn't have thought of it," she said.

"And so," he said, scooting his chair closer, "Mother Nu't went to Father Nu'h and begged him to petition God to make them lights. She was a woman of faith, but a practical woman as well. She and her sons went to the mount and from molten rock she fashioned 24 small stones, just as you hold in your hand." Then Narmer placed the small marble back into her palm. "They were round, as clear as glass, transparent, not too different in size from the hazel nut."

Cala held the small orb with a new respect, turning it about with her fingers.

"Mother Nu't took these 24 glass stones in her apron and came to Nu'h with the humble request, 'Ask God, the Lord God, to touch these stones with his finger that they will shine forth into the darkness and make light so that our journey will not be in fear, but in hope—in the sure hope that when the travail is ended we may be free to worship the Lord God as he commands us.'"

Narmer paused and looked at Shamar. He was as fixated by the telling as was Cala.

"Have you heard it before?" he asked.

Shamar shook his head. Narmer smiled and continued.

"Father Nu'h did as she asked and went to the mount and begged of the Lord God to touch the stones to make them shine. And the Lord God reached out and touched them, one by one, imparting a great blue light that you see here. They are called Lordstones because they are touched by the hand of the Lord."

"And you're letting me keep this one?" she asked.

"It's yours," he said. "In fact—mother?" he said, turning to Kiya. "Have you that necklace from your aunt that you never wear? May we—?"

Kiya smiled. "I know just the one," she said, stepping to the back room. She returned with a delicate silver chain with a green stone of no unusual interest. It dangled freely, clasped between a pair of ornately detailed talons made of thin bronze.

"I've never known what to do with this, I would be honored if it went away from this house as a gift," she said, handing it off to Narmer. He promptly produced a small pocket knife and pried away the green stone and carefully laid the Lordstone in its place. After some adjusting, he crimped the talons and tested its security.

"There," he said smiling, and handed it over to Cala. "With great affection and respect for your father and his daughter who is cut from the same rock of integrity, honor, respect and strength, please remember the day you received the Lordstone on your long journey into Egypt."

Cala took the necklace and turned the stone about. She held it to her cheek and closed her eyes. "It's not warm—it gives light but no heat."

"But it does give light, and for that you'll have its help always," Narmer said. "Just remember to let the Lordstone bask in the sun in the day and she will work harder to bring that light to the night."

Draping the necklace over her head she let the Lordstone hang respectfully around her neck, an elegantly simple adornment that made her feel clean and bright and beautiful again.

"I'll treasure this, treasure it always," she said, her hand cradling it carefully. "I'm most grateful Narmer, for your many kindnesses tonight."

"Kindnesses indeed," Narmer laughed. "Why, there was a time when I was running a route check for Abdali-ud-din south of here, a new caravan headed to the dark jungles beyond the White Nilus—many weeks' ride—snakes, great water beasts, cats as big as a grown man, strange hairy creatures in trees, stronger than ten men—I've seen them myself, fearsome beasts. And on that trip . . ."

And just like *that* the conversation shifted back to adventures shared best between the adults.

For Cala, the hour had grown late and her eyes were heavy with fatigue. It didn't take long to lose interest in the bravados of manly one-upmanship, and she closed her eyes and leaned her head on a cushion, dreaming of a large dark boat filled with the nervous rustling of wild animals crowded below decks, as clouds and winds and rains blew violently on the outside. On the inside the great boat was safe and dry and secure, carrying the only life that the eight souls knew of, preserved from the black watery void and held in hope by a few faint blue lights reverently set aglow on each of the decks. She could imagine such glowing stones carefully dangling from beams at either end of the vast chambers, gently swaying like a friendly wave of greeting, assuring all that could see them that everything was prepared, everything was safe, and everything was secure—that God was giving them his loving comfort with the peaceful and calming miracle of 24 little stars—the Lordstones.

ANCIENT TREE

Cala awoke suddenly having forgotten her whereabouts. It was night, no candles or lamps except for the moon that cast a brilliant white light through the window. It must be the end of second watch. *How long have I been sleeping? How did I get here?*

The moon gave such illumination she thought it almost day. There was a busyness in the courtyard. She heard voices and went to the window. Narmer and Shamar stood below on the patio pavers exchanging excited ideas in quiet discussion. Narmer pointed into the distance and Shamar listened intently. *What is this?*

"Shamar!" she called in a strained whisper. "What are you doing?"

The two men looked up as if caught in a secret.

Shamar smiled and approached the window. "Cala!" he said. "We thought you asleep. Did our scheming awaken you?"

"Scheming? What scheming?"

"Look!" Shamar said, pointing to the moon.

"What of it?" she asked.

"Don't you see it? An eclipse! Ready to begin. Have you seen it before?"

Cala shook her head.

"Come see. It's a wonderful sight, rare."

Cala joined them in the courtyard. The beautiful glow of her Lordstone gave a soft blue blush. She held it close and hurried to them.

"You won't hide in the dark with that," Narmer said. Cala smiled.

When she found her place, she realized the moon was indeed unusually brilliant, a perfectly shaped orb filling the southern sky.

"It almost hurts my eyes," she said. "What do I look for?"

"You'll see it soon enough," Narmer said. "A bite from the disk appears to grow, small at first, as black as soot, and before it's finished the moon turns red rust. Most people miss this because they're asleep when it shows."

All the region was bathed in silvery white, giving the landscape the feel of some faraway fantasy land, devoid of color and life.

Shamar smiled, looking into the sky. "I knew those great thinkers had it all figured out, Narmer. They probably conspired with the Greeks to understand the night sky. Do you know much about their myths, these warriors and gods who do nightly battle in their fixed places?"

"Maybe not conspired," Narmer said. "Simply learned. It's the Greeks who figured out much of it. But long before their science, the Egyptians got their gods involved."

Shamar pointed. "Look! It begins!"

"I see it!" Cala said.

They stared in silence for several long moments while the black bite appeared as a small black line, then slowly widened until a curved edge could be seen.

"It's the shadow of the earth—it moves slow, takes some time," Narmer said. "Do you want to stay and watch? You'll pay for it come sunrise, but you decide, I have nowhere to go as do you."

"I want to see more," Cala said. "Shamar?"

The old guide grinned, his eyes filled with the bright white spots of reflected moonshine. "Let's watch for it to cover completely, then I'll be ready to retire."

By the time the black bite had consumed a full third of the moon, Cala noticed gradual dimming of the light around her, from intense white to softening silver, a strange change cast its pall over the land. She fell quiet to watch the black shadow creep slowly across the moon's face.

She suddenly realized the men had wandered far ahead of her. She pulled the blanket about her shoulders and hurried toward their voices. At that moment, she stepped on something large and round that gave way under her foot and smoothly smashed. What is this? She stopped to investigate. It was a squashed fruit flattened under her sandal. A sweet crisp tartness wafted into the air.

What is that delicious sweet? She picked up a piece to examine. Is there more?

An old hedge to her right was broken open in one place and she could see just beyond it the gnarly, twisted limbs of a sturdy little tree. It stood thrice her height and bore few leaves. It scratched at the night sky with five old limbs, like crooked fingers, reaching toward the stars. Its dried branches appeared long since dead, but its curious shape made her stop.

"It looks like a hand reaching for heaven," she mused. "Is this moonlight playing tricks on me?"

At the end of one low-hanging branch, a cluster of leaves nested a white-skinned fruit the size of her fist, just like the one she had stepped on. It looked enticingly ripe in the moon's weakening light.

"I think I need to try this," she said. "A midnight snack for the eclipse." Just as she reached the fruit fell right into her out-stretched hand. "Oh my!" she exclaimed. "It's the peak harvest time for this old tree . . . Do I know this fruit?" With wonder, she brought it to her mouth and took a small, cautious bite. The thin skin broke easily and sweet juices flowed around her lips. "Delicious!" she whispered, and took a second bite.

It was neither bitter nor tart, but lightly sweet, pleasant to the tongue, satisfying and refreshing. "Not too much, not too little," she said. "Thank you, mother tree. This will make my night go better," and she continued through the dark.

When she regained the men at their hill-top perch, the fruit had been eaten to its core.

"Where did you go, young lady?" Narmer asked. "I thought I had bored you with my talk tonight."

"I was going to fetch you," Shamar said. "We thought you were right on our heels."

"I stopped to watch and I found the most delicious fruit. What is this?" she asked, holding out the fruit's pit.

Narmer sniffed and held it up to the partial moon. "Strange to find that here, look how white the pit is—I've seen similar fruits among the Greeks, but nothing like this. It's too hot around here, never seen it before."

Shamar examined it, smelling its sweet fragrance. "You shouldn't eat wild fruits, Cala," he said. "You could get sick," and handed it back.

"No, I feel fine," she said. "In fact, I feel energized! It was an old tree, certainly old, hardly a leaf growing, but this fruit practically fell into my hand! I'll show you on our way back. You should try some, delicious!" She wrapped the pit in a cloth and put it in her robe for safe-keeping.

For almost an hour longer the group exchanged idle comments and story telling until finally the last of the brilliant light vanished. The moon was engulfed in a black-reddish shadow almost the color of old blood. The landscape was eerily black with a faint reddish glow. Only the horizon remained midnight blue.

Cala found a place to sit and they watched until the reddish hue had glided all the way across the moon's grey face and slipped off. Suddenly a brilliant splash of white erupted on the moon's opposite edge, like a fiery white gem.

"Beautiful!" Cala sighed.

"What a display," Shamar said. "You don't realize how bright that is until it suddenly appears."

"That was a real treat, Narmer. Thank you for waking me," Shamar said.

"You are lucky visitors! I'm glad you saw it. These students of Ra, they are good at the science of stars and planets."

Narmer led them off the slope and through the date grove. The landscape brightened as the moon shed the shadow, returning a normal silvery illumination to the path.

Cala felt for the fruit pit in her robe. "That tree is over there," she said pointing. "May we stop?"

They found the thicket but no such tree stood—not anywhere. Narmer glanced around. "Maybe in the daylight?" and continued to the house. "It's a curious thing," he called over his shoulder. "I don't recall any such tree, not around here, anyway—maybe another thicket? I'd like to taste it—smelled wonderful!"

Cala was wide-awake back in her room. She finally had some time to herself—alone. She lit a lamp, and for the first time in these many months, put ink to stylus, and stylus to papyrus.

"My Dearest Bassam, my journal has laid empty these many months, but every painful day that I have been removed from the bosom of your parent's love is recorded in detail within my heart. I can tell you all the details later, but for now I will say that for this long ordeal I have lingered in fear and sadness. I was trapped by the vilest people who took me thousands of stadia from your smile, your laugh, your loving care, and warm embrace. How I have missed you.

Now I'm safe. I trust the goodwill offer from a steward of Abdali-ud-din to deliver this private message by whatever means she finds possible.

The treachery that took me chases me hard. I was taken for ransom, but by God's gentle benevolence he brought me to a relative who helped me escape. He leads me to freedom.

We crossed the Egyptian Sea to a place named Al-Jarf. Do not look for me there. We took a riverboat for many days to Akhetatan and No-Amon, do not look for me there. And now here in Cyene. Here I make plans to continue south to Korosko, Atbara. We take camels. The Nub'an Port is best, but which way there is safest? The steward tells us the Korosko Road is best. We think Atbara is safer. We're deciding it now.

I pray daily in my heart that God's kindness will find you and guide your steps. No matter what befalls me in the journey ahead, my heart is yours forever."

Your Rasha

BROKEN SCROLL

Quite suddenly, the reading came to an abrupt stop. "What is this?" Henri said, finding four separate insertions of loose parchment tightly wrapped in the scroll's coils.

"That's unusual ... what, an addendum or such?"

He lifted the curled pages to the light. They were papyrus cut to size with writing on both sides. The ink showed through.

"Cheap material . . . brown ink? No, no, oxidized, a cheaper formula . . ."

Then he spotted a strange marking at the top of each—a cross with two dots, one dot larger than the other.

"Ah ha!" he grinned. "Al Kalimat! It must be . . . so, look at that—that's their actual secret mark. Seems pretty simple to me, but that usually means something hidden as part of something plain. Is that not their purpose?"

The writing was of a different hand, but he could read it just the same—

NUB'AH

Al Kalimat verified — +:
Intercepted dispatch, see separate note:

Report of the First

I am Jabari.

My bargain with Master Rakbah for the silver is attested to by this record made by my hand this day, in fulfillment of the contract I am now embarked.

Master Rakbah told me he learned of the treachery of his guide and the theft of his property, the slave girl, on that day of their escape. Others who had been watching that morning told him how three people were seen boarding the trading boat to Al-Jarf. I know of it, a well-traveled route across the sea, but all barges were departed when Rakbah discovered the ending place of their escape. He told me they had gained a day's head start. I was contracted to help in their recapture.

By my oath and this written account, I, Jabari, am promised a fourth talent of silver for my labor, to be shared equally with my two companions who join me. He urged me to recover his stolen property and, as a token of his trust in me to fulfill this order, gave me a tenth of a talent of the promised silver in three leather pouches as a sealing of our covenant.

His instructions were direct. Upon making them prisoners, my payment would be in full if they are dead and I bring back their bodies. But, he said, it was not their death he sought and would reward me another fourth talent if I captured them alive. He told of a meeting place in Noph that I should find when my contract was accomplished.

I agreed and we boarded the boat. It was two days when we tied off at Al-Jarf. Others at the docking place told Rakbah that three from the east—an old man, an old woman, and a girl—had arrived the day before and hired to the caravan that drives for the Nilus River.

Rakbah showed us his map. He knew the river and its troubles. He showed me that twists and turns going south make a long trip, and I was to continue south along the coast before making land, to go forward in haste. From the coast, I should expect a week-long camel trek to reach the river. I should arrive before them by three weeks, and lie in wait.

If they did not go south, Rakbah said he would go north thinking the thief would drive for Ale'ksandria, to the West Sea. He was sure they would go north, but covered his doubt by hiring me to go south.

The river is quicker, he said, and to expect them on a boat. His spies would tell him if they went to a village. Rakbah promised gold and silver enough for all when the capture is finished. To that oath and promise I inscribe this testimonial.

Thus it was that we took a fast-sailed boat south, and Rakbah with five others, took the camels inland.

For 13 days the winds favored us to the port village of Nub'ah.

I hired with a caravan to cross the Kush for six days more and arrived on the seventh at the river Atbara. By nightfall we had reached the village of Atbara. It's a green, prosperous place where two rivers meet. The water is sweet. Here I write my journal for the contract, and I spy on the river traffic for the three of them to come.

Henri set the page aside, then scratched his head.

"Not part of the original," he mumbled. "Why?" then scanned once more the faded pen of Jabari's report. "It's like some sort of criminal action is being prosecuted, and this evidence is part of that, for some reason . . . but why bury it in a sarcophagus in some pit tomb when everybody is long since dead?"

He lifted the second sheet carefully and began reading.

SAND AND WATER

Al Kalimat verified — +:
Recovered channel dispatch, see note

My Dearest Bassam,

We are two more weeks on the river, and stopped tonight at this quaint portage village. I thought of you when we arrived. It

*was just before sundown, and the most beautiful sky presented—
low clouds, grey and flashing with storm. Their edges were afire
with yellow and orange, a glorious sight for all. It didn't last long,
and when the sun was gone, the flashing continued but we heard
no thunder.*

*There's no reason to believe Rakbah is following us, but I feel
like we're being watched. We compete for portage space at the
cataracts, and having no goods to trade, the portage masters make
us wait until the end. They serve the best paying customers first.*

*Shamar tells me our choice to Atbara was wise. The caravans
are escorted at this place, not in the north. The bandits are more
active there, so most of the trade goes south.*

*We have another decision to make about the river or the desert.
It's a difference of weeks or days. It's a beautiful land, but nothing
I can notice because you're not here with me. I pray God's help for
you no matter where you are.*

*I will leave this message in the good hands of the steward
here. We haven't met him yet, but tomorrow we will try before
departure. I am yours always, Rasha.*

"I need a good map," Henri said. "These river villages come and go, and
have different names today . . ." He scanned the rows of bookshelves.
"There must be an atlas . . . somewhere . . . it is a library after all."

A few minutes later Henri sat back, laying a thick oversized book on
his lap, flipping through to Egypt.

"Too far north, where's Nubia—what's this, oh, Sudan, yes, Sudan
. . . that puts them about here," he mumbled, running his finger along
the river's long path, stopping before the third cataract. "No, that's not
right. Let me see, going upriver under oars, what is that? About, say, 4
knots in low flood, then it would take them how many weeks?"

He closed his eyes and made the mental calculation. He let out a low
whistle. "I'd go for Atbara," and reached for the third parchment.

TWO

Al Kalimat verified — +:
Intercepted dispatch, see separate note:

Report of the Second

I, Jabari, write this record of the second part, according to my contract with the man Rakbah.

My wait of five weeks at the village of Atbara failed to discover the stolen slave girl. Diligent we were to learn of the trade, the merchants and their wealth that obligated me to make the bribe large for information about the girl. For a tenth of silver, I bought many of their promises to look.

My men did not endure the wait and devised a plan to travel down river to the Fifth Cataract and the Baggara Cataract to spy. After three days, I, Jabari, took passage and joined my men and set camp at the portage village.

Many long days in wait was testing my men. It was a week of heavy shipping, large boats, and barges. In weeks two and three, many hundreds of smaller boats passed, but only four commissioned for Atbara came to the portage village.

In week four we saw only one such boat.

On the fifth day of the fifth week, as the sun was near setting, we observed a lone boat, small with sail, afar off making its approach well upriver of the cataract. It was distinct to us because the surge of the routine afternoon traffic was long since docked. As it neared we saw a fair-skinned man and a fair-skinned girl seated in the shadow of their sail. As they came to dock, I, Jabari, believed them our contract. My companions were not persuaded.

"Jabari, there are only two," said my man.

"That's not a strong reason," I told him. "Would not the man kill the woman at first chance? Why would he want food for three when two would do? Why would he port a boat for three when a smaller boat would do? That little boat, is it not small enough? It must be those we seek."

The evening breeze pushed their boat quickly toward our watching place. They carried few things with them. More proof, I told my men, that these are not sellers or buyers.

"No trader would waste such trips empty-handed. Neither would a traveler risk such travel with no victuals or supplies."

Having thus convinced them to postpone their plan to leave for the next cataract, we made a strategy.

Tonight, I write that they are in the portage village at the fifth cataract. I was not close enough to follow them to their inn, and told my men to watch the pier.

I, Jabari, write that I will capture them thus, on the river where fleeing is made more difficult because of the current, and more dangerous because of the cataract, and more futile because of me and my men.

CURRENTS

Al Kalimat verified — +:
Intercepted dispatch, see separate note:

Report of the Third

I, Jabari, write this record of the third part, according to my contract with the man Rakbah.

It was not yet light when my men saw two people hurry to the boat we had been watching. So deliberate was their departure we hardly had time to reach our boats to begin our plan.

The light was dim, but the water polished gray, making our intentions difficult to hide. My companions pushed off, each in his small boat, while I guided them from shore. The man discovered us and was quick to react. The air was still so he abandoned his sail and locked oars.

I saw that they were aware of us because the girl hurried to tend the sail and the man hurriedly steered toward the middle of the river, going down instead of continuing their route of yesterday upriver. More proof, I told my men.

My companions were fast to react and gave chase. Their only option was the far shore. I went downriver to block his retreat should he attempt it.

I have measured the map. The Nilus is five stadia wide from Baggara to Atbara—too far to escape. When the old man turned west I saw there was place enough to outpace my men. I, Jabari, saw that his plan was superior. The great draw of each stroke made the distance grow longer from the small paddles of my men. I shouted urgently to pursue.

Suddenly the old man's boat jerked sharply right, directly down river. It was the power of the water, as if a great hand had grabbed his craft by force.

"The current!" I shouted. "He is steering for the current!"

My men did not hear my order. "Go after them!" I shouted, waving my arms in the air and pointing. They began pounding the waves in pursuit.

We could see the old man was stressed. He sat tall working his oars, pulling hard to maneuver within the grip of the water's strength. He was swept downstream. I saw his boat bobbing high then low in the waves, his oars doing little but sending up a mighty spray each time they touched. I saw his fatigue by shorter strokes. He had not the strength to fight the river.

I stood on shore to watch them, a thousand paces away. It is my report of the straits, that they are strewn with boulders, a long gorge that roars at low flood. Such was the condition that his boat headed toward. I, Jabari, saw the old man did not avoid it. He held his oars out of the water except to correct his course.

Then the man made a deliberate turn directly toward the chasm. He was going to run the cataract in his boat. It was madness! I shouted to my men, but the great distance to the roar of the water buried my call.

I, Jabari, saw his craft thrust toward the great stone walls that funneled the river to the narrow gorges below. There are sharp protruding rocks and steep drops. A rolling cloud of mist remains there always, smothering the piles and edges and funnels and chutes in the jagged rock wall and submerged boulders.

I shouted to my men. "Go! Follow!" but they couldn't hear me. I believed my men more capable on such rapids, but they became caught in the same current.

I, Jabari, saw the old man's boat leaning to one side, then drop silently from view behind tall boulders.

My men saw it and began paddling to avoid the same fate, but it was too late. The river was too strong and they could not escape. My first man's boat turned sideways then dropped from view, then the second right after.

From my vantage, I could not see where the cataract ended his punishments, the place where he spits the refuse into calmer waters.

I, Jabari, hurried downriver to see what became of my men.

The transfer station was deserted and there was no spare boat to take me to the spillway in search. I hastened down the pathway that descended some distance around the river's stony escalade. For half an hour I hurried, stumbling and breathing hard with fatigue until I came to an ending place with a large grove of acacias. There I took shade from the morning sun.

I was much closer here. I could see polished boulders piled in a great obstacle some 50 paces into the river. They glistened black and wet under the splashing torrent. I, Jabari, was diligent in my search. I searched and hunted, but no sign of my men or the man and the girl.

I ran 500 paces to the stagnant waters of a small lagoon where the wash dumped his debris—small green branches, pieces of broken wood, the floating carcasses of dead river fish, the smell of rot. There was no sign of them.

At a thick stand of papyrus I saw something floating toward shore. It was my lead man. Dead. He was broken and twisted, punished severely by the river's awful anger.

In another few minutes I found the broken front of the old man's boat piled against black stone boulders 200 paces from shore. It was wedged between rocks, a brush held shredded fabric—a piece of sail, perhaps clothing. I tried to see it closer but the current threatened me. I searched an hour more and found none other. Thus ends my report.

—I am Jabari.

Henri removed his glasses and rubbed the little indentations on his nose. His eyes burned and he rested them a moment, trying to assimilate the puzzle pieces into some purpose that would justify the additional parchments.

"There's a reason for this report, this Jabari fellow," he sighed. "Too much detail, too much story, there must be a strategy at work, perhaps it will present itself soon." He resumed with the main scroll—

AVALITES

Fawzi pushed off the last line and waved to the captain. We felt a hot wave of humid air wash over us as the boat caught the current, and we hurried for shade from the blazing sun. They said it was a calm trip through the straits for this season. They were an uneventful two days in calm seas. And as promised, just a few hours before sundown we bumped into the dock of Avalites.

"Follow me," Ammar said, leading out across the pier. "We need to find someone from Medewi. Anyone will do."

I followed behind, acting the tourist, looking at the amazing scenes. The surrounding hills were low and scorched. There wasn't a green thing growing except a few fields and nearby farms being quenched by some muddy ditch water. This was hardly the jungle I was expecting.

The land was cracked with flat islands of rocky plateaus standing atop broad bases with sloughed-away sides, as if washed away by a gushing deluge some eons ago. A few wild camels were pushing for position at a pond and herds of goats were fighting at some brush. Lines of weary men in loin cloths crowded the docks to take away goods while others loaded them anew. I saw massive lahpaš tusks shouldered by two men apiece, and heavy chained wooden chests carried by others. There were live animals, camel-loads of black-spotted skins and golden-striped furs, and much more that I couldn't identify. It was a noisy, crowded maze of activity.

"What's a man from Medewi supposed to look like?" I asked.

"Egyptian," Ammar said. "Or Nub'an."

I looked about and shrugged. "They all look just like that to me," I said.

"You amateurs," Fawzi scoffed. "Wait here. Get a drink. I'll be back." He strode away into the teeming masses.

"Does he know where he's going?" I asked.

Ammar smiled. "Nope. And that's Fawzi. He does it alone and nine times out of ten he succeeds even when Al Murrah fails. It's an uncanny gift."

We bought slices of yellow melon and sat under some shade as the sun completed his trip into the brown haze of sunset. Long shadows crept over us. Torches were being lit along shore. Suddenly we heard laughter coming our way. There was a sight I never expected on this trip—Fawzi was joking with an enormous black-skinned woman draped in a flowing cotton wrap.

"Here are my friends," he smiled, gesturing toward us.

The woman's face was round and her pudgy cheeks broke open in a huge smile. Her teeth were as white as a lahpaš tusk, with a laugh just as trumpeting. She walked right up to us as we stood to say hello and threw her large meaty hand out for greeting.

"I'm Falak, like the stars," she said, taking our hands in turn and rigorously shaking us into submissive smiles. "Pleased to meet you," we said.

"You've got a journey in front of you. Have you a place to sleep tonight? Will you need a caravan? Have you eaten? You should. You look too thin. Are there others in your party?"

I wondered which question to answer first. Ammar was grinning ear to ear. He thought the woman delightful.

"Falak, my pleasure. I am Ammar, and our young companion here is Bassam."

"Bassam! A happy name for a boy. And Ammar, you're the navigator, no?"

My eyes widened. How did she know that?

She laughed again. "Oh, you stargazers, you can't fool me. You're all the same. I can spot you a stadium away. That's why mother named me Falak, like the stars! So the stargazers would gaze on me with a dowry sparkling like golden sunshine." She bellowed with a laughter so full that others turned to look.

We couldn't help but laugh with her. She slapped Ammar on the shoulder. "Do some gazing here and I'll tell your wife on you," she said with a flirtatious wink.

Fawzi was grinning like he'd caught a whale in a pond and didn't know what to do next.

In those few seconds of greeting I had come to like Falak. I looked into her warm face and watched her eyes as she engaged the others. Behind her sandstorm of words and laughing, she showed intelligence and perseverance. I could see she had tasted her bitter share of life, and as such, had grown a kind and generous heart willing to help strangers like us.

Before the evening was spent, we had agreed on a price to join Falak's caravan to Tana Lake. She promised that with early departures and travel after sundown, it was a two-week trip to the river.

"It feeds the Nilus," she said. "A beautiful place after a long desert trip. You'll always want to travel this way with Falak, like following the stars," she said and let out another hearty laugh.

It was pre-dawn when Falak arrived at our inn. The keeper was awakened to fetch us.

"I thought you wanted an early start!" she laughed.

Ammar smiled and shrugged. "They stayed up late," he said.

"Then their punishment is that we won't wait. Let's go," she said turning away.

We scampered down with our things and followed Falak to her waiting caravan. I gasped. "What is this?"

A group of 16 short-legged white donkeys waited impatiently, each loaded with passengers and baggage, except for four at the end.

"What?" was all I could say. These animals are our caravan?

Falak looked over her shoulder and smiled. "Meet the best-footed transportation this side of the Nilus," she said. "These are our jungle camels. I know you desert people are accustomed to something much different, but not around here. I've seen Abdali-ud-din come through plenty of times with their hundreds of intimidating swords and war camels. Well, not here. This is the best ride you'll find! In fact, I'll wager that you'll want to trade all your bakras for a mating pair of Nub'an donkeys—they love the desert, they are sturdy, they honk when they're angry, and you'll find in them a faithful friend."

We secured our baggage and saddled up. Unaccustomed to the ride, I did the best I knew how and threw my leg over the back. The donkey sighed and steadied himself to my struggle. It was a strange sensation to have my feet dangle so close to the ground.

"Bassam!" Fawzi scolded, steering his beast next to mine. "Just because these are your close relatives, I can't believe you'd be so rude. I thought you would know better," he said.

"Know better?"

"These are no bakras, donkey dung. You sit over the hind legs, the hips, not their backs, would you really want to kill your own cousins?"

I scooted back and found an easy place to hang my legs and work the stick he handed me. The beast calmed down immediately.

"Be nice to him," Fawzi drawled. "It's not often you can have a family reunion like this . . . "

I tapped the donkey on the neck and he jolted forward, falling in behind the others. He took short choppy steps but the ride was smooth and easy. How long the beast could keep up this fast pace I didn't know, but it was certainly faster than walking.

With her group fully assembled, Falak took the lead and we followed a path directly west out of the city. The road took us toward a shallow valley between vacant rolling hills. The burned land was dotted with patches of acacia trees and euphorbias that scented the air with a thick perfume. I breathed a lung full—delicious! It truly was a new and strange land.

By midday Falak made sure all of us had become acquainted. Her companions included her two younger brothers, equally rotund but hardly as talkative.

I pulled alongside Ammar.

"Those other travelers," I said, pointing to the men who rode behind Falak, "are they Medewi?"

"Yes, all of them," he said. "I think they are like us, finishing a journey that takes them back home."

"I'd say they look more like the Medewi that you were looking for," I said.

He smiled. "Yes, but who would want to miss out on an adventure with the likes of Falak?"

I had to agree.

There was no breeze but those flies that had been pestering us since we left Avalites remained.

We traveled single file along a dried riverbed of packed sands. The wasteland was rocky and uneven except for the occasional sprawling grasslands where thorny trees stood in large bunches. We passed a herd of flop-eared goats. They stopped their chewing to watch suspiciously as we passed.

Though the river had not seen water for a thousand years, it presented us every portion the proof that a living river once flowed here with shorelines and cataracts. Long stretches of bone-dry boulders were just as much an obstacle as an actual flowing river.

"This is the hardest part," Falak said. "Three days and then we find some watered lands south. Cool shade! Oasis! Life! Our star attraction, like me, Falak!" She turned to make sure we were listening, then winked at Ammar.

As it turned out, Zafir's shortest route to the Nilus was not the best route to take. Falak informed us the Atbara River does not flow heavy all year round. This time of year it dwindles to a mere trickle in places. "Not even a stick of wood gets a ride," she laughed.

"The Blue Nilus is your quickest way north," she said. At one of our stops Ammar produced his map for more specific directions. "It will probably take you three weeks, maybe a half more, to reach the Nilus," she said. "Much better we go this way. It's how we travel in the hot months. The good news is, on the Blue, you drink any time you please, if first you don't drown!" She laughed at the joke, but I wondered just how dangerous that river might be.

MISSING MESSAGE

Al Kalimat verified — +:

URGENT: Recovered dispatch

Kaaper to Zafir, eyes only with attachment

Master Zafir,

Urgent update. Open immediately. A personal message from your daughter to the youth Bassam is attached. The pouch was stolen en route to this office from Cyene. It was dated 6 weeks ago, and was recovered by Al Murrah. The cover letter and personal letter are attached.

I did not delay acting on the information contained—messengers were departed to Port Nub'ah the same day we received the dispatch. I will send word.

The exact transcript follows, the last sentence of urgent attention.

I am your humble servant,

Kaaper

Attachment:

Dear friend Kaaper,

God's blessings to you and Tiaa and your family. We expected your customary visit before the inundation, and feared you were set upon by a difficulty. Should we anticipate your arrival again in the next 90 days? We look forward to your visit. All is going well.

Amthara of the Oromo desires the preferred transport. The manifest describes 45,000 debens of skins and 60,000 debens finished metals to Makedonia, and seeks transport from Djanet or a port close by. I quoted the standard carry rate through Lower Egypt but he objected to the over-seas surtax and fee. I explained the Roman merchants have tripled their carry fees, and he refused it. We need to discuss.

The trade caravan from Nok did not deliver their contract. Our pilot returned through Abu Ballas with no profit. I recall to your memory this is the third time in three years. I believe the time has come to terminate the route and consider instead either of the coastal routes west.

I'm enclosing a private message intended to Zafir of Rekeem, and addressed to Bassam of Rekeem. Please forward.

—I am Narmer

Letter from Rasha to Bassam (the original has been forwarded to Rekeem). The other message that she references should already be in your possession:

My Dearest Bassam,

I trust you received my message about our trip south to Atbara? We have elected to pass through Korosko and reach for Atbara before going east. We believe it a safer way. Yours always, Rasha

ROUND

Twelve days into the trip we found the land green and wet. The climate was desert but a multitude of streamlets and creeks flowing toward Lake Tsana produced an abundance of desert trees, grasses, and shade. The streams were plentiful. We were energized to see the green of life more abundant now, but the impatience to reach our goal grew almost as fast as the grasses and trees around us.

"Bassam!" Ammar called, "Get over here. You need to know this."

I steered my beast next to his. "What is it?"

He produced his map. "I hadn't planned on this when Zafir gave us instructions," he said, "but look at this . . ."

The Nilus was clearly marked, a snaking line pointing northward. His finger stopped on a place marked Cyene. "This is a famous place, an important place, the last of the cataracts on the Nilus going out of Egypt—it sits on their southern boundary."

"What's so important?" I asked.

Ammar turned the map so it was facing me.

"Notice up here, this place, Ale'ksandria," he said, tapping the parchment where the Nilus emptied into the West Sea. "And Cyene down here, two cities 5,000 stadia apart, the one directly below the other."

"I see them," I said.

"One day I will tell you how a Greek used these two cities to measure the distance around the earth."

"How is that possible?"

"A water well in Cyene where there is no shadow at noon on the first day of summer—they say on that day the sun shines on the well's water deep down in the earth. It is directly overhead. But 5,000 stadia north on that very day at that very hour, a stick in the ground does cast a shadow. Why is there a shadow up north but none in the south? We should visit this famous place when we get to Cyene."

"Tell me now, how did this show the distance around the world?"

"Have you heard of Eratosthenes, the famous Greek stargazer...?"

I glanced over to see if Fawzi was interested in any of this. His donkey was a few paces behind the pack, trudging along as best it could. And Fawzi was slumped forward, perfectly balanced, fast asleep, and snoring loudly.

Day 727—Dear Rasha,

I'm writing you in the hope that God has preserved you and that I'll find you to share my travels. I know in my heart that you live. I can't believe this world would let you pass from us. Be safe, have faith.

We're crossing many larger streams now. Our guide says the river is not far ahead. Tonight we took star readings. The polestar is low. Ammar started a new string of knots to record locations for this land. We compare them with shadows at noon that he measures with a stick. I'll tell you about this when I return. Ammar doesn't know if he'll ever get back here, but says he can sell his string and map to others who do travel here. We've been on these little donkeys for two weeks. They are sturdy and loyal animals. We'll switch to boats at the river. Do not despair. I am coming for you. —Bassam

TSANA RIVER

The shallow brown hills that kept us company these many days finally melted into the slope of a vast green plain that funneled us directly to the Blue Nilus valley. The old dirt wash led us around a slow steep bend, and suddenly, there it was—the famous thundering falls of the upper gorge surrounded by a rolling green carpet of lush trees and shrubs.

"Welcome to the beauty of the Blue Nilus," Falak announced with a bright smile. "Above those falls is a village, that's where we spend the night," she said, waving her hand at a thick patch of trees on the ridge. "Now listen to me carefully. Some of you go north to the lake. Don't go this way alone. I'll show you why—after breakfast. Those going south— and that would be you, my handsome boyfriend," she said, winking directly at me, "—there's a small dock by the river. I'll take you there so you can negotiate passage on a boat. But first! Let us get settled. You'll like the inn here. They are my good friends and they give you good prices. Follow me!"

Fawzi leaned in close. "I think she likes you," he said.

"Certainly, are you blind?" I said, "And I do like Falak. I like her a lot," I said. "She's like a mother to me—maybe even a grandmother. And that would make her what for you? Your sister?" I hurried ahead before his retort could gather some wit.

The falls were loud and spectacular—foaming, rushing, pounding, a non-stop rumbling overflow from Lake Tsana's southern outlet. The torrent cascaded over a jagged shelf of broken rock and tumbled at least 100 cubits to rocks below, an enormous curtain of water gushing without rest.

"I can't imagine a boat going over these falls—and those enormous boulders there," I said, pointing.

"I'm sure many have," Ammar said. "A trip you don't return from . . ."

Even the river couldn't withstand the impact, obliterating itself into a massive frothy spray of boiling mist.

"The locals call them the smoky falls," Falak said. "The breeze brings you the droplets. You'll feel them. I love this place! Perfect for hot days like today. Do you feel it?"

I did feel it—a refreshingly cool mist that moistened my face and arms. I removed my headdress to let the elegant luxury begin dripping off my chin and nose.

By late afternoon we arranged accommodations and put our animals to feed. It was good to be walking again. Falak led us down-river to a small wooden dock that smelled of old fish and sour flotsam. Several suitable boats were tied, but none for hire. "For the fishing," they kept saying, waving us away like we were so many swarms of nimits.

"For the Nilus, a short time, nothing more!" Ammar insisted. "We have gold!"

"Not enough, not enough," and turned to their net-mending.

Fawzi was watching the fruitless negotiation. He pushed past me with a long, bored sigh. "You two—watch and learn," he said, stepping into the negotiation.

We both went quiet and let Fawzi work his magic in private.

"You two," he said returning. "I bought tomorrow's catch from the old man, and for that, we may use his boat to the next cataract. There's a village with others for hire."

The old man and his son removed their belongings and handed the rope to Fawzi. They walked away counting their coins, pleased with the exchange.

We walked around the boat to examine.

"Larger, I like that," Ammar volunteered. "Slats, good long oars, a pair of paddles . . . a nice sail and mast, plenty suitable should the current run slow."

"It looks light enough for the three of us. We could drag it around the cataracts," I said.

"Tight build, no water in the hull," Fawzi observed. "It looks sturdy enough."

"Do you want to row while there's light? An hour or two?" Fawzi asked.

"No, let's rest and eat, I'm tired," Ammar sighed. "We'll get an early start in the morning."

We agreed and took the dirt path to the village. Somewhere up there was a diner with sweet bread, good drink and fresh fish cooking, and we were determined to find it.

The river flowed no less this morning than when we put it to bed last night. Fawzi had first turn at the oars.

"Where does it all come from?" I asked.

Ammar gazed thoughtfully as the shoreline disappeared. "Those mountains in the distance. I imagine there's a runoff this time of year. I don't know enough about this land to say, Bassam."

We watched in silence as the current caught hold, pulling us along for an easy ride. This far below the falls the river was peaceful and wide, almost too far to see either shore in the grey dawn. It felt like some gentle power pulling us downstream.

When the sun finally cast his lights, everything came alive. The squawking alarm of a hadada ibis swept by, startling us with its screech. Then I spotted the small green humps of soft-shelled turtles floating quietly near shore. I counted eighteen.

"Ah, breakfast!" Fawzi said, pulling lightly to steer us center again.

"Breakfast? Turtles?"

"No, shell head," he said. "The eggs, the eggs! Find them in the grass, near shore—boil them. Makes a good meal."

I scowled and looked over at Ammar. He looked up and nodded. "Delicious," he smiled.

"I guarantee you, Bassam. They taste better than those roasted termites we had at Babilu, or the locusts we ate with the Nub'ah. Even little girls like them, so what's your problem?" Fawzi said.

"But watch out," Ammar chimed in.

"Oh yes," Fawzi nodded. "If they're not new eggs, well . . ."

They saw my disgust. Ammar grinned. "You're protecting a palate much too delicate for these parts," he said. "You'll learn."

Ammar was at the oars when the river narrowed, moving faster. "I think we're getting close to the cataract," he said. We studied the route ahead. The swifter water was flowing closer to shore. Ammar steered us toward it.

The Blue was a different river here with its banks narrowing, closing in like a trap if anyone wanted to catch us. To either side dense green stands of papyrus walled us in, thick and solid. Behind were thickets of tall leaning far over the water.

"The local people make boats of this," Ammar said, wiping a glistening brow.

"Those sticks?" I asked, pointing.

"Yes, they make rafts—lighter and cheaper than logs."

"Living off the land in so many ways, ingenious," I said.

At this point the river slowed and appeared to divide into several branches around some small islands.

As we neared we discovered these were no islands but natural rafts made entirely of water plants entangled together—bulrushes, reeds, papyrus, more ambatch.

"Ah! And there you see, nature makes her own," Ammar said.

Several had pushed together and formed large floating islands. I imagined they must take a hundred years to form, and some appeared to have dropped roots, anchoring themselves to the river bottom.

Our boat brushed too close and we heard the scratching of old roots against the hull. The noise startled unseen life on the little floating islands. A few birds turned to look as a hazy plume of blood-sucking secroot flies rose to torment us. A dozen cormorants stood perched on sturdy stalks with their black wings spread out to dry.

"They've been diving for eels this morning," Ammar said. "Probably exhausted."

I swatted angrily at the insects, cursing them to a painful doom. "Do you think we could walk on these little islands?"

"Probably," Fawzi said. "But why?"

"I don't know. I was just wondering. It seems you could step across them, like a floating bridge."

"I doubt it," Ammar said. "They're not as solid as they appear. Your foot would punch through to the water. And besides, there are things living there you wouldn't want to meet."

"Like what? Meerkats, monkeys, Fawzi's relatives?"

"Not around here," Ammar said.

"On second thought, I think you should go find out for yourself," Fawzi said. "I'm sure you can count on finding, oh, I don't know, some thick poisonous water snakes, stray carnivores, large spiders, your usual man-eating kroks. Why don't we stop a moment and let you explore? Let me know what you find."

"Never mind." He was right. I ached inside for my Rasha. I was letting every diversion and distraction creep into my world to numb my worry for her, to consume my attention, to hurry me to her, to give me rest. But it would not.

Just ahead was an enormous raft that stretched almost the entire width of the river, nearly blocking us from moving forward.

"What way do we go?" I asked.

Ammar directed our attention to the flotsam. Several pink petals passed by, following some threads of white slurry around the near side of the raft. It quickly slipped away into the swifter current. "I'll let the river take us the right way," he said.

Another hour of intensive pushing through thick overgrowth finally freed us into the main flow. We decided it was a good time to make shore.

Ammar steered us to the nearest bank, but it was a mistake—immediately the air grew uncomfortably hot, and the humidity became thicker. We labored to breathe.

"What is this terrible place?" I asked. "Do you feel it? Let's get out of here."

Ammar's face was flushed with small beads of sweat glistening, but still, he had to explain it. "It's the radiated sunlight," he said. "It comes at you three ways, from above by the sun, from the reflection off the water, and the reflection from this growth."

I wasn't listening. I was trying to gulp the stagnant air. The papyrus lined the shore, making a solid wall of cane standing three times a man tall, bowing their long lacy heads low, brushing annoyance into our faces. The tree roots were shallow, bumping us with occasional jolts.

Despite our persistence, no suitable lagoon presented. The riverbank was too congested, and our boat almost mired into the clog of reeds and fermenting rot that formed a black gooey sludge along the shorelines.

"I don't think we'll find anything along this stretch," Ammar said.

"Yes, let's see what's farther down river," Fawzi agreed.

"Why don't we just pull ourselves in?" I offered. "I can jump out and hack away an opening . . ."

"Perhaps," Ammar replied. "Watch for a thinning in the reeds, I'll try to get close."

We rowed away from shore into the cleaner air. Its cooling freshness blew away the oppressive heat and scattered the insects. We could breath again.

After a good half an hour of attempting a landing, we finally resigned ourselves to the center currents.

"The next village is a few hours away," Ammar said. "If we can hold on 'til then, it might be best for now."

We stayed in the cooler part of the current, keeping a good lookout. A strong breeze found us, so we basked in its refreshment for the time it lasted.

"There!" I said. "That's one over there, the large grassy bank."

The dense foliage parted, revealing a wide opening just ahead, a good 300 paces of cleared shoreline. The large domed awning of acacias shadowed the bank. It was perfect.

Fawzi steered us near. The prow of our boat pushed aside large clumps of water lettuce and sent lazy ripples through a green carpet of water lilies that bobbed up and down. Their distinctive blue blossoms danced gracefully. I reached out for one and snapped its stem. It was large, spreading across my lap and drooped on either side.

"If Adam and Eve were told to make them coverings of leaves, this would be the best," I mused.

"Yes, Bassam," Fawzi drawled. "That's why they picked out a broad-leaf plant."

KROKODILOS

The shore seemed peaceful enough—tall grasses matted down in mud, a scattering of water fowl scurrying away, so far so good. Ammar turned for a landing when there was movement. A large fallen tree partly submerged in water suddenly came to life and slipped into the murky calm without a splash.

"What?" I asked.

"Uh-oh," Ammar said.

"Yeah," Fawzi agreed. "Back us up. This is not the lunch stop I had in mind."

"Krokodilos?" I asked.

"They must be related to you, krok face," Fawzi said. "They've come for that leather purse you've been carting around, probably a distant cousin of theirs."

The enormous beast measured larger than our boat.

"Do they attack boats?" I asked, my concern growing.

"No, that's a river myth," Ammar said. "They've snatched people on the banks, or people thrown into the water, but they don't go after boats."

Just then something hit the keel of the boat, sending a shudder from stem to stern. My heart raced and I reached for the rails.

"Yes, I'd say we just met him officially," Fawzi said. "And that was his hello."

"Or hers," Ammar said.

Fawzi rowed hard, then drifted a moment as we scanned the waters. The light was just right so we could see their long dark shadows on the bottom of the river. Then a massive dark shadow passed directly beneath. I reached for the sword of Suoud and Ammar put his hand on his knife. Fawzi held the oars out of the water, not sure what to do next.

"Probably a cow and her hatchlings," Ammar said.

Fawzi nodded, watching over the edge. I looked off toward the muddy bank with its wall of bulrushes, wondering if there were more.

"They'll want us far from the nest," Fawzi said. Ammar nodded and dipped the oars to drive us away as quickly as he could.

We examined the shore with a different alarm in mind. Several more shorelines cleared of growth seemed safe and inviting, but each was claimed by the kroks—sometimes three, sometimes six, or ten, in assorted sizes, all of them basking in the sun. They awakened at our passage and slipped quickly from view into the muddy shallows.

"They are ambush feeders," Ammar said, "lying in wait to spring upon a zebra, river horse, cheetah, birds, smaller kroks, and men who wander too close unawares."

"And that big bite?"

"It's enough to crush a cow's skull," he said.

I shuddered, wondering if a man could ever best one of the beasts.

"No chance with a knife?" I asked.

"Or your sword," Fawzi said.

"They usually feed after sundown," Ammar said. "Otherwise it's to defend their nesting areas, their young."

The short splashes turned all of us left and right as assorted numbers of the great-tailed beasts slipped into the water.

"Most animals have poor night habits," Ammar continued. "The kroks take advantage of that—they'll grab their prey who come to drink and drag them into the water. Drowning kills it first if the bite hasn't already."

I shuddered, wondering if my knife could find a vulnerable spot before my lungs gave out.

"What are they doing then, when they dash off the shore like that? Are they running or are they coming for us?" I asked.

Fawzi's rowing was steady and strong and seemed to speed up with all this frenzied talk.

"No, they're shy, like most wildlife," Ammar said. "They're not looking for a fight unless they can beat you to the punch, but they do keep track of what you do, Bassam."

"They watch?"

"Oh yes. They study the habits of their prey," he said. "It's the most intelligent animal in the Nilus. They watch behaviors and know when a herd comes to feed and drink. They'll plan their feeding around these habits. They'll even hunt in groups and herd their prey into a trap. I've actually seen them join with 3 or 4 others and start swimming around a school of fish in a great circle to scare the fish into the center, then each takes a turn to feed."

"Fascinating," I said and shuddered.

We passed several basks of kroks, six to ten for the most part. One group had a dozen, of all sizes. We steered as far from them as we could, watching to see if we were being followed.

"It must be their nap time," Ammar said.

Over the course of an hour we passed 60 or 70. All the older kroks rested with their eyes shut and their mouths set ajar.

"To dissipate the heat," Ammar said.

I watched a pair of Jacanas spryly stepping across some lily pads where an old krok floated between them, his lazy brown eyes watching with disinterest.

"Fawzi!" I suddenly blurted. "Look at that!"

There on the bank was an old fat male, wrinkled on his knees with a full, bloated stomach. He was spread out next to a tree, the warming rays of the hot afternoon sun lulling him to sleep. His mouth stood agape, not spread wide, but certainly enough to swallow a man. And there, right there in his mouth, a small blue-gray bird sporting a black crown was hopping around inside.

"Is it dead?"

Ammar chuckled. "Well, will you look at that! I've heard about the krokodilos bird," he said, "but didn't believe it until now."

He slowed the boat. "This is nature in its most wonderful state of give-and-take."

"Why doesn't he bite?" I asked.

"Watch her peck at the teeth—that krok has just eaten. Look at his stomach. He needs his teeth cleaned. The bird needs her food. Together they serve one another in ways understood only by nature."

The little winged fowl hopped across the jaw, gnawing between the massive shredders, then pulled a gangly strip of pink and tipped back to swallow it whole.

"Do you think they ever bite down?" I asked.

"I doubt it," Ammar said. "Not the big ones, not on a full stomach, anyway. What's a meatless ball of feathers to those powerful teeth designed to take down an impala or rip into the hide of a river horse?"

We watched for several moments more as our boat drifted past. Just then I saw the old krok slyly open one eye. He watched us a moment, then closed it as the bird continued her work.

32

QUWWA

We could hear the mighty falls long before we reached the village. The distant thunder of the gushing torrent rolled toward us like ten million heavy hammers pounding the boulders incessantly, wearing away the obstacle as frantically as possible. I was anxious to see this wonderful spectacle, but Ammar reminded me business first.

The small village was not on the river, but nestled among some trees a short way up the mouth of a slow stream. We would have missed it had Fawzi not spotted a slender column of smoke.

"What's so blue about the Blue Nilus," I asked as we dragged our boat to shore. "It looks green to me—I'd call it the green Nilus."

"And green it is," Ammar said, huffing.

We lashed the boat secure and looked for the path.

"It's a translation problem," Ammar said. "The Nub'ah use the same word for black as they do for blue. Why we call it blue no one knows, but it certainly starts out blue, as blue as the sky. When it drains into the White Nilus, it has gathered enough sediment to make it dark green, even black."

"And the White Nilus, it's probably black, too?" I asked.

"Nope, milky green," he said. "Grey sediment carried away in the rainy season makes it look creamy white compared to the Blue, and it all changes when things dry up . . . ."

Just then, three men with spears emerged from the jungle.

"Here come your escorts, nimit noggin," Fawzi said. "The chief wants you to meet his daughter." That joke was wearing old. I didn't even think to scowl. My thoughts were on Rasha and her whereabouts. Would any of these tribes remember seeing her? Would her captors bring her through these treacherous jungles safely or lead her into nature's traps? My Rasha is strong but is she strong enough?

The men seemed more curious than menacing, and began asking questions.

"They want to know if we're Greeks," Ammar said.

"Greeks?" I asked. "And how would they know anything about them?"

The leader pointed to a metal buckle adorning his leather breeches. Ammar studied it.

"My goodness!" he said. "This is Greek—fine workmanship, too. Looks bronze but the goat head, that's probably silver."

Fawzi bent over to see. "So, they've had some traders pass through," he said.

Ammar stumbled through his limited vocabulary to explain our urgent mission, and that we were not Greek. The men seemed satisfied and stepped away to examine our boat.

"Do they want to trade?" I whispered.

"No, just wondering," Ammar said.

The men poked at our belongings, seemed satisfied we posed no threat, and gestured us to follow.

Their village had more than 40 homes with some outbuildings and a large central meeting place. Each structure was built the same—circular with poles upright and thick walls of intertwined twigs and branches plastered over with mud. They were colored in white and light blue. The chief's home was particularly elaborate, painted with images of animals and hunters with spears, and large letters in a language none of us knew. A large rendition of the man's belt buckle was painted in the middle of the wall, standing alone in blue and brown.

"It probably says, 'I'm the boss but so's my wife,'" Fawzi said.

I laughed but Ammar gave us that familiar 'I know something' look. "You might be closer to the truth than you realize," he said. "Matriarchal societies are not uncommon in these lands—even among the pharaohs! This might be one of those."

"Women pharaohs?" I asked.

"Certainly," Ammar replied.

We found hospitality and kind hands among these Nub'ah. They were pleased to take our coins for a meal, and another for a good night's rest. They were masters of cooking the river fish, and adorned it with a few dozen fat roasted locusts, giving it a nice nutty flavor.

"If I don't think about what I'm eating," I said to no one in particular, "this tastes pretty good."

"Eat it, cricket breath," Fawzi said. "People around the world depend on these winged creatures."

"I doubt that," I said.

"Wake up, fish brain," Fawzi said. "They've saved whole villages from starving, something a mosquito beak like you hasn't faced."

"But I've seen those nasty vandals mow down an entire field in a single morning," I replied. "You call that saving a village?"

"Starvation is a hard taskmaster," Ammar said. "I'd like to see how they capture them alive, and in such quantities."

Fawzi grinned at me. "Cricket breath," he mouthed and continued eating.

"Even when they're not starving," Ammar continued, "I've heard they make a roasted powder for flour and a special hard bread. Quite tasty, I'm told."

I looked at the flattened black loaf on a wooden cutting board in the middle of our table, half eaten and still warm. I looked closer for little bits of insect legs and wings, and began to wonder.

Ammar stayed up late to update his map and tie another knot on his string. "This place might serve Abdali-ud-din," he said. "Trade moving west on the Blue would exchange well here, a good junction for the overland to meet shipping boats. We could guide them to the coast and avoid those bandits and their fees."

"I agree, but Zafir seems to have an aversion to water trade," I said.

"I suspect he knows the limits of his enterprise," Ammar said. "I don't know if aversion is the right word—probably business savvy is closer. Maybe he is looking to you to help him expand trade to these climes. I'll be interested to see how you might want to develop that."

I had given it thought, thinking that a new trade route from the south to north to east could cross through here, deliver to the West Sea, then on to parts west—it could be a rewarding experiment.

That night I dreamed of being with my Rasha in the shade beneath large palms on a warm sandy dune, and would not have awoken had Fawzi not kicked my foot.

"Huh?"

"Bassam! Get up!" Fawzi ordered.

"Is it morning?"

"Better get up," he said. "The chief wants you to marry his daughter."

I leapt to my feet and was the first out the door. Fawzi and Ammar followed, both of them laughing at my panic.

The pre-dawn mists hung heavy along the river-valley floor. A man and his animal pulled our boat down the slip way, his head bowed in regret that he agreed to the portage for only a deben.

The trail around the cataract led close enough to give us a wonderful tour of the great river boulders and stone shelves. They shed the rushing sheets over a thousand silky falls. The refreshing mist enticed me to chance a morning swim had we time to tarry.

A large raft big enough for 40 men sat just off shore, tied to a tree, empty and bleached from lack of use. We paid the porter his deben and were on our way before the western sky could surrender its last remaining stars.

We were an hour down river when the morning breeze came, pushing us north. Two of us worked the paddles while the third worked the sail. We rotated turns twice an hour to avoid monotony.

None of us were talkative. The scenery was beautiful, and we were too focused on the tasks ahead for much idle chatter.

In the sky behind rose a massive cloud formation. It bellowed its rumblings from afar, flashing a warning as it teased and taunted with boiling threats. The morning sun rays turned the storm's black edges to a beautiful pink, then orange, then faded to dark as the deep canyons and crevices of grey tunnels and passages formed and folded and built up again. As the sun climbed higher the massive cloud bloom rose majestically and more lightning flashed within, illuminating the great plumes in bursts of yellow and white, followed by a long drawn out rumbling. A wide grey curtain of falling rain appeared, darkening a portion of the horizon but then rewarding us with a beautiful rainbow covering most of the sky as it watered the luscious green jungles below.

"Is that headed for us?" I wondered aloud.

Ammar was enjoying this, caught in the grandeur of the great floating spectacle.

"I don't think so," he said. "See those tops? See how they are sheering off to the west? That's the high wind at work. I expect it will carry the storm west while we travel north. We'll miss it, but what a beautiful, powerful display . . ."

Our travel seemed faster through these parts, and we were encouraged by a positive wind. At one large bend that took us closer to shore, Ammar pointed out a thick cluster of short berry trees close to shore.

"Ah, the quwwa," he said.

I looked but wasn't impressed—more trees, more strange fruits.

"You don't know the quwwa, berry brains?" Fawzi asked.

I shook my head.

"This will excite you," Fawzi said. "I mean it! Ammar, tell him the story you told me."

Ammar settled into his place, letting Fawzi take the brunt of the paddling.

"It's the most amazing berry," Fawzi said. "You'll get energy from it, Bassam. It wakes you up!"

"I don't need energy," I said. "I'm just tired of this long trip. Enough of rivers!"

"Then I'll tell you," he said. "Long ago a man was tending his flock in the highlands of the Blue Nilus. He came upon these same berry trees growing along the river. When his flock chewed the berries he saw they suddenly filled with vitality and energy. The effect was so vivid that the man plucked the berries to test their powers. They were bitter and he spat them into his fire. As the berries burned, they gave a delicious roasted smell that made the man more curious. He used his stave to rescue the berries, and saw the fire made them dark, almost black. He tried to eat them again, this time they were hard like a nut. The inventive fellow decided to try softening them by boiling them in water. That was the great breakthrough! That same roasted aroma teased him to grind them to a powder. And that's how wild goats taught an old shepherd a thing or two about these wonderful berries, the quwwa."

"I've never even heard of quwwa," I said.

"You had to be Greek or in the Egyptian priesthood, part of their worship," Ammar said. "The people think it's a sacred drink—medicine from god that only the shaman may drink for visions and prophecies, to heal the sick, and—"

"And stay awake during Ammar's long stories," Fawzi said.

"Why don't we have it in Rekeem?" I asked. "I think they'd love having more push to their pull. Can we get some?" I said, pointing to the trees.

"You go play with the kroks, stork legs," Fawzi said, "and I'll get a bag's worth. Must I do everything for you, goat face?"

DEBS

Just as we rounded a lush bend thick with overhanging trees and vines, there was a tremendous flapping of startled wings that exploded to flight right in front of us. Dozens of water fowl rose suddenly into the air, wings flapping and squawking, making us jump.

The green canopy was full of birds of every kind, fluttering from nests and shadows, flaunting the grandeur and variety of wing and color in warning to predators or inviting a mate.

Fawzi pulled in the oars and we coasted for a while, enjoying the scene.

Ammar could hardly keep up with the variety. "See! Plovers, a hawk, that's a vulture, see the grey herons! Pelicans? Here?" He knew them all, even a yellow beaked fish eagle that swept by hunting an unaware early feeder.

The deep fishers dove for their catch, and were followed by others looking for missed prey.

"Watch," Ammar said. "The lucky hunters are challenged, see that fight?"

Just then a smaller bird driven to defeat dropped her catch as payment to the larger pursuer who broke pursuit to steal the morsel. Thus outmaneuvered the smaller bird turned for shore and the trees to find a meal elsewhere.

A few moments more and the morning scurry ended. Fawzi resumed his turn at the oars.

Life on the water was difficult on some days, and this was one of those. As the day wore on so did the humidity that became thick and sticky, sucking energy and life from our best efforts. The sun was hot, burning our skin. And then came those rabid nimits that stung and bit their way to the least bit of wet or salty opportunity. We endured as best we could for several hours, searching for that right place in the river where relief from their buzzing frenzy could be maintained.

By mid-afternoon the heavy sludge of fatigue and hunger drove us to rest on shore. We spotted a clearing near a village to stretch our legs.

No krokodilos here, but we were not alone. A Nub'an mother was washing on the banks with her young daughter. She didn't seem markedly alarmed by our arrival.

We pulled our boat to shore, and Ammar made gestures of friendly greeting. They eyed us with mild interest then bundled up their things and placed them on their heads. We watched them walk a path into the shadows of a great green wall of towering Nehet and Mama trees, and quickly disappear into the shadows.

"It's an ideal place for a village," Ammar said.

"Perfect," Fawzi echoed. "Guarded with this green fortress to fend off attacks, a wind break, hidden—the perfect place."

Then Ammar looked around and became suspicious. "Look," he said, pointing. A dozen poles stood haphazardly and neglected in the overgrowth, the skulls of animals and humans mounted on their tops.

"What's that supposed to mean?" I asked.

"It means they don't like strangers," Fawzi said.

"Might the woman and her daughter be rousing an unwelcome company from the village?" Ammar asked.

We agreed there were too many signs of hostility, so we erred on the side of caution and cut short our rest. We gathered fruits, replenished our water, and pushed quickly away from the little cove.

"That was odd," Ammar said. "I've seen trophy bones in some island cultures, the Indus interior, but here?"

"Is it a warning?" I asked.

"Yes, but for other things too," he said. "Good crops, happy marriages, successful hunts. In these waters it might be connected to the afterlife, some obligation on the dead to serve the living."

I watched the display shrink as we rowed away, wondering why anyone would make trophies from the bones of the dead.

With just an hour of sunlight remaining we scouted a place to camp. Ammar suggested we could resume our trip after the moon rose, but it meant waiting somewhere in the dark for an hour. That would let us eat and stretch, so we steered for a landing.

The shadows grew long, stretching across the water, turning green to black. Fawzi spied a broad lagoon sheltered on one side by a large bamboo thicket and steered there.

"Look!" I said pointing. "Are those more turtles? I'm game for trying an egg dinner . . ."

Fawzi brought us closer.

"Is it safe?" I asked.

"Looks good so far," Ammar said.

A small gathering of saddle-billed storks floating in front of us were startled and took wing in urgent gracefulness.

"Oh no, those are no turtles," Ammar said.

"Egyptian debs," Fawzi said, and immediately dropped his paddle to turn away.

"Debs?" I asked.

"River horses," Ammar said. "The Egyptian word."

"Dangerous?" I asked.

Neither answered but peered hard downriver, plotting a new path.

Then I spotted a cluster of debs standing on shore watching.

They were enormous—large round bodies and bulging necks. I saw a baby deb next to its mother soiling itself. It's little tail was flinging it everywhere. I pointed and laughed.

"You're a foolish boy, tusk bucket," Fawzi said. "These are man-eaters," he said, snapping his teeth and scowling. "Crush a man in half if you make her mad. Now, I'm talking about men, Bassam, so you're safe here."

"You said her—?"

"More nesting grounds," Ammar said. "The females are ferocious if threatened. They'll come after you, and the bulls will protect his cows. They don't swim."

"They float?"

"Oh no, they gallop along the river bottom and when they're close they'll leap for the surface. Quite frightening. And you thought the kroks were our greatest threat. Wait until you see deb's mouth open wide to bite your boat in half, and you with it. She won't eat you—but they'll kill just the same. Then you'll know who is Queen of the Nilus."

Fawzi steered far from the bobbing grey bodies. It was a long labor to cross against the current but seemed the best way to avoid them.

"It's getting dark," I said. "Shouldn't we find some place soon?" We steered away from shore a while longer, none of us sure about our best next move. Another clearing appeared and we made an approach.

Just then, a squirm of kroks slipped off the bank, disappearing among the gray walls of papyrus, sinking silently into the dark water.

"Never mind," I said, seeing a pair of man-eaters gliding in our direction.

Ammar stood as lookout, guiding Fawzi's rowing away from shore. I helped by paddling from the rear.

Another wall of papyrus rose to either side as the river turned, blocking the nearest length of shoreline. It stretched away as far as we could see. It was almost dark and we realized we had to stay on the water a while longer.

"Looks like we're stuck," Ammar said.

"With some heavy company," Fawzi added.

"Heavy, indeed," Ammar sighed.

"Should I make fire for the lamp?" I offered.

"Yes, good idea," Ammar said. "That might help."

I produced my bow drill, and after a few moments a small yellow flame stood up on my board. I fed it little twigs and prepared the Egyptian lamp. Soon, a bright flame took hold casting strong dancing shadows in all directions.

"That's more like it," Ammar said.

"At last, you've earned your keep, deb dung," Fawzi said. "Better stay low lest those flying fish find you," he said.

"There are no flying fish on the Nilus," I muttered.

The oil lamp did little to calm our nerves. We could hear the restless splashing and grunting of more debs that seemed to surround us in the dark.

A great blow sounded, then another closer. I thought a dozen were headed right toward us, and then all went eerily quiet. Great puffs and splashing rolled our boat side to side. Our drifting didn't satisfy their agitation. It was impossible to discern—were we floating into their nests or away? How could we know in this pitch?

Then without warning two tremendous blows sprayed so near we felt the mist rain on us from the shore-side of our boat. I grabbed the railing with both hands.

"Do they sleep in the water?" I asked nervously.

"Not at all," Ammar said. "That's what worries me. They'll take safety in the water, but at night they should be on land foraging—far from shore, far from here."

"Why don't they just go away?" I asked.

"When we're gone, they'll be gone," he said. "Keep your sword close. You have it with you, right?"

I held tighter to the rail, stealing a glance heavenward. We were in total darkness except for the dancing flicker of the lamp. The stars shined blankly, framed by towering black trees to either side. The lacy jewels shined distinctly, a familiar reference point that made me feel better. If nothing else we could see that heavenly channel above, winding broadly to guide us through the pitch.

"Bassam?" Ammar said. "Did you hear me?"

"Uh, yes," I finally replied. "I have my sword."

The words had barely left my mouth when a ferocious explosion of water erupted directly in front of us. The enormous bulbous head of an angry deb rose out of the river, his nostrils blasting a great spray, ears erect, and beady eyes staring blankly with murderous intent. In that paralyzing second, he opened his cavernous mouth with mighty tusks glinting wet and crashed down full bodied across the front of our boat, crushing it to fragments and scattering us into the cold whirlpool of churning froth and blackness.

ANOTHER BREAK

Henri stopped reading. There were three sheaves of writings inserted into the scroll.

"More?" he whispered aloud, lifting the small squares from the coils. "You'd think the scribe would have all this together before embarking on a long transcription..."

He held the sheets to the light.

"Skin," he said, focusing on the opaque striation and pale translucency. "Same markings of Al Kalimat. I see that a less patient hand inked these words, must have been in a hurry."

The cross and dots were written more deliberately than the text. "This was no hired scribe. Field documents perhaps? Are there more?" He lifted the scroll to check.

The squares were too stiff to flatten. "This needs a professional touch, maybe I can open it just enough to ..."

Al Kalimat verified — +:
Dispatch by currier – Urgent
Inscribed – 14 Mechar

Master Zafir,

The enclosed message was received through the resourcefulness of a barge captain in Abu Zenime' who is friendly to our cause. Al Murrah ensured the integrity of its delivery from a steward through controlled channels into our secure keeping. The message appears to be from the man Shamar, a relative of yours, with direct mention of Rasha by name. We surmise it's addressed to his wife and was handed off the night of their departure:

My dear Pageti,

A most remarkable blessing of God has unfolded and I know not where it leads. I have discovered, by the most impossible happenstance, the youngest daughter of my cousin Zafir. You'll recall you met him and Rasheeda in Rekeem some years past.

Their daughter Rasha was the kidnap victim of that raid we heard of and was taken for ransom. This kidnapping I did not know about, thus making this encounter more remarkable. She confided of her plight and we are tonight on the run from her captors. For this reason, I must be brief.

I leave this note in the care of good friend Sadad who takes us to Al-Jarf where we'll embark on an unknown journey into the coastal deserts of Egypt.

The man Rakbah will be in pursuit come morning, but we are already departing on the sea, a full day ahead. Rasha is afraid, I am afraid for our safety. I will, therefore, be somewhat delayed, my dear Pageti, from returning. We put our escape into the hands of God and beseech his kind benevolence for a quick and safe return.

With all the loving affection as your devoted husband, I call upon God each morning and night to watch over you and protect you until I return.

Your loving husband Shamar

The delivery place is provided on the original message. I have dispatched a courier to deliver it in person, and to convey our best wishes and your personal expression of concern for the safe return of Shamar to his family.

The facts to the above are verified through priority channel participants. The pilot Sadad has not been located, but estimates to time and place of the original writing is Abu Zenime, some 40-50 days prior to our receipt of the parchment. A steward has been sent to find Sadad for an investigation.

Additional queries as to sightings of a man and a girl have been dispatched to all contacts. Pending additional information, this is my report.

I am your servant,
Nefermaat

Al Kalimat verified — +:
Dispatch by courier – Urgent
Inscribed – 2 Phamenoth

Master Zafir,

The pilot Sadad has not been found. Witnesses at Abu Zenime' confirm a sighting of the criminal Rakbah and three or four men seeking passage to Al-Jarf. Their accounts are not consistent on some of the minor details, but agree as to the overall substance of his sighting.

As requested, I can report to you that friendly resources are now converging on Egypt's eastern desert portages, the region of the first and second cataracts, and Noph.

Pending additional information, this is my report.

I am your servant,
Nefermaat

Al Kalimat verified — +:
Dispatch by currier – Urgent
Inscribed – 19 Phamenoth

Master Zafir,

I write with important new information—I have just received word the conspirator called Sutekh, one of those who took your daughter, was captured by Al Murrah in the outskirts of Noph three weeks ago. He was interrogated and provided the following before he died:

Your daughter was the ransom target, betrayed into their hands by her acquaintance, the youth named Faris. She was given over to the criminal Rakbah to be delivered to Noph.

Ransom conditions set for Avalites was a deception to draw our resources south.

The conspirators are presently hiding in Noph, awaiting delivery of your daughter.

Sutekh claimed the Tauri of the Pontusl is regrouped under new leadership and have taken a village near Tadmor. Access to the main trade routes has prospered them.

The attack against Rekeem included local bandits who had knowledge of the city and its layout.

A network under their control intends to smuggle your daughter from Noph to the Western Sea and then to lands north, perhaps Tadmor. He claimed he was not told of the destination. The ransom demand was calculated to continue for many months.

Sutekh was leader over an active group of 10 or 15 men bound to service of the Tauri of Pontusl.

Sutekh's true identity was not discovered. He wore the blue crescent behind his left ear. No additional information was obtained before his death. Al Murrah conducted the interrogation.

We have no reason to dispute the information taken from the criminal. It's consistent with known facts and supports the theories put forward about the attack and subsequent events.

Pending additional information, this is my report.

I am your servant,

Nefermaat

Henri returned the squares to their place.

"That's a good network for those times," he said. "But to what end are these scraps of history—some sort of evidence or story, to prove something?"

He rolled a few more inches of parchment and continued.

TREE

Bubbling chaos roared around my head as thick water dragged me down. I reached out for anything, feeling my lungs compress, my heart race in panic. I spread wide my arms and frantically clawed for air. I kicked and struggled, breaking the surface just as a massive body rammed against me from beneath with such violence that I spun over, inhaling a mouthful of river and plunged deep again. Pain shot through my shoulders. Instinctively, I flailed against the swirling madness to find the surface. A great weight pulled relentlessly at my hip, taking me deeper. I swung my fist through the water to pound away its vicious grip, finding, to my great relief, it was not clenched teeth on my robe but the weight of my sword pulling heavy in the water.

Kicking my legs for a last push, I broke the surface and the cold night air rushed around my dripping head, then sudden relief as I inhaled air at last. I coughed, inhaled, and coughed again, each compression shooting white flashes across my vision.

"Help!" I shouted. "Help! Ammar! Fawzi!"

I heard a splashing behind. Ammar surfaced, coughing and gasping. Then another in front of us, lost to the darkness—it was Fawzi, cursing as he cleared his lungs.

"To shore!" Fawzi shouted. "Bassam! Where are you?"

"Here," I struggled blindly toward him.

"Ammar?"

"I'm here," he said, straining to stroke toward the sound of Fawzi's voice.

"The shore," he said. "Look up, the stars, the trees, that way, the shore, follow me."

"I can't see you," I gurgled.

"Follow my voice."

We took long reaching strokes, peering in vain for where the vague outlines of treetops cut silhouettes against the starry backdrop.

"I see it," I gurgled, choking and coughing between strokes.

"Follow me!" Fawzi shouted. "Ammar!"

"Here," he said, gasping.

I felt my foot kick against something hard. Had the deb come to bite off my leg? No, it was the sandy shallows of the shore.

"Ground," I gasped. "I feel the ground, the shore."

"Yes, keep coming," Fawzi said.

I pressed harder against the tide, clawing even more anxiously against the great swells toward nothing I could see.

Fawzi was first to stand and then reached for me. He found my arm and pulled me to my feet.

"All right?" he shouted.

"I think so," and coughed up more of the river.

"To the shore, hurry," he said, thrusting me past. I slogged through the shallow bog, almost slipping in the thick slime. The slender papyrus stalks appeared suddenly in my face, yielding stiffly as I stepped through them. I waved about blindly for the tree whose top I saw cast against the stars. It towered over as a massive black shape that assured me I was almost within reach. Reaching dry ground, I swung my arms in the dark, slamming my left hand against a trunk.

"The tree," I shouted. "I found the tree, over here, hurry."

It was a massive baobab with a trunk larger around than the span of three men.

Coming toward me I could hear the sloshing water where Fawzi helped Ammar to his feet.

"Over here! This way," I called.

Breathless and panting, they found their way to me at last. We all felt about, assuring each other we were intact.

"Are you all right?" Fawzi barked. "Are you hurt, Bassam?"

"I'm okay I think. I'm all right," I said. "I have my sword. I'm not hurt."

The truth was, I hurt everywhere. The cold, the anxiety, the panic had numbed my entire body. With motion, it was awakening and the sting of burn came alive across my back and left hip. I felt a great tear in my clothing and cuts in my flesh. It pained when I touched it, but I felt no slick of fresh bleeding.

"I think I'm hurt," I said, touching the wounds.

"What's wrong?" Fawzi commanded. "Where? Can you stand?"

Yes, I could stand. Yes, I could walk. I could—just then a great chill washed over me.

"I'm cold," I said trembling, and sunk to my knees.

"This is no place to rest," Fawzi said. "Get in the tree. Come Bassam, I'll help—the limb, there's a limb here. Give me your hand. Do you feel it? Hang on. I'll push you up."

I reached for his voice and he pulled me to my feet again. My cold wet clothing clung to me like heavy chains. I could hardly move.

"Move it, deb dung. This is no time to whine like a little girl," Fawzi barked, and drew me to him. Then he placed my hands on the limb so I could feel my way in the dark. He grabbed my legs and hoisted me up. I found smaller branches to pull myself onto the great limb and out of the way. Fawzi helped Ammar in the same fashion, then climbed up himself.

We felt about to test the boundaries of our precarious perch, finding thick branches to lean against.

"Anyone bleeding?" Fawzi asked. "Bassam? Where are you hurt?"

"Something hit me in the water," I said, reaching to my back. "My clothing is ripped and I can feel cuts."

"Do you bleed?" Ammar asked.

"I don't think so," I said.

"Then it's not severe," he said. "Cold water helps—washes a wound, closes it off, you should be all right until we can look closer."

"Sunrise is just a few hours," Fawzi said.

"Our things . . ." I said.

"We're alive," Fawzi whispered.

"We'll know more in the morning," Ammar said. "I'll wager the deb has our things on the bottom, so let him have it."

After a few moments of adjusting and turning about, I could hear Fawzi peeling off his shirt.

"What are you doing?" I asked. "Are you crazy?"

"Good idea," Ammar said, and sat up to remove his clothing.

"It's cold," I said, "why . . ."

"You'll warm up faster, feather brain," Fawzi said. "Get 'em off, now."

"Your skin dries faster than your clothing," Ammar said. "You'll sit in cold all night in that wet clothing, get rid of it. You'll be fine in a few minutes."

I handed my sword to Ammar while I wrung out the water and blindly spread my clothing over some tall suckers. Somewhere in that wadded-up bundle, I hoped was Rasha's hand-embroidered veil—I would check in the morning.

I curled up shivering, trying to get comfortable. After several minutes I felt warmth return. And then for the first time, I noticed all the wild sounds of the jungle—hooting night birds, chirping tree frogs, slapping of the river against the sandy shore, Fawzi's rhythmic snoring, and somewhere out there in the dark, the defiant blow and puff of a bull deb patrolling the safety of his pod.

DISCOVERED

The dawning sky melted from shady grey to deepening blue when I heard the sound of human voices. I sat up, startled. Fawzi and Ammar awoke at the same time. Below us, looking up in surprise, was a group of seven naked warriors in loin cloths standing around our tree with broad-blade spears. Their heads were shaved bald and each of them sported strange patterns of small round welts dotted in lacy lines about their shoulders and faces like a decoration.

I supposed they had been there a while—at least two of them were standing on one leg, the other bent with foot on inside knee, using their spears for balance.

"Look how they stand, like a tall-legged bird," I whispered to Fawzi. He shushed me. "Act friendly, fish face," he said.

"Hello!" Ammar said, lifting his hand in greeting. And then thinking a moment, he spoke again.

"Iiti!" He said.

The men stopped their murmuring and stared with unblinking eyes.

"What was that?" I whispered to Ammar.

"I think I told them hello," Ammar said. "Aksumi warriors, Aethiopian. I might know a few of their words." And then he tried another.

"Dua Netjer en etj!" he said with a smile.

The men acted confused and did not set down their spears.

"I'm not sure you're helping," Fawzi said. "Try something else."

"What did you say?" I asked.

"I'm not sure what I said," Ammar whispered. "Oh, wait, I said it wrong."

He turned to the men again and cleared his throat.

"Dua Netjer en ek!" he said.

At this the men laughed, pointing at us.

Ammar was blushing, even in this light we could see it.

"So, what was it?" Fawzi asked.

"I said it wrong," Ammar scolded himself. "I told them, 'thank God for you women.'"

Fawzi and I snickered.

"The word is 'ek' for man, not 'etj,'" Ammar said. "Thank God for you men is what I meant."

"I guess it worked," Fawzi said smiling.

It appeared the warriors understood us to be of no threat and the circumstance of our strange happenstance seemed clear to them. They laid down their spears to help us out of the tree.

As they set me on my feet, I noticed a smattering of animal footprints in the muddy grass—several sets were padded like a lynx, but as large as my hand. I elbowed Fawzi and pointed.

"So that was our company," he said, catching the eye of a warrior and pointing to the large cat print. The man looked at us with a quizzical expression as if to ask, "Is that new to you?"

We noticed our belongings in a pile along with some of the planks from our boat. The warriors had gathered it from the shoreline—my journal pouch, Ammar's map bag, the leather skin of oil.

A warrior offered them to Ammar, asking in the confusing, tongue-rolling sounds of his language if they belonged to us.

"They floated!" I said, watching Ammar accept our property from the outstretched hand of the warrior and clutch them to his heart. He bowed his head in the universal sign of gratitude.

"Dua Netjer en ek!" he said again, smiling kindly.

To this the man returned the greeting and all of them smiled with newly relaxed looks. Then they peppered us with questions. They pointed and gestured and touched our clothing and skin. I turned to Ammar for help.

"Iiti [eye-EAT-ee]!" He said to one. "Iiti! Iiti! Iiti," he repeated, personally greeting each man.

Their leader replied, "Iiti seqdew." This meant "hello sailor," but we didn't learn that until much later.

We were led to the warriors' village, comprised of three dozen homes similar to others we had seen—circular, walls of upright sticks tightly packed, covered in thick mud, baked hard in the sun. The roofs were peaked in the center with rafters of palm ribs covered with a thatch of grass and straw. A stand of tree ferns cast shade over the dwellings, and well-worn dirt paths beaten into the red clay guided the barefoot villagers from dwelling to cook fires to shore and places between.

Our escorts understood more about our accident with the bull deb than we had managed to tell them, making us wonder if they had witnessed the attack from shore.

From Ammar's feeble attempts to communicate, we came to understand this pod of river horses was particularly large and selfish, and that same bull we encountered had killed two people this season already. His viciousness was widely known among other tribes. Our warrior friends made gestures of attack with their spears, showing us they tried to kill him several times.

While Ammar and Fawzi engaged the village elders, I became the anxious focus of the village women. They had taken special interest in the great scrape down my back and were fussing and arguing with their medicine man about how best to treat me.

Then suddenly they just lifted me to my feet and hurried me away. I looked back at Ammar who just waved me on with a smile.

They took me to a hut with no windows. It was dark and cool inside, a small smoky fire giving the only light. The underside of the roof was as black as soot. Long cobwebs hung in the corners.

There was no furniture, just bed rolls and mats for sitting. An old man lay prostrate near the fire, tended to by a younger woman.

A few dry sticks were added, and yellow flames leapt to life. My caregivers tended immediately to my wound. A single long cut into the skin with red abrasions the width of two palms extended from my waist halfway down my leg. It was not deep or serious, but painful like I had been dragged across hard ground. The shaman made biting motions, pointing to his lips and teeth. I gathered he was saying the bull had grazed my hip with a tusk and the rough of his upper lip had scraped against my skin. I shuddered to think how close I might have been to the bull's crushing bite. The beast made quick splinters of our boat. What might it have done to me?

Their medical treatment was not much different from Humam's— warm water, cleaning out the old blood, a liquid wash and some more cleaning, then application of a paste made from pounded leaves and berries. The poultice actually felt good, numbing the burn with a tingling sensation at the same time.

They wrapped the deepest slash with fabric torn from my robe and then stood me up. I tested my leg. It felt much better.

I thanked them by clasping my hands to my heart. They chattered instructions and scolded me about something, then led me back to Ammar and Fawzi.

By this time the villagers had all gathered at the main huts to greet us. The chief ordered a welcoming meal, inviting us to sit and tell about our adventures. The food smelled delicious.

The women presented a platter of freshly stewed meat they called wat, and gave me a scoop of soft, lumpy cheese. A slice of flat, stiff bread served as our utensil. There was an orange fruit sliced with some gray green legumes, and clay mugs with some type of intoxicating wine that smelled as wretched as the river bank. But these were offered with smiles and kind hands.

I dabbled at the wat, wondering what animal had sacrificed for us, and what part of that animal was before me. The meat was in a sauce that was spicy and hot. I quenched the fire with a sip from the mug, an equally unsatisfying mixture of new flavors that burned down my throat, making me gag and cough at the same time.

"Eat it, bowel brains," Fawzi said. "Look at these people. Look at them watching us. They're doing us an honor. Eat!"

"Tasty!" I said, and scooped some of the crumbly cheese into my mouth. "Now this is an interesting flavor," I said.

"It's a unique cheese. They call it ayib," Ammar said. "I've had this before. Use it with the wat. It cools the spices."

I took another scoop with a piece of bread and found it wonderfully soothing to my throat and tongue.

After the meal, the chief elders wanted to share stories of battles, near misses with the deb or kroks and other dangers of the jungle. Fawzi and I had no idea what was told, only that Ammar was having a good time building his vocabulary.

The sun finally broke above the tree line, warm and bright, and melted away the morning haze. The rays splashed across the mat where I sat cross-legged, luring me to lie down. I wasn't sure the protocol, so I remained upright, closing my eyes.

A hand rested on my shoulder. I opened my eyes to see that several women were clustered about.

With the meal finished I supposed they thought it an appropriate time to gather. No, not gather—they crowded me like a swarm of nimits—talking, pointing, pinching my skin, nodding and conversing in hushed feminine voices.

I caught Fawzi's eye for help.

"Seduction for whatever reason comes in all languages, good looking," he said, stifling a laugh. The teasing would come later. I knew it.

The elders appeared upset with the women's chatter and the chief raised an arm for silence. An older woman scowled at the chief and the women continued fawning over me.

Without Ammar, I was lost in their attentions. They peppered me with questions and gentle smiles. They kept touching my hair, stroking my arms, and fingering the fabric of my robe. They were discussing something between themselves that I couldn't understand.

Standing quietly behind them were children of all ages, nervously giggling and snickering.

One woman kept gesturing. I surmised that she wanted to know my name.

"Bassam," I said, pointing my fingers to my heart. "Bassam—Bah-SAWM."

She repeated it as best she could, "bru-sch-wam," and smiled.

Fawzi's face was growing red.

"What's so funny?" I asked.

He shook his head.

I was actually enjoying the attention and the chance to meet new people. But Fawzi was up to something. I could tell. He rocked back with his knees pulled against his chest and shook his head, aware of something that I wasn't.

And then it became clear.

Immediately behind this woman stood her two daughters, one about my age, the other a couple of years younger. The woman brought them forward.

"Abaynesh," she said smiling, gesturing with open palms to the eldest.

"Ah-Bayn-esh," she repeated. The girl made eye contact with me and smiled, then looked at the ground.

Then the woman brought forward the younger daughter.

"Adey," she said. "Ah-Day," and smiled as if I should succumb immediately to the beauty of her daughters.

"Ah-bun-dish," I stammered. "Uh-day," I said, and smiled uncomfortably.

"Bassam!" Ammar came to my rescue. "She's introducing you to

Abaynesh, a word that means the Nilus, or like the Nilus—giving, fruitful, prosperity."

I looked appreciatively at the mother and her daughters, but felt an embarrassment that I'm sure was transmitted to the mother.

Fawzi couldn't contain his amusement at the situation and had to stifle his laughter by burying his head in his arms.

A few months before, he had teased me about having "a girl at every dock." This situation wasn't helping. When a third mother came by with her daughter, it was apparent I was being courted as husband material.

"Hey, I can't help this!" I blurted out and scowled at Fawzi. "I'm not asking for brides. I'm on a mission to find Rasha!"

I looked upon these fair daughters from a culture so removed from my own. I could see the sweetness in their eyes, and their worries about love and rejection—a universal look, I had seen it everywhere: a longing to be accepted and loved by someone. But it wouldn't be me. I was missing my Rasha, my choice, the shining light of my life.

"Why are we waiting around here," I growled at Ammar. "Let's get going."

Fawzi buried his face and shook again with his suppressed laughter.

"It's your youth, Bassam. Don't worry, just be pleasant," Ammar said.

"The younger one, Bassam," Ammar continued, "Adey, I believe that means something like a flower that comes in the spring, lovely name for a lovely young women."

I nodded then looked into the kindly eyes of the mother. I smiled and nodded my head. "What's the word for 'nice to meet you'?" I called over to Ammar.

"No idea," he said. "Why don't you try 'dua netjer en etj?'"

"What does that mean?" I asked.

"Don't you remember? At the river this morning?"

"No!" I said with growing strain in my voice.

"It means 'thank God for you women,'" and then he smiled a big toothy grin.

Fawzi broke out laughing so hard it brought tears to his eyes.

"Get me out of here!" I shot back in an angry hush.

TRADING

Ammar managed to explain to the Aksumi our need for a boat, and the desperate nature of our journey. The elders expressed a willingness to trade.

Since most of our belongings had been lost the night before, we had little to offer. Fawzi suggested they leave me at the village as collateral for the return of the little boat.

"No, we must not disappoint Zafir by losing him again," Ammar said. "Maybe your bow drill, Bassam?"

"Do you think they want it?" I asked.

"Try it," he said.

I set it on a piece of wood. The elders gathered close. Fawzi peeled some shavings from a dry stick and I piled it up around the little shaft.

As I worked the bow, a rhythmic squeak sounded and the children started swaying to the rhythm. The harder I worked the drill, the louder the noise, and the more the little ones shook their shoulders and smiled.

Finally the tip became hot enough for small ribbons of smoke. I blew the glowing tip to a tiny flame and the shavings caught fire. The group responded with an amazed, "Ahhhhhhh!"

Ammar smiled. "Good job, Bassam."

"What now, Ammar?" I asked. "Should I offer it?"

"Let me," he said, taking the bow and drill.

He presented it to them, and then pointed to the papyrus reed boats floating in the water. He made motions of us paddling down river, and offered the bow drill.

The elders spoke among themselves in hushed voices. After a few moments, the chief took it, smiled, and nodded his head. He pointed down river and repeated the word "titu, titu, titu."

"What does it mean?" I asked.

Ammar looked at the warrior a moment.

"I think he's trying to say we may use the boat to Titi Island," he said.

"Where's that?"

"Another few days, where the White and Blue meet, an important place in our journey."

"Then let's do it," Fawzi said. "You can make another of those fire starters pretty fast, right, ash head? Or do I have to show you like a little girl?"

"You make bow drills like a little girl?" I grinned.

"Well, that's not—No, what I meant was—"

"That's exactly what you just said. Shall I repeat it?"

Unbeknownst to us, our warrior friends were offering more than the use of their little boat. They would also escort us to the confluence at Gartoum. We were nervous about the four warriors with spears.

"No worries, just like the Xiongnu," Ammar said, "just like old times."

The chief made it clear they had other business on the river, so we would travel together provided that an occasional stop was acceptable. We agreed.

Bidding the villagers goodbye—seeing the longing looks of several mothers watching their catch escape—we loaded into the papyrus boat. As we paddled away, a wave of gentle relief washed over me and I sat back smiling for a long, long time.

The warriors led the way, steering us far from the three-dozen gray humps sitting still in the river. A lone bull raised his head and blew hard from his nostrils. We were pleased to see that he didn't wish to abandon his herd, and watched us paddle away.

RITUALS

Finding villages was easier now that we knew what to look for—
papyrus cut down to beach level, trees reduced to stumps for
paths, and columns of smoke. We spotted one such landing place where
a group of five hunters were anxiously dancing about a krokadilius,
trying to entangle him in ropes. He was thrashing about, giving them
quite the fight.

"What are they doing?" I asked.

"Catching it, or killing it? I can't tell," Ammar said.

There was great shouting as the beast rolled, throwing sand everywhere.
Then it lunged toward the river, but the ropes snagged its retreat. The men
came at it again, spears thrusting, others pinning it with poles until at last
the animal was subdued. Then they took out their knives.

When the commotion died, our escorts explained our purpose for
the visit, but the villagers were suspicious of our fair skin and strange
language. Ammar stepped in and we were soon trusted, even to the
point of being offered chunks of the beast's flesh as a gift. We gestured
to relay our gratefulness, and they led us to their village, dragging the
carcass behind.

"There are a dozen races in this great land," Ammar said. "If you
could travel to the places Zafir has led me, you'd see fair-skinned to
dark, small to tall, even giant people whose women tower over by head
and shoulders, yet greet you with such kindness you'd think they were
long-lost friends."

At the village, we saw these people wore paint. The men had war
paint on their faces and shoulders, showing status of some kind.

The women wore ornaments on their wrists and neck, around the
waist, the arms, legs, even long strands of golden braids laced about
their heads. Some of the designs matched their pottery.

"And the men find this . . . attractive?" I whispered to Ammar.

"That's an interesting question, I've been watching," he said. "But if they're like all other women I've encountered, you just watch—you'll see they really dress for the other women. Watch the men, they hardly notice."

"Don't ever deny your Rasha the chance to look beautiful," he said.

"Oh, no! She will always be beautiful to me," I said.

"I know, but it means something to be beautiful among other women. That's a good thing to remember," he said. "After 31 years of marriage, I can tell you it's a good thing to remember. And if you can figure out why things work that way, send me a note—and use Al Kalimat!"

Had I ever let her know that I thought her beautiful? Did I even say it to her? I couldn't recall a time—no, not once. My Rasha has been preparing all her life to be a companion to someone, and she chose me. The very thought made my heart swell, bringing again the wonderful glow of my deeply-felt love. Memories came as flashes. Things I did to tease and set myself above her—silly, selfish actions, not realizing her feelings toward me. But that all changed. The life I wanted for her now would be secure, protected, away from the dark designs of evil, and filled with beautiful mornings, busy days, relaxing evenings together, and nights undisturbed by taunts of danger. A family, she always talked about a family. "More than just me and another," she told me one time, "but daughters I can teach the way of the home, the joy of learning—and sons who can strengthen us. Isn't that your dream, Bassam?" I remember the look of disappointment when I blurted out my own dream, to explore and conquer. "A family?" I blurted out. "Well . . . yes, but to be trapped in a house?" Her disappointed look was crushing. I didn't say a word about it, but that look—Oh my, I never want to make sadness darken her face like that ever again. I would die first. I should have acknowledged her dream as my own. That much was true . . .

The villagers saw my pensiveness so a few of them gathered around and encouraged me toward a pair of women artisans. They were grinding pigments for the paint.

Ammar followed and helped translate. "They do it for the dead," he said. "The tokens and emblems connect them to their dead ancestors, and to the Great Creator—for good crops and healthy animals."

Others we saw along the river were nomads, living temporary lives, but not this group of families. They were here to stay. They had farms and pens, grain, cattle, sheep, and goats. Their homes were permanent—walls of mud and thatch, large cut stones for fire pits and storage areas.

"Fishing and herding is their source of income," Ammar said, "but all this grain should earn them something, I'd think."

"Maybe it's a transportation problem?"

"Yes, probably."

The village greeters wore loin cloths while the chief was adorned with the skins of a spotted animal. The spear bearers carried wide-blade weapons crudely fashioned from hammered iron.

I saw the most beautiful necklace around the neck of a young maiden. I caught Ammar's attention and pointed it out. "I want that for my Rasha. She'd love it." The long double-strand held assorted polished colored stone beads with tiny carvings and works of bone, animal teeth, and tusks, strung with colorful shells and hammered bits of copper.

She saw me looking so I pulled out my leather pouch and pointed to the necklace, smiling. She snatched it right out of my hands.

"Oh! Well! Yes, you may," I said politely, hoping a deben or two would be enough.

Ammar and Fawzi looked over. "What are you doing?" Ammar whispered.

"I think she'll sell it," I said.

She studied the pouch, turned it over and ran her finger along the sewing of the seams. Her mother stood by watching. The girl opened the pouch, revealing nothing inside.

"No coins, but may I trade?"

She handed it off to her mother and lit up with a bright toothy smile and removed the necklace, handing it over to me. The mother took the pouch to examine.

"All this for a worn leather pouch?" I whispered to Ammar, showing him the necklace. "I just traded for this!" I bragged.

"Don't presume you're a skilled trader," Fawzi said, and walked away laughing.

"What? Didn't I make a good trade?"

Ammar was in conversation with the chief. Ammar smiled, then shook his head with a grin. "Bassam," he said, starting to laugh. "They think you're trying to buy her."

"What?"

"For wife! The empty pouch is an emblem of your heart's empty longing for love, for the young woman you just traded with. It was a sign that you wished to fill a vacancy in your life with a bride, a proposal of marriage. Normally the young men use a woven basket or a clay vessel for such proposals, filled with something of value—your pouch the same, that's what she thinks—and her mother."

"They think you're really poor, lover boy, and they're right!" Fawzi grinned. "You're good at this, Bassam. Wait 'til Rasha hears about your great skill with the young maidens."

I shot him a death look. "Oh no," I exclaimed. "How was I supposed to—? I'm just trading, not proposing a thing to—I'm getting out of here."

Ammar and Fawzi couldn't stop laughing, and the chief was grinning at my embarrassment.

"Always ask me first, Bassam," Ammar said. "Had that gone differently you might have turned our triple into a quadruple."

"Or a double," Fawzi said. "Less trouble that way."

"But—but she snatched it out of my hand, I didn't offer it," I said. "In fact, I was looking to see if I had any silvers, and . . . "

"But you're lucky. The chief says when a maiden rejects a young man's advances, she keeps the offering but gives something personal. So my wayward friend, you just lost the pouch, but you got what you wanted—that beautiful necklace instead."

"It makes no sense," I said.

The chief was now laughing and pointing to the ground.

"Oh, you'll love this," Ammar said. "It's their custom—for your burial."

"My what?"

"To dress your wounded heart," he said. "To comfort you in her rejection when you're dead."

"What rejection?" I exclaimed. "That's not what I was . . ."

Fawzi had me cornered. "Try it on donkey face, let's see if you look beautiful."

I turned for the shoreline. I couldn't walk there fast enough.

MISPLACED

Al Kalimat verified — +:
Dispatch by currier – Urgent
Inscribed – 2 Pharmouthi

Master Zafir,

A message from Rasha since her escape has come into our possession from your steward at Korosko through the expedited channels. Per your instructions, the original is sent to Rekeem. The attached note explains how the message was misplaced before the regular dispatch, and was sent 16 days prior to the date of my relay to you.

We surmise it was written in Cyene within the past four weeks. The transcript follows:

> *My dearest B., I am free. Cousin S. escorts me to A. for the dawn. God has prospered me, and I come to you soon. I am well, cared for. Do not despair.*
> *Yours forever, R. –Cala*

Analysis by Al Murrah establishes these points:

1-The lettering indicates Bassam, Shamar, and Rasha. This validates earlier reports that your cousin Shamar is escort.

2-The name "Cala" is unknown. Some offer speculation Rasha feared the integrity of Al Kalimat, choosing to remain under disguise.

3-Travel to Cyene would be a logical passage from Al-Jarf. Atbara is the most logical choice for an overland connection to the coast for an east-bound barge.

4-The passage "for the dawn" is best interpreted as traveling eastward from Atbara, or eastward by ship from the coast.

WATCHED

We labored 18 days down the Blue Nilus. Our most difficult passage was where the river dropped into a great gorge then flowed through a long canyon of twisting obstacles. Our escorts were adept at managing the white water, but not us. We spent our desperate moments just trying to stay upright.

I was not accustomed to long stretches of heat and humidity. Overhanging limbs offered brief shade, but each time we veered close we were driven away by the insects.

"I thought they were used to it," I said, pointing to the other boats and the warriors who ignored our meandering.

"I say they're away from the shore because they know the habits of nimit better than us," Ammar said.

I watched them basking in full sunlight, but well removed from the unbearable swarms that lived in the shade. I dunked my headdress in the river and pulled it over me, it's cooling wet instantly broke the logjam of oppressive heat. At last, some relief.

Carrying our boats around rapids, sometimes long fields of dangerous boulders, was made so much easier with the little light boats.

"Maybe we should use these for the rest of our trip," I suggested, huffing my way down a slope under the weight of the rear end of our little conveyance.

"You need to eat more meat," Fawzi panted as the load became heavy. "Get some muscle on you, put some weight on your frame Bassam— That's why deb took only a taste and let you go, skinny butt. Speed it up, you're slowing me down."

I felt for the wound on my hip. It was mostly healed but the great bruise remained, faded to a large yellow stain covering most of my leg. So close. I shuddered.

Just then we ran into the back end of an ivory caravan. More than 50 natives blocked the trail ahead, laboring down the portage path with a harvest of great white tusks. They carried the smaller ones balanced across their shoulders, the larger tusks slung from ropes on poles that required two men to carry.

We made no effort to communicate, only an acknowledgement with a nod and smile. Our warrior friends just watched, impatiently trying to get around them. They indicated they'd meet us in a day or two, and rushed ahead.

Some 200 paces more and we rounded the end of the long boulder field. Lovely still waters ahead. The tusk caravan turned inland.

"That's the great ivory trade," Ammar said. "They're headed to the coast, and from there, a fortune at every stop."

Near our last day, Ammar calculated the jungles were largely behind us, and the desolation of the arid deserts of Kush and Egypt were not many weeks ahead.

I had heard of large cats in this land, ferocious man-eaters. Except for prints in the mud, we had not encountered any and I had no interest in discovering them for myself.

It was near sundown, and we had just found a suitable place to make land for the night. We floated through a shallow papyrus marsh to solid soil and a patch of grass. Fawzi alerted us to fresh tracks in the mud, several in different sizes that matted down the grass.

"We might have spooked 'em away," Ammar said.

We were not too concerned because other boats were ahead of us, seemingly safe and unconcerned.

"They don't like humans," Ammar said.

"I thought people were lunch," I said.

"You're too skinny, bone brain," Fawzi said.

"Yes, they'll go deeper into the jungle, but don't disturb their territory," Ammar said. "They'll rarely defend themselves from the likes of us."

Fawzi already had personal experience with cats so his sense of caution was particularly sensitive to the mud prints.

"I'm not going to be bait for them tonight," he said, almost threatening.

That's when I spotted the alarming glow of eyes just up the hill in the tall grasses. The setting sun was just right to ignite their shine.

"Look at that!" I said pointing.

The two bluish-yellow orbs looked right at us, unblinking. We watched without moving, awestruck that we couldn't see more of the animal crouched in the yellow growth. The eyes remained unmoving, then suddenly disappeared. A moment later, they reappeared a few paces away, and then were gone.

NAMLA

With cats nearby, we decided the village was safer than sleeping on shore. Kindly tribal leaders invited us to their campfire. We enjoyed festivities, a delicious fruity drink that burned down my throat, and the use of an empty hut for the night. After a peaceful rest, we left gifts before our departure the next morning.

A few days later we had an encounter that scarred me for life. It was our usual time to get off the river, and our warrior escorts had joined us again. As we dragged our boats to shore we heard the bellowing of an animal in great pain. Ammar and Fawzi looked puzzled. Our escorts glanced with disinterest and proceeded to a village some distance over a small hill.

We were cautious, thinking a large cat might be killing its prey somewhere near.

An injured water buffalo came into view, seeming to have fallen just moments before. It lay on its side less than 100 paces from the river's edge. To our horror, he was covered with a thick brown blanket of swarming namla. He was thrashing about under the biting and couldn't gain his footing to escape. There were thousands, crawling into his nostrils and mouth, biting his eyes, his lips, making him bellow and foam. The tiny mob took away little chunks of flesh in large pincers.

"They're eating him alive," I gasped.

"What can we do? What can we do?" I begged of Ammar. "How can we stop it?"

Ammar just shook his head. "Stay back, Bassam. There's nothing we can do," he said. "We shouldn't get any closer, we don't want to attract their attention."

"We can't help it? Oh, I can't watch," I said turning in disgust.

"We're not equipped to put him out of his misery," Fawzi said. "I suppose if we had your bow—"

I backed away.

"It's awful, Bassam, I agree," Ammar said. "But think on it this way—namla serve an important purpose in the jungle. This animal fell, weakened or injured, and here we see a balance unfolding to the benefit of all. Namla keep the jungle clean of carrion that would otherwise fester and spread filth, and by this they make a cleaner place for other forms of life."

He saw from the horror on my face that I wasn't convinced.

"Some acts of nature are not to be witnessed by compassionate people," he said.

I thought about such a horde descending on a village. Could any escape? "Can they kill humans?" I asked.

"It's been rumored, but the rumors are more vicious than reality," he said. "Yes, there have been human victims, but only those unable to move—the sick and elderly, the injured, infants. Those events are rare. In fact, some villages entice namla to their huts to do just what you see here, to clean up the refuse."

"You can bet the people are long gone," Fawzi chimed in. "They take a short vacation with their foodstuffs, and when they get back, all tidied up, spit-spot clean!"

"It's an amazing cycle," Ammar said. "These little soldiers hatch thousands every day. They'll grow about the length of your thumb joint—but they're blind."

"That doesn't look blind to me," I said.

"The movement, that's what makes it work," he said. "Even the mighty lahpaš can be felled."

By this time the animal had stopped moaning and lay still as the swarm upon him grew.

"It'll take weeks to strip him to bone," Fawzi said, "so no sense standing around to watch."

I turned away, squeezing the images from my mind. "Okay, enough," I said. "Can we leave?"

They agreed and we left the sorrowful scene to find the village and join our warrior friends.

MEDEWI

A day and a half downriver from the sixth cataract was the landmark city of Medewi. Our escorts bid us farewell and left us standing there alone. We were weary of river travel and disembarked for food and a safe place to get our bearings. We hoped to find a boat more accommodating for our journey north.

Ammar seemed distracted when we landed, looking far to the horizon. He insisted we take a short side trip to the outskirts of Medewi, for reasons, he claimed, that Zafir would approve. We were just so happy to be on solid ground again, none objected.

Ammar hired two donkey carts for a trip to a small settlement hidden behind strange stone pyramids, ancient, and long abandoned. There were dozens—partly covered by sand—brown, broken, and alone.

"Burial tombs, Bassam," Ammar said. "They say there are more than 200 just like these."

"More sight-seeing—" Fawzi huffed.

Ammar smiled. "You'll want to see these."

Ammar directed our ride through the little market, slowing for the shoppers who ignored the clip clop of animal traffic coming up behind them. It was a poor village—many dozens of skinny chickens pecking the ground, wheeled carts with wilted greens, or small fish from the night's catch, and curious people watching us pass, hungry for a coin.

"It was an empire," Ammar said, waving his outstretched arms. "It stood as Egypt's great pride, their capital until it fell to invaders. Then, a couple of centuries ago, iron was discovered and it became a great center of production. See these vast barren hills?"

There was so much the desert, I didn't really notice the hills.

"Trees! This used to be a great forest," he said sweeping his arm across the horizon.

"Really? Where did it all go?" I asked.

"Furnaces! Hot furnaces to melt the ore for iron production. Highest quality, famous!" he said. "Famous through Rome and Greece, the Nafud, all the way to C'ina."

"So, they cut down all their trees?" I asked.

"Yes, it must have been a great harvest," Ammar said. "Melting the ore demands great heat. It's the ideal place, too—not far from the sea harbors, the ports—they had excellent access to all of the major trading routes."

I remembered Ziyad and others telling me of such loads. "Zafir said the caravans hauled inland thousands of loads of iron products, a great shipment each time, but it gradually died away."

"A rich load, indeed!" Ammar said. "And here, more than just iron— there's gold, gems, pottery, the great tusks and all that can be crafted from them, traded away to grow the empire rich."

As the animals bore us farther east, we found ourselves on a sandy path seldom used. The dry heat intensified the more we drove inland. I tried imaging all the land filled with trees. It didn't seem possible.

Beyond the village we came upon massive ruins more typical of what I expected in Egypt and the land of gold—great columns ornately carved.

"This rich empire," Ammar said spreading his arms, "fell into decline a couple of centuries ago. By depleting the forests they also destroyed their iron works. But while they had it, the wood, the ore, the prosperity—it was their great rise to strength—and then, no wood, no iron, no trade. The caravans stopped visiting, and the land died. And those relentless sands came to bury the glory to forgetfulness."

We walked among the pyramids. They were built shoulder to shoulder, poking from the shallow dunes like the teeth of a giant's stone saw. They stood four times a man tall with steep sides, made of thousands of sun-baked bricks the size of large bread loaves. We touched their sides, strolling among them in silence, wondering how many thousands, maybe millions, once passed through here, lifted up in wealth and pride just a few dozen decades before. Ammar was stooped over making a rubbing of some carvings.

"Shouldn't we be going?" I asked.

"Yes, yes, one moment."

Fawzi rolled his eyes. "Scholars," he scoffed, and kicked at the sand impatiently.

Along the ridge a thousand paces beyond were more little pyramids, built in clusters—same design, neatly staggered and trimmed to fine points at their summits. Some were 10 cubits high, others 30 or more.

"I wonder what's in them?" I said.

"Probably a forgotten king or his queens," Ammar said. "But not any more, see over there, the robbers have been here?"

Fawzi was off making his own discoveries, and found a large flat-shaped boulder the size of a man's bed. It appeared to be singled out, to lie in its own place of distinction.

"Hey! Come see!" he called. "Watch this," and picked a fist-sized rock and dropped it on the flat of the boulder. A beautiful note range out as clear as a bell.

Ammar smiled. "A rock gong!" he said, hurrying over. "Very rare, do it again."

Fawzi dropped another, testing different parts of the boulder. Near its center was the clearest tone. "Music!" He said, dropping several rocks at once.

The tunes attracted the interest of a few natives who stopped their labors to listen.

"I'll bet they didn't even know this existed," Ammar said. "So easy to lose history and his purposes . . ."

He examined the rock and brushed off the sand. "Look at this, it's been worked by hand," and ran his fingers over the flat surface. The table showed vague indentations of carved images. He took Fawzi's water skin and poured life onto the carvings. Instantly, a whole display of distinct carvings appeared, images of cattle and wildlife—the lahpaš, large cats, giraffes, birds of many kind. Another portion showed images of stars and the sun and moon.

We stood in amazement. "They knew about the night sky, and look—an entire story here, that tells of this people and their lives," Ammar said. He poured more water on other parts and strange cursive writings appeared.

"I wish we had the time," Ammar sighed. "I'll get just this one, then we should be on our way . . ." He pulled from his bag one of his charcoals. "Bassam, I need another of your writing sheets, will you?"

I was just about out of my sheets for this very purpose, and reluctantly surrendered one more. Ammar pressed one of them to the carvings and held it still while he rubbed his charcoal lightly over the papyrus.

"I wish you had that rice paper, that would be perfect," and worked the image as best he could. "I'll fill in the details later, see if I can learn this language." He laid the sheet across some lettering and rubbed the charcoal until a rough copy appeared.

We walked a few minutes more among the memorials, looking to make a discovery.

"Look at this!" Ammar said, calling us to the wall of a large pyramid. A tall stone stele was mortared right into the wall. "Look, many women rulers, do you see this? A throne, and that means female. Quite unusual." Other carvings showed images of crops and farmers. "A fertile place, certainly giant farming operations once filled these lands . . . "

"How old do you suppose these little pyramids are?" I asked.

Ammar looked around. "I was told maybe a thousand years, maybe half. The Nub'ans adopted the Egyptian traditions—not as elaborate as Khufu (coo-ew-foo—each as in "<u>too</u>"), but the patterns are similar, so they're not far removed in time from them ..."

For me these tombs seemed futile. The land they trusted was now a burial ground for kings and dunes—deserted by trade and manufacture, a stopping place for impatient travelers, and home to herders of goats and sellers of wild camels.

It was time and we had to drag Ammar away, back to the village. The journey was made shorter with his telling the story of Medewi and all that had transpired here. It was a rich part of history I'd never heard.

Back at the village we traded for some greens, cooked chicken and rice. We chose from among willing owners to pay for his boat down river, and assembled the needs for our voyage north.

By early afternoon we were well fed, well rested, certainly educated, and finally back on the water, drifting on the sparkling smooth river where the current did her best work. A slight breeze blowing in our favor hurried us along, saving the back-breaking labor of rowing.

Ammar produced his maps and we calculated our path. He pointed to Medewi and traced a route that was several weeks in front of us—with five great cataracts standing in our way to Noph.

ATBARA

It was the dry time when we arrived at Atbara. The low water greeted us to a terrible scene. So much river life was crowded into shrinking ponds. It was a fight to the death for the creatures that depended on it. We witnessed several fights—gruesome and cruel battles.

We drifted past the outskirts of Atbara and Fawzi steered toward a large harbor where other vessels with tall sails were tied to its stone pier.

"A good starting place to ask about Rasha," Fawzi said.

"If they took the caravan to Nub'ah, this is the best departure—if they came this far south," Ammar said.

"Yeah, probably our best bet," Fawzi remarked, scanning the village for an inn. "We should get settled then start asking."

"Keep watch for anyone familiar, anyone eastern," Ammar said. "I can't say if we have a steward here, but maybe a traveler."

"What does Shamar look like?" I asked.

"About Fawzi's height, modest beard down to about here," Ammar said, pointing to below his neck.

"About 10 years younger than Zafir?" Fawzi asked.

"That's about right—probably a gray-streaked beard. I wouldn't know if he's a frail man, but he's light skinned."

"And speaks our tongue?" I offered.

"Yes, our language, probably the same accent," Ammar said.

Fawzi steered past the boat berths and drove onto fine white sand where we tied off. The shallow water lapped lazily over the wet sands, sparkling in the afternoon sun. That's when I saw tiny yellow flecks in the reflections.

"Gold," Ammar said. "Not much, but inland, in the red soils. They took out enough to build an empire."

I was fascinated. I'd never seen gold in nature like this.

"Gathering it is a long labor for many, but not ours—at shore it's neither in quantity nor a value in time."

I pinched some sand and swirled it in my palm, trying to isolate the golden fleck.

"If this is how God has shared it, no wonder they come upon it so rarely, and in such morsels."

A strong breeze blew past, churning the waters. A cloud of dust rose obscuring our vision. It seemed a storm was descending, but the sky was bright with no clouds.

We continued into the village and I found myself scanning every face—at the pier, the market, the rod-bearers, fishermen, anyone who was eastern, taller, of lighter flesh, with an accent, or anyone who might recall a slave in haste, a young maiden named Rasha. I was suddenly even more desperate to find her.

CLUES

It's like searching for sand in the desert," I said. "So many people, where do we start?"

Neither man answered. They just pushed through the crowds to an inn where we made arrangements for the night.

"Will our boat be safe?" I asked.

"I paid the man to watch. It should be secure," Fawzi said.

Our room had a small empty window, a thick wooden door, and a table to sit. We found our sleeping accommodations passable.

We piled our belongings in a heap then sat a moment to get our bearings.

"I've been trying to decide whether to divide or stay together," Ammar said. "I think it best that we split up. Bassam, you'll stay with me."

"He likes you better," Fawzi said.

"You just figured that out?"

We sat down in a diner, typical of the hundreds I'd been in before—noisy, smoky, busy—plastered walls always painted blue or yellow, a kitchen in back, two dozen tables, stools for chairs and linen of flax showing wear, covering bare wood. There were potted plants in the windows and a veranda in back, feeble attempts to lend a modest formality to the impoverished place. Yes, all was the same except for one important difference: the smell.

Oh, the unique smells of such diners. Curry, garlic, roasted chicken or fish, sometimes roasted red meat, fresh breads, spices—each smell created a unique memory of a land near or far. Yes, that part did change, and I was happy for it.

For this evening's meal, we entered a diner in Atbara proper, in a prominent place facing the market. It was sparsely filled, and an old woman shuffled from table to table, taking orders.

This was our first chance to enjoy the amenities of a large river city in Nub'ah. The meal wasn't much different from our earlier stops—a fish, fresh from that morning, with a heavy helping of chopped herbs and ground spices. It was served with a cucumber and cabbage, chopped radishes and some onion. They brought slices of melon, a bowl of figs, and some dark bread. We feasted well and we spoke little. The task ahead had come upon us at last. We were now faced with the urgent search for Rasha.

"The harvest time," Ammar said. "That's the time to be in these parts!"

"It's so hot," I said. "Seems they would be growing and harvesting all year round."

"Makes sense," he said. "But here, the Nilus floods but once, and that sets the time and seasons for the planting and harvest."

"So far south?"

"Certainly," he said. "The floods are more violent here, but the river is their blessing."

"It must be nice to have water in the desert," Fawzi said, frowning at a fish bone he pulled from his mouth. "Rekeem would do better with more rain—or a stronger spring."

We shrank into memory, each of us reflecting on the strong, but infrequent rainstorms in our desert home of Rekeem—storms that crept up with a wind bringing fresh smelling air that washed through our canyon and stirred the sand. People would run for cover and children would laugh and play in the puddles. Gurgling streams flowed into gutters and troughs and cisterns, pouring down the rock walls in sheets, captured and funneled to safety in our underground storage. They never lasted long, but it was a wonderful time when the rain fell. It was wonderful to live in Rekeem, the home I was missing a lot just then.

After meal we enjoyed a delicious barley drink that filled, but didn't sit heavy. The sun had set and darkness filled the streets.

I looked at the shadowed faces of people milling. "Who might have noticed Rasha and Shamar?" I asked. "Why would anyone remember?"

"Good question," Ammar said. "I think it best we start at the shore, those working the pier."

"Since you must be tended like a baby girl, moss mouth," Fawzi said, "I'll check with merchants and inn keepers. Where will we meet?"

"Yes, good plan," Ammar said. "Let's start early, meet here midday, then decide the next step."

That next morning Ammar led me to a fish broker who seemed versed in several tongues.

"She's not Egyptian, but hails from Rekeem," Ammar explained. "Young, maybe 15, slender, long dark hair, with a man old enough to be her grandfather, gray beard, also from Rekeem. They were running for safety."

The merchant shook his head. "We see many such," he said. "You believe it was four or six weeks ago?"

"Perhaps longer, eight weeks," Ammar said.

"That's a long time to remember anything," he said. Then he narrowed his eyes and asked, "Where were you eight weeks ago?" There was something accusing in his tone.

I thought back. Eight weeks. I tried to remember—we were . . . we were still on the sea, hurrying for Saba' with several weeks more to go.

The man broke into a big belly laugh. "Do you see it?" he said smiling. "And you think I can remember two from two hundred thousand? At my age?" He laughed and turned, waving us away.

A magistrate acting the authority for Atbara was more accommodating.

"We have many asking about their escaped slaves," he said. "We do our best to help, but it's difficult. There are many passing through. Perhaps you'll have better luck down river at the cataract. It's too busy here to take much notice."

Ammar offered some silvers to hold a message should Rasha come through, but he refused it. He knew of Abdali-ud-din, with respect, but couldn't help. "Don't waste money on me," he told us, "look down river."

We returned to the market thinking he was probably right.

"It's just as well," Ammar told me. "If Rasha and Shamar are hurrying away, they won't stop to inquire of magistrates for messages."

We found a dairyman busy in his crowded shop, turning over his cheeses. He told us of other men seen hurrying with high demands, but remembered no such visitors as my Rasha or Shamar.

"Yes, we outfit the caravans," he said. "We are famous for them. You should try, we give you a good deal. Others wishing to rent a journey to the coast are quick clients. You'll need to hurry if you require our services."

Ammar glared at him impatiently, awaiting a single answer to his question.

"Ah-em, yes, well . . . certainly," the dairyman said, "but a young girl and her father?"

"Her uncle," Ammar corrected.

"Yes, her uncle—no one matching that description came through here," the dairyman said, and turned to continue his work.

"Why does he do that?" I asked as we stepped away.

"Do what?" Ammar asked.

"Flip his cheese over," I said. "Didn't you see it?"

"It keeps it from going rancid—keeps the oils moving. Good way to make it last in this heat."

He scratched at his whiskers, staring at the crowds of people meandering through the market. "We need a better way," he said.

I agreed. If Rasha and Shamar passed through Atbara, where would they stop—and why? To join a caravan to the coast? For supplies to continue south?

"Let's check with Fawzi," Ammar said, and led me back to our diner.

Fawzi was already at a table with a view of the path. Another barley drink was clutched in his hand, already half empty.

"I don't know that we'll have much luck this way," Fawzi said as we approached.

"We learned nothing," Ammar said, pulling up a stool.

"What about the other boat drivers?" I offered.

"I asked," Fawzi said. "They are clever with news that people want to hear—people running and chasing, and when I probed deeper they were happy to invent any story I wanted for the right price. A nest of bedowi, those cheats."

Ammar nodded. "The same."

"If I was on the run I would stay in the shadows and do as little as I could to alert others of my plight, lest Rakbah have conspirators watching and listening," I said. They agreed.

"What about the caravan drivers?" I asked. "Did you—?"

"Way ahead of you, snail brain," Fawzi said. "I asked at the broker's shop. One driver was no help, two others now on trek won't be back for another week."

"The magistrate made a good suggestion," Ammar said. "At the next cataract, there are fewer entertainments, simply a way-station for travelers—a greater chance to make an impression on the porters."

"That sounds right," Fawzi said. "Should we save our troubles here and get back on river?"

"After some rest," Ammar said.

"I'm fine. Let's leave now," I said.

"Listen, moss gills," Fawzi said. "It's another two days—why leave a nice bed just because you want to paddle for a couple of hours? There are no villages until the cataract. Do you want to sleep with the deb again?"

Day 773

My dearest Rasha,

We finally arrived at Atbara. No one knows of you, but we're not discouraged. We're headed to the cataract in our search, and we'll continue north until there's no farther to search. If you came this far, if you left any hint of passing through these parts, we'll learn of it. Do you know we're coming for you? Be strong, have faith. Nothing will stop us. —Bassam

BAKETAMON

Al Kalimat verified — +:
Baketamon to Zafir

A communique to Zafir, regarding the search for his daughter.

My dearest Zafir,

I am your most humble servant in the cause of Abdali-ud-din at the port of No-Amon.

I am saddened to report that neither I, nor my sons, have seen your Rasha or Shamar. I haven't met your daughter. I can imagine she's lovely, a striking image of her mother. I am, however, acquainted with Shamar from years ago. I would recognize him if he passed.

To your request I am diligent. The time you expected her to pass through is six weeks ago. We will be looking and asking among our contacts.

With sadness I report that Amenken, your faithful servant, my husband, and the voice of Abdali-ud-din in No-Amon, has written his name into the Book of the Dead. It was a year ago, after a terrible accident that he was slow to recover from, that Anubis called his name at last. Since then my sons and I have performed his business labors.

I dwell here with my two boys and a daughter. They serve me honorably in the business at hand. If you can find your way here, you will enjoy what's left of No-Amon. It is much destroyed, but its temples remain. We live in the acropolis on a hill, a guarded place, although our numbers are steadily declining. We're obligated to leave in the coming years, maybe sooner. We'll seek a home in Noph.

We beseech Amun-Ra to guide the safe return of your Rasha.
—Baketamon

AMENEMHET

Al Kalimat verified — +:
Amenemhet to Zafir

My dear friend,

It's my terrible burden to report on horrible news from shippers at the fifth cataract.

A watch and a trader independently have informed me of unfortunate news that may be a black feather at your stoop.

A man and a girl were seen perishing on the waters of the passage at Portage Village near the Baggara Rocks. Their descriptions matched those given in your message.

I have interviewed the witnesses myself and learned to my satisfaction these facts—

A small boat with sail and oars carrying no load but two passengers stayed the night at our village.

I was told by a trader of his encounter with the killer Jabari and his men. They were most anxious that night for knowledge of an escaped slave girl and her thief. The trader told me he responded to the men that he had seen no such pair.

Another source, two men of the watch, informed me they witnessed a late arrival to the harbor that carried no trade. A man and girl left their boat tied and went to the village. The watch gave them no thought. At the morning hour, he was dismissed for home. And upon leaving, he spotted the man Jabari and his fellows running to their boats.

At this same time, the watch saw that the man and the girl had already departed, and were being pursued by the men of Jabari. The watch suspected something was amiss and returned to his post and the two men hurried to the shore to chase the pursuers for questioning.

Before an alarm could be raised, the men of Jabari chased the man and the girl into the currents of the cataract.

The man Jabari was seen hurrying to the spillway. The watchman and his relief man chased after. They discovered nothing except some pieces of a boat matching that of the chased man and girl, and clothing snagged on the splinter of a large boulder. Jabari was not found and is presumed on the run.

The magistrates were notified, a search conducted, but no other was found. We speculated Jarbari's men rowed to the other side and escaped. Not knowing more than this, the magistrates terminated their pursuit.

I am here to serve you at this difficult time. That is my report.
—Amenemhet

PORTAGE VILLAGE

I could hear the rushing waters of the fifth cataract long before we saw them. They made for a glorious sight in their torrential pounding against the granite walls. The rock was unmoving, as if to mock the water's futile persistence.

"These rapids run a dozen stadia," Ammar said, writing a note on his map. "I've been told they are navigable in the high water, but a death trap this time of year."

Finding the village, we pulled to shore and tied the boat to a stone pillar. We were among eight other boats, all of them wooden like ours.

"This is more like it," Fawzi said. "This is perfect. Look down there. These rapids run a long way. If Shamar made it this far, that's a long haul to drag a boat—might as well hire a caravan. He'd be exhausted from rowing. And Rasha? Why she would . . ."

I shot a warning glare at Fawzi.

"Why she's strong, and could have carried the old man herself, bless her heart."

I nodded, making it clear she would not play a part in his mockery.

Ammar looked up river. "Yes, fatigue. They'd need help. They'd be anxious for help and that plants a memory in most men's heads. Let's ask around."

We found half a dozen boat captains who couldn't recall anyone matching the description, but spoke of slaves and laborers who were moved through the area on a regular basis. They couldn't recall anyone who was fair-skinned and as young as my Rasha.

We stopped a goat herder driving his flock to market. "You should check with Abdali-ud-din. They have a steward here."

"Where might we find such a man?" Ammar asked.

"A woman," the herder said. "She's at Atbara."

"Atbara?" I said. "We just came from there."

"Then the luck is with you if you're so anxious," the old man said. "She has been here this week. I saw her." The old man gave a toothless grin with his scraggly, unshaven face as if expecting a coin for this information. "She comes often, one week in four doing business. She's most busy."

"Will you take us?" Ammar asked, producing a deben.

His eyes widened. "Certainly. Yes, I can for the silver." He barked at his goats and they bleated discontentedly as he spooked them onto a patch of green.

"Follow," he said, taking great strides toward the market square.

"It's the widow Bunefer," the man said, gesturing toward a clay brick structure. "She lives here when she comes to do business."

Ammar thanked him and made our approach.

"Hello?" he called at the entrance. It had no door or drape.

"I know that accent!" a voice called from the shadows. The figure approached and stepped into the full blaze of the afternoon sun.

She was about Fawzi's age with bright eyes, a seasoned smile, long black hair, and kindness in her face. She stood firm and professional in her posture.

"Ah hah!" she said, "Friends from a familiar land, welcome so far from home, and I'll bet you have business with Abdali-ud-din. Am I right?"

She was pleasant to look upon and I saw Fawzi grow interested.

"How's your wife?" I elbowed him and whispered.

He put his foot right on mine and bore down hard. I winced.

"Yes, far to the east," he said, waving his arm to knock me in the head, but I ducked.

"You are the widow Bunefer?" Ammar asked.

"I am, but you can drop the widow part. That was four years ago," she said, motioning us inside. "I am now Bunefer from Atbara, and you're fortunate to find me here today. I'm headed back in the morning."

"Then yes," Ammar said. "Our home is in Rekeem."

"Rekeem? Certainly I have heard of it, we see many travelers from the highlands come through."

There were chairs with cushions, a table, and a large clay pot with some wild flowers by the window.

"Tell me why strangers are so far from home at this most remote part of the Nilus?" she asked. "Are you traders? Do you buy or sell?"

"We're searching for a girl and an older man. It's most urgent," Ammar said.

"Then tell me, who are you? And why do you seek these people?" she asked.

"She was kidnapped for ransom and brought to Egypt."

"She's 15 or 16," Fawzi added. "The man must be in his late fifties. He's an old man, gray beard—operates a for-hire caravan service."

"He's named Shamar. He helped her escape," Ammar said

"Yes, yes," Bunefer said, waving her hand. "I know Shamar. He has been here two maybe three times, but I haven't seen him for a long while, maybe a year."

"They are running for their lives," I blurted. "Someone is chasing them."

She looked at me, then at Ammar. "Chased by whom?"

"The kidnappers," Ammar said. "After their escape north, we think they might have turned south. We're hoping to learn of them."

"And you discovered this how?" she asked.

"Our master Zafir dispatched us some eight weeks ago. We've been traveling downriver since then, and that brings us here."

At the mention of Zafir, the woman's countenance changed. We could tell she knew of him.

"And where is your Zafir now?" she asked.

"By now he has returned to Rekeem," Fawzi said. "But we parted company at 'Adan. He has family in Saba."

Bunefer nodded and smiled, then looked down at the table. "That's correct. That's in the messages. You are indeed true travelers. We were told you were coming. Dispatches from Zafir arrived several weeks ago saying you were coming in search," she said. "Yes, the stewards of Abdali-ud-din know about you, all along the Nilus. But I'm afraid your quest has come to a sad ending."

I froze. Sad? No. Oh, no. I felt that tired knot start to form again in my gut, the possibility that … that my Rasha was …

"Ending?" Fawzi said.

"What do you mean?" Ammar asked.

She removed a few curled papyrus sheets from a wooden box and spread them on the table

"Yes, here it is," she said. "Amenemhet left this."

"Should we know him?" Ammar asked.

"No, not yet," she said. "But soon enough if you continue downriver. He serves to the fourth cataract—he contracts with the caravans west, and . . ."

"What do you mean about the girl?" I blurted out.

Bunefer went quiet, scanning through the text.

"Yes, here, read it yourself," she said.

The three of us crowded together as Ammar read aloud.

"A man and a girl who matched the description you gave in your message were seen perishing on the waters of the passage at Portage Village near the Baggara Rocks . . ."

"Perished?" I whispered aloud. Perished? I groaned, feeling the blood draining from my arms and legs. A giant fist started squeezing my heart and I stepped backward in shock. My throat tightened and I searched the woman's face for answers.

Ammar and Fawzi were speechless. They tried to retain their composure.

"A small boat," Ammar continued, clearing the emotion from his throat, and fighting a tremble in his hand, "with sail and oars, and carrying no load but two passengers stayed the night at our village." He went quiet and skipped ahead. "Men watching were led by Jabari, a cohort of the killer Rakbah."

"We must go there and see for ourselves," I whispered hoarsely. They all looked at me, but I was looking at the ground.

"This Rakbah has been at the dirty end of many murderous plots. Did you see this man, this Jabari? Could you identify him?" Fawzi asked.

"I remember an ugly man with empty eyes, average height, a trimmed beard, strong, angry, always shouting. Oh, yes, I remember it. His finger. He was missing a finger," Bunefer recalled.

Fawzi almost stood up. "Which finger?"

"His little finger, right hand I believe, last finger, gone."

Fawzi turned to Ammar. "Then it's not Rakbah."

Ammar nodded. "That means he's north, but how far?

"This Jabari fellow, would you recognize him?" Fawzi asked.

"I'd never seen him before, but I would know him now," she said.

A thousand thoughts started crashing into my heart like great slabs of stone. The room began churning and a crushing weight bore down, knotting up my stomach, my throat, my muscles.

Ammar reached behind and put a comforting hand on the back of my neck. I felt nothing but ice cold.

"May I keep this dispatch?" he asked.

"Why?" Bunefer asked. "It is official communications to your Zafir."

"Yes, but I would like to study it," Ammar said.

"What else can you tell us about this accident?" Fawzi asked.

"Not a lot," she said. "Only what is in the letter. I arrived here a few weeks after this happened."

Hot tears began to burn at my eyes. My throat constricted again and I couldn't move.

"Perhaps," Fawzi said, "perhaps you could take us to the place where this happened?"

"I think I could do that, but we can't tarry long. I leave tomorrow."

"Do we have time before sundown?" Ammar asked.

She looked at the open window.

"If we go right now," she said. "Walking is too slow. Donkeys would be best."

TUMBLING

Our little donkeys carried us half an hour downriver to the spillway where the river dumped into the churning froth of waters. It grew placid after another 100 paces.

"Somewhere along here," Bunefer said, looking out toward the large boulders and cascading white waters. "The report tells of a chase up there," she pointed. "The man was making for the far side, but the current caught him and pulled him in. There's no way to survive this. His pursuers perished also. Two of their bodies were found."

"And Jabari?" Fawzi asked.

"No, he was last seen running the footpath to this location, right around here, wading into the water," she said. "We surmise he hunted for his men. Others said he was most anxious to find the man and the girl."

I was listening, but I wasn't hearing. My eyes stung and I felt nausea boiling in my gut. I left the group in their rehearsal and wandered, almost staggering, down the path to study the place where . . . the place where my Rasha . . . NO. It couldn't be. I clenched my fists and my heart pounded in my chest. "No!" I shouted.

Ammar and Fawzi turned.

"Bassam?" Fawzi said. Ammar put his hand on Fawzi's shoulder, said something, and then the two left me alone.

I shook my head, gesturing that I was okay. But I wasn't. I had to be alone.

Oh my Rasha, my Rasha. Is it all a great lie? How do they know? How could they know? I won't believe it. I am dead without you. Thick salty tears rolled down my cheeks.

Gone?

Gone?

My gut, oh my gut. I felt its acid fire burning me from the inside out. I was shrinking into myself, a relentless swirling darkness funneling my life down a black hole of despair. It couldn't be true. There's no proof. It's a trick, a plot, a horror beyond belief. No, she . . . she . . . she is not dead.

I watched the frothy white torrent crashing against the immovable stretch of boulders, boiling whitecaps smashing into them, unending. I looked more carefully. There were no broken remains of a small boat, no fabric caught on the dead brush, no sign of any accident at all.

In my mind's eye I could see Rasha's boat sucked into the gorge, a tiny craft pitifully out-matched against massive walls of stone, rushed along the foaming brown waters with no escape, the great powerful current drowning her silent screams.

"Bassam!" Ammar said, taking me by the arm. "Bassam," he repeated, his voice softening. "It doesn't end here for us," he whispered. "Fawzi and I have been talking, and we wonder if Jabari found her alive in the water, and took her with him to Noph, took her there to Rakbah to complete their plan against Zafir. Isn't that possible?"

"Think on it," Fawzi said. "Why else would the man leave so quickly? The magistrates had no claim on him. He broke no law. It was the river that took them down that gorge, not his men. It would easily be justified. Jabari could say she was his escaped slave, a thief running from justice. They would believe the silver tongue of a monster manipulator. Isn't that more likely what happened?"

"There's no other logical reason," Ammar said. "He fled because he had his prize. He had to leave—with her."

Yes, it was possible. It might be, but the image of Rasha slammed into boulders . . . I squeezed more tears from my eyes, willing the nightmare away.

Ammar could see the anguish raging inside of me. He put his hand on my arm. "We're not finished," he said. "We must not lose faith now. We still don't have all the answers."

"That's right," Fawzi said. "We can go after Jabari. He can't have traveled too far from this place, not in just a few weeks. Maybe he's caught up with Rakbah already. We have to learn more."

"And we can hasten our travels," Ammar said. "There are caravans to cut across the bends of the river. Men do it all the time. It's quicker overland."

"And we should do it, Bassam," Fawzi said. "We should find the man responsible, and discover for ourselves the truth, beat it out of him . . . and find Rasha. There's much yet to learn about this."

I looked into Fawzi's eyes and saw a new kindness. His face was taut and determined. He didn't want this ending either.

"Fawzi," I said, choking back tears and clearing my throat. "I can't believe it."

"Believe what?"

I looked up at him, fighting my emotions, and drew a sleeve across my face. "I can't believe what you just said."

"What?" Fawzi asked.

I sniffed and girded up my courage. "You just called me Bassam."

RESOLUTE

We returned to the village just as the sun was setting, and Bunefer directed us to a good inn.

I declined to join Ammar and Fawzi. I wasn't ready for sleep. I was too upset; I wanted to be alone.

After soft words and gentle prodding, they reluctantly agreed to leave me to myself. Fawzi offered to take my things to the inn, but I declined and threw them over my shoulder like a pack. I'm sure they noticed I carried the sword of Suoud, so their worries for me would be assuaged. Their silence was their consent to let me sort things out in my own way.

I had no direction in mind. I just wandered as far from the village as I could.

The moon was rising, lending his help as I navigated narrow passages and alleyways. After some time, I passed through the remains of the old city wall and found a well-worn path that led along the river and then turned toward the hills.

I kicked lonely stones in front of me, wanting to exert at least that much control over something, anything, even if it was just a stone that must obey my will. Everything else in my life felt as if under the strangle hold of other people and events, good and evil, deliberate and accidental, all of it holding me hostage to their will.

But not this stone. The stone was like me, put upon life's path, powerless. And with that I kicked hard and the stone went flying off the path into tall weeds.

I must have walked alone for more than two hours, sobbing, angry, wanting to hit, to scream. I kept rehearsing over and over the last moments of life for my young Rasha. "Drowning is the most merciful way to die," my father once told me. "When your lungs stop fighting for air, everything suddenly becomes relaxed and peaceful. You grow numb and everything around dissolves into a dream—simple, detached, accepted. It's easy to fall asleep when you're drowning," he said.

But that was his near-drowning accident when he was boy. This was different. What if a powerful current is punishing you underwater, pushing you along the rocky bottom, hitting boulders with such force that . . . *Stop it Bassam!* I pounded clenched fists at my thighs. *Stop it! You don't really know . . .*

I was panting again and my heart was racing. I looked to the sky, more tears came, I took a breath and let it out slowly. *I can't go on like this. There is enough doubt, plenty of doubt, I must discover the truth for myself. I must turn off these thoughts, I had to stop them, I had to find resolution or I would go mad.*

"Oh my Rasha, wherever you are, please, oh please speak comfort to me?"

And then suddenly, ever so quietly, the remnants of a long ago thought surfaced in the black forgetfulness of my young memory. It brought calm to that acid feeling in my gut, that same horrible emptiness of loss that overwhelmed me when my heart was broken like this, back there in a faraway village, a dirty, shadowy place where I slunk behind a barrel in the putrid darkness of a back alleyway, looking desperately for help. Yes, I remembered it, and from nowhere that memory stealthily rose into my thoughts, without wanting it or asking, it came back to me—I remembered it in every detail.

Why am I recalling this . . . ? And suddenly a physical and psychological jolt tore through me like a bolt of lightning. And that is all it took. I knew I needed some tender help, I would try to ask God.

I broke from my stupor and realized I had walked far away to some place I didn't recognize. I was standing alone in the moonlight shadows of a palm grove, neatly spaced in rows and nestled on a slight rise just a stone's throw from the river. I was obscured in darkness with only the moon illuminating the tree tops, making their green fronds look black. Their straight pillar-like trunks bristled with the pruned stubs of old leaf bases. It all looked eerily grey, freckled with white and speckled with black.

Without thinking on it more, I fell to my knees and poured out my heart.

"Oh God," I whispered, "Please help me. Please. Where is my Rasha? Is she gone? At the hands of evil? I am so filled with hate and dark and anger. Please give me peace. Please make in me a new hope and take away this horror. I can't live with this. I can't live without my Rasha, my companion, my life. Have you brought me this far to come upon . . . to come upon this? Please dear God, I will promise you anything. Take my life for hers, please let her be alive, anything you ask of me will I do, anything. Can she be found? Please, please help me."

I knelt there in final surrender, my head buried in my hands, tears squeezing between my fingers. I searched my heart, pushing away the dark, twisting about between denial and anger and despair. I couldn't accept it—I refused. I wouldn't surrender, so I purged all of my weaknesses before him, my flaws and confessions and promises and aspirations. I wept until there were no more tears, then prayed until finally, I was empty.

My surrender was complete. Now God knows, I thought. Now he has my burden. He will help me carry it no matter how much heavier it must grow.

In the silence, I became aware that all about me was beautifully still. The river lapped softly against the shore, a breeze blew at the perspiration on my scalp, cooling my tormented thoughts to a peaceful acceptance.

In this state of collapse, I felt the gentle stirring, as if my senses awoke from a difficult journey. I listened to the silence around me with eyes shut tight. The distant roar of the cataract blended with the night sounds of sleepy tree frogs and the rustling of small creatures and crawling things finding homes, food, shelter. I realized my knees hurt against the hard ground. I felt granules of sand embedding in my skin.

A chill went through my body and I wiped my eyes. The cooling desert breeze came once more, this time from another direction, blowing toward me from across the Nilus. It was gentle and kind, caressing my face to dry my tears. I could smell the fresh green aromas of life and growing things, and whiffs of stagnant rot and waste caught in the small ponds formed along the banks—it was the smell of life and its mighty circle of birth to death, the highs of youth and growth, and the lows of expended life, weakness, of dying. It was the scent of the ending, the place to where all things are lovingly called home, warmly, to their mother earth from whence they first came. Death is a blessing to end all suffering, I decided. To end all pain and anguish. And should my Rasha be so called, I would accept it with all the tender love that was intended by her life, all the love I wanted to be hers. It was clear to me that my soul needed repair. I would need knowledge about her ending place. To that end, I would make for my Rasha a memorial.

The sleepy stands of papyrus that framed this part of the shore hardly rustled their feathery heads in the night breeze, and a distant plop of a fish gulping an insect drew my attention to the shore. Reflected in the water were the same stars that had become such dear friends, staring down on my plight, as they had always, giving guidance and comfort. I counted eight of the great ones standing still in their usual formation overhead, the same as I had seen them so many hundreds of nights before.

The time? I estimated it was after second watch, perhaps I should return.

I searched my heart for any sliver of guidance. I glanced toward the river and realized the shore was just twenty paces from where I stood.

The place I had absentmindedly wandered to was near the end of the portage path. I stayed a moment to get my bearings. I let my eyes rest upriver on the great spillway's ending place. The cascades and whirlpools were quieter under the magic of the glowing moon. The waters seemed tamed into a calming peace as they passed over their blurry falls. When the fury reached me on shore, it was reduced to ripples and a thousand lazy sparkles from the moon reflected back at me.

For some time, I had been absentmindedly eyeing a plank-boat abandoned on the beach. It had been dragged to shore, but left unsecured. Inside was a full-sized mast and sail and oars. This traveler must have been sailing upriver, but this was the end. Now he must get help portaging—no easy chore, especially for a heavy boat.

What if . . . ? What if I took that boat and . . . A thousand ideas darted through my mind, unthinkable ideas presented themselves like a flashing vision full of real possibilities, striking me so abruptly to overflowing that I held my breath until the mental cascade reached its ending place.

Almost instantly everything became sharp and clear. I knew exactly what I had to do.

"This is why your boat went missing," I said aloud, "as if in proxy for some official officer of the village speaking to an angry boat owner. "You should know that a river is an untrustworthy servant, and a stormy rain from last night or yesterday or last week, a storm a hundred stadia upriver or a thousand, might have sent a swell to float away your boat. It happens all the time. How could you be so careless as to leave your rope untied?"

And with that, I threw my belongings into the boat and looked around for watchers in the dark.

"Please help me, Rasha," I whispered, and leaned hard against the boat to push. It broke free and slipped into the water. I hoisted myself over the rail and ducked low thinking I was being watched or someone might come running.

A few moments later, I sat up and scanned the great mirrored expanse that spread peacefully before me. It seemed I was witnessing some great law that nature enforced on the Nilus, a decree that its waters be calmer away from the cataracts, as if the torrent that first exhausted itself from its forceful compulsion through the rocky mazes then must find rest in an ending place. It was that calm the current carried me toward, and I dared not row. I let the craft find its natural path and float me along as it would any other log or frond accidently freed from its mooring place to be carried away as a river must.

The first thing I noticed was the smell of the water away from shore. It was fresher here. I took a deep delicious breath. A breeze filled my face and sifted through my hair. Straight ahead, shining brightly on the horizon was the pole star, smiling as if to say, "This is your way home, I will guide you."

I took inventory of my immediate circumstance and realized I was wet from catching the boat at shore. "I'll heat myself with work," I said, and locked the oars onto the pins and pulled for deeper water. "An hour of this and I'll be dry as a bone," and began the oarsman's labor, looking for a tune to hum, an ancient rhythm of a lonely work on the Nilus.

The shore was distant, the village was sleeping—no lights or fires, just the white wash of the moon. And somewhere among those shrinking shadows were my two great friends, probably asleep and not aware of my escape into the night.

It was a wonderful fantasy drifting through the heart of the Nilus, alone, skimming along under a beautiful starry sky, quiet to my thoughts, in control of my destiny at last.

"Oh that my Rasha could be with me to see it," I said. "Perhaps you are!" And with that simple thought. I was able to smile at last.

NEAR MISSES

Suddenly there was a lot of shouting and I awoke to a blinding sun in my face. *Had I fallen asleep?*

A massive boat with sails was bearing down on me fast. Men were shouting with long poles, pushing me from disaster. With just cubits to spare, they pushed me out of the way, nearly sinking me had I not leaned hard the other way to restore balance. The great sailing vessel glided by with not even a touch; its crew spat at me and cursed their displeasure.

I tried to slow my panicked heart and catch my breath. What was that? They would have splintered me to kindling. How could I have slept? What is this place?

The sun was high, well past third watch, and already hot on my face. Its reflection sparkled brightly off the water, shimmering with blinding flashes that danced everywhere.

I spied a village surrounded by palms a quarter hour downriver. I began working my way toward it. I would stop there and learn of my whereabouts and what lay from here to my future. I had put my foot on a new path I couldn't depart, and determined to do my best. I was all on my own—again.

My stomach ached for food and my mouth was parched. I should have packed food. But a drink? Not a problem this time. I drew in my oars and reached with my hand to scoop some water. I washed life back into my face. It was deliciously cool with a mossy taste. My brain began to awaken.

"The sails!" I said, suddenly recalling that the large boat that almost hit me had sails. They were taking the wind south, against the current. What did Ammar tell me about that? "There are tricks to reading the river," he said. "When you see their temples, take time to study the wall carvings. Pay attention to the images of their boats. You can learn a lot." The key, he said, was . . . what was it? "When you see many men at oar then you know they drive their barge north. That's with the current, Bassam. And when a boat is with sail, then you know it drives south. If it's a warship, it tells of an invasion. If it carries goods and animals, the sail will tell you if they go to trade or return from it." Ammar had been so excited about it. "There's much to learn from their figure writing, even if you don't know the language," he said.

The memory gave me thought. Had Ammar and Fawzi discovered my absence, and how did they act? Fawzi would call me names, Ammar would be concerned but will be first to guess my choices.

The river was different here. It was bordered to either side with reddish brown sand, and beyond was green farmland—sure signs of healthy irrigation.

"At least the debs and kroks don't like this heat." There were no killers shading beneath the patches of palms that I passed. My greatest danger was the great walls of papyrus that blockaded the gentle bends and turns of the river. They posed an old challenge I had grown weary of avoiding. How many more days of this?

"Ah! I saw this on Ammar's map," I said aloud. "Yes! The *bad water* near the Fourth Cataract—headed west and south for a dozen days. This is where boats fight the current and the wind—a bad place in low flood, he said. This must be where I get off!"

I needed to discover what the village offered the overland caravans. When I asked Ammar why we shouldn't just stay on the river he gave me that look again. "Don't let the water fool you," he said. "Men speak of six cataracts but there are dozens more to slow you, especially at low water—that's the month we're in. Be cautious, my boy, be cautious." My worry was the safety across land. He assured me it was secure and well traveled. My challenge was to find where those caravans mounted up and see what it would take to attach myself and find Rasha.

I realized that somewhere along here Jabari or Rakbah had taken the same route. They must have. Any other place would be too slow, not the route of fleeing criminals. But what of my Rasha? Did he pass through this place with her? Did she see the same vapid landscape of sand and plateau? Did she wonder what grew in the green patches far to the other side? Did she wonder how she might signal someone that she was in distress?

I determined to ask about Jabari and Rakbah at each village, each harbor, each market seller, and would follow their footsteps even if they were a month old. And every day saved on this shortcut would bring me that much closer to the truth about my Rasha.

I pulled harder on the oars just thinking on it. A large encampment was just ahead.

KURGUS

I knew the little village was the right place as I drew near. From a few stadia away, I could make out pens of camels, a crowding of boats, columns of smoke. This was it. I was sure of it.

The sun was just touching the horizon when I pulled my boat to shore. I was approached immediately by three men desperate to answer my questions; they were clearly accustomed to travelers with coins to rent a ride.

"Ah, a young man on a great trek!" he said. "And you seek Noph or the West Sea, am I right? Come! You must ready yourself. The next caravan is preparing to depart."

I was caught by surprise. "Now? So close to nightfall?" I asked.

"Ah, so, you're not from here," the skinny man said. "I know it from your voice. You're from the Sinai, am I right? No, no, not that, Ah! You're from the high deserts?"

I smiled and nodded.

"So! I am Babak [bah-BOCK]. It means, "little father." I am little, am I not? I have a daughter and three sons, do I not? And you, what do they call you?" he asked.

"I am Bassam," I told him smiling.

"Bassam, yes, Bassam. You are smiling. That is right. I am Babak and I'll help you get to your home. You're not here to stay, am I right? You're traveling down the Nilus to return? Where do the gods take you, Bassam?"

I sighed wearily and breathed an empty response. "He takes me where he must have me, and then I go home," I said.

"Ah, you follow *the* God. It is the Hebrew God? Of Abram? Of Moses? That is wise," Babak said. "Then you must obey, and God will make a manager of me to make that happen. See, come," and he beckoned me to follow.

The Hebrew God. Is he different from their gods? I thought it was all one, all the same just different names. I'll have to ask Ammar about that when he catches up with me.

Just as Babak had promised, a train was already mounting up to leave. He engaged a pair of men who appeared to be leaders of the group. He gestured toward me and the men nodded.

"You, Bassam, you must leave now!" He said breathlessly. "Here, I'll fetch you the camel. And you have coins for this? I cannot fetch the camel if you do not have coins." He held out his hand impatiently, avoiding my eyes.

I had some debens in my bundle, and dug around for a few.

"Babak," I asked, "where am I? What is this place? And why are they leaving in the dark?"

He took the coins and walked briskly to the assembly place, motioning me to follow. "Stand right here. I bring your camel. And I tell you this quickly—this is Kurgus, the way station taking men from the Nilus to Korosko and back. It's three weeks faster than the river—and safer. When the moon is with us, we travel at night—even faster. This is the Uaret train, and you're just in time."

"Uaret?"

"Yes, the 35th, every ten days. Do you not know it?"

"No," I stammered. "Is that your calendar?"

"Certainly, ten days. You must leave or wait ten days, then you take the Phu-hor train. If you're in a hurry, it's better on the Nilus if you miss the Uaret. Will you go tonight or wait?"

"Oh no, this will do just fine. Let me pay and I will go," I said.

"Then we take you on the Korosko Road, busy, famous. You have heard of it?"

I shook my head.

"It's the elbow of the Nilus, the great bend. It will take you north," he said pointing, "to Wawat—Korosko, Iken, or go south, the second cataract, Mirgissa, you decide. I'll tell you, go to Iken. There you'll get a boat. Iken is a good place, down river from those long rafts of stones, and islands, confusing, a thousand stadia, dangerous stumbling place, so broken with rapids that boats may travel it only in the flood. But there are many boats for you. They will show you. Don't get a boat until you're sure you're out of the rocks. They will cheat you there. When you're far enough for your boat, there you will continue God's quest." And with that he turned and hurried away.

"What about food and drink?" I called after him.

"Included, not to worry," he said without turning around.

"When do we sleep?" I called again, but he had disappeared.

I was left alone by a crude fire laid out on the flat sand. A wrinkled blanket was left in a dusty clump with an abandoned mug tipped to its side, and a sandal with a broken strap.

The caravan waited on me impatiently. It was small, maybe 30 camels receiving loads, and 10 or 12 riders. I saw large skeps of sorghum, sesame, and peanuts slung to the sides of a few of the camels. Standing near were four riders clustered in a group. These had black skins, from Aethiopia I guessed, and talked with such animation. The others were Egyptian; they were lighter in skin and smaller in stature—seasoned travelers and less talkative. They acted as if this trip was just a routine part of business. They looked impatient and bored at the same time, watching me as if wondering why I made them wait.

As for me, I felt conspicuous. I was young with an eastern accent, large stature, fair skin, blue eyes, and no beard.

The sun had just disappeared into a layer of orange haze swallowing the western horizon, but the sky was still bright. I enjoyed its beautiful reflection in the Nilus. To the east I saw the strangest shape standing above the sand. Its great walls reflected the fading orange with sparkling wonder as if made of broken glass. It had all the angles of a poorly constructed pyramid, most unusual for the Egyptian builders.

Babak returned towing a feisty camel chewing at the rope, and saw me staring east.

"It's the Rock of Quartz," he said, hitting the beast with his riding stick to kneel. With a great grunt, the camel knelt and breathed a long sigh.

"That's the great landmark in Kurgus—old, famous," Babak said.

"Famous?" I asked.

"Oh yes, ancient pharaohs carved their conquests into the stone," he said. "Seventy, eighty, eighty-five stories. I have lost count. It marked the southern border of Egypt's power in ancient days. You can see the carvings another time, no time now. Here, this is your ride."

"Are there images of boats?" I asked.

"What?"

"Never mind."

Babak handed me a pouch. "Some food to start," he said. "These are your things? This is all you are bringing?"

My sword hung to my side, but the pouches with my journals and some clothing lay at my feet. A blanket was wrapped across my left shoulder and an empty water skin slung from a rope on my right.

"This is all I have," I said. "Should I fill my skin?"

"Yes, three days," Babak said. "You'll eat what they eat and drink what they drink, and rest at the wells. Then three days more. It's part of the bargain. You know how to use that sword?"

"Yes . . ."

"You won't have to," he said. "You won't need it. I can buy it from you. Good price. Will you sell it?"

I smiled and shook my head. I liked Babak. He would make a good negotiator for Zafir in these parts.

"It has work to do, I must keep it," I said, placing my hand on its hilt. "Have you any recollection of a man of the high deserts like me, but perhaps 50 or 60 years, and a young girl, maybe 15 or 16, slender, black hair, traveling with him?"

Babak stopped in his tracks and scratched his head, looking at the ground. "That's your quest? Then no, I'm sorry. Was it recent?"

"A month ago," I said.

"That's too far," he said. "I can't recall anyone stopping here from the high deserts, not for a long while."

"How about a man named Jabari? Rakbah?" I asked. "They are missing a finger, each of them."

"Never heard of them, are they kin?" he asked.

"No, but one of them has taken the young girl, and that's the business I'm about." I put my hand on my sword again.

"Ah, then you must not be kept waiting," he said, taking my water skin. "Here, take him. He's your ride," and handed me the rope. "I'll fill this for you."

Babak returned with the skin dripping full and handed me his riding stick. While he loaded my things, I approached the beast with an angry expression and the stick held high.

"I'm tired. I'm anxious. I'm in no mood for trouble," I said to the camel. "If you give me grief, I'll slay you at the fire and eat you to the bone, and be pleased to walk the rest of the way on a full stomach. Do you understand?"

Babak laughed at my speech and came to my side. "That's the way, young Bassam, that's the way with this old man. Be mean and he will obey. Be soft and he will ride you on the road to Korosko. Get it?"

WATER

Preparations for the arduous six-day trip to Korosko were more extensive than I had imagined. For the longer methodical trip, I was accustomed to more simple preparations, suitable to those conditions. For this, a fast march, they began with conditioning the camels.

Four or five days before departure the Egyptian drivers fed their camels a diet of maize stalks—nutritious they said. As for water, they provided none until just before the start when they let the beast drink his fill. I could sense that the animals knew what was coming. I could feel it in the air—a quenched thirst meant a labor ahead, and they growled and stirred in anticipation to get on the road.

As for me, my goatskin was filled to the brim. A second skin was offered. I purchased it even though more than half our camels carried only water as their singular load. I knew the painful ordeal of thirst and had no intention of that experience again. My silver for the water was a good bargain no matter the reason.

"Not a drop until Mûrr-hàt," Babak said. "You must be light and swift. Shed your worldly possessions, except what is necessary. Do you understand me? No tent, no bedding, just a blanket. Carry necessary stores only."

I nodded, and told him I had already shed all that I could.

"If you want to carry more, if you must keep these bulky worldly things, then take the next barge on the Nilus, they will take your coins for the slower trip—but do not bother us here with such things, here we are swift, this is the Uaret train. You slow them up, they leave you behind."

I smiled and nodded—Babak's nonstop sandstorm of orders blew past my ears so quickly I decided his commands were swift enough for all of us combined!

Abar and Anen were brothers, and owned the train. They made this round trip to Korosko all year round. As for Babak, he was more than a promoter. He was their "little father." It was his job to steer a wandering sojourner to the family business so other caravans would not snatch him, just as I had been steered. And so, it all fit together nicely.

This evening of my arrival was called First Night for the Uaret train. Barely was I loaded on my camel when Abar ordered us up and out. It was then that I learned about my old camel and had to fight him fiercely to stand his load. After some hard whacks with the stick and kicks to the ribs, he finally fell into place.

"So this is how it's going to be, is it?" I held my stick just enough in view to let him know there were more beatings where that came from.

"You're a smelly beast," I told him. "Smelly with a black heart filled with laziness, and you're a stupid camel. I may have to break my stick on you! For that I'll call you 'Saafil [saw-awful] The Camel,' he who is loathsome and filthy—that is you. I may have to eat you after all, but will you make me sick on your meat? Yes, you would do that to me. So instead, I'll feed you to the lions."

For that First Night we marched immediately, pushing hard with only two short breaks. The moon made our pathway bright and we plodded in a single file at a fast pace. I had never run at such speeds before, and felt tired to the bone.

An hour before dawn Abar called a stop with time to eat and toilet. Then it was back on the camels, no delay.

Saafil cooperated with the removal of his loads at each of our stops, but for mounting back up, two others in the group had to beat him into submission to take again his load.

When no one was watching, I scolded my camel for his reticence. "You're looking a lot like my dinner right now, old man Saafil."

An hour later we passed the bleached bones of a camel skeleton poking from a sand drift. I pointed them out to my stubborn camel. "One more rebellion like that," I warned him, "and I'll leave you tethered to the bones of your cousin and pick another for a ride."

He snorted and flicked his tail.

The wind was calm but the air was filled with fine sand, so thick we put on scarves to breathe. There's something marvelous about charging into the unknown, making by day's end a grand memory of places and events passing so quickly I could hardly record them into my journal. At this pace, I expected to be at the second cataract in a short time; though, a week was their promised delivery schedule.

The rising sun brought rising heat, and it was intense. As with the smith's hammer, the sun beat on us like an anvil, pounding us into surrender, threatening us to turn back or face certain death. We refused. In defiance, each of us erected little tents made of our robes to create shade. The camels didn't mind the heat, even Saafil. He chewed as he marched, seemingly content in the middle of such oppressive heat.

At midday, we stopped for a short rest. I expected a longer layover, but Abar and Anen ordered us up.

"What?" I exclaimed. "It's the worst time to travel, the heat of the day!" and looked around to see if others agreed. None did and loaded the camels as usual.

The camels seemed just fine and hurried us along as though there was no sun and no heat. I had never imagined such a march possible in these conditions.

As the heat bore down, I thought to conserve my water by saving my portion. The Egyptians would not have it. They scolded me about drinking, slapping me with their riding sticks and jabbering something cross. I took the rebuke and obliged.

On the second day, I learned a lesson about pure water. In my haste, I had paid good money for a water skin made of new leather. After that much time with my pouch exposed to the sun, the water was tainted with a foul goatskin taste. I scolded myself for being foolish. "Newly stitched skins, not seasoned. That's what I get for spending my debens in haste. Next time, Bassam, consider your purchase."

The daytime march continued into the cooling hours of evening. When the sun disappeared, we dismounted for a good two hours to eat and sleep. I learned to fall asleep fast at each of those stops, but it was easiest in the cool of the dark.

The Nub'an desert was without shame. Not a green thing was growing—no vegetation, no palms, nothing. Even the plague of maddening flies that had pestered me at Kurgus had wisely abandoned me, no doubt returning to the human buffet that awaited them at the river. Did even the flies know something I didn't?

The terrain on Korosko Road was much different than other deserts I had traveled. Strange rounded mountains of black rock rose up in long stretches, polished with age and standing immovable. I imagined them to be the enormous carcasses of a thousand giants—all of them fallen by some terrible army and left prostrate in the rigors of agonizing stagnation.

The wadi was enormous. I guessed it was 1,000 stadia wide, probably more, as far as the eye could see. To the sides we saw smaller, sand-clogged tributaries of scarred earth turning away toward lower ground. Even though this desert was drier than a bone, everywhere I looked were signs of tremendous flooding. What caused it, no man could say. It stretched in all directions, and was as flat as a lake on a windless day.

"If I had a goatskin ball," I whispered, "I could give it a swift kick and it would roll undisturbed for a week!"

The wadi was perfect for the phantom images of the distant mirari. Ammar told me about the mirari. "Two kinds to fool you," he said. "Know both and you won't chase yourself to death."

He explained the lesser mirari was most common. A reflection off the hot sand of the blue sky, making it appear a lake lies ahead. These images were plentiful on the Road to Korosko. Each day toward middle watch, far to the horizon we saw a deliciously blue lake materialize from nothing—too far to reach, too inviting to ignore.

He told me I might witness the greater mirari at sea. "I've seen it myself," Ammar said. "Distant boats appear in the haze, just above the water, stretched, enlarged, ghostly. You think they are large boats, or a distant coast of mountains standing above the mist. Don't be fooled by it," he warned. "There's nothing at sea that floats over the water. It's all a mirari."

The evidence of water was no mirari. Like all rivers, the wadi had shorelines and small islands at high ground. Its bed was strewn with round, river-worn pebbles instead of the usual sharp-edged rocks. From all appearances, I would say these lands had not seen water for thousands of years. But it was undeniable—somewhere in the past a great flood had passed through.

The two hours' rest ended too quickly and we were called for departure. Only two hard days and already I felt a week had passed. It was night with a partial moon, the start of the third day.

I watched the stars as the drivers pushed us hard, and began to wonder—can they guide by the stars or do they have the south pointer? A man riding next to me had exchanged a few polite words. Maybe he would discuss it.

"Excuse me, but I'm curious. You've taken this road many times. How do you know that this is the right path?" I asked.

He looked up and then glanced ahead. "It's this way all the way," he said, pointing at the bleached bones of another camel half buried in the sand.

"The dead?" I asked.

"The bones of those who do not prepare mark the way for those who do prepare."

The bones were everywhere but I hadn't expected men to use them to mark a path. At any given time we were stepping through the graveyard of a dozen or more skeletons.

"There must be thousands of them," I said scanning the landscape, noticing, suddenly, their abundance.

He swept his hand toward the horizon. "You'll see it yourself. It's just like this before we arrive at Mûrr-hàt, and it's no different afterwards. A dangerous place for the ill-prepared."

We passed another pair of camel skeletons, brittle bones casting sharp, black shadows under the moon's bright light. Curled up next to one of them were the bones of a man, stripped clean of his flesh and clothing. His skull was looking right at us, half buried in sand, but watching just the same.

WELLS OF MÛRR-HÀT

I was astonished that we had traveled 900 stadia to the halfway point so quickly. The trip to the Wells of Mûrr-hàt had taken just three days. We might have paid a hard price for the brisk pace, but it certainly cut our time in half.

The landmarks ahead were vague, useful only to those already familiar with the great flat basin. Abar and Anen pointed my attention to a valley.

"The wells," Abar told me, pointing his stick. "Water and rest for a short while." Great black-stone mountains slumbered to either side.

They called the great basin the waterless sea; though it was without a single rock or boulder to offer shade. For three hours more, we suffered under the relentless heat before turning west to a great range of dusty hills. There, somewhere in its furnace-like belly was a dry, narrow valley with water.

The camels could sense we were getting near. They seemed to know, or perhaps they remembered.

I felt Saafil pull on the reins. He had caught wind of something ahead.

An hour later we passed small patches of sparse vegetation, some camel-thorn bunched up in small clusters. Yes, water was near. About 20 trunks of dead date palms protruded from the sand like skeletal sentinels in neat, man-made rows, guiding us in.

The valley was narrow, only ten stadia across, surrounded by more of the same black hills to the north and south. Along the base of the foothills were small mounds of dirt, the excavations of ancient wells. The wells were scattered about haphazardly, some glistening, others filled with sand.

"The wells of Mûrr-hàt," Abar called back.

Just then Saafil lurched forward and his pace quickened.

"Whoa, old man," I scolded him, pulling on the reins. It was no use. The other camels had sensed the same thing and picked up the pace like a mob, ignoring their masters.

They knew exactly what was ahead and stretched their necks forward as if dragged by some unseen force.

Helplessly we rode at a trotting speed that quickly grew to full gallop as all 30 camels charged the first small pond that came into view. I pounded Saafil with my riding stick, pulling on the rope to slow, but he ignored me. And then I saw it too, sparkling blue water peeking from between cracks in the crude walls. This was no mirari. It was the real thing! I was barely hanging on, my things flopping around. Saafil abruptly tucked his knees and fell to his stomach, sliding across the sand right to the pond's edge. A great cloud of dust boiled past—then he plopped his nose right into the water, lapping anxiously.

And me? I hung on for dear life.

I quickly slipped off the side to catch my breath. My arms were tired, my throat was parched, and I wanted my turn at the well.

Just then, a group of angry men rose from their tents and came toward us shouting, waving their arms and shaking their fists. I soon learned why—camels had their water and the men had theirs. Evidently our anxious herd had chosen poorly. The wells reserved for the animals were poorly dug and filled with greenish, brackish water. The people's wells were sweet and guarded.

The men pulled at the camels' ropes to dislodge them, but the beasts rejected the effort, looking up with drippy mouths, showing their teeth and hissing their spittle. The men let them be, and the beasts returned to drinking.

As the commotion quieted, I could look around at last.

So, these are the famous wells of Mûrr-hàt—

There was no sound here, no bird, no flies, nothing but the occasional bleating or growling of the beasts, and gentle speaking among the travelers.

The wells didn't distinguish themselves from my ground-level view for any special terrain or construction except for crudely piled stone walls, futile defenses against the encroaching sands. Everywhere else were mounds of boulders looking every part the protruding shoulders of sleeping giants.

I counted ten wells, three of them filled with brackish water and sparsely attended. Some goats didn't seem to mind the taste and looked up with mild interest at the new arrivals. I wanted answers to this mysterious place and sought out the man who earlier had spoken kind words. He was unloading his camel behind a large black rock.

"Excuse me sir," I stammered. "May I finally introduce myself? I am Bassam. I hail from Rekeem. May I ask your name?"

"I'm Nehi of Mirgissa, my home," he said.

"Mirgissa? Isn't that where we're headed? Korosko?"

"Not Korosko, but Mirgissa, more south. Yes, my home at the second cataract," he said. "Another three-day drive from here to the Nilus. You know that, don't you?"

I nodded and looked at his little camp for a place to set my own.

"Could you please tell me about this place?" I asked. "I have so many questions—how was it discovered? Why are there wells in the middle of this great wasteland? Who dug them? The pathway is so indirect and calculated. Were it not for the bones, what leads men here? Do not these wells dry up under this relentless heat? How did those goats get here?"

He looked up to see who else might be walking about, then arranged his things in the shadow of the tall rock. He pulled a blanket and spread it in the shade.

"Bring yours," he said. "Come, sit, and I'll tell you of this place."

The sun was leaning toward afternoon and the shadows were starting to grow. I found a place next to him and sat cross-legged.

"It was once a great land of milk and honey, a birthplace for all the world's living things—born here, raised here, sent to faraway lands. This was the beginning place."

I imagined a wonderful paradise built among the great rocks that had once been buried under a hundred cubits of rich soil. Basking atop might have been ten thousand flowering trees watered by blue rivers and streams snaking between the green mounds, bordered by blossoms and animals watching in wonder. The vision made me feel cooler.

"You can see the tracings of the great waters' paths in the wadis and washes," he said. "Its origins are lost to us, but we find pieces of the story and men try hard to compile them into a tale worth repeating."

He stopped to look about for a leather satchel, and then pulled from it some cheese, offering me a piece. I took it with thanks.

"The goats, they have lived here long," he said. "Good for milk and cheese and meat. Not all of the wells are sweet, some are brackish, not good for anything but washing."

"It seems peaceful here," I said. "Why not a larger community? A person could sell things here, and ..."

"No, not safe, it's a hotly contested place," Nehi said. "For many centuries raids on villages and caravans have been launched from here. Today the land is thick with a great deal of wealthy trade and prosperity, and the Romans look to spread their power. This keeps the bandit attacks an infrequent displeasure. You would do well to remember that coming here is not always safe."

"No mobs here now," I observed.

"Don't ever trust it. The thieves have been driven away, but this way station has become an important part of the trade. I'm sure they hide and contrive plans to profit by it."

The desolation surrounded like a great sandy carpet for hundreds of stadia in every direction. It made me wonder how anyone could survive hiding in this miserable place.

"Anyone know how it was discovered?" I asked.

"Much speculation," he said. "One tale is a rainy season of long ago. Sojourners passing through saw water captured by the great rocks. In stopping to collect, they found vegetation growing, signs of underground springs. Others believe it was the remnants of a lush tropical place that slowly succumbed to the sands, yet the wells still survive. This great secret has been passed from mouth to ear for a thousand generations—and thus has it been handed down to us today."

"What do you think?" I asked.

"Ah, what do I think . . ." he said, letting the question drift away. "My theory is not fact, but I'm fancied by the ancient people of Sumer. Do you know of them?"

I had heard the term, but not anything more.

"They are a people of the great rivers in the east, the land between the Tigris and the Euphrates. The people of Sumer are an ancient tribe whose great king Gilgāmeš impressed into clay tablets a mighty tale, an epic adventure as a poem. Have you heard of it?"

I shook my head.

"He lived after the pyramids and after the great flood," Nehi said. "At one time he displeased the advances of a goddess, and she tormented him. He embarked on a great journey to find a survivor of the Great Flood. It was said this man held the secret to eternal life. The gods failed Gilgāmeš and ordered him a new course. I believe that new course brought him far west of Urak and the two rivers, all the way west to Egypt and the land of Nub'ah. I believe he traversed the Nilus upriver, then tiring of his quest, cut through the deserts to this place where the gods spared him with this spring of waters."

"Where did you learn these things?"

"Ah, you're not familiar with the holdings at the library at Ale'ksandria, are you?" he asked.

I shook my head. "I must get there some day."

"Your trek, young Bassam," he said, "if it takes you north, then you must stop at the great library. You never know when you might return to this place. Do not miss this great center of learning."

He was right. Ale'ksandria was another three or four days beyond Noph. Perhaps I could make it work—but not without my Rasha, one way or the other.

"Now tell me. What brings you here?" Nehi asked.

"I'm searching for a young girl and her escort named Shamar. Have you heard of him?"

Nehi shook his head. "I don't have much dealings with the traders. I have my purposes and they have theirs."

"They are not traders. They are running from evil," I said. "A killer named Rakbah."

"Rakbah . . . No, I haven't heard of him," he said.

"If I find the killer, I find Shamar and the girl," I said.

"And so you have searched Nub'ah and Upper Egypt, and now you travel to search Lower Egypt?"

"There are reports of a sighting, and the reports are not good," I said.

"And so you must learn this for yourself, whether it be a good or bad report," Nehi said.

I said nothing, but he knew the answer already.

Day 786

My Dearest Rasha,

I am crossing a great desert to find you as quickly as I know how. I am traveling on my own, hoping to speed my way. I have heard the rumors at the Fifth Cataract. I have heard of Rakbah and his men. I have heard it all. But in my heart, I know it, I know it, I just know, you're not far from me. I have traversed the hot furnace of the Nub'an desert, and I come for you. We take rest at the wells of Mûrr-hàt, then a few days more to the river. Be brave, be well, and know that I come for you.

—Bassam

54

KOROSKO

My thoughts turned to Ammar and Fawzi. They were, no doubt, in pursuit. But I'd made so much more progress without their analysis and decision-making. Three heads are not better than one. My choice was a right one, but I didn't want to lose them in the mission. I decided to leave a marker. When departure was called, I lingered just long enough to find a low place on the shadow side of the boulder and scratched the symbol for Al Kalimat with my first initial. It was a remote gamble. But if they come to the wells, and Fawzi looked for shade like

he always does, they'd know I was here first. With that, I loaded up
Saafil for another three-day sprint.

A few hours' travel from the wells of Mûrr-hàt and we found
ourselves in the unprotected glare of the sun's lethal rays. It was another
vast, flat basin.

"The Waterless Sea," Nehi said, "the name they give every other flat
sandy basin in Egypt. See the marks that a real sea once lived here?"

I could. Even a stretch of boulders we passed was carved up with
little caves, the action of water not sand.

And just as he said, this region was a vast field of bones. Thousands
of them twisted and splayed in every visage of death-agony that I could
imagine, marking a path unmistakably clear. "Memorials," Nehi said,
sweeping his arm. "Silent markers to the thousands seeking salvation
at the wells."

"And so close," I breathed.

Two more hours and we passed another curious formation that I
called headstones—thousands of heavy black rocks the size of human
heads. Some were stuck together, others alone.

"They almost look like more bones," I said. "So much like river rocks,
but what river? Not even a million sandstorms in a million years could
carve such shapes, could they?"

Nehi shook his head and raised his hands to the horizons. "There's
no other way. It must have been a wondrous sight, a massive inundation,
a mighty flood," he said. "Could the Nilus create this work? Did she
wander from her path to this lonely desolation? If she did, it was an
adventure she played out long ago. Perhaps it's the last remnants of
carnage from the Great Flood. I have always wondered about that."

Our journey eastward was no different than our rush north to Mûrr-
hàt. We kept the same schedule and hurried along with short breaks at
the same intervals. The nights melted into day, making the duration feel
as if it was a single stretch of time. Abar and Anen pressed us hard until
our ending place was finally in sight.

Upon seeing our ending place on the horizon, I was startled at the brevity of the trip. I was exhausted and thinner for the endurance, but the vision injected me with new hope and energy.

The air was different as we neared the Nilus valley. The animals could smell the water, and a few lazy birds came to investigate, the first we had seen in a week.

As we entered the ruins of Korosko proper, I was actually disappointed. "This is hardly the oasis I was hoping for, not after that horrid desert."

"It's not the best landing place," Nehi said. "Mirgissa is better, but I don't run their business. Mirgissa is the oasis you long for."

The village was sparsely inhabited—barren, hot, with a scattering of low mud-brick buildings baked rock hard in the sun. They were white and dusty with shadowed entrances covered with faded awnings. No one left the shade to welcome our train as we paraded down the main boulevard.

Korosko was wedged in by steep, barren mountains that directed all the sun's heat onto its valley. There was no escape from this miserable condition except to make tents from our robes.

Rounding a slight bend and climbing over a shallow rise, we saw the most beautiful sight I thought possible. Far below the glistening Nilus stretched wide. A handful of peak-sailed boats followed the wind. Lush green vegetation and palms lined the shores, but beyond that, the sandy landscape was pure desert, lifeless and flat.

"Your new journey begins here at the river," Nehi said, "and I will go to my home, two days south by boat," he smiled. "You have two days north, just follow the river. Cyene is not far, the first cataract, then you may get on the river again. May you travel in safety, young Bassam. And for what you find, may God grant you wisdom to deal with it accordingly."

I thanked him and paused, wondering if I should take the risk.

"Nehi," I said, "I must tell you that I'm connected to Abdali-ud-din, on an official quest in the service of one of its leaders. One day I'll be back. There's much trade to do among these many villages."

"Ah, yes, Abdali-ud-din, you should have mentioned it before. I know them," he said. "Your traders have passed through these passages many times."

I had kept my affiliations to myself, having learned that not everyone had fond regards for the largest trading dynasty in the world.

"The Romans have longed to displace Abdali-ud-din," he said. "They want your business."

"I've heard," I said. "But for now, it's too strong and too widespread to fall for the Romans' tricks, so I continue a most important errand."

"That's well enough, then," he said. "Then let me tell you of Narmer. If your mission takes you to Cyene then you must give my regards to Narmer and Kiya. He is the steward for Abdali-ud-din—fine people, good friends. We did business some years ago. I see him every few months."

"Narmer? That's good to know. I'll find him and extend your greetings," I said. "They say Cyene has a famous well."

"Ah!" Nehi smiled. "Eratosthenes, yes, famous. Look to Abu Island for the famous well. I went looking myself, as a boy, long ago. You might get there in time to see the amazing feat—famous experiment, don't miss it!" He smiled again.

He raised his hand in a friendly farewell, turned his camel onto the dusty path, and trotted toward the river's shore where a dozen tall-sail boats awaited him.

AMMAR AND FAWZI

Fawzi returned to the inn breathless.

"Bassam is nowhere," he announced.

Ammar stood up from his chair. "Nowhere?"

"No sign, no suspicion, nothing," Fawzi said. "I've asked everywhere."

"Could Rakbah's men have . . .?" Ammar could not bring himself to finish the question. "No, certainly not. They wouldn't know who Bassam is, and they have no reason to suspect we're pursuing them."

"I wonder the same," Fawzi said. "The village is too small anyway. Anyone would notice. There's got to be another answer—"

Ammar hurried his things together. "He left with his sword. I'm not as worried about an ambush or thieves as I am the passions of an angry young man thinking to take this on himself."

"Would he be so foolish...?" Fawzi wondered.

"Not foolish, but passionate, yes, very," Ammar said. "I should have dealt with this more carefully. I noticed he has been unusually quiet these last few weeks. I wonder if he decided to give chase, either to find Rasha or kill the man responsible. Our young Bassam has been different since the Taklamakan. It changed him."

"Yes, yes, the desert," Fawzi said. "But that's not the same as hunting down a band of kidnappers skilled at finding ransom."

"Certainly not," Ammar said. "We need to learn about last night."

"I'll go downriver and meet you in an hour," Fawzi said. "Find me if you learn anything."

"Sir!" Fawzi called to a man directing workmen at a boat. "I'm seeking a young man, just taller than me, 17, 18 years old, from the high deserts, a long sword on his side."

The old sailor shook his head.

Next, he stopped to talk to a pair of guards watching the pier. They were busy collecting dock fees and didn't want to be bothered.

"I'm searching for my companion, a young man 17 years old, dressed for the caravan. Have you . . .?"

"Not today," one of them said. "You might try down there, the portage trail," he said pointing. "They were unloading before dawn. They might have seen something."

Fawzi hurried down the path. Six boats were tied to stakes and men labored to load them with bundles and sacks.

"A question for any of you!" he called out. "I'm looking for my friend, a young man from the east, just taller than me, a long sword to his side."

The loaders stopped to look, then continued about their business. But one man remained in place, rubbing his whiskers then stepped forward.

"Man," he called. "I came here late last night and left my boat over there on shore, you see the track? This morning it is gone," he said. "Did your friend take it? If he did I must be paid. I am missing it for my return trip. Much business lost, and much money. You must pay if he stole it."

Fawzi looked downriver. "If my friend took your boat then we'll pay you, but I must find him first," he said.

"There's only one way to find out," the trader said. "Go down river to the fourth cataract. Four days, three if you row hard. He has a head start, but it is my boat, *my boat*. You must pay me!"

"Not so fast, friend," Fawzi said. "You should have tied it up, not left it lying around on the shore. Why, anybody could take it. Why didn't you use the slip? Everyone else did."

"It was late—no animals, no help," the man said, growing angry.

"Even the river could be your thief," Fawzi said, growing annoyed. "If my friend has taken your boat, and if I find it, I'll pay you." Then he hurried up the path to find Ammar.

A thousand possibilities raced through Fawzi's head. "Perhaps our Bassam did decide this mission was his alone," he thought. "It may well be—for his Rasha. Would I do the same? Perhaps. Oh Bassam, now I must find you and save you from yourself, bat brains. Oh, when will you ever learn?"

HOUSE OF KHNUM

Just as Nehi had suggested, I bought passage with a caravan to pass the great cataract to Cyene. It was the right choice as passage on the river was poor. Halfway to Cyene we were visited by boatmen who told us the river was high enough at that place. Some of our company continued on land, I opted for the boat. The craft was wide with a shallow keel, nicely designed for low-water travel.

I was on the boat for almost two days. Perhaps the camels would have been faster, but on the boat I could walk about, sleep, and catch my meals fresh by hook and net. I didn't like the infrequent stops at river ports while the shippers moved their goods. I was impatient with their casual motions, as if their sense of haste feared the pyramids more than they feared the anxiety of my worried quest.

Late on the first day, a family boarded with a young boy about twelve years of age. He introduced himself as Irsu, and befriended me right away. Both of us were anxious to fight our boredom. His parents were glad for the diversion and didn't seem to mind their son consorting with a friendly stranger.

Despite our language barriers we communicated rather well. Irsu had a board game he wanted to play, and I was delighted for the distraction.

"It's called Senet," Irsu said. "A game about dying."

"Death?" I exclaimed. "What happy play is this?"

"It's not hard, just a game of passing to the next life," he said. "Don't die with evil giving chase to curse you," he explained.

"I don't intend to!" I said, patting my heart. "How does this work?"

Irsu's game consisted of a rectangular board a cubit long. It had three long rows, each divided into 10 squares. We took turns moving the pawns through all 30 squares with little clay figures.

Senet was more complicated than I thought. Each time I moved my pieces into the second row, Irsu promptly replaced my front piece with his own, removing my piece back to the beginning. His face glowed with delight that he bested someone so much older than himself.

"You beat me again!" I laughed, pushing him on the shoulder. "I don't know how many more of these defeats I can take!"

"You are a slow learner," he laughed.

Early in the day we passed Pilak Island with large beautiful temples honoring the gods of the Nilus. We saw pillars, tall and majestic, standing perfectly straight along long porches of stone. Their capitals depicted the water plants—the lily and papyrus. They bore the weight of enormous stone slabs.

"How did they lift those all the way up there?" I asked.

"We're a creative people," Irsu's father said. "They used ramps for pulling, canals for floating, towers for cradling."

Even from that far away I could see their beautiful artistry carved into the pillars and walls, hundreds of tales and histories, bragging accomplishments and pleadings to their god Khnum for another good year of sowing and harvesting. I wanted to explore.

"Bad place," the father said. "Too many cobras make their nests in those temples, but there will be more to see. For now it is best from a boat."

Approaching Cyene was a curious study in opposites. The scorched honey-colored sand hills to the west were covered with strange barren structures carved from the rock itself, and others rising with rows of sun-baked mud bricks—bleak, unfinished, broken to ruins. The intelligent artistry of the more noble temples was missing from these block houses.

"Tombs of the nobles, that's why they're different," Irsu's father said. "Not much power, do you see it?"

It was a desolate place. The hills rose high enough for a panoramic view of the river but were also eroded, proving it a dead place for dead people and dead memories. We passed them without much notice. Just beyond the necropolis we found ourselves maneuvering around small lush islands and grassy mounds. The shore was crowded with great rounded stones and swaying palms. It was, at last, the first cataract.

There were temples everywhere, and ruins of temples—an amazing city of ancient glory and power as far as the eye could see. My new friends tried to explain the significance. Most of it was lost to me. I was enamored by the magnificence of their engineering and elegance. They stood in defiance, as if to challenge the gods themselves.

"And this is the Temple of Khnum," Irsu's father announced with pride, pointing to a large block structure with ornate battlements atop its walls. "It's an important temple to plead our cause, for the flood, for a good enrichment of soil, a good harvest—the worship and appeasement of Khnum."

We floated past a large doorway cut in the temple's wall that was framed in stone. Leading out were steps cut into the stone right down to the river.

"To measure the water—do you see it?" he asked. I saw that each step had a large number on it. "To measure the mud," he said.

"The mud?"

"They read the clarity of the water, the sediments. The darker the water the better the harvest, and pharaoh taxes the people according to it—and this he does months before the water is receded, before the land is even dry! Months before the sowing! Months before harvesting! It's clever of him, but the people do not approve. Dark water means rich harvests and more silver into pharaoh's treasury. These are the many gifts of Khnum, and pharaoh taxes us for them."

As we passed the end of the island, I saw lining the shore clumps of massive gray rounded rocks rising ominously at the water's edge. "Look at that," I said. "Like so many lahpaš herded together to drink!"

Irsu's father smiled. "Indeed, that is its name," he said. "Anciently it was Abu, our word for lahpaš. The Greeks changed it to Elephantine, the name of this Island. It's famous for the ivory trade. All of it must pass here for inspection and fees. They keep an army in garrison to enforce it."

Across the river we passed dozens of green farms and orchards. Even in this oppressive heat their laborers were hard at work.

"You see? They finish for the season," he said. "They prepare for the three months of no labor when the flood comes."

I licked my dry lips. The heat was taking a toll. Oh Humam, where is your goat fat now?

"It's such a hot place," I said.

"Yes, the water, the Nilus—the only salvation for man and beast for a thousand stadia. That's all, no magic—it is, simply, the water!"

Perhaps Irsu's father was right about me acting the ignorant tourist. What would Fawzi say to me at times like this? Probably poke my ribs and say, "Oh Bassam you big lahpaš brain! Go pack your trunk and leave."

I missed my friends. I might have told them my plans, but at the time I *had* no plans. Ammar is too methodical, Fawzi too abrupt. They act much the part of old men. But they're my dear friends. Were they faring well? Certainly they would've discerned my actions. Certainly, they'd be hot on my trail. If not, I pray God's protection, not to worry or be angry with their younger brother. Perhaps Fawzi is right—I am just a lahpaš brain. But lahpaš is tenacious. If they want to help me rescue Rasha, they have to catch me.

KIYA

We arrived at the river port of Cyene where I bade goodbye to Irsu and his family. The trip had been gentle enough but the warnings were true—a few rapids, the occasional scrape against boulders, some short stretches of sand bars dragging the keel. Even so, it was a calmer part of the river—I was glad to be in Cyene.

Upon stepping from the boat an overwhelming sense of loss and loneliness washed over me as a cold chill. It was an enormous task I had set in front of me, and I stood wondering. Where to begin? It was a strange land, a strange language, a wide and unknown path.

"It's risky to follow the crowd, Bassam," I said to myself. That was Zafir talking, telling me about mindless conformity. "When you follow the crowd, remember always that you go no farther than the crowd— therefore, my son, execute all of your choices with thoughtful purpose."

My purpose, then, is to get into the city center. And if the crowd can take me there, then it is a purposeful choice. Perhaps I'll find those who can direct me forward, to the steward of Abdali-ud-din.

An hour later I passed through a long avenue of 30 or 40 ancient pillars, some as tall as a tree, others fallen into pieces. Strange figure writings covered them all. The anxious trade of modern commerce busied itself acting forgetful of the empire that these monuments represented. "Ammar will love it here," I smiled.

For several stadia the sprawling city hugged the Nilus. It rested on a great granite plateau with sparse patches of green and clusters of trees. Manual irrigation with the old Persian wheel was in full operation, methodically drawing water to fill canals and water the fields.

Scars in the surrounding hills bore evidence of quarrying, the birth place of red granite blocks for the temple builders. Who could count the millions of stones hauled away over the centuries, making deep pits deeper and flat hills larger. It was a place I wanted to visit again with time to explore, when my errand was not so urgent.

But now I had to find Narmer the steward.

I made my first inquiry at the shop of a businessman whose shelves were filled with imported glass and metal works. The proprietor was kind to my plight and knew exactly the name of Narmer and his home.

Half an hour's walk north, I found myself among farms and orchards. The home of Narmer and Kiya sat behind a lush garden surrounded by a squat brick wall. *Keeps the goats out,* I thought, *but welcomes the strangers.*

I rapped on the door and Kiya answered. "May I help you?"

"Uh, yes, hello!" I said. "My name is Bassam. I'm looking for Narmer, a steward for Abdali-ud-din?"

She was kind but curious.

"You know my husband?"

"Your husband!" I said. "Then you must be Kiya?"

Her smile relaxed. "Yes, I am Kiya, have we met?"

"It's a long story, but an urgent one, may I share it?"

Over a sweet-cake and tea I unfolded the story of Rasha and her kidnapping, and how we interrupted my great business trip with Zafir to rescue her.

"And so I journey to Noph in search of Rasha and the men Jabari and Rakbah who have kidnapped her," I said.

"And you wonder if I have seen her?" Kiya asked.

"Oh yes, any sign of her? She's about my age, a little younger, long black hair to here, slender . . ."

"We have many visitors all the time," she said, "young and old, coming with others, parents, traveling companions, young husbands passing through to set up a business. My husband is constantly busy helping them. Perhaps he will remember someone like your Rasha."

"May I talk to him?"

"When he returns," she said, waving her arm to the south. "He's away on business, and should be back in 3-4 weeks. But that's not soon enough for you, is it?"

"Sadly I must be on my way," I told her. "If you haven't seen her, I must hurry to Noph."

"Rasha—A beautiful name," she said.

"Yes, after her mother."

"Is she alone?" Kiya asked?

"No, another man is helping her."

"No, there is no one by that name come calling," she said, "but I'll certainly be watching. We do our best to help travelers when we can. There have been many in recent months."

"And no one named Rasha," I repeated.

"No," she said. "I'm so sorry. I'll watch for her and I'll ask around. Perhaps others can help."

Her countenance brightened. "Do not lose hope, Bassam! Noph is large, a place where evil may hide. You should continue your search. If the men you seek want a hiding place, it is in Noph. Look for the steward there—Pepi. He will help you. He's Egyptian, a short man, about this tall, thin, gray beard, brown skin, funny sense of humor," she said measuring his height at around my center chest. "You won't miss him. He teases my husband about his fair skin and hair. 'I am well baked, you are not,' he says. 'But be patient my friend, Egypt will cook you just right. Then will you be perfect!'" At that we both laughed.

Her words were encouraging. Perhaps I had raised my hopes too high. How could I expect Kiya to remember just one young stranger from hundreds? But then Rasha is one out of a hundred, a million— no one could miss her face, her lovely presence, her kindly spirit, her energy and tease. For that I would continue my promise to God to listen for his guidance.

"Have you a place to sleep?" she asked.

"Oh no, I couldn't," I protested. "I'll find an inn for tonight, or . . ."

"Nonsense," she said, waving away my objection. "I'll have Betresh make up the bed in the guest room."

"But I'm filthy on the trail these many weeks, and . . ."

"The road from Kurgus? Yes, yes, everyone is dirty and skinnier after such a trip. My goodness, Bassam," she said laughing. "How much harder will you make this for me? Come, I'll show you the room upstairs and you may clean yourself at the well. It's a short walk to the orchard. Come, I'll show you from the window." She stood with her arm extended. "Evening meal in an hour. We need to fatten you up! And there's a moon out so you can find your way there to wash. Don't get lost. Betresh will have the meal ready when you return."

FRESH OLD FRUIT

The night air was filled with the pleasant smell of cut grasses from harvested grain fields and desert fragrances drifting softly over the ridge of the hill. By moonlight I could follow the path easily. It led beyond the well between some shrubs and wove itself along the slow rise of a shallow hill.

All the land was bathed in the moon's brilliant glow. I squinted into the sky, noting the moon was full, giving the landscape the feel of some faraway fantasy land devoid of earthly color and life.

I continued past several rows of stacked stones scattered among the trees, ancient dwellings once home for someone here, but now in ruins—overgrown and forgotten.

I loved the quiet and the fresh outdoors. The scene was perfect—a sparkling night sky, a friendly moon, warm breeze, and pleasant perfumes of nature's cycles. Negotiating my way around a hedge I stepped on something large and round that gave way under my foot.

What is this? It was a squashed fruit flattened under my sandal. A sweet tartness wafted into the air.

"What is that delicious sweet?" I wondered, picking a piece to examine. "Is there more?"

An old hedge to my right was broken open in one place and I could see a couple of paces beyond it the gnarly, twisted limbs of a sturdy little tree. It stood thrice my height and bore few leaves. It scratched at the night sky with five old limbs, like crooked fingers reaching for the stars. Its stark branches appeared long since dead, but its curious shape made me stop.

"It looks like a hand reaching for heaven," I mused. "Is this moonlight playing tricks on me?"

At the end of one low hanging branch, a cluster of leaves nested a white-skinned fruit the size of my fist just like the one I had stepped on. It looked enticingly ripe.

"I need to try this," I said. Without even touching it, the fruit fell right into my outstretched hand. "Oh my!" I exclaimed. "It's harvest time for this old tree. Do I know this fruit?" I smelled it then took a small, cautious bite. The thin skin broke easily and sweet juices flowed around my lips. "Pleasant! Delicious!" I whispered, and took a second bite.

The mellow flavor was lightly sweet, pleasant to the tongue, satisfying and refreshing. "Not too much, not too little," I said. "Thank you, Mother Tree. I'll discover your goodness when the sun is up. This will make my night go better," and I continued my stroll under the beautiful night lights.

When I reached the top of the hillside, I had eaten the fruit to its core.

"White," I observed, turning the pit around in my palm. "I'll look at this closer in the sunlight," and I tucked it away in my robe.

I glanced at the moon. "I'd better get back."

Day 791
My Dearest Rasha,
*   I have arrived at the first cataract and found a good friend in the family of the steward who live here. The wife gave me room and food. It's a hot, dry place.*

I have asked about for you. Did I miss finding you? No one has seen you. Are you somewhere south in hiding? I pray to God every day and night you are safe. I won't rest until you are safe and Rakbah is dead.

—Bassam

PURSUIT

"Rowing the Nilus," Fawzi grumbled, pulling the oars. "Makes me feel like a galley slave on a Roman long boat. Why can't the wind blow with us? It's like every cubit forward is two cubits back."

Ammar smiled. "No, you're making excellent progress. I'll take my turn..."

"Not yet," he said. "Not for a while. At least the current is going our way."

"There's a season when the wind does blow north," Ammar said.

"Let me guess—It's any other time except right now?"

"Right!" Ammar said. "You'll get help in a few days when the Nilus turns west, about half way between the fourth and fifth cataracts."

"I know that tone in your voice, Ammar," he said. "That's a good-news, bad-news announcement. What's the bad news?"

"No bad news," Ammar said. "If we're on the right path, and if he did decide to continue north, I'm just wondering what path he took."

"Okay, what paths could he take?"

"There should be some villages that rent overland camels to bypass the river's great loop," Ammar said, holding up the map and pointing so Fawzi could see. "See here? Turns south, west, and the caravans cross the Nub'an desert through here. It's a horrible land—high risk, much death."

"That sounds like exactly what Bassam would choose," Fawzi said. "What else?"

"After the fourth cataract is another overland road to bypass the river's bend, though not used as much," Ammar said. "This one joins the Nilus one or two days below the third cataract."

"What's after that? Good rowing north for another month, I hope."

"That's where our young Bassam may have difficulty," Ammar said.

"Why?"

"From this second bypass there's another 150 stadia to reach the second cataract, but it's the most difficult section of the entire river."

"All right, I give up," Fawzi said. "What are the horrors I don't want to hear about?"

"Just before the second cataract, The Belly of Stones," Ammar said.

"Oh, that sounds just great," Fawzi said. "And how long is that stretch?"

"A thousand stadia, give or take."

"A thousand?" Fawzi exclaimed. "That's no river, that's torture."

"Yes—not passable this time of the year."

"That would be an awfully long slip-way," Fawzi whistled.

"Or canals. I'm told most people go over land from here, to other boats on the far side of the cataract."

"So the time to sail is, what, another few months?"

"Next month," Ammar said, dragging his finger along his map.

Fawzi shook his head in disgust. "If Bassam has anything more in his brain than great mounds of black bat dung, he would ask around before jumping at those cataracts."

"Agreed. Let's go to shore at that village and ask. Maybe we can second-guess our friend and catch him before he encounters trouble he can't handle alone."

ALOLI

They said the trip from Cyene to Noph is 17 days in normal weather, on normal water, with normal loads. That wasn't good enough for me. My impatience was agonizing. I paced the deck more than I slept, and I slept more than I ate.

Twice a day, sometimes three, I offered to take an oar to hurry our time, but they scolded me each time into retreat.

"I have urgent business in Noph," I told the captain. "It's life or death!"

He acknowledged my angst but explained his men were rowing as steady as they could. "Fastest way," he said. "Better to make hours of back-breaking labor than hurry the oars only to make men fatigue."

He was right.

I found myself seated in the same place by the railing near the bow. I watched the keel ply through the water as the current carried twigs and grasses rushing past us. I couldn't believe this large boat could go so slow that even the river was quicker.

I passed the time composing letters to Rasha in my head.

"My dearest Rasha, Are these the same scenes that you saw in your distress with Rakbah? Did you see them going to the north or coming south? I have hunted for you in Upper Egypt. Will I find you near?"

The oarsmen pulled to a tune they sang among themselves, sometimes with a drum to push them along. The repeated pattern became a measurement of stroke and duration, like the men who built the wall in C'ina. After a few hours, I found myself humming along.

The passing land held little but flat monotony. An occasional pyramid could be seen in the distance—small, large, sometimes in a group. One man told me there are more than 100 in Egypt, but counting them from the boat would be only a third.

"You'll miss most of them for the trees and papyrus," the man said.

The papyrus stood tall in these waters and stretched across the land for as far as I could see to the horizon—millions of them, a living lake of shimmering silver—enough to make a thousand boats for two thousand warriors to hunt for my Rasha. If only I could wield the power of pharaoh.

"They call it Ta-Mehu," another passenger said, "the land of papyrus."

Of such hopes were my dreams made, finding rescue for my Rasha and bringing her to safety. It was eating at me, made worse that I was powerless. The long hours left me vulnerable to imaginations that were dark and evil, and whipped my passions into an angry procession of hate and vengeance and rage. I was left exhausted after a bout of such mental duels. Then I'd revisit them again. I had distressed myself for so long it was beginning to violate my idle thoughts. I renewed my deepest resolve to not get distracted again. Rasha needed me.

Day 798

My dearest Rasha,

Tonight I witnessed a scene so beautiful, that only in Egypt could such a calming majesty unfold. I so wish you were with me to see it. We rowed into a long stretch of no bends where papyrus thinned to sandy shore and long rows of palms stood still to either side. The sun was sitting low, almost touching, making the layers of thin clouds boil into yellow and orange. The deep blue sky framed the images intact like a painting—rich, full, alive, breathtaking. And right there, exactly where the sun was setting, some thousands of stadia away rose the perfect dimensions of a distant pyramid, seated flatly on the horizon. Its pointed apex met the sun exactly on its tip, perfectly balanced, holding it from setting for just a few amazing moments. Then dipping behind, it became eclipsed, igniting golden rays of sunshine that radiated outward across the sky like a flaming fan of shimmering light, lasting for several counts of the oarsmen's draw. All of us watched in silence, absorbing the spectacular ending to another long day's journey down the Nilus. Had I a brush and paints I would have spent the night capturing it forever.

—Bassam

On Day 5 the nimits found me. They acted pleased to add me to their menu. They didn't just sting, they bit hard enough to draw blood. I continually swat them dead, but other nimits come looking to see what all that excitement is about and the torment continues. The locals didn't seem bothered.

On Day 6 I met a girl named Aloli and her little brother, Adjo. They were traveling with an escort named Bast to Ale'ksandria. We made fast friends and exchanged stories about our different quests. During one afternoon of idle talk, I noticed Adjo playing with a sling. It reminded me I wanted to learn.

"Would you teach me?" I asked.

He was bashful and grinned, then handed it to Aloli, pointing to her.

"All right then," I said. "Aloli, could you teach me the sling?"

"You don't know how to sling?" she asked, surprised. "How is it you are a great defender of a caravan and haven't learned the sling?"

"I suppose it's because we don't have much opportunity to use them," I said. "When the enemy comes, he comes fast in a cloud of dust, his sword drawn."

She thought a moment, conjuring the circumstance in her imagination.

"A camel is no good. It's better when you're on foot," she said. "But I will teach you."

"And I suppose you swing it around your head until it's going as fast as you can?"

"Not at all," she said. "Once is enough so you don't lose your aim. Treat the strings like making your arm longer—release the string where you release a rock at a lion's head."

"Like a lion's head," I mumbled, whirling it around a few times. I envisioned a lion charging me, then swung it hard toward the rail, making a swooshing sound.

"That's good!" Aloli said. "Try it with a stone, the weight helps."

That night the four of us went to market for food and materials to make a sling. We found a nice spool of hemp for a deben. Aloli said that would be fine for a beginner, then pointed out a diner for evening meal. The offerings were uniquely Egyptian. Aloli ordered tubers of the tiger nut, cooked eggs, jamiid cheese, and barley bread. Her brother wanted fish, which came with a mass of greens, onions, garlic, figs and dates, celery, palm nuts. I went for chicken, and Bast ordered her favorite— nabk berries with honey in goat milk.

"What awaits you in Ale'ksandria?" I asked.

"My father is in the medical arts," she said, "and has taken residence there to improve his skills. We go to join him."

"Very good for you and him!" I replied. "You must miss him a lot. Humam is our medical expert for the caravan, and it seems there's no end to the knowledge he must consume to be of best help."

"That's my father's life," she said. "But he's different from the others."

"In what way?"

"He believes the body has many solutions to its trauma. He looks for its own powers to solve problems, while others turn to the gods with spells and enchantments."

I was thrilled to hear this. "Your father is the kind of man I want helping me," I said. I relayed my injuries from the knife wound and other cuts and sprains, some stomach ailments after Fawzi pranked my food with an herb.

"Yes, and that's why he's in Ale'ksandria," she said. "He tells us the study is good—herbs, plants, mixtures of different powders. It's all a mystery to me, but those solutions work better than appealing to Ra." She looked around sheepishly to see if anyone had heard her heresy.

I smiled. "My good friend visited a medical man who used needles to correct his broken leg," I said.

"Did it heal?

"It certainly did! It took almost nine months, but he's walking almost as good as new."

"Then I'll tell my father of it," she said. "There's much knowledge— my father is hoping Ale'ksandria will help him find it."

"Then it is settled. When I come to Ale'ksandria, I'll look for your father, and Aloli, Adjo, and Bast. I'll bring my worst ailments for your father to resolve. So how do I pay? May I pay him with camels or would you like instead my slave Fawzi?"

She looked at me confused and then laughed. "You own a slave? Is he a good slave?"

"The camels are good, but Fawzi? He's stinky and fat. He sits around on his brains all day and calls for his mommy," I said. "And he picks his nose. Disgusting."

"Then I'm sure he would be a good trade," she laughed, and broke another bread.

SLING

I took most of Day 7 to finish making my sling.

"Oh my goodness Bassam!" Aloli said. "You do fast work. You're good at this."

"I have good teachers," I said, thinking as much about Zafir's patient guidance through sewing the scroll bag as what Aloli showed me. "Now I need to give it a try. Will you show me?"

I had 30 small stones gathered from shore. Aloli placed one in the pouch, faced the railing, then turned to her right.

"Addressing your target correctly is important," she said. "A teacher told me to practice on a circle in the sand. Divide the circle into 12 equal sections and number them. The direction of your target is number 12, but you face 2."

I watched her arrange herself.

"At number 2. Do you see it?"

And then she quickly spun the sling and the rock went flying 50 cubits across the water and plopped.

"Nice work!" I said. "Show me again."

After several days, my skill at slinging had greatly improved. When we reached No-Amon, I could hit almost any target within 20 cubits.

"You've got a really good aim," Aloli said.

"Maybe . . . but I still couldn't hit the broadside of a riverhorse!"

"I suppose that depends on how close she was," Aloli said smiling. She had no idea what horrible memory sprang to life. A rock in deb's face would just make him angrier.

Adjo had warmed up to me over the past few days. He was treating me like a trusted older brother, and one day brought his collection of slings and projectiles to show.

"And this one is made of lead," he said, proudly handing an oval bullet with engravings on its sides. A winged thunderbolt was cast in its side with some writings on the other.

"What do these say?" I asked.

"Sister knows," and he handed it to Aloli.

"Oh, yes," she said. "These are gifts from our father, from the Greeks. This inscription with the thunderbolt means 'take that,' and on the other side, see these figures, father says they mean 'catch.' Very funny for a bullet meant to kill you."

GEBTU

Two days sailing past No-Amon we came to a great departing place named Gebtu. It was here that I gained the first glimmer of hope I was on the right track to find my Rasha.

It was dusk when we pulled to shore and tied off to an expansive pier. Many large boats were there, already in the throes of unloading.

Aloli had traveled to Gebtu and became my guide.

"An important place," she said as we stretched our legs and looked for a place to eat.

"They tell me every place in Egypt is important," I said.

"It depends in what century you want to live," she said. "This is where the trading and mining expeditions left for the Egyptian Sea, an important part of history for a long time."

"The Egyptian Sea?" I said with renewed interest. "This is the shortest route?"

"Well, yes, is that not good?" she asked.

"No, no, it's just fine," I said looking eastward. "Tell me more, please!"

She explained that there were two main roads for the sea. One went north to a coastal village called Myos Hormos. That port city had a major trading pier where commerce traveling for the north could be transported over land to the West Sea. That was the quickest way to the Romans and Greeks. It was also the route that long-haul trains took when returning from the high deserts.

"That's the way to Rekeem," I told her.

"The high deserts?"

"My home."

"The other road is longer going south," she said. "There's a port about halfway down the coast named Berenice. From there the ships depart to 'Adan, the Indus and C'ina. Do you know of them?"

Two roads east—this could be the place Rasha might escape to the coast! I created a map in my mind showing caravans choosing between two directions. Was Shamar taking my Rasha north or south? If Rakbah had overcome them, what would his black heart decide? Yes, this could be the crossroads. Perhaps the shoremen had seen—?

"Bassam?" Aloli said shaking my sleeve.

"Sorry, I was thinking," I said. "I'll need to excuse myself tonight. You and Adjo find some dinner. I've got to leave for a while."

Bast smiled. "Are you sure, Bassam? You've got to eat something—"

"Thank you, you're kind, but I have things to do. I'll see you on the boat tomorrow," and excused myself.

The boardwalk was empty of traffic except for three guards leaning on a large empty cart, and done for the day. They were chewing something and pointing up the river.

"Sirs!" I called as I approached.

They looked at me carefully.

"Sirs!" I said again. "I'm looking for someone, a girl about 15 years, fair skin, long black hair, from the high deserts who speaks that tongue."

The men looked around, shaking their heads.

"Sorry," one of them said. "They come from everywhere. We don't give any of them much heed unless they make trouble."

"Ah! Then maybe—" I paused, thinking about the right way to ask about Shamar or Rakbah and his men.

"I'm also looking for pair of bad men who must pay for their evil," I said. "One is Jabari, the other Rakbah."

They looked at me blankly as if waiting for a bribe.

"Rakbah is a big man, my height, heavier," I said. "Black beard, scar across his cheek. His hand, his finger is cut off, a distinctive mark," I said.

"The finger?" the first man said.

"Yes! Cut right off."

"To about here?" he said pointing to his own hand. "The pointer finger?"

"Yes, yes! Cut off there," I exclaimed. "Did you see him?"

"There was such a man here about a week ago," he said. "I only remember because his friends started a fight."

"How many friends?" I asked.

"Oh, three, I think," he said. "They were arguing, then a big fight. We dragged them out and made them pay a fine."

"What way did they go?" I asked.

The one man pointed east to the sea. "They took the north road, right?" he said, looking at his companions.

"No, no," said the third, "I saw them take the boat, sailed north."

"To Noph?" I asked.

"I don't know," he said. "I don't ask, I'm busy here. I have much to do."

"Yes, yes," I said, "I'm sorry. I just need to know. And a black beard, with a large scar on his cheek right here?" I asked pointing at my left cheekbone.

"Well, yes, that's about right," the third man said. "But that finger, I remember it. I was surprised he could hold his sword—seemed pretty angry."

"He pulled a sword?"

"Well, yes, that's why they called for us. Big fight. He wanted to take matters into his own hands."

This sounded like Rakbah—the finger, the beard, the scar, the temper.

"Thank you, thank you!" I said.

"Why do you hunt this man?" asked the first.

"He kidnapped that girl, and I must find them."

"There wasn't any girl," the second said

"Yes, that's right," said the first. "We didn't see any girl when they boarded for Noph. This half-finger man, three other men, but no girl."

SCRATCHED

"Where are you off to now?" Ammar asked.

Fawzi didn't answer. He headed right for that single tall rock, the only real shade near the wells. The miserably hot Mûrr-hàt valley had but one place for shade this close to the water and Fawzi was going to claim it.

He threw down his belongings in the shadow and stood over them like a great cat claiming its kill.

Ammar shook his head. "Fawzi, there are women with this train. They should get the shade."

"Yes, they should," he said, "but they won't. Besides, they hauled those tents. The workers will set them up as usual." With that, he spread out a blanket and kicked off his sandals.

"There's room for you," he said. "Better get your stuff over here. I don't know how these fellows run their schedule, but you better get some rest before we leave again."

Ammar removed the saddle from his camel and dragged it to the shade. "All right," he said. "Move over, I need to sleep."

Fawzi pulled his gear to the other side leaving just enough room for another blanket.

Ammar dropped his things and began smoothing out the wrinkles.

"Oh, Ammar, you are such the woman," Fawzi said, shutting his eyes and rolling to his side.

"It takes an awful lot of work, including a neat blanket for a nap, to spare myself from becoming like you," Ammar said.

Fawzi growled and reached for his bundle, pulling it closer for a pillow. Then, rehearsing his usual errand of caution about scorpions or camel spiders, he glanced at the rock's shady underside for any crawling visitors. That's when he saw it. "What? What's this?"

"What's what?" Ammar said.

Fawzi got up on an elbow and jutted his head back for a better look. "Look at this . . . scratched into the rock."

Ammar leaned closer.

"Do you see it? Isn't that a cross?" Fawzi asked. And the two dots down here," he said, running his fingers over the marks. "That sure looks like . . ."

Ammar laid flat for a better look. "YES! I think it is," he blurted. "And look, Oh! Look at this," he said pointing. "Isn't that a 'B'?"

Fawzi dropped his chin to see. "That's a 'B,' 'B' for Bassam?" Fawzi said smiling.

"Al-kalimat—he remembered it," Ammar said with a surprised smile.

"That big desert donkey butt of the sandiest kind," Fawzi said, grinning his toothy smile. "Our escaped desert dog has left a mark!"

"And those are fresh scratches," Ammar said, running his finger over the cross mark—fragile powdery dust fell onto Fawzi's blanket. "I'm going to ask the driver if he can tell us the last time a caravan made its stop here. Perhaps we can . . ."

"Yes! How many days ahead of us," Fawzi said, and both men stood with hands to eyes, shielding the bright sun.

"Now, just where is that skinny old man?" Ammar asked.

"I'll bet he's dead asleep under one of those tents," Fawzi said. "And snoring like a bloated camel—as usual."

"Babak!" Ammar called. "Where are you, little man? We need to talk."

THE RICKETY BOAT

I switched boats at Gebtu for a smaller one, to be with a crew as anxious to move as me.

"I must be in Noph in one week. Can you do it?" I asked.

"If you'll stop wasting time and get on board," the captain said, "We're wasting light. Ten debens silver, take it or leave."

He was a short man, barrel-chested, heavy black beard, balding head, and smiling eyes—alive, anxious, spirited. This was the hurry-up "do it yesterday" attitude I had been searching for, and surrendered the silvers with gratitude. I even offered my services at the rowing. The captain took note but told me to sit down and stay out of the way. I did, taking a place toward the back near the cargo.

The boat was slender, twelve cubits long, five across, with four men rowing and a rudder station left empty. A long split mast and coiled sail were tucked under the wooden benches.

The load was sizeable but not overbearing—several stacked boxes and baskets covered over with a large net. The captain, the rowers, two other men and myself, were all the passengers the small boat carried.

We pushed off almost immediately upon my arrival. And just like at Kurgus, I was barely on time—and glad for it.

The boat pulled from the pier and quickly steered toward the center currents. I felt the pull grab hold, lunging us forward as the oars began their work. "What's your name?" the captain asked.

"Bassam," I told him. "Rekeem is my home."

"Rekeem, eh? That's the city of caves, am I right? A long way from here. And the scrolls of treasure, right?"

I nodded. "That's home, and the scrolls, yes, I've been taught that story all my life."

The captain smiled and looked at me as if I might know. "They lead to enormous caves filled with the treasures of the ages—caravan riches, bricks of gold, skeps of gems, satchels of stones, only the finest, only the rarest, too much for one man, too much for one nation!"

"So I've heard," I said.

"And you know nothing more?" he asked, eyeing me with suspicion.

"Sir, if I had access to those scrolls, would I be buying a trip from you on this rickety boat that smells of old fish, old goats, and old men?"

He tried to look offended, but it wasn't his nature. He let out a great big laugh, and slapped me on the shoulder.

"Right you are, right you are—'rickety old boat' indeed! Why it's not even a century older than a millennium!"

"This is my crew," he said. "I'm Tachus. I own the boat. I am boss of these old men." The others chuckled.

"Hail Pharaoh," said one.

"Leader of goats, follower of his wife," said another.

"All the same," called another.

Tachus shook a fist and everyone laughed. "A mutinous band of cutthroats, I'll soon throw them to the kroks. It's how I lighten my load," he said. "Just for that, double rations for everyone!" They laughed and made gagging noises.

"Now, here you see Aka and Nekht, rowers on the left, Oshe and Ursha on the right." The four men smiled and raised a hand. "They're good. They'll get us there quickly. And we feed them well. They earn it every day, except for when they sleep. Then they cheat me—you cheat me don't you? You jackals in disguise as dogs!"

The rowers shrugged. By this time I was laughing.

Tachus gestured to the other two passengers. "These old men have bribed me for 12 years to drive them up and down the Nilus. This is Pabas and Ursha. Why they put up with me I wouldn't know, but they force their silver on me and I'm obliged to take it, so it suits us all."

The two men nodded with smiles behind long gray beards—Ursha was frail and elderly. Pabas looked about the same age as Fawzi, in his early forties, healthy, strong, and carried a long sword to his side.

"Father and son, actually," Tachus said. "They see their family in El Silsila for the harvest, and then I hurry them home to Djedefre before the flood, it's their little ritual."

"Then I'm pleased to be a galley slave for Tachus," I said. The others chuckled. "And for the right bribe, I'll tell where the scrolls are hidden."

They all laughed out loud and Tachus slapped me on the back again. "You, Bassam, you are a treasure."

I sat back in my place smiling. This is a great crew, I decided. When the time is right, I might invite them into the work of Abdali-ud-din. Such good-hearted integrity is hard to find.

Some two hours had expired according to the sun shadows, and Ursha produced a pouch of jerked goat meat.

"This goat meat is Ursha's offering to the gods that his move to home is a safe one," Tachus said.

"A kind offer, and good meat," I said.

"At sundown, the moon guides us on the river," Tachus said. "We'll continue north for another few hours, then we'll rest. It is how we do it."

Tachus produced his knife and a piece of wood that appeared to fit as part of the rudder. His was a repair work to create new from old. "Tell me Bassam, you have a look of pursuit in your eye. Do we help or hinder you?"

"You help me a great deal," I said.

"Will you tell me of your quest?" Tachus asked. "You don't need to, but I'm happy to make new friends and help where I can."

I thought a moment and wondered just how much I could safely share with him. He might benefit me if he understood.

"There's a wicked man," I began, "a murderous man in Lower Egypt. Perhaps I'm just behind him. Many months ago he attacked our Rekeem."

"Ah, yes," Tachus said. "I have heard of this. The Tauri. We all thought them disbanded until news came. A terrible attack. Did you suffer from it?"

"I was away when it happened," I said. "I have come to find a girl who was kidnapped and brought here for ransom."

"Who is this girl?" He asked.

"Her name is Rasha. She's the youngest daughter of Zafir. Perhaps you have heard of Zafir?" I asked.

"Not Zafir," Tachus said. "Should I know him?"

"He's a chief with Abdali-ud-din," I said.

"I know of the great Abdali-ud-din," Tachus said. "They do a lot of business in Egypt. So, she has been brought here?"

"That's what we were told," I said. "Zafir dispatched me and two others to find her."

"Do you know where to begin your search?" he asked.

"We came ashore from Avalites," I said, "thinking it faster to start there and search north if she was going south, to find them somewhere in the middle."

"Avalites!" Tachus exclaimed. "My fire-breathing gods of the netherworld and beyond! You have been traveling a long way for a long while, my young friend. This is no small quest. Where are the others?"

"They follow behind," I said. "I hope we'll meet in Noph."

"Then you have the best boat to get you there, this rickety old boat," he said.

I laughed. "Well, it's done you good this far!"

He smiled and put his hand on the railing. "We've seen a lot of stadia in this old pot," he said. "So you must tell me, who do you seek, these kidnappers? Have you their names?" he asked.

"They say he's named Rakbah, with three other men, one named Jabari."

"Rakbah? *The* Rakbah?" Tachus said.

I nodded. "I suppose there's only one," I said.

"Oh yes, we know of him—a horrible man. We've heard of his treachery. There are many who want his head," he said. "Big man, a scar on his face, a missing finger. He was seen going downriver a week ago. Word spread quickly but he disappeared before anyone knew it."

I sat tall taking a breath. "You saw him? A week ago? Was he alone?"

"I didn't see him myself, but I was told he had three companions," Tachus said.

He could see disappointment in my face that my Rasha was not mentioned.

"My young friend," Tachus said. "He's a vile man, a clever man, wanted for many crimes for many years. I didn't know he was part of the Tauri. That would explain a great deal."

He looked at his men, then cast his gaze down river. "See those lights? That's as far as we go tonight. We're behind because we left late, but we'll go ashore. My men must rest. Tomorrow we'll leave early. You must be careful with this killer, Rakbah. He's a most cunning man. He has much blood on his hands. But if he took this girl for ransom she must be a great treasure. Otherwise, he would not have let her live. You can be sure that he has her put away some place while he maneuvers his plan. That's how he works. Have courage and peace, my friend."

STONING THE SHADOW

I passed the daylight hours practicing my sling. Each time I wound up to let one fly, the boat would absorb the throw by rocking, a disturbing motion that awakened the complaints of others. Aka suggested I practice another way.

"Sit in the back," he said. "Launch your bullets directly behind us. Every throw will help propel us forward, and you won't rock us side to side. Try it!"

It was a great idea. Straddling the keel-board by the rudder guide, I set a good stance, rotated a sixth away as Aloli had taught me, and my wild flailing bothered no one. I picked for targets any passing flotsam—sometimes a stick or a lily, and worked them to perfect my aim. I was getting pretty good and could almost decide what part of a target to hit—if they were close enough. My confidence grew with this simple little weapon.

"Now you qualify as goat herder!" Oshe said between pulls on his oar.

"Oh? How is that?"

"Unless you're David of old, don't expect to fell a man. But scare some goats? That's what you've learned!"

I still didn't understand, though he was smiling as he rowed.

"The herders," he said, "They keep their goats in line by tossing a small rock or a shower of pebbles just beyond where a goat wanders. It scares them back, and they return to the herd."

"Oh!" I said. "I always wondered how they kept such herds together. That's a nice trick."

"Sheep are different," he said. "They are content to follow their shepherd and his call. But brainless goats? They are like you, Bassam! They wander away on their own—and get into all sorts of trouble."

Oshe didn't know it, but he was more correct than he could possibly know.

Our trip on the river grew quickly routine and I felt the boredom come to pester me. My slinging was greatly improved and it was tested just two days later in a very real and lethal way.

It was dark except for the sparkling jewels spread across the sky, their patience reflected a thousand times on the dark water. The moon was late tonight, but we could see he was on his way—maybe another hour. Tachus ordered that we continue in the dark until the moon could help, and then, to row a few hours more. "The ruler of the night could let us continue another few hours north," he said. "This is how we get you there in a week."

We traveled without lantern so the rowers could better watch the black silhouette of the palms on shore to keep us on course.

We had just entered a turn when the shores narrowed and the water rushed faster. The men struggled to stay in the middle current. They shouted orders back and forth as we all peered into the black, blindly calling out obstacles and direction. Our only reliable reference points were the stars, and I clung to the railing as we rocked side to side. Right after the bend, we were suddenly dumped into quieter waters. The shores pulled far to both sides, and black flatlands rolled out in all directions. From that vantage we could see to the east a slight white glow growing above the horizon. The moon was not far behind.

Just then Oshe shouted an alarm.

"To the right, to the right, Attack! Attack!"

Appearing from nowhere two black shadows were coming right at us.

Aka dug his oar in the water making us pivot hard left, then all four pulled hard away from the approaching mystery. Our boat was too slow in the turn and suddenly with a great shouting roar the pirates were upon us. The first boat bumped into ours and the attackers threw ropes and hooks. A man tried to lunge but missed and splashed into the black water. There was shouting and yelling, and in that confusion I had just enough time to rack a stone and take aim at the shadows. I spun the sling and let the rock fly as hard as I could. There was no sound of contact, but a man screamed out in pain. It gave me courage.

The men of Tachus waved their oars at anything moving, and we unhooked the ropes as quickly as we heard them go taut. I racked another stone and threw it at the other shadow. There was a loud clunk against their boat. I mounted another and let it fly. This time I heard a hard slap sound, then a splash into the water.

Meanwhile, our men were successfully pushing the two boats apart. Another attacker had grabbed an oar and was pulling it from our man when they broke his grip and he splashed into blackness. Two more were at our railing trying to climb aboard but they were beat upon and disappeared.

I let fly another rock into the shouting and a man let out a sharp groan and went quiet.

Tachus shouted back. "Is that you, Bassam?"

"Yes!" I said breathlessly and let fly another. Another man shouted out in pain.

"Keep it up boy!" he shouted. "Let 'em fly!"

Each time I hit flesh, an attacker let out a scream—the sound helped me target my next throw. It was like they were telling me where in the dark to point my aim.

The encounter didn't last more than one minute, if that. After another three or four more stones, we heard more whimpering and then heard paddles in the water moving away from us into the dark.

My heart pounded. I could hardly catch my breath. I just stood there with my sling loaded and ready.

"Are they gone?" I whispered.

"Listen," Tachus said. There was distant moaning and cursing, some hushed, hurried talking, and paddles scraping the sides of their boats as they retreated into the shadows.

A sense of cautious exhilaration began to settle.

"I didn't know there were pirates on the Nilus!" I exclaimed.

"That's the first in a long time," one man said.

"Our boat was faster," said another.

"It's Bassam," said a third. "His sling! Not a goat-herder's sling after all!"

"Indeed!" said the first. "A lethal weapon."

"We need to get one of those," said another.

"Bassam, you risked your neck for us and drove them off!" Tachus said.

"Well, I suppose I discouraged them," I said, putting my hand to the hilt of the sword of Suoud. I was relieved that I didn't have to use that in the dark—sword fighting creates a much more dangerous selection of targets.

"Discouraged them?" Tachus laughed. "I expect Queen Krok is dining right as we speak, thanks to your sling."

The other men laughed and began chatting more casually. I sat down at my usual place in the back, my arms and legs shaking from panic. I felt the cool of the night bring a shiver. The rising moon was now visible and cast a million soft reflections across the Nilus behind us. I could see that no man or boat was in the water to follow.

"Let's not tempt the kroks," I said. "Let's just keep going, hard and fast."

Deep inside I knew things should have gone badly. I vowed to keep this encounter a secret. I felt positive we were watched over by powers unseen, and for that I needed to express my sincerest gratitude, and not be tempted to boast. We were, after all, outmanned at least two to one by bandits more experienced in nighttime water raids than we were in defending ourselves. We should have perished.

A few hours later we entered a beautiful stretch of river where it grew pleasantly wide. The scene was delightful—its sleeping expanse swelled wide, a black velvet reflection of the starry sky. The gentle light softened the turns and spread the shores far to either side, while the pole star stood calmly in front, beckoning us to follow.

All around was peacefully quiet except for the steady movement of the oars. The moon was brilliantly white and round. Its glistening trail paved a wide highway to shore. I looked hard to see the distant land and could barely discern the scruffy heads of teeny date palms standing dark against the lighter-colored sands. To the west was a distant mountain peak cutting out a perfect black triangle above the great desert sands.

"That's no mountain, is it?" I asked Tachus, pointing into the darkness.

"Indeed!" He said. "Welcome to the mysterious pyramids of ancient Egypt—Lisht, Masghuna, Dahshur, and over there—I think that's Saqqara. And Abusir should be near. Those smaller ones between, I can't identify. Maybe in the daylight."

To me these looked no different than what I had been told of the great tombs of Khufu—man-made stacks of stone echoing a theme that spoke of ancient Egypt in all of its pomp and glory. The distinctive shapes jutted above the gray landscape, sharp and distinct against a backdrop of stars and sandy dunes. Some of them reflected the moonlight in lighter shades of grey, others were pitch black with a mysterious ashen glow.

Signs of human habitation were sparse along these parts, but each was revealed by groves of date palms and man-made walls. Desolation stretched between the habitations. These, too, were scenes distinctly Egyptian. Sometimes the square shape of a village or farm was nested closer to shore, but wisely built on a rise, protected from the annual flood.

"Ordered by the gods," Tachus said.

"What?" I said, caught in thought.

"The villages, their place by the river," he said. "The gods ordered their places. It's their way to endure the coming blessing with the inundation."

The desert air blew softly past our little boat bringing the smells of the dry desert, a delicious reminder that we had returned to the land of sand and dunes. *Oh my Rasha. I am coming, I am closer, can you hear me?* To that gentle thought, the caress of the warm breeze, and the steady rhythm of the rowers' faithful work, I was rocked into a deep and restful sleep.

NOPH AT SUNRISE

I was so grateful to Tachus for pressing his men to hurry. They kept rowing through the night, and just as the moon set, the eastern sky brightened. As promised they had completed the trip to Noph in just a week!

"Then we must part ways," Tachus said.

"I'm most grateful to you and your men," I said, gathering my things.

"We're in your debt," Tachus said. "Had I known I carried Al Murrah on my boat, I would have treated you with more respect."

I shook my head and smiled. "No, that would have been no fun. I know you meant no disrespect. I should have told you sooner. I'll always count you a wonderful friend."

Tachus smiled and shook my hand. "Certainly, and God's blessings on your quest. All of us know you head into danger. All of us want you to find your Rasha and return her to her home in safety."

I had barely stepped out when Pabas rushed right past me with his belongings bundled in his arms, and hurried up the planks. I raised my hand to bid him farewell, but he ignored me as if on a sudden emergency. I looked back to Tachus. He and his men were watching with puzzled looks.

"What about your father?" Tachus called after him. "Should we continue without you?"

Pabas hardly looked back and raised a hand as if to give consent and disappeared.

I looked at Tachus and shrugged. He watched a moment longer, then bent down to exchange words with Ursha. The old man just sat there not moving. Tachus nodded his head and stood, resuming his send-off with a hand held high.

"I suppose all is just fine. We'll continue to his home," he said. "Safe journey, young Bassam!"

Facing Noph at last, I knew I had an enormous task in front of me. The man Rakbah would be hard to find, if he's here at all. As for his men, I concluded I could remain anonymous long enough to discover them, and be led to my Rasha if her hiding place was indeed here in the city. That would take a great deal more cunning, but what choice was left to me? And if not here, then where? Ale'ksandra in the west? Or Buto in the east?

So here I was, another city, another unknown. I stood looking at the mingling strangers, did one of these carry the secret? I needed help looking, it was too large of a quest for just myself. Somehow I needed to get word to Ammar and Fawzi.

My first instinct was to find the gair house, to send a message to Cyene, tell them where I am.

A merchant pointed the way, and it was easy to spot. It was a natural grotto just below street-level. On the outside it was surrounded by strays who strutted about bobbing their heads for scraps and pecking for food. They flurried away at my approach, and I stepped down to a curtained entry.

"Hello?" I called. It was dark inside and took me a moment to adjust. The whole chamber hummed with the gentle cooing of hundreds of birds, each in its own little nest in the wall—triangle holes shaped like little pyramids, so Egyptian.

The ceiling was held by stone Roman arches separating the chamber into several large spaces. There was a subtle smell of bird excrement and stagnant air. A single gair fluttered across the room passing right through a column of dusty sunshine, momentarily flashing brilliant white. His wings made a whistling sound. Another flew the opposite way as if annoyed.

A short round man in a brown robe looked up from a table and set down his quill.

"Who are you, boy?"

"I want to send a message to my friends. What is the charge?"

"Too much for you," he said. "Where are your friends?"

"Cyene," I told him. Everyone there knows Kiya. I could send to her and hopefully she could deliver it when Ammar and Fawzi arrived.

"No," he said. "Go away."

"No? What do you mean no? Why not?"

"No gairs for Cyene. All out. Leave me be."

"I don't understand. There are hundreds here."

"Listen boy, my man carts the birds from Cyene, Gebtu, Korosko, and leaves them here. I sell them. They fly home. That's how it works. I don't expect him back in another month. I have no more Cyene gairs. You can leave."

I wasn't sure I believed what he was saying. Noph is a central hub for a great deal of traffic and communication. Shouldn't he be better prepared?

I thanked him anyway and returned the way I came, careful to avoid the gairs strutting about near the entrance.

As the curtain closed behind me I heard voices. A coin was dropped on the man's table. "A message to Khufu, quickly, do you have a bird?" a man asked.

"Yes, several," came the reply. "I'll pick you a good one. What is your name?"

By then I was too far away to hear more coins drop on the table. "Show me your five fastest birds and the largest message scraps they'll carry, to Khufu, today—I have much to say. I'd been here before, you don't remember? I am Pabas, where is a writing quill?"

THREE DAYS

Kiya was gracious to the two strangers standing at her door.

"You must be Ammar and Fawzi," she said, inviting them in.

Both men looked at her in surprise.

"You're expecting us?" Ammar said. "I'm surprised."

"Your friend said you would probably look for the steward at Cyene, and you have found the right place," Kiya said.

"How long ago?" Fawzi asked.

"Three days," she said.

"*Three?*" Fawzi looked at Ammar. "That little river rat must be paying his way with gold. Nobody can move that fast."

"Nobody but our Bassam," Ammar sighed. "He has every right to leave us old men behind."

"Speak for yourself," Fawzi said.

Kiya smiled. "I understand—he seemed anxious to forge ahead, but he looked well and stayed here for the night. We had a nice talk."

"Then he told you of our important mission?" Ammar asked.

"Yes, to rescue a girl," she said.

"And to destroy her kidnapper," Fawzi said, putting his hand on his sword.

"Yes, he mentioned that too. You are welcome to my home. I'll enjoy some company. Will you stay for dinner? We'll have chicken if you can wait for Betresh to finish preparing it?"

It was a fine meal, and they adjourned to the great room for tea.

"Then you, too, are Abdali-ud-din?" she asked. "I know of Zafir, but I haven't met him."

"He's building the trade to the far east—Indus, C'ina, north and south, the main routes," Fawzi said. "We're sent by Zafir for just this purpose you heard from Bassam."

Kiya went quiet for a moment, studying the two strangers.

"Then you're aware of the dispatches?" she asked carefully.

"Yes we are, Al Kalimat," Ammar said. "Is there another?"

She retreated to the hearth and removed a stone, pulling from hiding a well-worn pouch. "I can't trust an empty house and prying eyes when my husband is away on business," she said.

"That is wise," Ammar said.

"This arrived the day after Bassam left. It was too late for him, but perhaps not for you?" she said, handing it to Ammar.

Ammar removed a stiff papyrus. "Who sent this?" he asked.

She wore a pained look on her face and forced a smile. "The usual," she said. "We have a trusted courier who has been with Abdali-ud-din for 13 years."

The message was creased, a corner torn. On the upper right corner was the cross and two dots. Ammar read it aloud.

"A dispatch from Lateef to Zafir, to your query just received. Confirming the earlier report with our own witness to an encounter of a man and a girl at the fifth cataract," he read. "Early morning pursuit on the water, three boats lost in the torrent, no survivors. Another who was possibly involved escaped downriver unidentified. We gave no pursuit, not realizing him to be a party to the attack. We were so informed by the witness already cited. He was a fugitive going under the name Jabari. We could not present ourselves at the scene to investigate until an hour after the accident, and upon thorough examination we found no survivors, fatalities, nor remains of the boats involved, concluding that all had been carried away in the current.

—by my mark, Lateef"

The message was dated seven weeks earlier.

Ammar bowed his head and handed it to Fawzi.

"Then Bassam is headed into a trap," Fawzi said quietly. "And that way he becomes Rakbah's new ransom."

"Maybe," Ammar said. "But only if they find out who he is."

"Oh, he'll do something stupid, that bat brain," Fawzi said shaking his head. "And then our real work begins."

Kiya's face was pale and pensive. "I wish I could help," she said.

"You have helped immensely," Ammar said. "We'll leave early and try to catch him before . . ."

"Yes, I'll send you with food," she said. "Some of the boats leave before third watch. Choose the Roman barges. They are the fastest ride to Noph, and there you'll find your friend."

PEPI-MERIRA

I was not well trained in the tracking expertise of Al Murrah, and proceeded through Noph with caution. Hunting down Rakbah without arousing the local magistrates was risky and I could afford no more delay.

My first challenge was to find the steward of Abdali-ud-din, probably in the business district. But first there was a portal with two large rod-bearers I had to pass. They eyed me suspiciously as I approached them directly.

"Stop," ordered one, "state your name and purpose and destination."

"Yes sir," I said directly. "I am Bassam of Rekeem on a business quest for Abdali-ud-din, and seek their official steward. Can you direct me to his place?"

The man looked at me with tired eyes. "Two debens," he said, holding out his hand.

I didn't dare question an entrance tax.

"Before the market," he said pointing. "Those long rows of buildings, half way down, the blue awning, the agent for Abdali-ud-din."

I thanked him and passed through the grand entrance. The busy throngs drew me into their flow and pushed me toward the market street.

The alley was a long passage of compacted sand, just wide enough for two wagons to pass. It was dark and cool with overlapping awnings on every building. Not a ray of sunshine touched the ground.

There was scarce activity—a man here, a pair of women there, no children. Some chirping birds sat along the overhead poles, others clung precariously to the ropes and awnings. They chirped angrily, probably about the heat, the smell, or perhaps me, a stranger in their midst.

Standing beneath the blue awning, I found the office empty. It had a narrow doorway wedged open with a large chiseled rock, and tall empty window with a potted plant facing the alley. The rock had figure writing on its flat side, probably taken from a ruin.

There were two tables and a dozen chairs against the walls, and a curtained closet at the back.

"A busy place when it's needed," I thought. On the table sat an ink pot and two quills. Some skins with writing were spread haphazardly.

At the shop across the way, two men were hunched over a table in deep discussion, not noticing my presence. They sat on wooden chairs, laboring over a large map with two mugs of drink keeping their company.

"Hello?" I said.

I startled them. "What do you want?"

"I'm seeking the steward for Abdali-ud-din."

I noticed the men acting strangely, looking at each other in mild panic.

"I am the steward," one said, pushing back his chair to stand. I sensed immediately something was wrong. There was an alert in his eyes that didn't match his smile.

"Your name?" I asked.

"Yes, certainly. I am Pepi-Merira, the official steward of Abdali-ud-din in Noph."

This was not the man Kiya described. Why the long formal name instead of Pepi, fondly known by all? This was hardly Egyptian, and hardly Pepi.

I offered my hand.

"Pleased to meet you, Pepi-Merira," I said. We shook. His hand was moist.

"I've been searching a long time," I said. "What do I call you?"

"You've said it already, no offense, everyone calls me Pepi-Merira," he said. "And your name is?"

"I am Aziz," I lied.

"Aziz. What do you need?"

"I'm here with business partners. They should be here any time," I said, looking up the alley in expectation. The men followed my glance as if measuring their options.

"We have much trade from beyond Upper Egypt," I said. "We're in need of transportation. I'm told you offer the safest caravans at the best prices, with armed escorts."

"Yes, we can help," the man said. "When will your partners come?"

"They should be here momentarily," I said, glancing again. "Unless they stopped at market for something to put out the fire from this day's heat."

They chuckled uncomfortably.

"Not to worry," I said. "How long are you here today? Will you be here tomorrow?"

"That depends on the time of day."

"Very well," I said. "If you're away, we'll leave a note on your table and set a time we hope to return."

"That's fine," he said.

I nodded my head and returned up the alleyway. I felt their eyes on me the entire way, curious, wondering, suspicious.

I disappeared into the market crowds and positioned myself to watch behind a rack of skinned rabbits—they smelled disgusting and were swarmed over by nimits. For several minutes I brushed away the seller's petitions and surveyed the scene. Had they followed me? After half an hour, I decided they had not.

"Now I know two of them," I thought, putting their faces to memory. "I wonder how many more are in the city?"

MURDER

I t was risky going back that next day. If these were Rakbah's men, if they had learned my true identity, it could mean ambush, kidnapping to parts unknown—or killed.

I would wait for the busy time tomorrow. Safer that way. I needed that little man. I needed to take Pepi into my confidence and let him know the kidnappers spoken of in the official dispatches were here in the city, I had met two of them, and the rest? Probably hiding among the alleys and ruins of ancient Noph. I was sure Pepi had seen the dispatches—he could guide me to safety.

At dusk I found my way back to the city center, hooded, lest the men from earlier find me. I spotted an inn with good access to several escape routes and took a room.

Day 808
My dearest Rasha,

I am in Noph looking for you. Do I look in vain? Here is where your father believes you have been taken. We learned you escaped and have been searching these ten weeks. I will look ten thousand more to find you, my Rasha.

Your father knows of the man Rakbah. He will pay the severest suffering for his crimes. I'm on his trail, I believe he knows it.

It won't be long now. Do not give up hope. Be strong. I am coming.
—Bassam

I arose early for morning meal. I planned to monitor from afar all the traffic around the blue awning until it appeared deserted. I bought some fruit and watched for more than two hours from a distance. I did not see the two men return. Thinking it safe I made my way casually down the deserted corridor. All the shops were empty including Pepi's.

Scanning up and down the corridor, I slipped inside Pepi's little office and hurried my search.

The sheets of papyrus lie on the table exactly as before—Pepi had not disturbed them. I saw he was an efficient clerk—the writing was neat, clear script, straight lines, even columns. The notes told of orders and goods and destinations, along with lists of owners and drivers and payment—completed, concise, direct. Nothing in the writings, however, spoke of Pepi himself or his whereabouts.

But . . . there was a smell. In my urgency I had ignored it, but noticing it finally, it quickly grew wretched.

Behind me was the curtained closet. The drape was covered with nimits. *What's this?* I wondered as I shook them off then drew it back.

"AH!" I shouted. A rush of rats exploded in all directions, dashing for cover, one of them scurrying right over my foot.

"No, Pepi!" I groaned, seeing into the closet the short Egyptian man curled lifeless on the floor in a large pool of dried blood—his throat slashed and the flesh from his face and fingers nibbled away.

"Pepi, Pepi," I cried, slamming shut the visage with clenched eyes. I stumbled backward to the doorway, tripping my way over a chair and pushing against the table that made a loud honking noise across the stone floor. I staggered into the alleyway and bent over to vomit.

But there at the top of the alley were two alert men walking my way. They looked startled to see me stagger out of the door. I knew immediately they were the same as yesterday, they were the killers. I was in danger. The alley's ending in the other direction opened to sunshine just 100 paces away. Without thinking more I took off running, and the men gave chase.

My vomiting would have to wait.

PREFECT

I had just rounded the corner when I spotted a prefect and rod-bearers just 150 paces away. I ran straight to them waving my arms. The five were engaged with a broken wagon and three men yelling at each other. Fruit was spilled on the ground.

"Murder! Murder!" I yelled, pointing.

The rod-bearers stepped toward me, spears in hand.

"Murder! They're coming for me, there!" I said breathlessly, pointing toward the alley exit.

The two men hurled around the last building in a cloud of sand looking for my escape. Seeing me surrounded by rod-bearers, they slid to a stop, then turned back into the alley. Three of the rod-bearers gave immediate chase.

I could still smell death in my nostrils and staggered a few paces to bend over and vomit. The prefect waved the arguing traders away with a stern growl, and approached me.

"Boy! What is it? Are you ill? Do you need a physician?"

I took a moment to arrange myself, wiped my mouth, and took a dizzy step forward.

"They killed," was all I could say between breathes. "Murdered him."

The other rod-bearer looked hard at my face.

"Don't I know you?" he said. "Yes, aren't you Bassam? You came in yesterday to see Pepi, right?"

I looked at him, remembering his face, and nodded.

"I checked you in at the gate."

"Yes! Yes!" I said. "And those two men, they have murdered Pepi. You must come see. He's in his shop, dead."

"Tell me what happened," the prefect said.

I unfolded the story quickly, telling of my two visits, the suspicious behavior, and how the taller one had pretended to be Pepi and arranged another meeting.

"They must have killed him," I said. "He lied, he tried to trick me into a trap."

The prefect went quiet for a moment. "Then we must question the men, for their side of this story."

"Sir," I said, "may I offer an idea—a plan?"

The two men listened as I proposed a means of entrapment. It was simple, but it had merit and they agreed to give it a try.

The three rod-bearers emerged from the alley with the two men in tow, waving their hands about, anxiously explaining and threatening and demanding. The rod-bearers gave no yield, and delivered them in front of the prefect. The two men took immediate notice that my hands were bound behind my back and that a spear was at my throat.

The prefect took the lead. "You," he said pointing to the taller man. "Aziz here says you are Pepi-Merira, the local agent for a trading concern?"

The impostor looked at my eyes, and then my hands. He wasn't sure how to answer. That brief delay confirmed all our suspicions, but our ruse continued.

"Why, yes, I am," he said. "This boy came to me yesterday telling of trade and transportation, and I was to meet him today."

"Then why were you chasing him?"

The impostor's eyes danced left to right. "He killed my assistant," he lied. "He murdered him! For what reason, I don't know. But he killed my assistant, yes, with his knife. He cut his throat and threw his body in the closet. And we, well, we just came upon him, just as he did it, and gave chase. He's a murderer!"

"And how did you know there was a body in the closet?" The prefect asked.

"Well, we . . . uh . . . there was blood!" the impostor said. "Yes, blood leading to the closet, all over the floor. So we followed it and knew immediately that Aziz had—"

"With what?" The prefect asked.

"Why, his knife, what else? He had a knife!"

"This?" The prefect asked, lifting up the sword at my side.

"Well, no," and began to stammer. "He must have thrown it away when we gave chase."

"Then it should be simple to settle," the prefect said. "Let us go, all of us. We'll go back to the blue awning, and my men will hunt for this errant murder weapon along the way. And then we'll see blood on the floor, and in the closet, a man killed within the last hour—bring them," he ordered, and we retraced their steps.

There was no knife and mine was spotless—as clean as Al Murrah would expect—and there was no fresh blood on the floor. Pepi's body was abandoned like a sack of discarded waste, curled on the floor in the closet. He'd been dead for at least a full day and night, chewed by the rats, on grim display.

"You ignorant fools," the prefect said. "Pepi was my good friend for many years. You cut the throat of a little man for your plan? What plan? You have the time it takes from here to there," he said pointing east, "to give my men an explanation. And then? If your answers don't satisfy, you won't see the sunset tonight. Take them to the beheading place, then bring me word."

The prisoners began begging and pleading as the rod-bearers dragged them away.

The prefect said nothing but his eyes were clouded with sadness. He untied my restraints. "That was a good idea, young Bassam, where did you learn such a clever disposal of lying men?"

That was a good question—where indeed?

"I have had many good teachers," I said.

The remaining rod-bearer stepped closer, looking at my sword. "May I see it?"

I unsheathed it and he examined it closely, then turned it over and let the bluish light glint off the shiny blade.

"Yes, Al Murrah, I know of them," he said. He went quiet a moment, reading each of the names neatly engraved near the handle.

"Suoud!" he said suddenly. "Suoud! *The* Suoud? Of Rekeem?"

"Yes," I said, shocked that a stranger would know him. "That's the same, the sword once belonged to him."

"I know of him! Not a friend, but an acquaintance from many years ago," the rod-bearer said. "He and I shared some drinks at a harbor diner on the West Sea, the delta. We met a few times over the years."

I broke into a big smile. "You knew Suoud? That's wonderful! He was a good friend for a short time, and I have been carrying his sword for him."

"Yes, we heard," the rod-bearer said. "It was most unfortunate, but I see now that your name is inscribed below his, after the manner of Al Murrah. Why, the last time I saw this sword unsheathed was when Suoud showed me his name inscribed here, right here. He was so proud. It was so many years ago. We were all so much younger then . . ." He handed me back the sword.

"Yes, a good and faithful man," I said, "and with permission I carry it in his honor."

The rod-bearer smiled then looked away, recalling distant memories and old friends.

"Then—we're finished here," the prefect said, putting a hand on the rod-bearer's shoulder and shaking him back to the task. "We'll attend to Pepi's body, and tell his wife and family. And you, young Bassam, you have a problem."

"What problem?" I asked.

"We have two killers who murdered this kindly man for reasons we have yet to discover," he said. "Do you have any reason to think why they wanted to entrap you?"

Yes, I did have reasons, but would I dare speak them? I needed more allies than suspicions, so I shared part of my story.

"A girl, the daughter of my master Zafir, was kidnapped long ago for ransom," I said. "When Zafir received word, he sent me and two others to find her. We have been searching for her many months and learned that a man named Rakbah and another named Jabari may have brought her here. She might have escaped. We're checking on that too. I believe the impostors were sent to destroy anyone trying to discover them. Pepi was an innocent victim in their deception. His death was probably triggered by my visit yesterday."

I looked down and sadness crept over my face.

The prefect listened quietly and shook his head. "No, it's not you—killers will kill when it suits them," he said. "You have no blame to share in this, it sounds like he was dead before your first arrival. Tell me about your friends. Have they arrived in Noph?"

"No, but they should be here tomorrow or the next," I said.

"Then it's dangerous to be alone. You must be careful. I would venture there are more than these two involved. I will alert my men to watch, and you will come tell me if you suspect anyone."

I nodded with relief. At last there was someone I could trust.

Three other men arrived with rods and a sheet to bear away the body. The friend of Suoud patted me on the shoulder as he turned to leave.

"You take care that your sword does him honor, young Bassam," he said. "There's danger in this city. It's where evil comes to do his evil deeds."

THREE SQUARES

I paced around town for the rest of the day trying to calm my nerves and focus. My Rasha could be somewhere in this city. How do I start looking for her among so many thousands milling about? What about others hiding from the heat—or hiding from me?

I worked my way to the market thinking I could spot other easterners lurking around—anyone fair-skinned like me, of large stature and speaking my tongue—or perhaps spot a man with a missing finger.

I hooded myself and stayed among large groups. Toward evening I drifted from diner to shop to animal pen to alleyway and boulevard—searching. Discouraged at my feeble attempt to find a diamond in the sand, I gave up the hunt and returned to rest.

I absentmindedly cut a fruit into thin slices and wrestled with a nagging feeling of discontent. There was something bothering me, something disconnected about those killers. "I can't put my finger on it," I said aloud. I could hear Fawzi retort, "Bassam you donkey-headed knuckle brain. It's not you that can't put your finger on it, it's Rakbah, he's the one missing the finger, you finger-fumbling numbskull."

It made me chuckle. I missed my friends. I hoped they were traveling safely and would make it here soon. I had learned what I needed to learn. It was time for them to rejoin me.

I reflected back on the happenings of yesterday. When I first saw the two men, they were examining a map. It must have been part of their conspiracy because they hid it when I came up behind.

Could I recall anything about that map?

I laid back on my bed, let my head lean back over the mat, and closed my eyes. In my mind I recreated the event. There was the map, two mugs, a stylus, a coin, what else? A satchel with papers poking out. Anything else? Not really—but that map, it was different from Ammar's. They were studying it, pointing to parts with a finger. The map was neatly drawn. I remembered that much, and it was on a skin instead of papyrus. The ink was dark brown, not black, and the skin looked pliable. It seemed to fold easily when they closed it. It had crease marks. There were holes to close it with strings. What else? What could I remember seeing?

Lines, there were lines on the map, not many, but in a grid pattern, much like the map of a city's roads and alleys. These were not so regular or dense. What else did I see? I remember some writing I couldn't read. But there was something else—yes, there were large squares. Two squares? Yes, two of them—no, that's not right. There were three, two large, one small, all in a row like the stars in Orion's belt. And a wide dark strip, about a finger digit wide. It was darker, filled in with color. That might be . . .

"That's it!" I blurted out, sitting up in discovery. "The Nilus! The strip was the river, and the squares were . . . yes! The pyramids! Of Khufu! There were a thousand places to hide—chambers, tombs, tunnels, quarries. That had to be it! It was the perfect place to hide, and hide a hostage."

I was sure of it, the place where they could hide my Rasha. And Rakbah's men? Yes, his men would supply Rakbah from Noph until such time they could spring their trap. I would need to be alert for anything.

I stood from my bed and looked around my room. "Where is a map when I need one? Ammar? Where are you?"

They said Khufu is 12 Roman miles from Noph. Miles. What am I to do with that? I detest these different measuring systems. They should just say 120 stadia, maybe a three-hour ride, and leave it at that.

It was dark, well past first watch when I made my way to the guards at the city gates. One of them recognized me and we exchanged friendly talk, reviewing the events of the day.

"They confessed to nothing," the one man said.

"Lopped off the head of the first," said the other, "and then the second man made a wild claim that there was no girl, just a hunt for the kin of Zafir. A trap, he said. Do you know a Zafir? I thought the fellow honest, but the prefect had given his order."

I was caught off guard.

"No girl?" I said.

"That's right, no girl," he repeated, "but said they were aiming for another prize, somebody related to a rich man."

I staggered backward and felt my stomach begin to knot. *No girl? How could this be? How could this be, unless . . .* I refused to think it. No! And felt the fatigue of loss wash over me, like a heavy blanket of chains, dragging me down. I stood there slouched, head buried in the futility of the hunt, wondering, was it all for nothing? "Oh my Rasha," I whispered. "Where have they taken you?" *And if that other prize was me, they could have me—over my dead body. I'll kill every man I lay eyes on, no matter how many. Those butchers, if they harmed my Rasha ....*

"Bassam? Are you listening?" asked the first.

"What? What? Oh—yes, I'm sorry. I can't think of who they might be seeking. I'll check out this report, this declaration that they have no girl. That would be bad for us if that's true."

"What is your plan?" asked the second.

"Can you leave word to your replacements that I need an official pass outside of the gates for later tonight? I depart for Khufu, to be there by sunrise."

"Certainly," said the first. "You don't have much time. You should leave by third watch if sunrise is your goal. Here, I give you this," and he knelt down by an official looking box with inks and papyrus. He scratched a short note, quickly applied a wax seal, pressed his signet ring, then handed it over. "If one of us is not here, show this to the others. They'll let you pass without question."

"That's an early start," said the second. "You'll have to arrange for a camel or donkey, and . . ."

"No, no camel. I'll go by boat. It's faster that way, and I'm a good rower."

"No, the best way to Khufu is by camel. Follow the path—I'll give you directions to the large boulevard to Khufu, the fastest."

He reached into his box for another sheet of papyrus. "Show this note to anyone tending the pen. It is your pass. They will take 20 debens for a camel. It's about three hours north."

I took the notes and thanked them for their kindness. I had much to prepare.

SUN OVER THE NILUS

The moonlight was a poor assistant for tracking, and I detected few fresh signs of traffic. If messengers had gone before me, I hoped their tracks would lead me to Rakbah's lair. It was difficult to see in the poor light. And then came stony ground and I lost sight altogether of things suspicious, and was left on my own.

The trail cut directly north through the desert. I tapped my riding stick on the camel's neck. She looked back, annoyed. "Ammar never visited this place but he hoped to, one day. If they're following me, maybe he'll get his chance after all."

I swatted the camel to hurry, thinking I was easy prey for ambush.

"Just look at that, bakra," I said. "The moon makes of a black path a grey one. We can travel a gray path. And ahead, it makes of those black hills silver ones so we know what waits us there."

The moon's reflection on the Nilus followed us the entire trip, a beautiful, serene vision of peace and calm. The farms and groves came as large black patches while the sand was silver and shades of gray. It was prosperity of the most amazing kind, here in the desert, hiding in the many shades of night.

Another few stadia's travel and the silvery shadows of night started exchanging duties with the coming day. The black desert haze to the east was turning dark orange. As more light revealed my whereabouts, I realized I had been climbing a long slow rise near some tall hills, and was now on the descent.

But wait! I yanked on bakra's rope dragging her to a dead stop.

"These are—these are no mountains, camel brains!" I said. "Why—they're ... could they? *Yes! The pyramids!*"

Rising majestically from the flatlands and marching right into the sky stood the most magnificent, mysterious structures my eyes had ever beheld—the mighty pyramids of Khufu.

They were massive. Three distinct peaks with perfect symmetry, shape, and balance—mystical, impervious, splendid. They towered above me in stagnant glory over these forgotten desert sands, a monument to pharaoh's supreme arrogance, or an unmoving tombstone to his inescapable demise.

"A million stones," I said. "No, ten million—no, more! Who could count them in a lifetime?"

With sides forming a thousand stair steps stacked together, the protruding layers of massive stones gave a path to the sky, climbing uniformly from all sides to a pinnacle that nearly touched the heavens themselves.

"No wonder people find in these such a mystery so mystical," I thought. "They're too big for words, too big for comprehension, and too big for life!"

The sky began to brighten and details of the massive monuments of Khufu took form.

Far below, the village spread over the grand plateau was just awakening. A small column of smoke near one of the smaller pyramids climbed lazily into the morning haze.

The village was nestled near the river, a quaint oasis in the middle of this strange desert graveyard. A small canal ran through its center, and thick clusters of palms and squat little buildings hugged its banks.

As the yellow rays cast their warmth on the pyramid summits, life took wing—little brown bats flew across the temple grottoes, snatching their fill from the swirling clouds of nimits and secroots. A few brave pipits joined the activity while a tree of sunbirds chirped about the coming day.

"Father Yosef!" I called across the centuries to the prophet of old. "Did you see this grand vista when you escaped your prison sentence to serve pharaoh? And you, Father Moses! Did you see this place when God freed you from pharaoh with the plagues so you could lead the Israelite slaves from their captivity?"

I couldn't imagine how they would miss it. Ammar told me the pyramids forever changed the horizon along the Nilus. "Khufu named his tomb Akhet-Khufu, meaning horizon of Khufu," he said. From its completion day onward, the horizon was forever changed, and filled the people's hearts and minds with obeisance to Egypt's ruling powers. The structures carved a lofty place among all of their ancient writings.

"Bakra! There I go again!" I said. "I'm wandering—fatigue, stress, the unknown, fear—don't let me do that!"

Yes, I would soon need sleep.

I dug in my pouch for a date and chewed it slowly while my camel stood impatiently, snorting a complaint. From this high vantage, I could see the whole layout—the village of Khufu, the three pyramids, six or seven smaller pyramids, quarry pits, the burial grounds and those legendary mastabas neatly arranged—certainly a necropolis in every meaning of the word.

I decided I should hide my arrival by entering the village from the north. "Less suspicion that way, bakra." More columns of lazy smoke from cook fires laced their way into the sky. Fishermen departing the harbor caught the morning breeze that billowed their tall peaked sails. The village of Khufu was awakening.

My best route was west, behind the pyramids, keeping me in their shadow for most of the detour.

"Okay old girl, let's go." I said, kicking her ribs and snapping my stick on her neck. "We've got another hour's ride, then you're free."

We turned west and hurried along the crest of the plateau toward the back of the pyramids.

After a quarter hour, I passed the point where all three pyramids should have lined up, three in a row—except they didn't. Then I remembered! Another of Ammar's annoying facts.

"Their peaks! Look at that, bakra! Their peaks! Do you see it? Do you see they don't line up, like the stars—the belt of Orion, just like Ammar said! They really do line up like the stars!"

No wonder they kept the name Khufu. I breathed with a big tired smile. "The 'horizon of Khufu' is more than a horizon rising from the desert. It's an earthly connection to the eternal night sky, a horizon from any direction day or night."

"Okay, camel, I won't hurry you any longer if you'll take me to a diner, and if you present me as just some random driver to Noph, so much the better—are you listening? Then help me hide from narrowed eyes and I'll set you to food and rest—is it a bargain?"

I was pleasantly surprised when my camel bowed and raised her head as if to nod her consent.

"What?" I leaned to her neck to see around to her eyes. "Did you actually hear me?"

The camel nodded again.

"This is marvelous!" I said. "I didn't think it possible, never in a thousand lifetimes. But here, right here at Khufu, I finally found another bakra as smart as mine."

FALSE START

The old Roman barge arrived at the pier of Noph just at midday. The rowers lifted their oars in unison and drew them in while ropes were tossed to the dock men. They towed the vessel into position and secured the ropes to iron rings embedded into massive stone pylons. After all these centuries, the old artifacts remained in good use for river traffic, a tribute to the civilization that first built them.

"Let's get off this thing," Fawzi said. "I can't stand another hour of this military regimentation and barking orders."

Ammar was too busy writing on his map to sympathize.

"Distances, locations, names, contacts . . . I've got to return some day when we're not chasing our young Bassam," Ammar said. "Look at these ruins, the majesty of a mighty empire once traded here."

"Yes, yes, like all the other stops," Fawzi said. "You fret over one ruin, you've fretted over them all, Ammar! Let's get off and go hunt for Bassam—just look at all the people up there."

The midday market was in full trade, and a long line had formed for entrance at the city gate.

"What will it be?" Fawzi asked. "Food or an inn?"

"I think we would do better to just walk around," Ammar said. "I suspect he's walking around the city right now."

"On the hunt?"

"Aggressively."

The line finally shortened and it was their turn to deal with the two rod-bearers.

"Five debens," said the first.

"But we're just passing through," Fawzi said. "Not to sell," he said, holding out his empty hands, "Is the rate the same?"

The second man smiled at the forthright honesty. "For you, a special deal," he said. "Two debens, and enjoy our hospitality."

Fawzi paid the man and they stepped their way around carts and people and stands to the main boulevard leading toward market. The noise of squawking chickens, honking donkeys, laughing children, pleading peddlers, and cussing customers melted into a great cacophony of life and activity in the central market.

"Does Zafir have a steward here?" Fawzi asked, brushing away feathers from a chicken cage that bumped him.

"I believe so," Ammar said. "Three or four in Egypt. We should try to find the man here. he might be able to help."

They worked their way past smells that delighted and smells that disgusted, stopping at a lone stand bearing fruit for sale.

"Maybe naranjs—I'll get those if you can get a bread," Ammar said. "Then let's sit and watch. I want to find the prefect and ask him about our young charge. He might know something."

By afternoon, Ammar and Fawzi had fallen on sparse results. They finally received directions to the steward, but when asking at the blue awning, found no one manning the post. Then they found the prefect.

"Yes, yes, I know all about Bassam," he said. "He was here yesterday. There was a murder, you know. He solved it for us, clever boy, smart."

"Murder?" Ammar asked. "What murder?"

"Not pleasant, not at all," the prefect said.

He related the whole story and how Bassam caught the impostors in their cheating.

"We executed them," the prefect said. "And then Bassam told me he had to travel to Khufu."

"Khufu?" Fawzi asked. "What's in Khufu? When did he leave?"

"Early this morning," the prefect said. "He should have arrived already. It's a short trip, the burial city for Noph. The great pyramids are there, too."

"Did he say why?" Ammar asked.

"Only that the kidnappers were holed up there, perhaps with the killer Rakbah, a man we've been searching for this long time."

"Then it's a trap," Ammar said.

"Indeed," replied the prefect. "I warned him. If there were two men here to spot him, then there must be more lying in wait. He was insistent, so we helped him all we could. One more thing. Before we executed the impostors, one of them said their plan was no longer to hold a girl for ransom, but they wanted to kidnap the kin of a rich man—Zafir was the name."

Fawzi looked at Ammar who looked at the ground and then to the prefect. "He's headed into danger. We must go help," Ammar said. "Will you guide us please to the best means for Khufu?"

DISCOVERED

I sat in the shade of an open diner with a cup of tea and slices of freshly baked bread slathered with a wonderful red jam. The food was perfectly satisfying on my empty stomach, and somewhat settled my anxieties about the work in front of me. I looked about casually, sensing that somewhere out there, evil men were hiding in this graveyard city, perhaps holding my Rasha in some dark place.

I had to plan my next step carefully. I hoped none of Rakbah's men knew what I looked like, and hoped that I was safely anonymous. I decided I should take measures to stay apart from crowds. But how could I discern them from others?

The server came by with some plums.

"You're not from here—may I ask?" he said.

"Certainly," I replied. "I trade in the high deserts and all those stops beyond."

"Ah, nice, many wadis and palms, not like our dry Egyptian deserts," he said.

I wanted to tell him about long stretches of dry, hot desert I had crossed that would shame Egypt's worst.

"You know, I've recently been through some sun-baked ovens that were far worse than . . ."

My attention was diverted by a man who came to purchase goods. The server paused my story and excused himself.

I took another sip of tea and cut the plum in half, digging out the pit with my thumb.

The customer presented some coins and asked about sweetbreads.

"A full or half?" the server asked.

"Full," he said, "and quwwa for this pot," and put a ballas on the counter.

The casual exchange had a certain edge that gave me an uneasy feeling. That voice sounded familiar. Holding my bread to mask my face, I took a quick glance at the stranger. I recognized him instantly—the passenger from Tachus's boat! He saw me look and remembered me. His eyes widened, and his coins fell to the counter, rolled off, clinking on the stone floor. We locked eyes and I stood.

"Pabas?" I said.

He said nothing, but his eyes narrowed like a cat dressing his prey. Then he reached to his robe. I saw the handle of a knife.

"No!" I shouted and threw my chair at his feet then dashed for the open side of the diner. I raced through dusty gravel around the blind side of the building. I ran as hard as I could across the boulevard into a shadowed alley. I slid around the first side street and continued west through rows of dwellings until I was into the tended areas with goats, gardens, and fields. I spied a grove of vines and fig trees overgrown with brush far to its end. The thicket was still in shadow so I ducked in, pushing past branches and thorns to it deepest parts. Morning shade swallowed me in darkness and I crouched listening. There were birds, a barking dog, bleating goats, but no footsteps.

Several moments passed. I couldn't tell which was louder, my pounding heart or my heavy breathing. I tried to calm both. Minutes grew to an hour. Sometime after that, I lost track of time. My fatigue overpowered my fear, and I drifted into a deep and forgetful sleep.

MOON SHADOWS

"It should be close," Ammar said. "We've been riding long enough. See anything?"

"These Egyptian saddles—much too small. My backside says it's been ten hours—no, twenty. I'll never walk again, Ammar, never."

"Look," Ammar said. "It's getting lighter."

"Ah, finally, the moon," Fawzi said pointing his stick at the horizon. "It's about time. That thing seems to come up later and later every night."

"Actually, you're right," Ammar said, "just shy of an hour each night, it all has to do with—"

"Look!" Fawzi blurted out. "Look at that!"

The men stopped dead in their tracks.

From the veil of night, three distinct peaks appeared in shades of black and grey as the moon's white wash drew down the sides. Their massive slopes took form as the details presented themselves in hundreds of rigid layers stacked upwards, perfectly level, to pointed summits touching the stars.

"Spectacular!" Ammar said throwing his hands in the air. "Magnificent! Marvelous!"

"They're enormous!" Fawzi said. "Huge!" and craned his neck upward.

The shadowed megaliths loomed over them as if from a dream, cutting into the star-lit sky—silent, ghostly, mystifying.

"I didn't think they were so—" Fawzi said.

"So massive!" Ammar breathed. "At long last! I've got to go see, I've got to explore them . . ."

"Oh no you don't, pharaoh," Fawzi blurted. "I want to end this thing and get back home."

"End it? End it? When we're right here, once in a life time?" Ammar said. "It wouldn't take long, an extra day or—"

Fawzi turned in his saddle and faced Ammar. "You're kidding me, right? The man who made me wait while he did charcoal rubbings of every figure-writing column and tablet and stone and ruin we passed, is going to breeze by these massive monuments because 'it won't take long?' You think I'm buying that?"

Ammar smiled. "Yes, yes, you're right. I wasn't thinking, we have our errand, and, well, we can't very well do anything sitting right here, you're right, let's get down off this ledge and . . . " Then he stopped. "Wait. Look there" he said pointing to the plateau.

Far below were five thin shadows moving over the sands, hurrying across the foreground of the middle pyramid. The runners' shadows stretched like single strands of black hair in the bright moonlight, rippling over the dunes, nearly invisible except for their movement.

"I see it. What do you think?" Fawzi asked.

Ammar studied the scene a moment. "Something's not right," he said. "At this late hour?"

Fawzi leaned forward and pointed. "Look—see that? They're running. Or chasing. Hey, you don't think . . .?"

"Oh yes I do—to the far pyramid. Do you see it? That's where they're going."

"Somehow I get the feeling Bassam is over there, the far side, in the shadow. That brainless mummy head. What has he gotten himself into now? I've got a bad feeling about this," Fawzi said. "Oh Bassam, don't you dare leave another big mess for me to clean."

"Not on my watch," Ammar said, slapping his camel into full gallop. "Let's go!"

BLIND STAIRS

I hoisted myself up the next layer. "That's 22," I whispered. I could see nothing in the dark to guide me, but the vague outlines of the pyramid's massive stone blocks—black against black, nothing more. I had to feel my way to the next layer.

How many courses to the summit? I looked upward seeing nothing but the great black shadow slicing the starry sky in half. It was like wearing a blindfold. The best I could do was feel about for the next layer, and choose a place with enough flat space to pull myself up.

"I'll have to be content with small progress," I thought, and climbed another.

The pyramid was smaller than some mountains I had scaled and not as steep. But none of that mattered in the dark. The moon was opposite me tonight. Without this black shroud of shadow I could dart up in minutes—but without it I was their easy target.

I hoisted myself up another. "That's 30," I whispered.

I took encouragement they were fighting the same obstacle. Every few minutes I heard someone below cursing at something—a misstep, a slip, banging of a shin. Perhaps I could work their fatigue to my advantage. I had to be first on top, God willing.

I stopped for a rest. Looking far to my right, the edge of the pyramid was starkly outlined against the starry sky, the block layers cutting a shape like saw teeth—uneven, steep, perilous, and nearly invisible. And standing beyond it, the second pyramid rose up in view, awash in moonlight. Looking to my left, the edge was too far away to discern details. It disappeared into blackness with the pole star and his companions shining steadily above.

I brushed the dirt from the next course and pulled myself up.

At each row I made an informal measurement—most of the stones were the same, reaching to mid-thigh. A few came to my hip, others to my knee, sometimes a palm or two higher. "This is where the builders corrected the angle of the slope," I decided. "If I were pharaoh, I'd drop the man into the bottom of the Nilus who maligned my pyramid with such sloppy numbers!"

Regardless, the stones were not uniform as mud bricks pressed in a mold. I found the stones misshapen and crudely aligned. Some blocks were placed right to the edge of those below, making a wall instead of a step. Others were split, chipped, uneven.

Each layer was covered with drifts of dirt, forcing me to clear a place before trying to climb. "This is no Roman marble stairway," I whispered. "This is like the mess of boulders in the cataracts—just as steep, just as jumbled, and just as unforgiving."

The next course was shorter. I hauled my body up the ledge, then paused to let the blood tingle life back into my arms. The next two layers were the same.

"That's 50," I whispered, staggering to my feet.

My sword and sling bag were growing heavier and I was really feeling the drag with each layer I ascended. I could stash them somewhere, but with what do I defend myself? No, they were a necessary burden.

I finished three more in quick succession.

"That's 60," I whispered.

It's quiet here—too high for birds, too low for clouds, but peaceful. A soft breeze whistled through the cracks and fissures, and a few diving bats made chirping sounds. I could hear the pounding of my heart like great drums in my head, and futilely hushed my labored breathing. Could they hear me climbing? My panicked rush made short order of any pain I was feeling. I refused to let my life fall into the hands of these wicked men and hurried myself up each layer. One slip, one noise, and they would converge on me in an instant, and to where could I flee? I mustn't lose courage now. *For you Rasha. For you I will fend my way up this impossible climb and face the men who know where you are kept.* And then? *And then they will be sorry they stole you away.*

I took courage from the struggles of Rakbah's men somewhere below in the dark—shouting, slipping, cursing. They had no reason to be cautious. They knew their prey was trapped, and by their shouts and calls they steadily chased me upward into their certain trap, directly to a place where death might well be my only escape.

But me? I had to remain perfectly silent. It was my best defense lest they have some other means to catch me unawares. These narrow steps were no place to engage in a blind sword fight.

The next layer came to my hip. I felt around to brush away debri, and hoisted myself up.

I turned about and sat, letting my feet dangle off the edge—not long, just enough to clean them of pebbles and sand.

"Sandals are not for climbing," I said, removing one and brushing the grit from my sole. "I suppose they help more than hurt," and rubbed the other. "Can't get blisters now," and made a mental note to be cautious about the wear against my skin. But no time for such bother.

Somewhere below I heard more mumbled exchanges directing their climb according to some arbitrary noise somebody heard. They were getting closer. I was shaking in my arms and legs—fatigue or fear? Without thinking on it more, I turned to my task and pressed upward. Death was breathing down my neck, I could feel it, and though careful to climb the next row in perfect silence, I hurried that much more.

I pulled myself up five more layers, each higher than my hip. Without a good visual reference point it was easy to lose balance. I crouched to keep my gravity close. The builders left little space to stand, and for that sloppiness pharaoh should have thrown them to the kroks.

The next row came to my waist. I brushed the sand, placed my hands and jumped, barely getting my knee over. I felt the fatigue setting in.

"That's 80," I whispered.

This will take hours. And when the sun rises, will they discover me still struggling to the top?

I brushed off the dirt from the next stone and pulled up with a groan.

"I think Father Time is having his way with these crumbling stones," I said brushing away the dirt on the next layer. "Could all this dirt get blown here? There must be three thousand years of wear—So, they aren't immortal after all."

I pulled up another layer and sat upright, panting for rest.

The next two courses were knee high. I scampered up as fast as I could, holding my sheath lest my sword knock against the edge.

Just then came shouting. Rakbah's men must have heard something.

"Left!"

"Left? How far?"

"Fifty paces."

"My left or yours?"

"Fool."

"Shut up."

All went quiet. Such shouts revealed their whereabouts. For more than an hour I had used them to adjust my position.

The moon was higher now, lighting up the sands but keeping me in shadow. I imagined the other sides were bright and easier to climb, certainly to their advantage. In moonlight a man could find all manner of shortcuts that I could never discern in this pitch.

I estimated Rakbah's men were still below me by several layers—the two on my right, about 30 rows below, and one on my left about half that. It was too close for comfort, but their shouting convinced me I was keeping pace with their climb—they were not gaining on me.

Then I realized why they were slow to gain on my position.

"Bassam, where is your brain?" I said. They have a chore that I don't—to clear the length of each layer lest they pass me hiding in a crack. They had to make sure I didn't huddle somewhere.

It gave me an idea.

"Bassam, you block head, you've been doing this all backwards!" So long as they thought me above they hurried upward. Why not make them backtrack?

I felt about for loose stones and kicked a chunk bigger than my hand. Too large; they'd know it was a ruse.

In a corner drift I felt some smaller rocks and waited quietly for the right moment. Just then, I heard pebbles scatter to my right. *Much nearer than before—four or five layers below?*

I estimated their place as best I could, took aim a short distance below and threw the stone far across to the other ridge.

When it hit, I heard strained whispers:

"There, there, over there."

"Too far."

"It was up"

"No no, straight across."

"Left! Left!"

"You go up, I've got this."

"Listen . . . are you sure?"

"Fool, it's a trick."

"Shut up."

"Hush."

Then . . . silence.

In the flurry of confusion I climbed two more layers, then another. I knew they were listening more carefully than before. And whether they were angry at being fooled or unaware, it would perplex them, make them doubt. And that would make them more cautious—and slower.

I had to hurry.

UNKNOWN BLOOD

The last time I saw Rakbah he was running toward me with a knife in his hand and a coil of rope slung over his neck. "Put it on, boy," he shouted. I wondered if he still carried that thick coil. By now it would be pulling awfully heavy—wearing raw on his skin.

The next layer was just higher than my hip. I positioned my hands flat, jumped, and hoisted my body to its top.

"That's 90," I whispered, rubbing sand from my palms.

I gave names to the different layers to stay focused. Those as tall as my chest I called "killers" because I had to pull my entire body using my arms alone. Those were especially hard. I had missed a couple at the very bottom—slipped and fell. I could feel a rainbow of tender bruises already forming on my shins, proof that these killers deserved their name. The jumping was wearing on the back of my legs. I felt some cramping begin—I needed water, I needed rest.

Just then . . . a sound.

And another.

It was coming from my left, maybe 30 paces. What was it? Had one of his men reached me already? I could hear sandals on gritty stone, cautiously crunching toward me. It sounded like he was on the same level on which I stood.

I crouched instinctively, frozen in place.

The steps slowed as if the man was calculating—or listening. *I've got to go up or down. Dare I even move?*

The crunching sound stopped.

He was listening. His breathing was labored.

Could he see me?

I unsheathed my sword slowly, and felt for a crack among the stones. I found a wide crevice between two great blocks and crouched into it as best I could. The tight opening was worn smooth, and was cool against my skin. I noticed my mouth was dry and I kept swallowing to prevent coughing.

He started moving.

Crunching.

Was it ten paces or five?

Slow steps—one, then the other—deliberate. *Was he right here?*

Suddenly, a large black shape appeared right before me and passed by silently, pushing a great wave of heat, almost touching as he went by. He was perfectly silhouetted against the whitewashed landscape beyond. He was bent over, knife extended, taking slow cautious steps.

They don't want me alive, I realized. *I must act now.*

I rose quickly, lowered the tip of my sword, calculated for his upper torso. I took one long step and thrust with all my might. The blade hit him squarely in the back, piercing flesh and bone so abruptly he couldn't scream. I pushed hard, driving the steel forward and through. His body recoiled against the searing penetration and he collapsed to his knees with a shallow "umph." I pulled my blade quickly and he crumpled to the stone. A gurgling sound drowned his cry for help, but he let go his knife and it fell to the next layer with a double clang.

"Yuny? Yuny, is that you?"

The voice was from below, maybe 20 layers down. I heard scuffling and anxious whispers.

I quickly laid my sword on the next stone, pulled myself up, rose to climb the next, then another.

Moments later I heard the faint thud of a body against stone, wheezing, and then all went quiet. He must have rolled to the layer below.

"Say something" another voice whispered. It came from five or six layers below.

"What happened?" whispered another. This one was much farther down to my left.

"You hurt?"

"Did you get 'em?"

"Say something . . ."

"Yuny?"

I hurried up another five layers. Then I leaned back to listen.

My hands were shaking and I was dizzy. There was murmuring in the dark and some quick movement over the stones. I climbed another three layers.

I breathed deeply and looked to the stars for composure.

I hated taking human life—even my enemy's. Yuny—that must be the man's name. Who are you, Yuny? Why were you chasing me? You don't know me. Did I just make your wife a widow and your children orphans? I'm sorry I had to choose me over you.

I wiped sweat from my brow and rubbed my hands dry on my robe.

And then I smelled it—that sweet metallic scent of fresh blood on my sword. I detested that smell, like wet rust. I felt around for a thick accumulation of dirt and pushed my sword several times to wipe it away.

Suoud came to mind. "That grit will cost you hours at the stone," I could hear him scolding me. Wiping the blade was dulling the edge.

"Very foolish, Bassam," he'd say. The thought made me smile. "I can't put a man's blood down my sheath, Suoud. I'll grind back its edge and polish it as new. I promise."

There was a foul taste in my mouth, the horrible aftertaste of pushing steel into a man.

That's one man dead. How many left? Did I see four men chasing me, or was it five? With Rakbah it was five. The odds are better now, but not good enough.

I put my hand on the next ledge and pulled myself up. "That's 120," I whispered.

I noticed stinging pain in my left palm.

"Blood or blisters?"

Both hands were raw and tender, I couldn't lose the use of my hands, not yet.

I quietly tore two long strips from the hem of my robe and wrapped my hands. I looked about wondering if the sound had carried. The wrappings made my hands feel better, but my grip was less secure. It would have to do for now.

The next dozen courses were easier. I took them like giant stairs, feeling ahead for my new perch each time. The summit was nearing. The black slice through the stars above me sloped inward, slowly closing from both sides.

I caught movement to my right. *What? Another, already?*

I crouched against a wall.

There he was, far to the south edge, creeping slowly, a black cutout in front of the backdrop of the middle pyramid. That massive stone structure was so ablaze in moonlight that I could make out exacting details of the man's body and head in silhouette. Younger, no beard, short sword. He looked in my direction. Could he see me in the reflected light?

He had the advantage by climbing near the moonlit side. Enough light spilled across the stones to guide him more carefully up the layers, choosing stones for an easier path. He stepped up another row and stood on my level. I could see his body turn, his head tipped to the side listening. Yes, he heard me. He started toward me, coming for the kill.

I reached into my bag, produced a rounded stone, and felt for my sling. I put the stone in its cradle and stretched out the strings to my side. I had one chance to make it work.

And then an idea—draw the hunter to the hunted.

With my free hand, I felt around on the ledge and gathered some loose rocks, aimed a few layers below the silhouette and threw. The figure was startled by the scattered clicking noises so near to him, and stood upright, presenting his full body as a target.

I whipped the sling around and the stone whistled through the air, hitting the stones directly above him. *I missed*! The man ducked and turned around to look.

I loaded another stone, aimed a little lower and let it fly. It hit the man somewhere and the form collapsed. There was movement, I heard him whimper, then he slipped to the layer below with a heavy ka-flump. I heard a stifled cry of pain, and thought to go in for a kill. Too risky and decided against it. Whatever the damage, he was stopped for a while. I turned and continued up the stones.

"Yuny?" someone called. "Setka?"

The man's call to his companions betrays his numbers! Yuny is dead, Setka injured, the odds are better by one more man.

Keep moving, Bassam.

I listened for the wounded man's voice. Nothing.

"That's 140," I whispered.

The backs of my arms were shaking with fatigue and my whole body was overheated and chilled at the same time.

One slip and I'd go tumbling. I had to stay focused.

The sides of the pyramid were cleanly tapered to the summit, I was almost there.

I took my next step, then a painful cramp—right thigh, burning knot. I fell to the stone, blinding pain, and gripped it hard, trying not to scream. I forced my leg out in front of me, stretching, and pressed it flat to the stone—grabbed my toes and pulled steady until the knot slowly released.

"Water," I whispered, massaging the muscle deeply. "I need water."

A few more moments of rubbing and I stood. The muscle felt taut and bruised. "This will slow me, must be careful."

"You're drying yourself out, Bassam," I whispered. "You'll have to climb back down at some point. Are you ready for that? Maybe I should reverse course now, fool them into finishing the climb while I make my way to safety?"

I looked down. Nothing but blackness lightly outlined by desert moonlight.

No, can't retreat now, there is less mystery upward. I proceeded gingerly.

The next several rows were each just higher than my knees. I cautiously hoisted my body, time and again, using my other leg for the work.

"That's 170," I whispered.

Zafir came to mind. I wondered if he was healed. He had to be doing well, probably reorganizing his forces to put down the Tauri. Maybe everything was calm now, and he was tending his farm with his family.

"The test of your true self," he told me one night in a faraway desert, "isn't in the accolades from grand achievements. It is in the privacy of your own struggles. Remember it my son. We all possess the vanity of the natural man and will pursue some difficult tasks for the public rewards they promise. Only the truly strong man will conquer his chore in secret for no other reason than to conquer his self. There's no other achievement that truly satisfies, my son, only those done for the good they achieve. Men's personal glory is never satisfying. Remember it always. Outward praise is short lived and fleeting, but inward achievement is strength for a lifetime."

I missed that great man's counsel. He had the wisdom for putting everything in its proper order.

The words renewed my courage. No matter the outcome, this labor is for my Rasha. I will take Rakbah by his ugly gullet and learn from him the truth about my Rasha, or I will die trying.

Just then a man screamed far below. My heart jumped and I turned to look. I saw nothing in the blackness, but heard scuffling, another shout, a sword clanging to the stones, and then silence.

"What was that?" I whispered as new fear took me in its icy grip. "More men coming? A fight below? With who?"

Then more noises, voices—something was happening down there in the shadows. A new wave of panic swept over me and I hurried my task, hoisting my body up one more course. "That's 190," I whispered. *Or was it 191?*

I held my breath, fearing discovery by this new threat. The summit was so close, within reach. I could see it clearly, a sloping blackness revealed against the stars, both sides coming together to a flattened top. I could almost throw a rock to its top. The layers were shorter here. I could almost step up like a staircase, a nice reward after such a struggle.

Fatigue was coming in great surges, washing over me like thick syrup. My brain was getting foggy. "Stay with it, Bassam," I scolded. "If Fawzi were here, he'd say . . ." Then it hit me.

I looked down where I heard the fighting.

Of course! It had to be! Fawzi! Ammar! They're here! At last!

MERCY AND JUSTICE

I raised my head above the last layer and the full blaze of moonlight hit me squarely in the face. I lifted my hand to shade it.

"The top! I beat them!" I whispered, panting heavily.

I rolled my body onto the stone platform, resting my back and legs, scanning the whole canopy of stars. *I made it!* Then staggered to my feet.

This amazing view! I drew my sword for ready and turned about slowly, surveying my new circumstances. A cooling breeze passed over the peak, blowing away fatigue and pain, sifting through my hair, calming my taut anxiety. I surveyed the magnificent scene. The panorama was breathtaking—ten-thousand stadia in all directions. I could see the village of Khufu snuggled in shadow—the great Nilus asleep from her labors, a black ribbon reflecting the moon's great light.

I could see toward Noph from where I had driven, and west to the great receding wastelands of desert sand and stone.

And then an overwhelming sense of exposure shivered through me, I felt so naked.

I'm too exposed. No hiding place.

The top of Khufu's pyramid was a flat stone platform, perhaps no larger than the deck of Tachus's boat—about 15 cubits on all four sides with another layer of a dozen stones linked together at its center. "Leftovers of an unfinished cap?" It was an uneven battlefield, but it would have to do.

My mind raced. "If they come at me from many sides, what is my plan of defense?"

Five chased me from my hiding place, I eliminated two. Ammar and Fawzi must have taken the third. Then there should be but one more coming up the shadowed side—and Rakbah climbing the moonlit side.

Perhaps Ammar and Fawzi could get here in time.

I sheathed my sword and reached instead for my sling. I retrieved a stone and placed it in the leather. I let it hang in ready, and cautiously walked the perimeter for signs of movement or an ambush.

Suddenly a hand grabbed my ankle!

"AHHHH!" I screamed and pulled away, escaping the grip just as a knife slammed into the rock, breaking its tip with a lightning spark.

I quickly backed away, noticing the broken blade glinting in the moonlight, illuminating his face. He rose slowly, grinning with spittle on his teeth and sweat beaded on his brow.

"Pabas!" I taunted. "You left your father to die?"

He snarled like a desert hyena cornering his kill, and pulled up a knee to climb the last layer.

"An old man, something you'll never be," he panted, climbing to his hands and knees, his broken knife gripped in one hand.

"No, that's not what I meant," I said. "I'll ask again. You left your father to die?"

"The only dying on this rock is Bassam, the kin of Zafir, unless—" He drew off the coil of rope from around his neck and threw it at my feet. "Unless you put this on. Then you live."

"I'm not his kin," I said. "But that will change," then swung the sling as hard as I could. The bullet missed his head and zinged off the great stone into the dark. I quickly loaded another.

Pabas looked surprised, then angry, and pulled himself up. He just gained his feet when I let loose the next.

This one found its target in the middle of his chest and he fell to his knees gasping in pain. He looked at me with acid hatred burning in his dark eyes.

I drew my sword and took a step toward him, then suddenly—a black shadow flowed across the stones, clouding over us like a spilled bucket of black ink. I turned to look.

Rakbah.

He pulled himself up from the opposite side, grinning like a crazed madman.

"Bassam! Bassam!" he huffed. "We meet again at last! And I see you have already met my associate. He and I have business with your father."

I clutched my sword with both hands in ready-attack posture. Pabas was just getting back to his feet when Rakbah took his first step toward me.

"It's over Bassam," Rakbah panted. "Just drop it, let's talk."

He was right, it *was* over, their trap was closing. I was compelled to act.

"Then take this with you," I said, lowering my blade and leaning into a wide, dramatic spin, swinging my sword in a wide arc, feigning first a swipe at Rakbah. He instinctively stepped back, opening up my real target. Pabas raised his broken knife and staggered toward me, right into the path of my blade. Its polished edge swept directly across his shoulders, beheading him instantly. His body slumped to the stone and his skull tumbled through the air, hitting the stones below with a dull crack.

Rakbah looked at the pool of black draining out in front of him, and stepped back disgusted. The similarity of this sudden event did not go unnoticed by me—a distant dune, a broken sword, two against one, different faces but just as wicked.

"That was rude," he huffed. "Listen, listen, calm down, I don't want you dead, boy. There's the rope," and pointed to the coil on the slab. "Put it on and we'll sell you back to your kin. Nobody get's hurt."

"I saw you kill," I said, raising my sword to shoulder height. The blade was streaked with blood.

"*Me* kill?" and gestured to Pabas' lifeless form. "It was an inconvenience," he grinned. "I am just a business man—"

"A cheap killer," I said.

"They are mistaken about me," taking sideways steps to position the bright of the moon squarely in my eyes.

I countered by moving to his right, forcing him to face me north to south.

"I'm told there's a great reward for your capture."

"I have much bigger prizes in mind, and you just filled my bill," he said. He swung at my sword, striking its tip, then smiled, taunting me by passing his sword from hand to hand like a toy. Beads of perspiration glistened across his forehead.

"You're tired, old man," I said, taunting. "You hauled your rope for nothing, was it heavy?"

He took another swipe at my sword, making a dull clang.

"You're so brave, Bassam," he said, circling around. The headless body of Pabas made for a strange barrier between us, obstructing Rakbah's lunge.

"Does your Zafir know I have you captured?"

"The hunted drew the hunter," I said. "And you're too tired for a fight. I can see it. You're done Rakbah. Give up and live."

"Never too tired to ruin another braggish boy," he warned.

"Then try me," I said, beckoning him with my other hand.

"My pleasure!" Then he lunged straight toward me, his sword flashing against mine in a flurry of heavy hits and shouting. I slid the blades together, locked down to the hilts then twisted hard and pushed him backwards. He tripped over Pabas' body and fell flat on his back, jarring loose his sword that went sliding across the rock and over the edge, clanging to the stones below. I quickly stepped forward and thrust my sword into his face and held—steady, unmoving, unflinching.

"One move, just one," I whispered, pointing its steady tip directly at his right eye.

It was all I could do to restrain.

"I will ask this once, where's the girl?" I said.

Rakbah froze, peering cross-eyed at the finely sharpened tip. I saw conniving stir in his brow. "What girl?"

I dragged the blade down his cheek. He jerked backward, wincing as a red line started bleeding. I put the tip on his throat.

"Kidnapped."

"Oh, that girl," he said through clenched teeth. "She's dead. Why do you care?"

My heart pounded, my trembling sword magnified my rage.

"Where?" I demanded.

"I don't know, I don't remember things like . . ."

I pushed harder. A drop of blood trickled down his throat, he leaned backward. Defiance paled to fear.

"WHERE?" I shouted.

He swallowed, trying to read my eyes.

"NOW!" I shouted, twisting the blade so it reflected moonlight across his face.

"All right, all right, south—far south, the river, you know, the cataracts—I don't remember . . . Atbara, yes, it was somewhere near Atbara."

"What did you do?" I demanded.

"I sent my man, Jabari, he went to . . . it was ours, to reclaim our property—a stolen slave girl, we meant no harm, just wanted her back."

"And then?"

"Nothing," he said, trying to shrug. "He followed them to a place, an inn, the girl and a man. He watched. When they left he chased. But the boat—all their boats—caught in the current, all of them dead. It wasn't my fault, I didn't want them dead, I sent him to bring them alive."

The dispatches flashed through my mind. Could they possibly be right? *No, no, no!* I refused to believe it. My jaw tightened and my grip was tiring. He had to die. What use was there sparing him longer? I felt my eyes wetting.

"Listen to me carefully you *ibn el-sharmoota*. A great man gave me power over your life—to know when death is certain and life just the same. Those are his words," I said and pushed my sword harder at his throat.

"So? What is that to me?" he gagged, twisting his head away.

"It is the wisdom of the father of the girl you murdered."

"It means nothing. It's stupid."

"Only to stupid men, *ya zebbala*. Tonight you'll wear the ropes you lugged up this mighty mountain for me. Then I'll show you life that is certain because I wished it so, and will deliver you prisoner to the hot blood that comes after you. They'll get their justice, and you'll feel their wrath."

I stood back.

"Get on your knees," I ordered. "Hands high—"

Rakbah squared his shoulders with a calculating frown and righted himself to his knees, his hands high over his head.

"Higher."

I knew he wasn't finished with me, and kept my sword pointed at his face.

"Your rope," I ordered. "Take it off slowly, hands behind back. I'm not sure how much longer I can keep this blade from your lying throat."

The man obeyed, but I could tell he worked a plan. Instinctively, I took another step back.

Removing the coil, he quickly twisted about and threw it into my face, lunging for my legs, screaming. I raised my sword and knocked him hard on the head with the butt of my handle. He collapsed at my feet with a heavy groan, limply grabbing for my legs. I stepped out of his grasp.

"Wickedness makes a man weak, Rakbah—you're weak! You're caught! You're mine! Try it again and I'll use the pointed end."

Blood dripped down his face.

"You're bleeding, Rakbah, but I am also merciful."

I pointed my blade into his face. "The ropes!" I commanded. "On your knees, hands behind your back!" I circled behind him with my sword pointing to his back.

He remained, clutching his head with blood now running freely through his fingers, then rose to his feet. He was bent over and moaning, and staggered sideways in a dazed stupor. Then quickly he turned to me with bloodshot eyes, growling like a rabid dog, and lunged one more time. I was too quick and stepped aside. To my horror he tripped again on Pabas, lost his balance and went stumbling right off the eastern edge.

"NO!!" I screamed and threw myself toward him, stretching for anything—his hand, his foot, his robe, but landed on my stomach to watch helplessly as he fell away cursing his hatred. Four layers down he slammed face first into the stones, then flipped over for another half dozen layers and slammed again, then picked up speed, tumbling faster and faster, arms and legs limply flailing about. The horrid slosh of flesh and shattered bones shrank from sight as the tiny, formless object disappeared into the shadows below.

The roar in my ears was my own screaming. I lay on my stomach, reaching into empty air for the killer now escaped. I was numb, gasping for air. My sword lay to my side, unstained by the blood of this monster as I had vowed. Only a crimson path glistening in the moonlight bore testimony of his demise that was now splattered across stones for a thousand paces below.

I lay there frozen, shocked, disbelieving. A thousand thoughts collided in my head in search of consolation. There was none. My hopes of a revelation about Rasha were gone, empty, escaped, now dashed on the ancient blocks below.

I had failed her.

My heart hurt. I was too exhausted, the fight gone out of me at last. I opened my heart to let the truth finally extract her terrible toll, and let the tears finally come—great salty drops that blurred my vision. I let them roll down my face and fall onto the dusty slab below.

The cold rock pressed hard against my body—I didn't care for myself any longer. I stared forlornly at the dim ghost light washing about the pyramid's foundations below, sensing the ancient heartbeat of a million setting suns, a million human lives, a million heartaches, and a million sorrows cast at the foot of the great stone monolith. I wanted to die.

"Oh, my Rasha, my dearest Rasha. What have they done with you?"

I closed my eyes and sobbed.

SIXTEEN

Ammar and Fawzi came upon me some time in the night, and finding me unharmed, did not disturb.

When I awoke, a cloak was covering me and the sun was blinding my eyes.

"What?" I said, sitting up abruptly.

Ammar and Fawzi woke up startled and looked over.

"Bat brains!" Fawzi said smiling. "You did it! You did it!"

Ammar sat up rubbing his eyes. "Are you all right?"

The nightmare was distant and disjointed, but slowly the pieces assembled.

"They killed Rasha," I said.

The men looked pained and said nothing.

"Yes, we know, Bassam," Ammar said gently. "We received another message. Witnesses saw the accident, near Atbara."

"I refuse to believe it," and pulled my knees under my chin, staring across the Nilus and the vast desert wasteland beyond.

They remained silent, waiting on me to define the moment.

"Look at that amazing view," I breathed. "I had no idea—last night in the dark . . ."

Ammar and Fawzi exchanged a brief glance.

"I just didn't think," I said, "I didn't think that God would lead me this far only to—to . . ."

Far below, columns of smoke rose from the village of Khufu. There was a stirring of activity in the market. To the east, the Nilus glistened green with tiny boats hoisting their graceful sails.

"Just what is this place," I asked blankly.

"What place?" Ammar asked.

"This pyramid," I said. "Whose is it?"

"Ah yes, a pharaoh, a couple of thousand years ago," he said. "Khufu, same as the village. I don't know a lot about him, an important king who commissioned this massive building project. This pyramid over here," he said pointing "built by his son. And that over there, the smallest? His grandson."

"What about those little ones down there?" I asked.

"The queens," Ammar said. "Not sure whose, but I imagine they were the first wives of the pharaohs."

I fell quiet for a long while, and then looked about searching the stones. "Where's that broken knife?"

"Oh, that," Fawzi said, pointing. "We pushed everything over the ledge, with the body."

I stood and filled my lungs a moment and stretched my muscles.

"He tried to kill me with it."

I saw pain in their eyes. Neither knew what to say.

I eased myself down and retrieved the knife. Fawzi gave me a hand and pulled me back up. "Was that your excellent work?" he asked, pointing to Pabas' headless corpse.

I nodded. "He kept calling me camel breath," I said.

Both men smiled cautiously. And then, as if by open invitation, Fawzi assumed it appropriate to take his usual liberties.

"We were there about 50 levels down when Rakbah went by," Fawzi said. "We met, but just in passing."

Ammar furrowed his brow at the bad joke and shook his head at Fawzi. I wanted to smile but couldn't. I sat down on the platform with my legs dangling off the edge, letting the morning sun warm me.

"It seemed he was head over heels to meet us," Fawzi said.

I felt a slight smile work its way onto my face.

"We asked why he didn't clean up for breakfast, and he said he was going to wash up in the Nilus."

Ammar gripped Fawzi's arm and shook his head more vehemently. Fawzi pulled away and scowled.

That did it, and I laughed. I laughed and then I cried, and cried some more. The tears came rapidly until I was weeping, and buried my face.

It hurt, oh how it hurt. The two men bowed their heads to wait.

I was so glad to have my friends back—my best friends.

Finally, I dragged a sleeve across my face and took Pabas' knife and started scratching Rasha's name into the stone.

"This is no longer the tomb of Khufu," I sniffed, scraping away tiny rock chips. I worked it in large block letters. "It is the Temple of Rasha," I said. "Forever will I tell my family, my children . . . well, my family, that it's a secret that only the sphinx knows. It is his great secret, and anyone who asks will hear him whisper it, that it was built to celebrate the life of my Rasha. It may be the village of Khufu down there, but from today forward, this is the Temple of Rasha. I give it to her as my gift because today is special. Today is her birthday celebration—today she has turned sixteen."

HAPU

Al Kalimat verified — +:
Hapu to Zafir

I am Hapu, steward-agent of the Abdali-ud-din by my seal (the validation impressed hereto), keeper of the tablets, writer of the scrolls for the treasury. By my hand I inscribe this report as requested, to Zafir, may God bless his soul.

My dear Zafir,

I am long absent from your company, but my family does well. Aneksi sends blessings to you and Rasheeda.

I'm happy for this excuse to write. It has been too long. Noph is much changed since you were here last. We are more than 300,000. The Nilus brings us more visitors every month. The people of Rome have sent ambassadors. They seek trade, but I believe they also seek power. We're ruled by Ptolemy IV, a strange family, a wicked warrior. There's talk in Upper Egypt of secession and installing a new pharaoh. Perhaps you have heard of this unrest.

Aneksi and I welcome your visit when your current difficulty is resolved. May God rest your daughter and her escort.

It pleases me that we can verify the earlier reports that the killer Rakbah is dead. His men are dead. His body was found at the great pyramid of Khufu, broken and dismembered. We suspect he was trampled by camels and became food for wild dogs. I'm told many of the bones, of he and his men, lie there still. At my order we're content to leave him that way.

My men continue to search for answers about your daughter, but with this report, I have nothing new to share.

Blessings on your patience. We will, by our oaths, continue to look until you have instructed us to end.

I am, —Hapu

LEUKE KOME

The village of Leuke Kome—I was almost home.

When our dhow pulled to shore, I could see all the familiar places. They were just as when we first left them for our great adventure more than two years ago—wattle and daub shacks, bleached white with age, hundreds of them, leaning against each other like sleepy cows.

At the camping grounds were the usual lodgings and a dozen caravan groups dressed for camp. Their clothing and manners spoke to me of lands and languages no longer foreign, but friendly to the ways of commerce in their own fashion and tongue and greeting. I had a new understanding of the world. I was glad to see them busy in the trade.

The city was no longer the great spectacle of adventure I longed to explore as a youth, and the sights and smells no longer held the mystiques of before. I could see it now for what it was—just another coastal village unique to the land where it was formed.

"The first man Zafir seeks here is Jamal," I said.

"Yes, yes," Fawzi said. "We all know Jamal. I think we can bypass a report and just get home."

"Bypass?" I exclaimed. "Not at all! We're here. We're official. We'll report in."

Ammar elbowed Fawzi. "There's going to be a new leader in town. I told you so!"

We found Jamal at his office in the marketplace. He bubbled over with joy at the reunion.

"Ah! My friends, my friends, my great friends!" he said, throwing his hands in the air. "You're back, you're back! So good to see you, so good! Zafir told me you had a difficult work, but you're back!"

Then he stopped to look at me.

"Bassam?" he said smiling. "Is that really you! My great heavens, you have grown!"

I felt embarrassed at the attention.

"I'm so glad to see you, Jamal. And I promise I'll be here more often," and showed him the ring on my finger.

"Ah hah, my young *master* Bassam! I suspected Zafir would entrust you with his greatest treasure! I'm thrilled. I'm delighted. It is a good choice. I'm pleased to give you whatever help you require. You just tell Jamal and I will make it happen!"

I wanted to finish the rest of the story about the ring, and, well, . . . the rest—but the pain was still deeply churning, so I left it at that.

Ammar saw my wound and quickly stepped in to offer the leather pouch.

"Dispatches?" Jamal asked.

"We were asked to deliver this from Al-Jarf," he explained. "I don't know who was faster, but we took an oar ship from Egypt, and . . ."

Jamal opened the pouch. He leafed through a few pages and turned them over.

"This is all?" he asked.

"Well, yes," Ammar said.

"That's what they gave us to deliver," Fawzi added. "Is something wrong?"

"No, other than you're many weeks behind."

"What does that mean?" I asked.

"One moment," he said. "Here, where are my manners, sit! All of you! I'll ask my help to get refreshments. Sit, and don't be bashful—relax! This is your home away from home!"

He stepped to the back room and returned with another, much thicker, pouch. He pulled out sheaves of papyrus, thumbing through each of them.

"There, here," he said. "To take with you to Zafir, some orders and reports, an accounting from the west sea trade that Zafir is looking for—and, oh, yes, the last dispatch from Cyene. Quite sad."

I knew what that report would say, and felt my heart heave to a stop, making my chest begin to hurt.

"I knew them," Jamal said. "Did you know that? I knew all of them well. I feel so sorry for Kiya, just tragic."

"Kiya?" Fawzi asked.

"Yes, yes," he said. "Zafir told me she returned to live with her aged mother—a grand woman in her 84th year! Isn't that just wonderful? She has her health at 84! Who has heard of such a thing? And she's in, uh, where is that? I don't recall, I think somewhere north, near the sea," he said scratching his beard. "I can find it for you, I probably have it written down here somewhere, a dispatch or something . . . "

"I don't understand," I said.

Jamal looked at me. "Oh, you didn't hear? So tragic, so young. I think just 13 or 14," he said.

"You said 13 or . . .?"

"Harmer, her husband. He was the steward in Cyene. Do you know him? And their little daughter, Ana. A terrible accident killed both of them. You didn't hear of this?"

The three of us froze and stared at Jamal.

"What? What are you looking at? Is something wrong? Food in my beard? Oh, that happens when I'm in a hurry!"

"Tell me that again slowly?" Ammar said.

"Mid-day meal, you know, fruit, a bread, usually bread, and . . . "

"NO!" Ammar said. "About Kiya, her husband, and . . ."

"Oh, certainly, well," he said, "Kiya's husband, you know, he's the steward in Cyene. He took little Ana with him up the Nilus, a trip to somewhere south, El-khartoum was it? I don't recall, but somewhere way down south—it was business, mind you, he often took her on several such trips, and—"

"What happened?" I asked

"I suppose they were late," Jamal said, "the Nilus, you know, it was running low. It's often dangerous on the Nilus. The floods were months away, boats are so much safer in high water, the rocks, you know . . ."

"AND?" Fawzi said.

"Oh, yes, of course, and near Atbara, close to the cataract, I don't recall. It says here in the dispatch, I can find it. . ."

"Jamal!" Ammar ordered. "Tell us what happened at Atbara."

"All right, yes, of course, Narmer and his little daughter were chased by pirates into the cataract and were killed, drowned. They never found their bodies."

I stared at him, not believing the words or hearing them either. Ammar put his hand on my knee. I wanted to ask but didn't dare open my mouth.

"So, it was not Rasha and Shamar?" Ammar asked.

Jamal looked puzzled. "Rasha? What are you talking about? Certainly not, no, she's back in Rekeem—terrible experience, just terrible. Did you hear, did you hear what happened to that poor girl? But she's home now, and—"

I leapt to my feet. "When?"

"When what?"

"When did she pass through?" I stammered.

"Oh, I think it was six weeks ago, no, maybe ten, no, eight—I can't rightly recall right now. I can look it up. It's in a dispatch. I'm sure I have it here somewhere. . ."

I was out the door, running for the camels.

Ammar and Fawzi looked at each other, huge smiles bigger than their faces spread ear to ear, and they stood extending their hands.

"Say, aren't you going to stay?"

"I don't think so," Ammar said. "We've got to catch up with Bassam."

"He's probably half way there already," Fawzi said. "That little bat brain, he's working me to death. I'm too old for this, Ammar. Let's go home and try to collect Bassam along the way. He'll get into some mischief, I'm sure of it, that camel breath."

THE SIQ

Kateb hurried to his usual place as the sun leaned toward the evening horizon. He wore the same faded, brown robe—frayed and worn—barely hanging by a few threads. His whole appearance made him look the part of the revered village scribe.

He brought his favorite walking stick that evening, working it to keep away the dogs and goats in his path.

Kateb had great instincts about the coming of the caravans, he knew before anyone else that another was already working its way through the Siq. He could smell it long before he could hear it. Not to delay, he sprinkled water on his clay, kneading it smooth and pressed it to his writing board. With his sharpened scrawl, he neatly inscribed *Ahad*, the first day of *Safar*, before dusk. It was the hottest time of year. The customary evening breeze washing through the Siq's snaking passages told of the traffic that descended. On this evening, the breeze revealed that a light train of just a few, long on the trail, was making its descent.

Kateb's long years at his post made him an expert at foretelling the loads that such caravans carried.

He discerned from the breeze as clearly as one might feel the carvings on the wall that this was the caravan of travelers familiar to Rekeem. Traveling lightly, their burdens did not include the tell-tale traces of oiled perfumes, the heavy aroma of seethed myrrh and incense, or the pungent sweet of pippali, ginger and cassia. No, this was a train of little size, perhaps a dozen? Maybe fewer. In either case it was a God-blessed day, an omen of good fortune for the people of Rekeem whenever a train came to visit their desert canyon city.

The setting sun just touched the hillsides and Kateb's patience paid off as the noise of distant jangling bells and the snorting, growling complaints of camels and anxious riders echoed from the Siq's shaded portal.

As the lead camels appeared to make their grand entrance, their clopping, plodding footfalls suddenly muffled in the sand of the plaza that served as Rekeem's large welcome mat.

Kateb watched carefully as they made their exit. Two camels emerged from the shadowed opening riding side by side and steered directly to Kateb.

"Kateb!" Ammar called.

"We're back! We're back!" Fawzi shouted, raising his hands heavenwards. "Yee-ha! Where's my wife?!"

"Ammar? Fawzi?" he exclaimed. "Is it . . . is it really you?"

"Hurrah!" they shouted together, and then smiling they steered their camels to the side.

I galloped past them and raced directly to the steps of Al Khazna.

"Father! Father!" I shouted with glee, waving my hands.

I drove my camel to her knees and leapt off, waving my stick and shouting. "Father! It's me! Bassam! I'm home. I'm home!"

Kateb could hardly react. His face broke into a great smile. He struggled to pull himself upright and greet me.

I lifted him right to his feet and was smiling so hard that tears came. We kissed cheeks and embraced.

"My boy! My Boy! You have come back to us. You're home! Oh, thank God you're home! Let me look at you." He held me at arm's length. "Oh, my son! You are returned!"

"Oh, father! I made it. I made it home."

Kateb embraced me. I felt his heart pounding, his old whiskers, now white with worry, scratching my neck. It made me smile and I hugged him tight.

"Oh you have grown," he said, holding me by the shoulders. "You've grown a palm taller at least. A palm, no, maybe two?"

"Probably," I laughed. "I was certainly stretched a few times, stretched to breaking!" We both laughed.

"I see some wisdom imprinted in this boy face of yours," he said. "Did you find the worst or did our prayers spare you?"

"Oh father, I have so much to tell. Yes, there were hard times, but I felt your pleadings and God has spared me to return home to you and mother. Mother! Where is she?"

"Oh, she's at home, my boy, at home!" Kateb said. "We'll surprise her, we will!"

Though father had aged, I could see his eyes were the same—beaming with joy, love, and relief.

"Much has changed," he said. "And much has not. We must talk of it. Oh, my boy! You're home!"

I held his hand and tried to restore my image of his younger self, the father in my memory. He looked older, but his eyes were the same. "I love you father," I said.

He put his hand to my face, a gentle caress of fatherly love. "I love you son. Welcome home!" Then a different kind of smile formed, with a new kind of twinkle in his eyes.

"What?" I asked.

He took a step back, turned, and gestured toward the steps of Al Khazna.

I glanced at the great stone steps and mighty pillars, and shrugged. "What?"

From behind that last pillar a radiant figure gracefully emerged, smiling as if to surprise me unawares. Her face, framed by long hair emblazoned by the setting sun, looked lovingly upon me as shadows teased the white robe that draped the gentle curves of her body. My heart stopped, my mouth fell open, I took breath but there came no words.

She extended her hand. "Bassam?"

A thousand worries instantly imploded together, dissolving to nothing under the revealing light of one great truth: *She lives!*

Tears came without shame and I took a step toward her.

"Rasha?"

"Bassam!" she said, reaching both hands.

"My Rasha!" I leapt the great steps, taking her into my arms tightly, swooping her from the step, and spun her around and around and around, holding her warmly to me. "My Rasha, my beloved Rasha. Oh, my Rasha. You're safe. You're alive, *you're alive!*"

She cried and kissed my neck. And I cried, and we laughed, and she hugged me close. "Oh, yes, oh my dearest Bassam," was all she could say, squeezing me tightly, her tears wetting my cheek.

I set her gently and held her to me, our hearts pounding together, to just breathe and embrace.

She inhaled the musky smells permeating my clothing, faded reminders of a long, painful journey now behind me at last.

I gazed on her beautiful smiling face, combed my fingers through her silky hair, and smelled the rich sweetness of her fragrance, feeling the warmth of her body close to mine.

"I was so afraid you couldn't come back to me," she whispered. Two large tears trickled down her cheeks. She looked up with those lovely oval eyes, so soft, so blue. She fixed her gaze searching my heart, searching my soul, then rested her cheek against my chest, smiling. "I am here," she whispered with trembling lips. "I am here, just as I promised. I am here."

I reached gently to her face and brushed away the tears.

"I love you," I said.

"You came for me. You came to find me," she sighed.

"I searched for you everywhere—deserts, rivers, the pyramids. I came to save you," I said.

"I knew it. I knew it in my heart," she said. "I knew you would come. I could feel it. That kept me alive. It kept me safe. It gave me hope—"

"I thought of you every day, every breath, every moment, and you're safe, oh, you're safe—you're home, you're here." I bent down to her soft lips and kissed them gently. She embraced me tighter, pressing her lips to mine with a sweet sigh, infusing her heart and soul into mine, safely in my arms.

Ammar and Fawzi clapped and whistled at our passionate reunion.

Kateb was embarrassed. He looked at his feet, kicking the sand, drawing circles with his stick, and blushing. "And of all places," he mumbled, "right here in the bright of the setting sun ..."

He tried to distract as best he could the few passersby who slowed to point, wondering what all the excitement was about. Kateb just nodded a pained but friendly greeting, tapping his fingers on his walking stick.

"Hello folks . . . Yes, nice to see you . . . Uh, yes, that is Bassam . . . Oh certainly, yes, he is returned . . . Yes, we're pleased . . . Certainly, I'll tell him . . . No, just got here . . . Yes, they'll marry soon. . . Of course you're invited, it will be nice . . . Thank you, you have a nice day too . . ."

We ignored them without shame or restraint.

Fawzi kicked his camel, and made a friendly wave toward the young lovers. He spread his arms wide toward Kateb. "At least you'll have this many grandchildren," he said laughing. Then snapped his stick to hurry past.

Ammar was fully engaged in the reunion, a joyous smile spread across his face. Kateb could only shrug and gesture over his shoulder.

"I think they're happy to see each other," he said dryly.

Ammar laughed. "I suppose they'll be done in a while. Maybe we should go for tea?" he joked. "My young student is finally home at last— and in the arms of his sweetheart. I couldn't be happier for him," he said.

"I can't thank you enough, Ammar," Kateb said. "Zafir has spent many nights at our table telling of the things you helped him through. I'm so grateful to you."

"I love that boy," Ammar said. "You have a fine son. There's a great life ahead of him. The world needs him. You and Dalal are the perfect parents, the best parents a boy could have."

"Oh no, no, we're new at this. Maybe we'll get a chance to try it again with a grandson!"

Ammar laughed. "Many, I expect," and gestured to the enraptured young couple.

"Well!" Ammar said, "I'm anxious to get home to my family." With that, he kicked his camel, steering her up the boulevard toward market square. "We have much to talk about, Kateb.," he called back. "Your son—amazing things. We'll talk, soon." And rode into town.

In whispers no one else could hear, Rasha and I exchanged vows of our love for one another.

I finally let her go and she started brushing the wrinkles out of her dress, paying futile attention to her mussed-up hair.

"You don't need to unruffle," I said. "You look beautiful just like that."

"Oh Bassam!" She tried to hide her blush by attending to my own disheveled hair and twisted robe.

I took her hand in mine. From my robe I produced the small veil she had given me and pressed it gently to her palm. It was dirty, spotted and yellowed, signs of love and attention through so many difficult times— but it was folded just the same.

She looked up, opening her mouth in surprise. "You have that still?"

"I carried this next to my heart every single day—it never left me, Rasha. Never. You gave me strength to carry through so many difficulties. I promised," I said.

She took the little veil and unfolded her handiwork from so long ago. It made her smile.

"I also promised to bring you a gift from Chang'an."

"Oh no, I don't need any gifts," she said. "All I ever wanted was you."

"Well . . ." I stammered, "I have nothing to show, except, um, now, I hope that my gift to you could be . . . that is, since we didn't . . . I mean, should the magic of your care for me somehow turn into the magic of love, then I want you . . . I need you to . . . Oh my heavens, Bassam! I had this all memorized and I can't even talk!" My heart pounded and I could barely speak. I took her hands in mine: "Will you my dearest Rasha be my bride? The mother of our children, the heart of our home, and the joy of my life—forever? Will you marry . . ."

"Oh, *yes*, Bassam! Yes! Yes!" And threw her arms around me, squeezing so hard I almost tipped over. I held her close for several moments.

Just then, another untimely interruption.

"Bassam!" Kateb called. "Are you two, uh, finished? Your mother is at home. We should . . . some time soon, when, uh, when you're finished . . ."

I turned back to Rasha. "Mother waits on us, but you must first see this," I said, raising my hand to reveal the ring Zafir had given me. It glinted yellow in the fading rays of the sun.

"My father's ring, why are you . . . ?

I lifted her face to mine. Her beautiful eyes sparkled with surprise. "It is his consent, Rasha," I said.

She threw her arms around my neck and kissed me. "I love you so much."

"I love you. You're never leaving me again."

"Hey," she said, pushing me back. "I never left you. You left me, remember?

"Well, you pushed me away. I distinctly remember it as plain as day. You put your hands on my chest and pushed."

"No, that was not pushing away. It was just the beginning of this." She grabbed me around the waist, pulled me tight, and kissed me again.

"Okay, now I get it!"

We laughed.

"Now, there's somebody I want you to meet," she said, pulling my hand.

"Oh?"

"Father told me you suffered a terrible loss, your Bakra, in a horrible accident," she said.

"It was . . . it was the hardest thing," and I shut my eyes, trying to squeeze the images from my memory.

"Well!" she said brightly. "May we help heal that wound? Follow me!"

"We?" I asked. "Who is we?"

She held her hem and let me help her down the steps of Al Khazna. My father followed as she led me to a tent. In front was a young camel tied to the rail and vigorously chewing a cud. She watched with curiosity as we approached.

I looked, then looked harder, and . . . "What is this?" I whispered. "Bakra?" I asked hesitantly.

"You'll need to teach her that name," Rasha said.

"But she looks . . . she looks exactly—"

"And she likes to be scratched between the ears," she said.

"This is not possible—How did you, I mean, where did you . . . she looks—every part of her, just like . . ."

"*Get her*?" Rasha laughed. "Bassam, this is Bakra's daughter. Before you left, remember?"

I thought back. "Yes—oh yes—we calved her! I completely forgot. And this is her daughter? Certainly it is! She looks—why, she looks exactly like my Bakra!"

"She *is* your Bakra," Rasha said. "Everything about her—her personality, her likes and patience and frustrations—she's a gentle and faithful soul. I have grown to love her."

The camel was of full stature, although she still wore most of her yearling coat. Beneath it showed patches of soft brown fur just like her mother.

I wrapped my arms around the young camel's neck and squeezed lovingly. It made her snort.

"My Bakra!" I said. "I know that snort!" She lowered her head to be scratched between the ears. I gave her a good vigorous rub and she leaned into my hand and sighed. "My Bakra, oh my dear friend, you made it back home with me after all."

Kateb gave a loving pat to the camel's neck. "Rasha took such good care of her," he said. "Every day she groomed and fed and watered. There's no better-loved camel in all the high deserts. And she needs a few good trips outside of our canyon walls. She's been asking for that a lot, you know."

I smiled. "Yes, I can see there's travel lust in her eyes. We'll get her on the trail soon enough."

Kateb took his walking stick and started down the path. "We should be going," he said. "Mother has dinner ready."

He let Rasha take him by the arm on one side to steady and I wrapped an arm around his shoulders in support. Side by side, the three of us followed the familiar boulevard toward home—with young *Bakra* following close behind.

"The seven scrolls, Father," I said. "Zafir let me read them."

"So he told me."

"It's amazing. They are secrets of such importance, secrets that can lead to prosperity. But I've learned there's no prosperity greater than family."

Rasha smiled and Kateb nodded.

"Then, my son, you have learned their truest meaning, a secret that few others have fully understood without the scrolls," he said. "That is their true message, my son—family. I'm so pleased to hear you say it from your heart. It's not complicated for those whose virtues help them get past the riddles."

What? The riddles? Virtues? How would he know about the riddles— unless . . .

"Mother will be thrilled!" Kateb said. "I hope no one has told her. I don't believe she knows you've arrived!"

"Then let's go surprise her!" I said. "After we eat, I'll tell you a story that will take the whole night to finish . . ."

"Does it have a happy ending?" Kateb asked, smiling.

I looked at the beautiful young woman at my father's side. She leaned toward him, guiding the old man's steps, then looked at me with a flirtatious smile—exquisite joy shining through loving eyes that wouldn't let me go.

"The best!" I said.

Girls. They are so much work—but there's no labor more worthy than winning the love of my life, my truest friend, my dearest, beloved Rasha.

I was home at last.

"Does it have a happy ending?" Kateb asked, smiling.

I looked at the beautiful young woman at my father's side. She leaned toward him, guiding the old man's steps, then

looked at me with a flirtatious smile—exquisite joy shining through loving eyes that wouldn't let me go.

"The best!" I said.

SUNRISE

Yellow Beard paused in the telling as he realized the eastern sky was swallowing the last remaining stars. It was the soft glow of an approaching dawn—and the end of his tale. *Oh, no,* he thought to himself. *I did it again—all night!*

He smiled at the four young boys. They had remained faithfully seated at the dying fire the whole time, captivated by a story they probably didn't realize was already legend among the villagers and nomads of the high deserts. *In a few years,* he thought, *they'll come to appreciate this history and relish the night I kept them up to hear these words from my own lips—and then the years will pass, they will grow old, and tell their own tales to a new group of young boys—I wonder who among them will become the next yellow beard?*

He sat up to straighten his back and dismiss the group.

"I've kept you all this whole night," he smiled, then noticed the other two men had not stirred, even with the sun in their faces.

"Thank you, Sir," said one boy, rising with a handshake.

"Oh no, thank you, my young friends," Yellow Beard said. "I'll be in big trouble with your mothers for keeping you. They're probably worried about you being gone all night."

"Yes, but the whipping will be worth it," said another.

"Well, well," Yellow Beard grinned slyly. "Maybe I can help." And with that, he took a long stick and poked Brown Beard in the ribs.

"Huh? Wha . . . ? Is it morning already?"

"Is it morning?" Yellow Beard laughed. "Where have you been all night my snoring faithful friend?"

"Oh my, don't you boys know it," Brown Beard said as he roused his faculties. "He's such a long-winded goat rope. I swear on the grave of Moluck, that story grows longer with each telling."

Brown Beard scratched his forehead and that's when the boys saw it for the first time—a double scar that ran diagonally over his right eyebrow. The eldest boy jabbed another to look.

Yellow Beard smiled. "I have a plan. Come here close boys. Maybe I can help you avoid punishment. Yes, come here close."

They all stood, stretching the knots from their legs.

Yellow Beard rolled to his knees and stood, revealing a spryness not usual for his age. "Maybe I'm getting too old for this!" he laughed.

"Now that's not really possible, is it, camel breath?" Brown Beard said. "That mass of goat hair hides a face only 30 years old," he said to the boys. "It's a miracle, I tell you, a mystery—the man never ages."

"Oh stop it," Yellow Beard said.

"And his wife, too!" Brown Beard said.

"I told you—*one* fruit," Yellow Beard said. "One for her, one for me. Had I known I would have shared, honest."

Brown Beard shook his head. "Yes, yes, that's what you always say. You've told that lie for years, fish phlegm."

Yellow Beard turned his attention to the boys and pulled a cold cinder from the fire. He rubbed it into the palm of his hand.

"When you arrive home," he said, curling his right hand into his left, smearing black soot over his ring, "I want you to show your mothers something. Tell them you were with me and my friends this past night, that we taught you the ways of the caravan. And show them this mark. They can reach me if they must."

He took the hem of the first boy's shirt and carefully pressed his ring to the fabric, marking it with a small pattern printed in black.

"What is this?" the boy asked.

"It's the crest of my wife's family, the ring of her father's consent."

They all fell silent, their jaws dropped open in surprise.

"The ring? Then you are . . . ?"

Yellow Beard grinned. "Your mothers will understand," he said as he imprinted the ring's crest on each boy's shirt, then urged them home.

"Run! Perhaps you can climb under your blankets before your parents awaken!"

They scampered down the long boulevard in the growing light, turning to one another with waving arms and hushed gestures to exclaim the secrets that only young boys will keep.

"Come back again—we'll talk some more!" he called after them.

"Really, Bassam," Fawzi said, picking flecks of bread from his brown beard. "You shouldn't keep young boys up all night with your l-o-n-g stories."

"Listen Fawzi. If you had only heard what I was telling them, it's like more and more details come to memory with each telling, but you so rudely fell sleep."

"Telling them? *Telling them*? What did you tell them, donkey brain?" Then turning to Black Beard, "Ammar! Wake up! Get up, old man!" he said, shaking his slumbering friend. "Bassam has been spreading rumors about us—again. Get up." Fawzi let go with a huff. "What'd you say, Bassam? Must I face my grandsons and undo your horrid webs of exaggeration *again*?"

Ammar rolled over and squinted. "What? Is it morning?"

"Come on Ammar. Our families missed us."

Fawzi and Ammar pulled their aching muscles into action and stood.

"Did you tell the boys whose image you had carved there in the Siq?" Ammar asked.

"Didn't have to," Bassam said. "They'll recognize her now that they know the story. Yes, they'll see my Rasha who greets all who journey here to enjoy this warm place. I didn't tell them about my Shrine of the Veil, but they will pass it one day and hear the story, and they'll remember—"

The men gathered their things and let their walking sticks lead them to the dusty pathway home. The early breeze was cool, and tugged at their headdresses as the sun splashed across the western cliffs. The two old friends exchanged a tired wave, nodded to Bassam, and went opposite directions up the boulevard.

"I'll see you tonight for dinner, right?" Bassam called. "After your nap? And then we'll plan our next trip! As we talked! As we planned, right? Did you hear me?"

Fawzi shook his head. "Camel breath," he mumbled out of ear shot.

"I heard that!" Bassam laughed.

He poked at the fire with his walking stick, spreading the coals to extinguish, then gathered his things for home.

I expect they'll be late tonight as usual. But they'll be there. They wouldn't miss it—they never do. Everyone knows there's no better cook in all of Rekeem than my Rasha!

Just then, the padding sound of young footsteps came up behind him. It was the eldest of the boys, breathless.

"Sir? Sir? Mr. Yellow Beard?" he said, tugging on Bassam's robe,

"Oh! Hello again. I thought you were on your way home."

"I was, but . . . something you said in your story."

"Yes?"

"I have been thinking . . . I don't know what this means, but it's a secret, I don't know what to make of it."

"So, tell me, boy. Tell me this secret."

"You won't be angry with me? Grandpa said I shouldn't talk of it, that he would beat me if I did."

"Angry? Beat you? Certainly not, boy! What foolishness is this? A beating from your grandpa? I'll want to talk to him about that! So what is it?"

"It is this," he said, folding his left ear forward.

Bassam took the boy's head in both hands, turning it so the rising sun would illuminate the back of his ear.

Bassam's eyes widened.

"How did you get this?" he asked, turning the head to see more clearly. He touched the boy's ear, gently tracing a thin, blue-inked crescent.

"Who gave you this?"

"My other grandpa. I was little. Please don't be angry with me. I didn't know what it was. He said it made me a man like him. It hurt. A needle and some ink to both me and my brother. We were to tell no one. He told us when we were older he would teach us what it meant. When we became men he had work for us to do, important work, when we were big."

"You must tell me," Bassam said. "You must tell me who did this. Who is your grandpa?"

The boy took a step back and looked at the ground. "He's my grandpa's older brother, a great uncle, I suppose. Do you know of him? He told us to call him Grandpa Sofian."

HENRI

Henri sat back in his chair and closed his eyes. The story had ended at last.

The long wrappings of the scroll lay curled in the cardboard box.

"Perfect," he grinned, looking about for signs of dawn.

"If there's more, they won't find it in this old coffin," he sighed, then started winding the scroll back to its spindle. "One day, it would be nice to know who's buried in there, and why this story was buried with her—or him." He glanced at the loading dock. "Maybe one day they'll figure it out . . ."

He returned to the souvenir shop for a sheet of bubble wrap, cradling the scroll.

"The problem with customs," he muttered, "is they work too hard to find treasure—and miss it when they see it. What do they call that? A blinding glimpse of the obvious? Yes, yes, that's it, blinding. This better blind them . . ."

He put the scroll into a long box and fumbled around for a price tag imprinted with *Museum of Natural History Gift and Souvenir Shop*.

"Let's see—I'd guess this looks like $65—no, more, something like $84.95." He jotted down the price in neat writing and tucked the tag into the box and sealed it.

"That's three—same shape, same price—gifts for my grandchildren. Will they stop me for gifts? I doubt it."

Looking about for his personals, he was content all was together, and hurried down the dark corridor to his office. He left his apron on the desk and pulled on his coat and hat. A quick look through the drawers for anything important, then turned for the door.

"What am I forgetting? Ah, yes, mustn't forget these," he said, fingering his apron for the pocket holding the small white fruit pits. He held them to the light and tested their smell. "Ahhhhh, sweet as before, delicious!" and tucked them into his pocket.

Back in the receptionist's office, he pulled out a sheet of museum stationery.

Dear friends,

Alas, my time has come. Thank you for these many years together. I've had a wonderful career, and made so many friends. And thank you for your faith in me. I will forever remember you and think fondly of you for the rest of my days.

Please accept my retirement not as an ending or parting of ways, but as a beginning because for me that's exactly what it is.
Fondly,
Henri

He placed the letter in an envelope and wrote "To My Friends," and propped it in front of the postcards.

"I'm late, better get going!"

He removed a second envelope, addressed it to a desert village in Jordan then took five postage stamps from the cash drawer.

"That should cover it," he said. "I'll send the money later."

On another sheet of paper he wrote—

Dearest Mother and Father,

I found it at last! This letter will reach you before I do. But please know that when I arrive, I will have with me your long-lost journal. I found three scrolls. Are there more?
Love, Han'rrah

He sealed the note and dropped it into the mail slot.

It was time to leave.

Henri pulled on his coat and hat, bundled the boxes into his arms, and set his keys where they could be found. For the last time he walked through the reception area into the grand hall and flipped off the lights. His footsteps echoed in the emptiness, a lonely sound that followed him across the great linoleum map of the world, up to the front doors.

He looked back once more.

"Goodbye old museum," he said. "You were a great part of my life. Thank you."

A blast of cold air rushed over him as he stepped outside, and the door closed behind with a solid click. He tested the icy latch, suddenly reminded he had left his gloves on his desk.

"Never mind. I won't need them after today."

Peering once more through the glass for a last look, he smiled and shook his head.

"So many years, so much searching, my heavens! That took longer than I thought," he said, taking the wide granite steps down to the street.

He pulled his collar up against the dampness then reached to his pocket, making sure the small pits were still there.

"It's an interesting word, from the Latin *genesis*—generation, nativity, birthplace. And the Greek—origin, source, production, creation, Vetus Latina, Vulgate, Tanakh, Mikra, γένεσις, not many variations over the centuries—but still, a good creative name for a book."

He breathed out a burst of puffy fog.

"They'll never guess it in a thousand years!" he chuckled. "People just don't read good books any more. But maybe. Maybe some day a curious soul will look to the Bible, to Genesis, to Chapter Three, and slow down long enough to creep through the verses at its end, to read about the Tree of Life. But who in his right mind would ever guess that I've got the seeds?"

END OF BOOK THREE

Important Note

The following letter of authentication to portions of the preceding text was received by the British Foreign Office of Affairs, Antiquities, from the signatory on behalf of His Majesty, King Hussein of Jordan, from the year past. It is reprinted here for the convenience of the reader.

June 4, 1968

British Office of Foreign Affairs, Antiquities
London, England

The Latin-to-English translation that follows contains the complete text of the so-named "Jordan scrolls."

Discovered in 1913 by British soldiers serving in southern Transjordan, the scrolls were found in a sealed clay jar buried beneath the altar box of a structure identified as the Shrine of the Veil. The shrine stands in the south-western desert region, as mapped, some 58 kilometers due north of the Gulf of Aqaba. It is an insignificant ruin that has no known history, pre-dating the second nomadic-Julien period by some 2-5 centuries. For details of the shrine's dimensions and precise location, see Lt. Col. William Tristan's report, HRA 29:115-119, 1912, Middle Eastern Holdings, Ministry of Defense, London.

Upon their discovery, the scrolls in their original jar were moved to the central British military camp in Amman and shipped to London with additional antiquities that held no particular interest.

The wars that followed obscured the
discovery until 1963 when it was rediscovered
in a warehouse and sent for translation to the
Department of Linguistics at the University
of Chicago, USA. It has since become popularly
known as the Jordan Scroll(s), and was returned
in 1968 to Jordan's King Hussein (1935-99).

There are few additional details available
regarding the Jordan Scrolls.

The events described indicate a time
period during the height of the first golden
era of the ancient caravan trade, 500-150 BC.
The original text is an early dialect of a
common Bedouin language. Some time prior to 150
BC the text was translated into Greek and some
100 years later into Old Hebrew. Small scraps
of those translations have been accurately
identified in various museums and collections
around the world. The original text has
disappeared.

Approximately 50-75 AD, a scribe who
signed himself "Yoshua-Ginat" translated a
version into Latin, probably in homage to the
Roman overlords of his day. It is that Latin
version that was discovered by the scouting
party at the Shrine of the Veil.

The University of Chicago translators
are in agreement for reasons of style, script,
verbiage, and comparative analysis that the
Jordan Scrolls are first-generation copies of
the original text.

The author of the original text has no
place in history, but was evidently a well-
traveled, wealthy man. He described himself as
an historian and a teller of true tales. His

writing style is narrative, but awkward and leaves some critical specifics missing. It is, nevertheless, detailed and moving.

Of particular interest is the author's examination of a small collection of writings he called The Seven Scrolls. It is evident in the record itself that he was probably the last man to handle said scrolls. Some portions were copied into his own record.

What follows is the complete translation of the Jordan Scrolls with all due diligence toward precision as provided by the University of Chicago. Original dialect that was not rendered into Latin has been phonetically spelt. The main characters' names and related words are correctly pronounced on their first use in parentheses.

Respectfully,

Dr. Al-ammar Assad
Director, Middle East Antiquities and Landmarks
Commission
Amman, Jordan

[Editor's note: The parenthetical pronunciations mentioned above were removed for purposes of style and brevity.]

Update on the Jordan Scrolls

Since the English translation of the Jordan Scrolls was first made available in 1968, more details about their discovery have emerged.

Excavations at the Shrine of the Veil in 2006 uncovered additional findings regarding the origin of the shrine and its connection to the Seven Scrolls.

A stone marker standing over the extraction place of the sarcophagus with poorly preserved writings was found at the one-meter level beneath the northeastern corner of the altar wall. (See Tyson, D., Kennedy, P., McConnehey, T., et al, *Excavations of Tomb 31, Jordan,* 2006) Four lines of an obsolete dialect of reformed Egyptian have been rendered as:

"Here find my tale.
For my beloved's last place, look to the Siq and her image there.
She guards the gate to the seven virtues, but not to my wealth.
The mystery sleeps in the house of the small veil with dreams of the
    Scroll of Eight."

In 2008 the State of Jordan approved supervised excavations at the Siq and more extensive diggings at The Shrine of the Veil.

Because of the translated text, the old ruin was officially renamed The Shrine of the Small Veil (Elisabeth, S., 2009). Maps were updated accordingly.

Excavations to locate the Scroll of Eight are presently underway.

–Editor

Acknowledgments

REKEEM

Much of the research on Rekeem (Petra), its history, civilization, and participation in the various trade routes across Eurasia is due in large part to the helpful body of research at www.Nabataea.net. This rich website contains, according to its creators, only a fraction of the painstaking research accumulated over the years by a devoted family of scholars. Much of that work, they say, will be forthcoming at some future time. Until then, the author is deeply indebted to the remarkable and laborious dedication to the subject of ancient history and the Holy Land by Arthur Henry Gibson (1869-1960), David J. Gibson (1904-1966), and Dan Gibson (still actively assimilating research on the Nabataeans as of this writing).

SELECTED SOURCES

Aside from a tremendous wealth of information available from Google Books and other Internet resources, some writings of particular value for The Search for Rasha, and a few smatterings of sources the author does not want to forget, include (partial list):

Ainsworth, William, The Illustrated Universal Gazetteer, J. Maxwell & Company, 1863

Bible, King James Version

Bridge, E.A. Wallis, The Egyptian Sudan: Its History and Monuments, in two volumes, 1907

Bruce, James, and James Ballantyne, Travels to Discover the Source of the Nile: In the Years 1768, 1769, 1770, 1771, 1772, & 1773, Volume 7, 1805

Budge, E. A Wallis, An Egyptian Hieroglyphic Dictionary in two volumes, London, 1920

Catholic Encyclopedia, 1907, three volumes 1912, master index 1914, Robert Appleton Company, New York, The Encyclopedia Press, 1912

Churchill, Winston, The River War: An Account of the Reconquest of the Sudan, Longmans, Green and Co., London, p. 200, 1902

Clagett, Marshall, Ancient Egyptian science, a Source Book. Volume Three: Ancient Egyptian Mathematics. Philadelphia: American Philosophical Society, 1999

Darnell, John Coleman, and Colleen Manassa, Tutankhamun's Armies: Battle and Conquest During Ancient Egypt's Late Eighteenth Dynasty, John Wiley & Sons, 2007

Durrant, Will, The Story of Civilization

Ebers, G. (translated from German by Clara Bell) Egypt: Descriptive, Historical and Picturesque,, Cassell & Company, 1887;

Faulkner, Raymond Oliver, A Concise Dictionary of Middle Egyptian, Griffith Institute, 1962

Gibbon, Garth, Blackwood's Edinburgh Magazine, Vol. CXLVII, January-June 1890, pp. 749-751 [Murad Wells], William Blackwood & Sons, Edinburgh, London, 1890

Gillings, Richard (1972), Mathematics in the Time of the Pharaohs. MIT, 1972

Goddard, John, Kayaks Down The Nile, Brigham Young University Press, 1979

Google Earth

Grant, Lieut.-Colonel J. A., Proceedings of the Royal Geographical Society and Monthly Record, Vol. VI, 1884, "Route March, with camels, from Berber to Korosko in 1863," pp. 326-335

Ibbotson, Sopie, and Max Lovell-Hoare, Sudan, Bradt Travel Guides, 2012

Isani, G. B., et al, Camel Breeds of Pakistan, 2000

Knight, Edward Frederick, Letters from the Sudan, 1897

Lobban, Richard A., Jr., Historical Dictionary of Ancient and Medieval Nubia, 2003

Lutz, H. F., The American Journal of Semitic Languages and Literatures, Vol. 37, No. 1 (Oct. 1920), pp. 73-75, University of Chicago Press

Payn, H., The Well of Eratosthenes, The Observatory, Vol. 37, P. 287-288, 352-353, 1914

Rawlinson, George, History of Ancient Egypt, Volume 1, Longmans, Green 1881

Rossi, Corinna, Architecture and Mathematics in Ancient Egypt, Cambridge University Press, 2007

Sarton, George, Hellenistic Science and Culture in the Last Three Centuries B.C., Dover Publications, NY, 1959, pp. 103-105

Smith, William, Smith's Bible Dictionary, 3 volumes, London, John Murray, 1863

Sudan Notes and Records, Volumes 1-2, 20, 1918, 1937

Taylor, Bayard, A Journey to Central Africa—Life and Landscapes from Egypt to the Negro Kingdoms of The White Nile, G.P. Putnam & Son, pp. 175-190, 1870

Torok, Laszlo, The Image of the Ordered World in Ancient Nubian Art, 2002

Willcocks, Sir William, The Nile in 1904, E. & F.N. Spon, 1904

Yang, Shang, The Book of Lord Shang (390 BC-338 BC), translated by J.J.L. Duyvendak, Chapter V, Weakening the People, 1928

THIRD SCROLL

The relationship between happiness and giving, as presented toward the end of the Third Scroll (Book 1), contains principles and ideas that were given by Arthur C. Brook, president of the American Enterprise Institute, in a speech February 24, 2009, at Brigham Young University.

FOURTH SCROLL

The Golden Mean as discussed in the Fourth Scroll (Book 1) is an idea originated by Aristotle. He suggested moderation in all things except knowledge. This idea has since been expanded upon by other scholars. An excellent source for application of the Golden Mean is a book by Nelson Hultberg, Dallas, TX, "The Golden Mean," prepublication, 2007.

QUOTE

Zafir's quote (Book 1) about this life being the time to prepare for the afterlife where no more labor may be performed is slightly rephrased, with thanks, from the scripture Alma 34:32.

AUTHOR'S PERSONAL STORY

Zafir reflects on his first and best teachers—his mother and father—and tells of a conversation he had walking his mother to the familiar entrance of her home. He quotes her musing about how it seemed like yesterday that she was the one helping him walk to that door as a boy. This experience is a direct quote from the author's mother to the author when she was in her 90th year one summer evening when they approached the back-porch door of her Berkeley Street home in Salt Lake City.

When Kateb, Bassam's father, was a young man traveling with others, they chanced atop a great plateau with plummeting cliffs that dropped at least 3,000 feet. Kateb tells Bassam about a foolish venture to the edge, to peer down the cliff. This is something the author did when he was 12 or 13 at Dead Horse Point, Utah, where the sheer cliffs drop off 2,000-3,000 feet or more in some places. Since that experience he has refused to step foot on that beautiful overview, even to this day.

QUOTE

The quote by Zafir (Book 1), "A man is not conquered from without until he first destroys himself from within," is due with thanks to the original quote from Will Durrant who wrote, "A great civilization is not conquered from without until it has destroyed itself from within." (The Story of Civilization, Vol. 3, Caesar and Christ Epilogue—Why Rome Fell)

TOPOGRAPHICAL DETAIL

Descriptions of the lands crossed by Zafir's caravan were made more realistic thanks to the good people at Google Earth. They made that part of our world available to a tired and fumble-fingered writer whose few visits to some of the locations described in the series were too short and limited to adequately absorb the beauty of those lands. He was left to struggle many thousands of miles and years away from actual locations and events to otherwise bring the story to life. Google Earth was an enormous help. Thank you to the U.S. and European satellite programs, as well as other assisting nations, and Google for their innovation.

MODELS

Zafir is modeled after the author's father, Dahlal after his mother, Rasha after his wife, Ammar after his high school buddy Ricky, Falak after the author's daughter's mother-in-law, Fawzi after all the great guys who teased the author but cared, and Bassam after the author's hoped-for version of himself in the resurrection.

NAMESAKE

Cala is named after Kayla, the author's granddaughter (parents Joe and Heidi Skousen). Dr. Lincoln is named after Lincoln, the author's grandson (parents Ben and Brittany Skousen). Suwr is a real Egyptian name that's meant to sound like "sewer." The name "Henri" is adapted from the cute Pocket Beagle owned by the author's daughter, Michelle and Peter Kennedy, and their family. Arja is patterned after Ozzy, the author's grandson (parents Jacob and Jen Skousen), Tachus after the author's son, Joshua, and Aloli, Ana and Kiya after the author's daughters Tricia Taylor, MaryAnn Doughtry, and Elisabeth. The personality and gentle patience of Bassam's beloved Bakra is patterned after the finest and most loving black Lab ever born into the Earth, Annie The Dog (June 6, 1997-July 31, 2008). Kalila is patterned after all the girls who rejected the author's requests for a date because they were too invested in finding the perfect man for them to see . . . well . . . to see the actual perfect man. Good thing, too. The author might have missed Kathy, the perfect woman, had things gone otherwise.

The decorations by each chapter heading are the Arabic (Book 1), Chinese (Book 2), and hieroglyphic (Book 3) renditions for "beloved," Bassam's oft-repeated term of endearment for his Rasha, and the author's for his bride, Kathy, of 42 years—and going. The supernal blessings represented in the Tree of Life are alive in her. She is, as Bassam declares at the end of the journey in the third book, "My dearest, beloved Rasha."

FRUIT

In Genesis 2:9, 3:22-24, Adam and Eve have already disobeyed God by partaking of the fruit of the Tree of Knowledge of Good and Evil. For this disobedience, they were cast out of the Garden of Eden. As protection to prevent them from partaking of the Tree of Life (as alluded to in Bassam book 3) and living forever in their sin, the Lord God has Cherubim and a flaming sword placed before the Tree of Life to prevent Adam and Eve from partaking of its fruit and living forever.

The Garden of Eden is long lost to history. Strangely, a certain old tree with five limbs like that of a hand reaching toward heaven is discovered by the two young adults of our story who have lived their lives in purity of heart, fidelity, and integrity. The tree presents its perfectly ripened fruit to Rasha and Bassam on the night of a full moon one month apart from each other. Why the tree just happened to reemerge at this time and circumstance is curious. Scholars continue to hunt for that answer.

For the purposes of this book, it explains the mission of Henri, of the scrolls, and serves as another curious intervention by the Creator of all things that he deems good and necessary. It is a gentle commentary on the loving but absolute aphorism from Isaiah: "For my thoughts are not your thoughts, neither are your ways my ways, saith the Lord." (Isaiah 55:8 KJV)

ABOUT THE AUTHOR

As a young child, Paul B. Skousen grew up mesmerized by a faded Asian carpet that hung high in the main hallway of his family's home. It depicted desert nomads seated on a rug spread over sand, camped between palm trees, their camels pastured nearby. A couple of hunting dogs stood anxious, awaiting their meal, and in the background rose the rolling desert sea of nondescript dunes, forever undulating toward the horizon, frozen in time. It was a destination he longed to see for himself—and over the years that followed, he did.

Skousen enjoys visiting the Middle East for archeology digs or just for renewing friendships. He is a journalist by trade, finished graduate school at Georgetown University, worked as an analyst at the CIA, and was assigned to the Situation Room as an intelligence officer in the White House. He is a professor of communications, married father of ten, grandfather to 37 (and growing), and is the author of the three-volume Bassam series and several nonfiction books on politics and history.

It is to "My dearest, beloved Kathy" that this trilogy is dedicated as a story suitable for many hours of reading to children and grandchildren, and for those millions of adventurers searching for true values in a confusing, chaotic modern world that seems to have forgotten the peace that comes from living the eternal values of trust, honor, and love.

Books in the *Bassam Saga*

Bassam and the Seven Secret Scrolls
Zafir and the Seventh Scroll
The Search for Rasha

CPSIA information can be obtained
at www.ICGtesting.com
Printed in the USA
LVHW04s1426161018
593788LV00002B/328/P